REYoung

Daaa ... SnowBiz!

Daaa ... SnowBiz!

By REYoung

Copyright © 2024 REYoung

This book is available in print and electronic format at most online retailers.

ISBN 978-1-7334461-3-6

TageTage Press

REYoung-author.com

BOOKS BY REYOUNG

UNBABBLING
MARGARITO AND THE SNOWMAN
INFLATION
THE IRONSMITH
ZOL

As always for Adria

There's no business like snow business

LAAAADIES ANNNND GENTLEMENNNN! Tonight! Live! On stage! For your delectation and viewing pleasure! We present to YOU! The blood *pounding!* Bongo congo drum *beating!* Bungle in the jungle *tom tom* of the heart! The lights, camera, sound and action *It's Showtime!* thrill of your life! Clown cars! Flaming hoops! High-wire walking African elephants in pink tutus! Right here! Under the big top! The big tent! On the big stage of the Bolshoi On Broooadwayyy *theatuh!* In the land of milk and honey! The honey pot! Sweet spot! How I love you, how I love you, *maaa-a-aaammmy*. The suck-suck-suckling mammary gland of wealth and power! The dragon hoard! The capitalist swagger! The dance of finance! I mean m-o-n-e-y *MONEY!* Prestidigitated, pilfered and pixelated before your very eyes! It's ... *daaa* ... *SNOWBIZ!!*

1
Pushcart

AN ANNOYING ON-AGAIN OFF-AGAIN squealing sound that could be a bad fan belt in the theater's heating system is accompanied by a methodical *slap, slap, slap, slap* and on the screen we see a pair of feet shod in frayed and crumbling leather and tire tread huaraches striking the pavement. The camera pulls back and through the simmering, fried egg morning haze we see a man in a faded Hawaiian shirt (palm trees and—*hula girls?*) and worn khaki cargo shorts pushing a classic three-wheeled ice cream cart with a top-hatted Frosty the Snowman in an identical Hawaiian shirt (palm trees and, yes, it is— hula girls) painted on the side. He's got a couple days of salt and pepper beard stubble. His dirty blond hair's infused with a watercolor wash of gray. Polarized wrap-around sunglasses hide his eyes but you can tell there's something weird about them. It's only ten a.m. but the sun is already burning in the sky like an industrial heat lamp. Membranous waves of moist hot air swarm around him. Rivers of sweat pour from his body, soaking his shirt and trickling down his legs like embarrassing streams of pee. The slightly lopsided left wheel of his cart squeals at regular intervals. He's been meaning to stop at the bicycle shop on Guadaloupe and ask Rick to have a look at it, maybe buy a new wheel if necessary. But instead of pursuing this idea in a logical fashion, like figuring how and when to fit this stop into his schedule, he drops down an etymological rabbit hole that begins with the word *bicycle,* which everybody and his grandmother knows is pronounced bi*sick*le, even though we say motor-*si*-kel and uni-*si*-kel as in *scythe* or *psychopath*. Although, let's face it, *Snowman*, bi-*sike*-al would sound kind of snooty, fucking *Brits*—'scuse my English—especially to the American ear.

This distinction or, maybe better said, *divide* between British and American English a subject he might have delved into deeper if only it weren't for these horrible shrieking sounds crashing against the velvet timpani of his eardrums like breaking glass, like fingernails on a chalkboard, like … *Snowman! Snowman! Gimme a PoPoPop!® Me too, Snowman!* It drives him fucking crazy, all this grabbing, all this *gimme gimme gimme*, all these painfully shrill cries of innocent childish glee shredding the finely veined membrane of his sanity. He'd like to throttle every single one of these little bastards with his bare hands. He'd like to slam the lid of his icebox down on their grasping, groping, filthy little fingers. He'd like to …

Why, helloooo little *friends!* Is everybody ready for a *PoPoPop!®*?

YAYYYY!

Arrrgh, I'm gonna kill ya little fuhhh … Here ya go, kiddos!

Infanticidal tendencies disguised by a crocodile growl of affection, he hands around half-a-dozen frosty, cone-shaped confections to the waving hydra of nose-pick, thumb-suck, sticky little digits, in exchange for which stay-at-home Mommy (but don't even begin to suggest she doesn't *work*) forks over a handful of Daddy's hard-earned but rapidly devaluing shekels, her ever wary mama tiger eyes searching behind this disheveled pirate of the pavement's opaque shades for any signs of genuine madness that might actually threaten harm to her precious, special and probably gifted (even if there's no quantifiable or qualitative evidence to back up such claims) little princes and princesses. Not that *he*, the *Snowman*, would *ever* in his wildest imagination do anything to cause the least reason for doubt in Mommy's double X chromosome-configured brain given the pair of pearl-handled Colt .45s she's wearing on her childbearing hips over a slightly faded chocolate brown cotton shift that reveals a surprisingly fit mommy body toned by 24/7 cross-training (i.e., child-rearing), or the very pointed toes of her fire engine red, ostrich skin Tony Llamas, which could certainly add a new dimension to colorectal cleansing. After a final socializing admonition—say Bye-Bye, Snowman, *Bye-Bye, Snowman*—Mommy dearest and her brood, tail-wagging Gala Poochie Pup included, wander off in their discrete family unit, followed by yet another chorus of gleeful screams as they give their *PoPoPops!*® a quick *cha-cha-cha* maraca shake and pull the paper tabs and *pop! pop! pop!* out pop these rainbow-colored mushroom clouds of tangy, brain-numbingly cold, fresh fruity sweetness they eagerly plunge their plump pink tongues into and lick and slurp with the exact same canine exuberance Gala Poochie Pup would if only—oops! Half a block down the street little brother drops his *PoPoPop!*® on the sidewalk, *splat,* poochie dives in, lap, lap, lap, junior's bawling, *boo hoo, Mommy, I want anudder PoPop!*

Too late. Even if the harried momster *were* willing to backtrack and hand over more loot to this drooling, depraved and most likely criminally insane reprobate (don't think she didn't notice those creepy eyes crawling over every inch of her voluptuous mommy body), who, surely due to some clerical error, has been licensed by the city (she read the permit on his cart) to extort money from already cash-strapped parents to satisfy the whiny whims of their (to be perfectly honest) spoiled little brats, *he*, the so-anointed *Snowman*, pockets full of grimy quarters, dimes and nickels and damp, wrinkly paper currency, is already off again, *slap, slap, slap, slap*, in fact, he's practically running, *slap!slap!slap!slap!* his face twisted in the desperate grimace of an escaped down-by-law convict, his cart tilting dangerously, the lop-sided left wheel squealing non-stop, the right wheel making a peculiar squishing, sticking sound as its tread grips the hot asphalt and releases again, and no wonder, he sees now. There's a wad of chewing gum stuck to the tire. Fucking pigs can't place their refuse in an appropriate container? Where's their goddamn sense of civic duty? Look at this shit!

Eyes on the ground, the vigilant citizen itemizing the detritus of society, cardboard and Styrofoam food boxes, plastic, aluminum and glass cups, cans and bottles still containing the root beer brown or neon orange or raspberry red dregs of coffee, sports drinks, diet sodas, craft beers, teas and designer waters, hopelessly out of date newspapers, cigarette butts, crumpled cigarette packs, big fat green and yellow loogies, pink pristine wads of bubblegum like little undeveloped fetuses, soggy, fully loaded diapers, unscooped doggie poop, bloody tampon applicators, surgical masks. Disgusting slobs! That's the problem with goddamn society today! Nobody gives a shit about fuck! And what's this crap? He sends out a sideways kick, a vestigial reflex from a year of karate in his freshman year in college, giving the boot, so to speak, to a row of electric scooters some *fucking moron* has left blocking the sidewalk and *whoa!* over they topple in a clatter of plastic and metal alloy uttering angry buzzing, beeping, flashing androidal cries of complaint. Murder! Mayhem! Help! Police! Take this scofflaw into custody! Slap him! Beat him! Teach him a lesson he won't forget! Fuck you, *machines!* he growls with bone-deep gratification that immediately evaporates because, well, he wasn't wearing one, a boot, that is, and, *ow! ouch! ow!* the overdue bill from his offending and offended foot has just now arrived at the central pain station in his brain where a chronic ache in his lower back has already filed a complaint. Goddamn it to hell, that's all I need is a broken fucking toe, probably have to go to the goddamn hospital and get a fucking cast or something.

And, yes, glancing left and right to see if anyone has noticed, he does realize that he has been muttering and cursing out loud not entirely unlike one of those scabrous, drooling street people you pray to God doesn't choose you as the object of his affection and, who knows, start licking or even *eating* your face. Although, really, *Snowman*, who gives a shit about some loony talking to himself when the whole fucking world's talking to themselves. Look at this asshole yakking on his EyePhone®. No fucking idea where he's going, who's listening in on his conversation. No, I don't wanta hear about your big score down on Sixth St. last night, asshole! *Brrrinnng!* Jesus *fucking* Christ, another one! Answer your damn phone, dickhead! Oh, shit … he reaches into the left front pocket of his cargo shorts, extracts an antiquated EyePhone® the size of a hardbound King James Bible, hoists it to his ear, and Iago's voice, tinged with a micro-measurable dose of radiation, penetrates his brain. In the second or two it takes for him to comprehend what is being said his blood pressure soars like the mercury in a thermometer stuck up the butt of a boiled lobster. Fifty thousand?! Are you fucking crazy?! Tell that sleazebag to go fuck himself! SLAM! (*beep?*)

Hmm, well, *that's* certainly interesting. Fifty thousand what—*bucks?* That's a lotta moola for an ice cream peddler. Is the *Snowman* up to dirty tricks? Dealing in a little sideline, i.e., dealing? Good fucking God, how did I get sucked into this shit? And, hmm, that too sounds ambiguous. Exactly what is this *shit* he's referring to? Given the circumstances one might guess it has something to do with *this*: the guy's gotta be near sixty and he's pushing a fucking ice cream cart? And you think that thought doesn't occur to him at least once every day of his life? But, oh no, you shouldn't have said that, *Snowman*, you're not supposed to think that. No negativity, remember? Unicorns and fields of fucking daisies? Too late. Psycho become somatic, a deep throb has started at the base of his thumbs, not quite as opposable as they once were, the various osseous and cartilaginous connections gone stiff and arthritic from years of gripping this damn push bar. His lower back feels as crunchy as car tires on a gravel road and *yeeoow* that spot in his hip feels like somebody's digging around with a rusty screwdriver. He won't have to get a fucking replacement will he? Maybe there's some kind of natural herbal thing. Well *of course* there's a natural herbal thing. Keeping in mind this *is* Texas and in this great freedom-loving state taking a toke can still pull a life sentence *if* you ain't the right kind (white, money) or your ma (black, brown, yellow, white trash) isn't sucking somebody's dick. Oh, but Snowman, Snowman (glancing left and right again before taking a quick toke from the baked clay chillum in his pocket), let's not be so harsh. There are fucking *ladies* in the audience. *Okay, okay!* I'm sorry.

This bitching and complaining more or less his morning mantra when he's still ironing out the kinks and hijinks, the aches, pains and ancient scar tissue in muscle, bone and gray matter. Only, Jesus Christ, just when he was really starting to dig in and, *c'monnn*, admit it, Snowman, *enjoy* this darkness, here's this little girl sitting on a bench at the bus stop, shiny black pigtails tied with red, blue and green rubber bands, little matchstick arms and legs sticking out of a faded, threadbare in places, but otherwise clean and starched pink dress with ruffles at the knees, bashful brown puppy dog eyes looking up at him out of puddles of uncried tears. Her poor mama sitting next to her works standing on her feet six days a week behind the lunch counter at Moiphy's Five and Dime and the same six nights a week with her aching back bent over a mop and pail cleaning the third floor of the Saddz Building while her daughter's at grannie's whom she loves dearly but … Mama looks so tired she could probably fall asleep right here on the bench but she knows if she does sure as shootin' some concerned citizen's gonna call the authorities (child neglect, abandonment) and they'll take her to jail and her daughter away, and besides she clearly doesn't have a penny extra to spend on whatever nonsense this grubby old ice cream man is selling. *Oh damn it all to hell*, he growls (inaudibly) as he extracts two *PoPoPops!*® from his ice box, gives them that quick maraca *shake, shake, shake*, and presents them to the little girl with a theatrical bow and an affected Liverpudlian accent (who knows why—all you need is love?). Here you go, Miss, one for you and one for yer mum, knowing full well the lady would never accept them herself, in fact, the little girl's already so well-trained by her mother's own stoicism and pride she's on the verge of saying, no thank you, Mister, in her little tiny peep voice when he gives her an encouraging nod and in his best Bogie as good guy (*Sabrina? The African Queen?*) says, Go on, little Missie, we're doing a free promotion today. But what's this, a sentimental streak in our grouchy old Snowman? And even a grizzled smile as he hears *pop! pop!* and sees the mother's and daughter's faces light up with glee as the rainbow-colored mushroom clouds pop out of their cones like frozen cotton candy?

2
Bums

HIS COUNTENANCE TURNS FROWNISH AGAIN when he spots a rugged wooden cross lying on the sidewalk. It's actually jagged chunks of creosote-soaked railroad tie arranged like a cross with strips of white cloth that *might* have been torn from a surplice crossed on top of that, which *could* be read as meta-commentary on the crucifixion and resurrection, or the death of a once great industry (no, not religious indulgences—*railroads*). A hundred feet farther he spots another cross, this one made out of glossy white pieces of shirt board placed on a manhole cover and held down with a large rock. A little later still, pushing his cart under I-35 (or DR-35, short for *Drive 35*, as jokesters refer to this stretch of the Interstate because everybody knows there's no way in hell you're going faster than thirty-five even on a good day), twenty-four lanes of traffic roaring over his head, exhaust fumes pouring down around him, the exposed aggregate walkway under his feet scattered with dry brown leaves, beer cans, plastic bags and food wrappers, he spies a pigeon decomposed into clumps of gray and white satin plumage attached to skeletal remains in which, yes, he does see evidence of the reptilian transmogrification into fowl. He also sees that on top of this pigeon carcass someone has carefully, one might even say lovingly, placed yet another cross, also made of white strips of cloth, and on top of that a bright red rose, a velvet plush of crimson petals, relatively fresh, which he just knows if he were to raise it to his nose (as he almost impulsively does except … *yuck*) he would inhale into his nostrils and smell blossoming again in his brain a rich rose scent that, thanks to GMOs and unbridled hybridization, has mostly evaporated from the face of the earth. In yet another example of meta-commentary, next to this memorial, someone, quite likely the same someone, has placed a shallow Styrofoam package containing the brown-breaded skeletal remains of deep-fried chicken *parts* that have also merited a cross and flower, this time a wilted yellow gladiola with sepia age spots that, like the rose, most likely came from the nearby Burnumwood cemetery.

The Snowman will see similar displays all over this part of the eastside he calls his haunt or even hood, but probably not barrio, depending on *whom* he's talking to (you know how that goes). Crude cairns, cenotaphs, crypts, tombs, monuments, memorials, mausoleums in miniature, graves, sepulchers, ossuaries, entire fucking cemeteries, towering Egyptian pyramids—who knows what this mad architect of public mourning spaces is capable of? Or is that just him, the *Snowman*, again? Well, yes, of course it is. His mind all over the map as he follows these equally desultory stations of the cross, which, seen from the police helicopter hovering five hundred feet above his head, look less like a discrete dotted line leading to—oh, who knows, buried pirate treasure? the bad guys' hideout?—than multiple intersecting trails resulting in stochastic patterns of crosshatching that largely obliterate any sense of direction or purpose.

But before he can go any further down *that* garden path his mind rubber band snaps back to this moment because there he is just ahead, the mortician of dead birds, the cleric of crucifixes. And in case you had in mind a cartoonish, child-friendly, gruff but lovable Disney character, he is not. Indeed, quite the opposite, he is a hunched-over, gnarly hobgoblin with a tangled black beard that is almost certainly home to various insect and possibly rodent species. Even in this heat and we're talking a hundred-plus degrees he's bundled up in a black wool overcoat, baggy brown corduroy trousers tied at the waist with a piece of rope, on his head a ragged but somewhat natty gray fedora. His small black eyes constantly dart left and right. He's muttering to himself, to God, to whoever's listening, whatever message he's trying to convey largely obscured by almost non-stop profanity *fuck you motherfucking cocksucking sonofabitch piece of dogshit.*

Bum. That's what the Snowman calls him, the name he has given him, ironically, *affectionately*, because, sure, he *is*, by definition, a bum, a vagrant, he does wander from here to there, he doesn't seem to have an established place of residence, he has been known (on rare occasions) to cadge funds, albeit in a silent, wild-eyed, slightly threatening pantomime that suggests some sort of transactional arrangement, in exchange for what isn't exactly clear—safe passage? But to suggest that he, *Bum*, is lazy or shiftless is anything but the truth. He's enormously resourceful, an urban survivalist, a finder of things. He's pushing a shopping cart permanently appropriated from the nearby HUB grocery store and loaded with an empty five-gallon paint bucket, a plastic broom missing half its bristles, two dissimilar hubcaps, a hamster cage with exercise wheel intact (no hamster), a rolled-up foam mattress, a white Styrofoam ice chest, a flattened cardboard box. Products of scrounging, scavenging, dumpster diving. Which might be why on occasion the Snowman also refers to Bum as the *Bumster*, although, being a word guy, the Snowman, that is, it's just as likely for that rhyme thing. He has also been addressed as Dirty, Filthy and/or Disgusting Bum (because he is, unfortunately, really filthy), usually by people in passing cars who feel the need to inform him of their opinion, probably impolitic and possibly even risky up close and in person because this gentleman, *Mister* Bum, if you please, has long ago relinquished any claims to politesse. Forsooth, he giveth twice as good as he gets, mutters vile-sounding curses at anyone who even remotely appears to obstruct his path, whether they're getting off the bus or exiting a store, crossing the street or just standing on the corner *you motherfucking cocksucking steaming pile of monkey shit!* The Snowman pre-emptively hands Bum a *PoPoPop!*® like he's passing off a baton in a relay race, pre-shaken, ring tab pre-pulled *pop*, a frosty rainbow-colored mushroom cloud already fizzing forth, for which the Bumster, whose attitude will change imperceptibly (not *quite* rainbows and unicorns) the second he takes a bite, shows his gratitude by snarling at his benefactor *fuck you, motherfucker* while simultaneously ducking his head like he's expecting incoming, which could be anything, a roundhouse punch or a foil-wrapped baked potato thrown from a passing car or an RPG.

This last possibility occurring to the Snowman as he approaches the intersection at 38th and DR-35 where he spots something at first sight a tad bit disturbing. It's a ragged black T-shirt stretched over a No Parking sign in a triangular shape that looks like a man with his arms sticking out as if he were crucified and wearing a hood over his face, albeit with a pair of cherry red sunglasses where his eyes would be, not unlike something you might see on a mannequin in the window of an alternative clothing boutique or in a hellhole prison freezing cold at night and suffocatingly hot by day where human beings are routinely subjected to acts of depravity (rape, torture and hopelessly mismatched casual wear) in the name of yet another noble cause (*lalala*). And, sure, maybe it is some scofflaw's attempt to park illegally *I swear I didn't see no sign, officer*, but just as likely it was placed there, the Snowman suspects, as some sort of social commentary (the sunglasses added as a comical afterthought), by a member of the homeless community who solicit funds (panhandle) at this intersection, also referred to generically by the public at large as *bums*. And in case you think that's some kind of slur, well, it is, but even the bums call themselves bums self-deprecatingly, or defecatingly, it's an inside joke, you know, like when you really gotta go and there ain't nowhere to go, you pretty much live out in public, you can't just pull down your pants on the spot (well, you can but—), stores don't want a bunch of goddamn bums using their toilets *Beat him up, officer!*

Mostly the bums on this corner are fungible, they come and go and no one notices. Over time, however, a few hang on, take root, become regulars. This crowd for instance, the Snowman sees them here all the time. It's Big Earl and the gang, Hop-Along, Peg Legge, One-Eyed Jack, Handsome John, Penurio. They're sitting on the dilapidated railroad tie planter outside Kamel's Kwik-Stop, smoking, drinking beer, laughing and bullshitting. What people in passing cars see is a bunch of bums mooching off society and, to all appearances, having a great time. And, sure, these folks are taking a break now, laughing it up, trying to boost each other's spirits. They've been standing on this concrete island awash in hot, smothering exhaust, the sun blasting off windshields, waves of heat rising around them, the ambient temperature about a hundred twenty-five degrees. Pretty sure you can imagine what that's like (maybe not). You look as miserable as you feel, your feet are aching and blistered, your knees hurt, your back's stiff and sore, you're greasy, grimy, dripping sweat, nearly delirious, on the verge of tears, you're holding up a home-made sign drivers have seen a thousand times. God Bless, Anything Helps, Homeless Vet, Bad Back, Bum Knee, Need Beer! You might as well be invisible, you *are* invisible. People sitting in cars right next to you are desperately trying not to see, acknowledge you, you gotta smile, you gotta shuck and jive and do your vaudeville act to try and earn enough for a bite to eat. And then if somebody does wave a dollar bill or a bottle of designer water out the window you gotta run or more likely hobble down the line of cars, banging your already bum leg on the metal guardrail and stepping on broken glass and loaded diapers to get to that car before the light changes and *Beep! Beep! Move yer fucking ass!* the car's gone in a line of cars and so much for that basket of fried chicken or bag of chips you were dreaming of. You just wanta collapse on the side of the highway and fucking die. What you really want is an ice-cold tallboy or a spike of fucking morphine, *please*, God, *anything*. But no one's listening to your prayers, no one in the world gives a shit about you, little turd. No one except maybe Mother Teresa, and she's, you know … well, yeah, *dead*, but the answer we were looking for is *a saint*.

And now here *he* comes, the fucking *Snowman*, schlepping his cart up the sidewalk. He sees this guy sweltering on the corner, his first thought's look at this poor schmuck. His second thought is, goddamn it, why the fuck is this my problem? Why am *I* the one who's gotta play the goddamn good Samaritan all the time? Because of course he's going to, isn't he? Trying to sound more benevolent than begrudging, he growls, Here ya go, pal, it's on the house, and he shoves a *PoPoPop!*® in the guy's hand (Let's call him Charlie). *Bam!* Charlie's eyes light up like he just copped the aforementioned ice-cold tallboy. God bless ya, Snowman, I been jonesin' for a PoPop! all week. (Attentive viewers will notice the truncated form of *PoPoPop!*® in the vernacular of both young children and certain mentally challenged adults. One might also begin to suspect there's something more to these *PoPoPops!*® than your normal FDA-approved summertime ice cream treat.) Charlie gives his "PoPop" a quick shake, one-two-three, pops the top *pop!* followed by a pop bottle rocket *fzzzzt* as the rainbow-colored mushroom cloud bursts forth and, man alive, you can see the process of rejuvenation at work before Charlie takes his first brain-numbing bite, that precognitive rainbow glow of euphoria in his eyes followed by that look of re-amazement on his face when he plunges his tongue into the sweet, tangy ice-cold bliss and *Wowie Zowie!* just like that he revives like a wilted ragweed after a cloudburst. A few more bites and he's standing as tall as a Marine fresh out of boot camp. Because you're not like the rest of these losers, are you, Charlie boy? You're one in a million. You're gonna get yourself back on your feet, you're gonna get yourself a job and you're gonna make it in this old town *New York, New York*. He's wired, he's awake, he's alert! He's clowning for the cars, waving to the kiddos, playing air violin for the drivers who hold up empty hands and mouth *I'm sorry*. He no longer looks like some down and out sad sack. He's got this rainbow aura and there's something just so darn *appealing* or *charming* or *je ne sais quoi* about him. He even looks like he might be somebody famous. Yes! It's gotta be! Brad Pizzoccheri, Hollywood heartthrob! And he's flashing that beautiful, bright, beguiling smile right at you! No way! Am I in a fucking movie or what?! Windows are rolling down, a flurry of ones, fives and even ten-dollar bills are fluttering at Charlie like leaves falling from the proverbial money tree. Polar pockets of AC wash over him as he grabs as much cold cash as he can before the light turns green and ... *Beep! Beep! Move yer fucking ass!* the whole line of traffic's off to the races again and Charlie's back at the curb with a hefty wad of moolah in his hands. Looks like the folks on the corner are going to be living it up later.

That's how it works. You do your time on the island, you pool your assets, maybe you got enough for a bucket of fried chicken, a super-size bag of corn chips and a couple twelve packs of Old Milwaukee's finest, and you retreat to a shady spot behind a building or in an alley for a feast, stuffing your face with fat and cholesterol, smoking weed and cigs and gulping beer and telling tall tales—man, that's the life (sorta). Meanwhile the Snowman's pushing his cart away like a bit actor exiting stage right after his two minutes of fame but you can see by his outfit that he's a cowboy—no, that's not it—you can see that something's going on in his brain, he's got this idea sort of half-assed bubbling and percolating in his head like an old-school coffee pot. It's that eureka thing, the *voila* moment. He actually says to himself out loud, *Man, if you could organize this shit!* so that once again we don't know exactly what he means by *this shit!* Guess we'll just have to tag along and find out.

3
They're Gonna Put Me in the Movies

IT'S LIKE SOMEONE'S FILMING THE SNOWMAN as he pushes his cart throughout the day. Well of course someone *is* filming him. As devoted cinephiles have suspected, it's that venerable maestro of the B-grade movie, Boone Weller, back in the saddle again (with some assistance), grown older, naturally, his visage more wizened, his face more skull-like, the silk threads of his thinning hair dyed black and waxed into a single licorice whip glued to his forehead, his mustache a grease pencil crow in flight, his true age unknown, birth records, baptism, schools attended, childhood illnesses, family, relatives, friends, all a cypher. He walks with a cane now, an Irish blackthorn with a staghorn grip. Mostly it looks like a prop but an Italian paparazzo with a fixation on obscure American film directors has captured a grimacing Boone leaning his full weight on this third leg (ask the Sphinx). He (the paparazzo) also has a knot on his head to testify that Boone is crankier than ever, his bitterness exacerbated by years of critical drubbing. Even his diehard fans (who number, perhaps, in the *hundreds?*) are questioning if he still has the chops. Even his crew roll their eyes at each other and whisper behind his back. Of course, they're mostly fucking *kids*, every one of whom thinks he's (very few shes on Boone's crew) gonna be the next big Indie thing. Boone would love to regale these punks with tales of *his* Indie days surviving on Campbell's pork n' beans and Wonder Bread sandwiches and selling his blood as often as FarmCorps allowed him on the gurney, pale as a ghost, barely able to stand on his feet, just so he could afford a cartridge of Super 8. But what's the use? Just inviting more abuse. *Save it for the nursing home, Old School!*

All that remains of Boone's original crew are his hoary-headed, Yosemite Sam-mustached, ponytailed gaffer Moot, who's almost as crotchety as Boone himself, and *his* "best boy" (something just doesn't sound right about that), the equally cantankerous, also sixty-something, bald as a beetle Jeef, who keep up a running commentary of snide and fossilized remarks about *these whiny diaper babies*. Lad thinks he should get a raise. Ya don't say? I do say. What, wiping yer own bloody arse is a special skill set these days? They're also not above directing their opinions at (but not to) Boone. Old blighter's fault for hiring out of kindergarten. Doesn't have much of a choice, does he? Nobody with half a mind and a month's experience would work for the old shite. (Not sure why they're speaking with a (questionable) UK accent—*Manchester?*)

There's also this residual tension between Boone and the Snowman who is convinced Boone's got him pathologically confused with this actor dude Billy "Plum" Bob Bengay, which may just be his, the Snowman's, perennial paranoia (see patient history). Any hint of a camera aimed in his direction and he's off and running like a two-bit street hustler fleeing a flatfoot copper *slap!slap!slap!slap!* Boone attributes this, um, recalcitrance to *Billy's* well-known erratic behavior. He's either off-script or off on another drug and alcohol binge. Doesn't show up on the set for days, Boone's gotta send out search parties, seasoned trackers with bloodhounds. His new young tech guy makes the job a whole lot easier. He's got eyes on the Snowman pretty much 24/7. Doorbell and security cameras in homes, stores, banks, cafes, barber shops, schools, porta-potties (*hey!*). Tiny drones that look like ordinary insects dogging (*bugging?*) the Snowman's every step. (Diehard fans will see a reference to Hunter S. Thompson's *Fear and Loathing in Las Vegas*, re: bats (think *Chiroptera*, not the Babe).) There's one in particular, looks like a fairly large yellow grasshopper (*Schistocerca americana*—Ed.). The Snowman sees the damn thing everywhere he goes. He can actually see its face and it does have a face. It even looks like it's grinning at him, like it's in on some kind of joke, which makes the Snowman wonder (as does just about everything). According to science, an insect has eyes but it doesn't know it sees, it doesn't *know* anything. It's essentially a fucking machine. But in an odd reversal, this really is a machine. He can hear its tiny electric *hummm*, which is nothing at all like the fishing reel unwinding sound a real grasshopper's wings make when it launches itself like a V-1 rocket in short, nearly horizontal flights. Thanks to recent advances(?) in technology, this tiny machine is having an AI epiphany. *I think I think, therefore … I think?*

And, completely absorbed in this existential crisis or, at the very least, conundrum, it loses track of its target and goes off on its own path into the Emersonian wilderness, which appears as a small and impenetrable-looking patch of urban sylvatica, at its center a huge sprawling live oak that's probably been around since well before the Alamo enclosed by a natural palisade of bamboo and overgrown with poison ivy, ragweed, gnarly hackberries, native grasses and winding, twining mustang grape. Survivalist plants. The faux locust's curiosity growing, it decides to have a peek inside this tangle wood and, hmm, this is interesting. In a small clearing beneath the mighty limbs of this ancient oak there seems to be some sort of encampment, tents, tarps, hammocks, sleeping bags, bedrolls. Indeed, here we have an example of Osberg's affordable housing initiative at work. And, man, this is the flip-side of that happy-go-lucky street life we observed earlier. Empty cans and bottles everywhere, malt liquor, Mad Dog 20/20, cherry vodka. Cigarette butts, drug paraphernalia, used syringes. Dirty clothes. Plastic milk jugs filled with water. Blackened garbage smoldering in a fire pit. It's over a hundred degrees, the locusts are singing their mechanical refrain *zinnnc zinnnc zinnnc,* the dead yellow grass and weeds give off a sour metallic smell. People are sprawled on the ground in varying states of consciousness and dress or undress. One is only wearing a dirty pair of shorts. Angry red fire ant bites cover much of his body. Maybe for that reason another guy—*gal?*—is bundled up in a hoodie, sweat pants, boots. Another's pants are stained an unmistakable brown in the rear. Another has his head in a Styrofoam ice chest. Most of them bear cuts and bruises from mostly unremembered fights, assaults, falls. Two of them are drunkenly, ineffectually taking swings at each other now. Another is lying on his back, moaning, his face battered, eyes swollen shut, nose twisted and clotted with dried blood. Wow. The drone's totally fascinated by this crowd of bottom feeders. Maybe even thinking of settling in, get a government grant, do a study. Hey, guys, got room for one more? Until, that is, one of the inhabitants starts swatting at it with a stick. Go 'way fuckin' cockroach! Hey, Joey, that ain't no cockroach, you fuckin' idiot. Fuck you, Bubba! I hate fucking cockroaches. I'm gonna kill the little motherfucker. Uh-oh. The drone's imprinted human instincts tell it to get its faux invertebrate ass outa here. Where the heck did that Snowman guy go?

The scene changes. Now we see the Snowman down on the Drag across from the University. How he got here isn't clear. He's pushing his cart past a buffet of Thai, Chinese, Korean, Vietnamese, Ethiopian and, no longer émigré of the moment, Italian restaurants. Past the Picassoesque graffiti on the corner of 21st street of a smiling hipster alien frogman with a black charcoal goatee and eyes on stalks who greets passersby with a friendly *Hi, how are you?* Past the University Co-op *book* store (obsolete information storage containers) where one summer when he was still in college about four hundred years ago the Snowman got a seasonal temp job shelving those containers and even on occasion scanning the contents in stolen snatches of five or ten minutes leaning into the shelf so the manager, Emil, couldn't see him on the security camera (he did, but not before the young Snowman got all the way through *Fahrenheit 451*). Past the open-air arts and crafts market (tie-dye rules, ya'll) and famous Osberg mural, a palimpsest of the city's incarnations from small-town outlaw-cowboy-hippie-punk-slacker paradise to warp speed AI and IT intergalactic hub with no room in the inn for anybody who don't belong to that club. Past the Kaos student Co-op whose concept of cooperation and shared living space did not appeal to the Snowman's individualist (sociopathic?) tendencies. Past the eternally on the verge of closing music and booze haven *The Hole in the Head*. Past Dirty Martian's Kum-back burger joint that, for reasons he doesn't remember, the Snowman didn't come back to after one burger (greasy?). Past the ghost of the original Conan's Pizza Parlor where, totally stoned, he pigged out on Chicago-style deep dish pies in preparation for all-nighters that had nothing to do with studying for tests or writing papers.

At the next corner he glances up at the virtual billboard where a shimmering holographic Maurice Phillips advertisement shows an athletic young couple in bicycle helmets, bright red, green and yellow cycling jerseys and padded black riding shorts, improbably taking a vape break sitting astride their mountain bikes at the top of a steep rugged trail (a reference, the Snowman recognizes, to a very early Hitchcock film and more or less the same scene set on a snowy ski slope). But what really catches his eye, in fact elicits from him a cynical, knowing snort, is that this advertisement is sponsored by the (purportedly) health and well-being oriented Schneeland Foundation. Which reminds him, the couple on mountain bikes, that is, that this might be a good time to stop at the bicycle shop on the next block and see about that bum wheel, but before he can follow up on that thought all it takes is something like, well, that word *cycle* and it's down the ol' rabbit hole again.

Because if it *were* pronounced bi-*sike* that assonance (*cy? psy? sy? çai?*) could come in handy if you were writing a poem or having a go at wordplay, *ass and ends*, for example, an assembly line of asses, trousers down, buttocks skyward, a salute to the heavens, to the divine buttocks positioned over the world ready to let go with an

eternity of clogged plumbing—*Well!* (Jack Benny) You
can just imagine what *that's* going to look like (um … the
Apocalypse?). *Besides*, there's always the danger he'll
get caught up in an hour-long and arcane discussion of
spoke and rim tensile strength and torsion or the virtues
of titanium over palladium alloys with Rick, the shop
owner, who did a postdoc in astrogeophysics and was
recruited by Berkeley, MIT and Johns Hopkins before he
dropped out of academia to take up residence in an Inuit
village, whence, having attained the Inuit's knowledge of
cosmology from the village angakkuq (sounds
suspiciously like *Chingachgook*—have anything to say
about that, Mister Cooper?) as well as native fluency in
Inuit, he rode a modified mountain bike (air foils,
photovoltaic cells, kinetic energy-generating knobbies)
down to Tierra del Fuego to measure differentiations in
the effects of telluric forces on the human organism (*his*)
as it traverses the longitudinal curvature of the planet
earth from the north to the south pole over the course of
one solar year by means of electrodes in his bicycle
helmet, riding suit and derriere padding, the resultant data
quantified and assigned values according to an evolving
set of algorithms Rick programmed into his
EyePhone®36 ProGro, none of which the Snowman
understands or will remember later, and besides, right
now his mind's strictly on business.

Midday on the Drag is his bread and butter. The
sidewalk's jammed with students, about ninety-nine
percent of whom are bent like religious penitents over this
month's avatar of the EyePhone®. Approximately half of
them (49.6%—the Snowman's into odd statistics) are
also packing some kind of heat, easy-going *Howdy,
pardner* types wearing low-slung, long-barreled Colt .45s

that hang down to their knees, edgy, borderline psychopaths carrying silver-plated .380 Smith and Wessons and 9mm Glocks in the gleaming, stiff black leather of *au courant* shoulder holsters. He hears the muffled *pop pop* of a .25 caliber Browning semi-auto, followed by the single loud and decisive *Bang* of a Smith and Wesson .44 magnum, no doubt a couple of over-caffeinated kids squaring off for what has become the routine high-noon shootout *Do not forsake me, oh my darlin'*. But most of all it's the girls! Good God, Snowman, *look at 'em!* All these beautiful young female faces glowing like lanterns, all these beautiful young female bodies straining against mere wisps of polyester and cotton. May Ah please have a *PoPoPop!*®, Mistah Snowman? this little blue-eyed blonde says in a honeyed southern drawl that makes her plump, pillowy lips do all kinds of squishy things. But, oh no! *Mister* Snowman's gotta affect paternal indifference to those sparkling blue eyes and those puckery pouty lips and that perfect innie belly button punctuating that bare and perfectly flat athletic midriff and those smooth creamy thighs and those jogger's firmly muscled calves. Tennis, anyone? Jumping jacks? Acrobatics? Legs wide, that bold white triangle sailing across the Mediterranean blue skies? And *pop!* goes her *PoPoPop!*® and *lick lick lick* goes her deft pink tongue and up into the clouds goes her fertile young mind, immersed in all sorts of lascivious acts (well, maybe *his* is, *she's* thinking rainbows and unicorns).

This first sale sets off a chain reaction. At the sound of the *pop!* a line immediately stretches half-way down the block (except for a couple of high-strung survivalist types who drop to the ground, guns drawn) and the business-minded Snowman quickly raises a large green and yellow beach umbrella over his cart (it's more of an advertising gimmick, the scant slant of shade it offers illusory). Most of these kids are here every day, he knows them by name. Hey, Austin, Travis, Cody, Mohammed. Hi, Ashley, Brittany, Lakshmi, LaShondra. And *pop! pop! pop!* one after another, the carefree young collegians' faces light up with delight, oblivious to the rumblings of WWIII, oblivious to Governor Bismol's nefarious scheming against women, minorities, trans kids, immigrants, democracy, freedom, the unhoused—we have an example right here, this young dude in hopelessly passé Steampunk grunge who should be in school but is sitting on the sidewalk with a shaggy, sad-eyed mongrel mutt wearing a red bandana around its neck, both of whom, the kid and the dog, may indeed be homeless, but there's also the distinct possibility the kid's just some privileged punk acting out (excuse me, sir, do you have time to take a survey?). No less visible to the college crowd, the herky-jerky guy in a brown corduroy winter coat with strings of drool clinging to his bushy black beard and his eyes rolling wildly as he proclaims to a very small part of the world at large the imminent arrival of Jesus Christ. Oh, and space aliens. Oh yeah, and lizards. Very big lizards.

Which, hmm, is about to lead the Snowman off on another track (that thing about birds and dinosaurs?), when *clack-clack, clack-clack* this dude comes flying down the sidewalk on a skateboard, surfer dude shorts, tie-dye T, tarnished brass and leather steampunk goggles with rose lenses, red and black tartan driver's cap on his head and preternaturally bushy muttonchop sideburns blowing back like smoke from a steam locomotive. *El Pájaro*, perennial adolescent slacker and fixture on the

Drag, occupation or source of income unknown, been boardin' since he was in diapers (he will tell you). Grinning maniacally, Pájaro raises his black slide-gloved hand for a passing high five, shouts *S'up, Snowman!* and flies on down the track like a ninety-mile an hour Casey Jones madman *clack-clack, clack-clack.* And then—it all stops. The *pop! pop! pop!* of *PoPoPops!*®, the babble of excited young voices, the noise of street traffic, gunfire, the light rail whooshing *byeeeee*—all disappear when the Snowman by dint of a random space-time intersect catches a snatch of conversation between a couple of coeds regarding a class wth, u knw, that wrd prof, *Dktr Levant?* it's, lk, rly *wrd?* Lk, sh mks u do, lk, rly wrd, u knw, *stuf?* Lk, w ur *fon?* Lk, trn it *off? OMG!* thts so rad! I mn, lk, ds nybdy get *sic? OMG!* Lk, ths 1 chk ws, lk, *hyperventilating?* (auto-correct is guessing here) And, lk, thy hd to tk hr to th, lk, *hsptl? OMG!* Thts so *awsm!* I knw, *rt?* Thts wy u hv to sine a *waver?*

4
Lily of the Night

HER FACE IS THE COLOR OF COAL, of ebony. As black as sable, onyx, obsidian. The wings of a crow, a raven. Pitch black, midnight black, jet black, boot black, lampblack, black as soot, black as black. But also infused with impossible shades of cobalt, jade, malachite, plum, mahogany and rosewood depending on the light, the mood, the music. If she were white she would look, well, white, sorta. More like a Nordic extraterrestrial. Her hair is closely napped. Her features, forehead, nose, eyes, ears, lips are as perfectly defined as if they were made of porcelain or blown-glass, not readily identifiable as Black, but not Caucasian either. There's definitely something about her eyes. They're a brilliant green, like sunlight on blades of grass or a deadly green mamba sliding through that grass. She stands at a chalkboard in room 221 of David Hall, formerly the English building, the camera looking over her left shoulder so that we see the back of her head, her slender neck, a wedge of her white cotton blouse, her extended left arm and the piece of chalk she holds in her hand as she writes in cursive as elegant as silver Victorian flatware the word *Invisibility*. The camera draws back slowly, there's a sense of anticipation, even apprehension and—okay, let's just say it right off the bat—it's gonna be impossible not to stare at her butt. Everybody does. She would herself if she could (well sometimes she has with a mirror but it's tricky). It's not just that it's *large* (not, mind you, as big as a VW beetle, but pretty damn close). It's also absolutely, unutterably beautiful. The mother of all butts. A steatopygous masterpiece whose taut global curves a geometrician or cartographer would be hard-pressed to fully describe. A pair of buttocks that looks entirely capable of squatting a quarter ton for reps or launching its owner over an eight-foot bar. This maximum gluteus has been likened to a huge ebony heart, a colossal black cherry, an enormous eggplant, a giant plum. More than a few honest souls have confessed to wanting to take a bite out of it. Even more noticeable in contrast to her wasp waist, slender arms, small, high breasts and petite torso. Dr. Lilith Levant. (Despite the suggestion of lilies, fragrant perfume, lunar whiteness, in Hebrew her *Christian* name means night hag, monster, demon, screech owl (In that sense also harridan? Virago? Maybe, but probably not in her case.); also associated with blackness, darkness, the underworld; also wind in the sense of a malevolent spirit (ill wind?); also, yes, the moon, as, perhaps, a malignant force (the tides of March?). One might also think of the yin and yang, the balance between positive and negative, light and darkness (and, if you must, good and evil).

Dr. Levant has seen plenty of darkness in her life, a childhood eclipsed by darkness, a penumbral adolescence, days of hunger gnawing at her stomach, of sleeping on the floor in a cold empty room, of waking to a strange man lying on top of her and falling asleep again from hunger and exhaustion and waking again to another strange man on top of her, sometimes men who are not strangers, uncle, father, priest (forgive me, Jeeeesuhhh …), po-leece (shut up, *bitch!*), *husband*, the one who was to save her, love her, protect her (*only sixteen*). A good man, *they* said. Sober, clean, upright, hardworking, *they* said. Tyrannical, she *knew* but didn't say, controlling, abusive, possessive. *He* was possessed, by the word of God, the rule of God, the tyranny of God, *his* God. At first it's just an angry word, an admonishment, why did you speak to that man? I do not want you to go out of this house in those clothes! You call this slop food? It gets worse and worse, the endless interrogations, the accusations, the slaps, smacks, punches, jealous of every man she talked to, disapproving of every outfit, pair of shoes, didn't want her out of his sight, didn't want her to have an education, the man of God, servant of God, pious, righteous, it's all there in the scriptures, everything you need to know, the woman shall obey, the woman shall do her conjugal duty by her husband, the woman shall not defy, speak ill, resist, even if she doesn't like it, even if *please, stop, it hurts*. Shut up, *bitch! Slap! Slap! Slap! Slap!* A familiar story, an old story, a very old story indeed.

Now enters the next player, Samuel—Sam'l, his thug bruhs call him, among his many other names on the street. She's heard his other names, she begins to pronounce them to herself, Wrath of God, God's Venom, God's Poison, Evil Messenger of God, Seducer, Destroyer, Angel of Death, *Brutha Grim*—she likes that one best. In other words, the baddest bad boy in the hood, the meanest muthafucka, the devil in disguise, the closest thing to pure evil, he, Beelzebub, mocked, laughed at anything good, reveled in, entrapped, seduced, manipulated, *destroyed*, didn't care who or how he hurt. Day after day on the corner, so handsome, a prince, king, his words sweet, hello, beautiful thing, how you doin' today my Nubian queen? He does this rapping thing, is it meant for her? *Dam bitch, thought it was doggerel, you know, vulgaral, also can't spell,* she *said, didn't know it was lexical, intratextual, dam and bitch being the same thang, a female dog, y'all, so you wanta file a complaint? Call it redundant—maybe.* And yeah, she knew he was bad, knew what happened to his girls, *hos* fo sho. She didn't care, she *loved* cheating on the cheating husband, snuck out during the day, more brazenly at night, slapped back *Slap! Slap! Slap!* Kicked, *hard*, in the balls. One day just walked out. *Oh baby*, she said. He made her feel so good, he pampered her with clothes, jewels, *Oh Daddy*, the high he gave her on this drug or that, that magical protracted orgasm that lasted lasted lasted until somehow it was in the past, gone, a memory she groped for, passing out and waking again with another strange man on top of her. She remembers doesn't remember trashed-out apartments, broken bottles, destroyed furniture, rotting food, pizza boxes, Chinese takeout cartons, cockroaches, rats, guns, *bodies?* That's right, *baby*, back to the same old *way it was* and then some. Woke with sledge hammers pounding on anvils in her head, angry rats ripping apart her stomach, pills, alcohol, razor blade lying next to her, she was going all the way, didn't make it, the cut, discovered she didn't want to die. She had to get out of that house, out of that life. She broke away from Sam'l, moved in with an aunt. Her *husband* (no exes except death in that belief system) saw his chance, the *good* Satan, he came begging, I'll treat you right, I'll treat you nice, my helpmate in the day, my queen by night. *They* all said, they who *knew better*, right? *Go back to him! Go back to him! Go back to him!* like a Greek chorus, coven of witches. She said, No way, Jack.

AGAINST ALL ODDS she held on, survived. Fortunately she wasn't dumb, *stupid bitch! dumbass ho!* On the contrary, she was smart, very. Her brain always at work, alert, when she wasn't fucked-up anyway, even without access to the internet, smart tech, no EyePhone® to call *my* phone, her mind like the web, gathering information from the matrix, *it's everywhere!* TV, radio, signs over shops, stores, advertising in windows, on the sides of buses, trucks, street names, numbers on digital clocks, glimpses of open laptops, words overheard in conversations, the odd wobble of the wheels of a dump truck passing in the street, the tension in the cables of a crane lifting an iron beam at a construction site, discontiguous bits and pieces of information she assembled into larger units of meaning so that when she was finally able to take classes at the local community college at night after hauling her tired and suddenly (what the fuck? where'd *that thing* come from?) burgeoning buttocks through day after day of low paying jobs, fry cook, maid, waitress, convenience store clerk, she immediately grasped concepts like resistance, inertia and force in physics class, absorbed literary texts almost by osmosis, wrote a thirty-page essay on "Echoes of Caesura from *Beowulf* in Contemporary Hip Hop" that stunned her English prof who had only asked for three pages and expected two written at a third-grade level on some inane subject like My Pet Dawg, aced the SATs (1600), got a full scholarship, did brilliant work.

That's one narrative. The other is that she was a pampered child of privilege who never wanted for anything. Who took piano and tennis lessons, who attended ballet and gymnastics classes, who traveled near and far, studied abroad, had private tutors, a healthy diet, a wonderful home life with love and support for her every endeavor. Who was, yes indeedy, also brilliant, spoke several languages, excelled at the university, BA and MA magna cum laude, PhD dissertation that blew the socks off everyone in the department titled *Non-Linear Perception and the Ineluctable Modality of the Visual; or: An Introduction to Invisibility* which came out a year later in hardback with a *few* amendments. Basically rewrote the whole damn thing, translated prerequisite academic horseshit (jargon) into brilliant prose, reduced the title to a single word *Invisibility*, spent three months on the NYTBSL, frequently referenced, often carried about, largely unread, a rarity for an academic work (the best seller list, not the largely unread—see Manley Formix's scathing critique on the Big Brilliant Book: Joyce, Gaddis, Pynchon, Wallace, Schmidt, et al.).

Regardless of the truth, her origin, fact or fiction, she was a star, appeared on Oprah, Colbert, every big-name university recruited her. What's not to like about a brilliant Black woman with a PhD in an exotic field who also happens to be strangely beautiful (although, true, even the politest pair of eyes in the room can't avoid blatantly staring, if only for a moment, okay, two— *three?*—at that incredible double-barreled butt) and speaks perfect white (this is what it looks like on the blank page:), non-Ebonic English without a trace of identifiable dialect, region, culture or national origin that puts everyone at ease, even the other Black faculty

members (you go girl!)—if only, if *only*, she could keep
her *fucking* mouth shut! Because, yeah, sure, she's prim
and proper, she laughs politely and sometimes even
heartily guffaws, she's friendly, a good listener, but then
there are these odd, completely out of character bouts of,
well, profanity, when she can be a real—what did we call
it earlier, not bitch, *virago*, which, according to the
Dickshunary, is a farrago of virtuous and heroic warrior
woman (archaic) and ugly, violent shrew, and how to
reconcile the two? Just a question of mood? When she's
feeling down and blue? When she says, yeah, well, fuck
you? When she raises up her sword and shield to the
heavenly blue and says to God is this good enough for
you as she steps over the bodies she slew? Except she
hates that rhyming shit, heard way too much of it *my
Nubian queen*. All the accumulated hurt, the betrayal, the
lies, the pain, whatever their source, it's all there in this
truth-o-meter in her brain. When she hears total bullshit
she just can't restrain herself and she spews forth ugliness
in martial arts proportions. No eye for an eye, tooth for a
tooth. No jab and parry, go ahead, hit me again, Christian
pacifist turn the other cheek. It's total war. You hurt me
this much and I hurt you this much more. And she is
indiscriminating, employs any and all weapons at hand.
"Polite society" euphemisms inherited from the ancestral
oppressor. Demotic, vernacular, gang language, ghetto
slang, street lingo, tribal code (e.g., ululations, clicks,
tsks, spitting, vulgar gestures, traditional insults), *mostly*
to herself, in the sanctuary of her head (one doctor has
described it as Inside Voice Tourette's Syndrome—to be
perfectly frank, Ms. Levant, quite preferable to the
outside version), which is the only place (inside her head)
she feels fully free to give utterance to her frustration and

outrage at the enormous *fucking* stupidity of the world around her, above all that of her so-called *colleagues*.

Egos inflated like hot air balloons, a fleet of flatulent blimps, dirigibles, schmoozing, oozing, self-promoting their way through conferences, dinner parties, departmental meetings. Their primary interest squeezing as much gravy out of the system as possible with the least expenditure of energy (and risk of getting called on the carpet). The few tenured profs who remain are fossilized, lapidarized, they've been working on the same book or paper or edition for years, *teach* one class, sometimes with only two or three students, one day a week one semester a year, for which they receive a salary equivalent to that of the entire staff of untenured lecturers, adjuncts and aspiring assistant profs (*buena suerte*). One's writing about Gomer's bones—the Old Testament guy? See, you didn't know, that's why it's important. So, I have this theory that his bones, which, by the way, I keep in a box in my office—give me a sec, I'll show you, here we go—as I was saying, his bones show signs of *poetic wear?* Exegesis written all over them—*see?* Those are teeth marks, Fred. Human, I'd say. Geez, Jerry, you paleontologists are so literal. Fucking losers, hypocrites, don't do shit and suck the well dry *not* doing it. Some of her sympathizers (fewer and fewer) describe these outbursts as expressing herself (not that compelling of an argument in a civil forum) or speaking truth to power (except the message gets lost in the language) or standing up to the man (definitely not gonna fly). Dean Dunge (no matter how you say it ...) judged it *damned stupid* of her—*he*, that fucking imbecile, calling *her* stupid? Can't even tell the fucking difference between his rectum and a hole in his head—yes, your fucking *mouth*, you ignorant asshole! Which, unfortunately, she told him, to his face, at an open departmental meeting, in front of fifty-nine faculty and grad students, as well as attendant secretarial, technical and janitorial staff (could ya's hurry it up here? we got woik ta do), when she herself was, as of yet, untenured, second year into her assistant professorship (although true, one book under her belt, contract pending on another), resulting in her abrupt dismissal (appeal also pending, *rotsa ruck*), to the relief of even her staunchest defenders.

Which is how twenty—is it really already fucking *twenty?*—years ago she ended up here in this fucking mediocre *institution* (despite the chancellor's claims to excellence, *top tier!*—it's the scotch talking), where all her talents, her awards and publications (at this point author of several books, all largely unread, everybody agrees they're brilliant, beautifully written, but also "obscure," "recondite," "possibly *too* smart" and, above all, "angry") mean nothing because she's a fucking lecturer in freshman comp in the lowliest department on campus (last in line for triage, first to take shit when it hits the fan), the combined Department of English, Foreign Languages, Literature, Linguistics, Classics and Advanced Finger Painting or, as it is known by some wise-asses, The World Made Easy for American Speakers. The language instructors teach the putative foreign language in English with fakey accents, sometimes tossing in a genuine word or two, *Ciao! Buon giorno! Je t'aime!* Hee! Hee! Hee! The students love it. It's just like speaking English but it's *foreign?* Like, I'm *Italian?* Like, my great-grandmother or somebody came *here?* So, I thought I should, like, learn to *speak it?* You know, like, *Capeesh? Bone Jorno! OMG*, that is, like, so *awesome?* Like, you're totally *affluent?* I know, *right?*

And, yes, they do write the way they speak, when they write. Any assignment Dr. Levant gives them is perceived as a greater or lesser annoyance in proportion to the time it separates them from their EyePhones®. They stagger into the classroom fifteen minutes late, just now doing wakey wakey at eleven am, ear buds blasting substratal musical frequencies, spilling double cappuccinos and lattes and dropping crumbs from the muffins or donuts or chocolate chip cookies they're equinely masticating. They collapse in their seats like they've just returned from a trek in the Himalayas, fumble with backpacks, set up their desktops according to individual spatial or OCD requirements, coffee here, pastry there, EyePhone® *here*, do a little thumb work, *tap tap tap*, take a bite of croissant, a sip of coffee, totally unaware anything's amiss until an awareness of *something* does begin to penetrate their interiorverse and they notice that, yes, *asshole*, everybody *is* staring at you and even then they're, like, totally *clueless?* Like, did I miss anything *important?* No, Trevor (*douche bag*), when do we ever do anything important until you show up? Oh, well, in that case. Wait—is that, like, *sarcasm?* Because if that's sarcasm I'm gonna fry her fucking big fat ass in the evaluations (and yes, he will say that, *fucking big fat ass*, and get away with it). But … uh oh, just the mention of this part of the anatomy and once again all eyes present glom onto the damn elephant in the room and that's all it takes for this egomaniacal gluteus maximus to claim the limelight, and, man, this butt's putting on a performance, it's like it's got a personality of its own, like it's running for office as an independent candidate and Dr. Levant's the appendage.

Cut! Cut! Cut! Stop the action!

And with these words all hell breaks loose as Boone Weller himself rushes onto the set looking every bit like Tony Perkins' agitated "Mother" in *Psycho* in what, at first glance, appears to be an ankle-length Victorian dress (it's actually an 18th century brocaded banyan) and boy is he exercised about something.

Camera! Destroy that film immediately! Costume! Can the big butt!

Apparently the Cultural Sensitivity and Cucumber Appraisal Board is in an uproar and Boone's the target of their ire. How dare this white-ass honky mofo perpetuate the stereotype of the big-butted Black woman? They've got a rope and a chair if they can just find some place to string up this hater bigot. Boone, who has never shied from controversy, appears completely nonplussed. He's spu-spu-sputtering, *Who, m-m-m-me?* Seems there's been a major fuck-up in communications between costume and the screenwriters, chronology's off, characters mixed up, *something*. Boone is even more baffled by his crew's reaction. *Ha!Ha!Ha! Ho!Ho!Ho! Hee!Hee!Hee!* It's a joke, you see? *Can? Butt?* No?

Turns out the damn thing's a prosthesis. Some dumbass newbie who did a stint at SNL thought it'd be funny as hell (well, Boone did too until he got his skinny old ass in a crack). Somewhat awkwardly—it certainly calls into question the film's credibility even among diehard fans—Dr. Levant will appear in the next scene with a noticeably diminished derriere, it's practically petite, as is she, but still *sweet as a plum* (perhaps in an effort to appease critics and smooth over hurt feelings, both Boone and the Snowman will be seen at different times later wearing this enormous butt, looking embarrassed as hell and constantly banging into things with their loose caboose).

Class starts at last. Dr. Levant asks a question about today's reading assignment. As usual no hand raises to suggest a possible answer, much less acknowledge her question or even her presence. The worksheet with half-a-dozen sentences they were supposed to correct? I forgot, the dog ate it, grandpa died, sister married, the alarm didn't, the doctor did. But heaven forfend she should say anything remotely bordering on criticism. Call mommy and daddy! Teacher's being mean to me! Report her to the dean! Call the police! Up against the wall, bitch! Shoot her Black ass!! Next thing she knows she's on a conference call with the parents and the Dean who assures the parents that in addition to going through a lengthy cultural sensitivity program (the irony does not escape her), *professor* Levant (did I get a *fucking* promotion?) will be only too happy to apologize and even give three hours a week of her own spare (in a parallel universe maybe) time to privately tutor the offended student (*spoiled punk*), which the parents are welcome to supervise.

And indeed they will. Parental involvement in children's education is all the rage. The helicopter moms (and yes, they're *here*, followed all the way from pre-K to high school and now, just think, *we're* in college) swarm into the classroom suspended from drones, hover like ungainly Tinker Bells over their little darlings (he's *only* eighteen, voice quavering), ready to deflect any difficult or uncomfortable questions (Do you think the ~~holocaust~~ … *Bleeeep!* Did ~~slavery~~ … *Raaaant! Is ~~abor~~

... *BLAAP!*). They don't hesitate to *share* with the *teacher* (so now I'm fucking demoted again?) that whatever she says is only her opinion uncorroborated by the Bible or Fuchs News. They're all armed to the teeth. How dare you speak to my little Tiffany like that! *Blam! Blam!* Now the whole room is in an uproar. Some students start to cry *waaah!* Others stomp their feet, tear up papers and throw tantrums. Harried momsters and a few stay-at-home dadsters are trying to calm their little lambs with candy, pacifiers, warm bottles, baby blankies. Calling up an ancestral mother earth spirit from *somewhere in Africa*, Dr. Levant begins to croon. It's a melody, a tune, no words or lyrics but full of intent, a mix somehow of keening and lament and at the same time an offering of love and reassurance and just like that everyone drifts off into slack-jawed, drooly, happy nappy land, snorting, snoring, occasionally flatulent, while Dr. Levant sits at her desk writing notes for the new book she's working on (tentatively titled *The Collapse*, it's about the end of society and, too bad for us, she makes a pretty strong case).

Despite the kid gloves, the space she gives to parents, the diaper changing tables she agreed to have installed, the powderpuff grading (call it the curve recurved, all grades cluster around some fractional gradient of A, not unlike the agglomeration of stars around the black hole at the center of our galaxy), her students tear her to pieces in their evaluations. I was intimidated! Terrified! Tormented by a sense of inadequacy! Reverse discrimination! The law of the jungle! But hold on a sec, says the admittedly nerdly Nell, adjusting her horn-rimmed glasses (she can see fine, she's just hiding). You know what? She's actually funny and her class is fun and

I learn a lot of cool stuff and maybe it's all a *mask?* You know, like a *charade?* Like that stuff they used to have in the *old days?* Satire? Sarcasm? *Irony?* So—Llewellyn, the intellectual in the crowd, Kierkegaard trending toward Kant leavened with Freud, adding his two pfennigs—it's obvious that she's, like, *projecting?* Like, she resents our happy *childhood?* And, who knows, maybe she does. If only she could convince these kids, just open the fucking book, just pick up a fucking pencil and fucking *start*, it's not so hard, it's no different than learning to ride a bike or play a new chord on the fucking guitar like Johnny in the corner who she knows will sit up all night hugging and crooning to his National steel gitbox like it's a dying lover (he doesn't have the licks for that yet—hasn't paid his union dues, the union of the blues) but he can't spend five minutes trying to construct a fucking decent sentence? She wants to say, what the fuck are you doing here with your life? Don't you know your time is already fucking running out?!

One day when she feels she really might lose it and possibly even start screaming at her students, out of nowhere she sees a hand raise and it really is out of nowhere. The hand is unattached, the wrist bone isn't connected to the arm bone, there is no arm, no torso, no head. And yet she senses the presence of such, or at least the physical mass it *uninhabits.* Yes? she says, glancing at her roster to see if she can tell from the seating arrangement who this inchoate person might be. No use, the kids are all over the place in this bedlam, drops, adds, chronic absentees, name changes following gender reassignment. The voice that answers doesn't help her much either, oddly melodious, also androgynous, not exactly male or female but also not, she's pretty sure, AI, and what it says is almost magical, not because it's in an elven tongue or it suggests otherworldly powers but because what it's saying is fucking *correct*. She can't fucking believe it. The disembodied voice of this faux student she can't even see is answering her question correctly and in simple, direct terms almost as if he-she-*it?* actually read the fucking assignment and did the homework.

I'm sorry, what's your name?

Oscar.

Oscar? Hmm, I don't seem to have you on my roster. Are you sure you're enrolled for this class, Oscar?

I registered late.

Odd, I haven't received any notice.

There was a billing problem.

While not a direct response to Dr. Levant's last comment, this answer does follow logically upon Oscar's prior statement. There is also an intriguing sense of practiced evasiveness about it. Well, okay, she says, I'll look into it. But she won't. Whether or not this kid's legit, he's a fucking gift next to these losers who *have* begun to look at each other, quick sideways glances like wild little bunny rabbits darting into the underbrush, I mean, like, who the fuck is she talking to? A few of the older kids roll their eyes. By now they assume this is part of her shtick, performance art, who knows, maybe she *has* lost her marbles, *whatever*, before bending back over their phones *tap tap tap*. The texting is so loud she can actually hear it. No, wait, it's a huge horned owl with large orange eyes and it's furiously beating its wings at the window and rapping its huge black beak against the glass in what could conceivably be an intelligible and even urgent message in, say, Morse code. Dr. Levant gives the great raptor her own furious glare, indicating with a sharp jerk of her head that it should go away or, at least, somewhere else, possibly even, one senses, for some sort of rendezvous, and then she casually strolls to the window and looks down at the Drag where she can see a snake-in-the-grass ripple among the crowd of students.

5
A Brief Revisitation of Old Wounds

WHICH DISAPPEARS LIKE A SEAMLESS STITCH as the Snowman instinctively turns down a narrow side street, instinctively because during his indolent senior year at the university he often took this street to the nearby Les Amis Café for a cheap lunch of buttered brown rice and steamed vegetables and a Shiner bock sitting at a table under the awning watching girls passing to and from class, usually stoned, maybe smoking an experimental Gauloise or Gitane, *The Glass Bead Game* or *Dandelion Wine* or *A Moveable Feast* bookmarked next to him, the waitress always French or German or Italian but exotic enough by his ne'er been nowhere American standards to give him a glimmer, a glow, a largely misguided romantic notion of sitting at a Parisian café or bistro. But Les Amis is long gone and right now all he wants is to take a load off somewhere in the shade and enjoy a quiet bag lunch (steamed vegetables and brown rice) when the squeaky left wheel's plaintive appeal for grease or other remediation reminds him he should have stopped at the cycle shop.

And wouldn't you know it, that word *cycle* (*sci? sei? sai? si?*) takes him right back down the old rabbit hole on a brief and ultimately painful memory detour that begins with an almost mythical chain of islands and the impossibly blue sea surrounding them, lapis lazuli, sapphire, turquoise, cerulean, cobalt, the blue of glassware in apothecaries, in ancient Mesopotamian burial sites, the blue of royalty, of a pair of eyes gleaming with androidal intelligence and with them a celluloid stream of images. Judith running toward him in a black storm cloud of hair, breasts bouncing pertly beneath a brown wool sweater, behind her protesters outside the snow-blanketed Old Main shouting fairly lame slogans (*Don't be loyal to Blimpford Oil! Don't be the "IS" in Capitalism!*). Judith in a multi-colored, Klimtian-print hoodie and pink flannel pajama bottoms bent over a screen at the kitchen table, coffee gone cold, cigarette smoldering into ash in a bowl of congealed oatmeal, her eyes glowing like LED lights on a missile launch console, her fingers striking the keyboard with robotic fury. Judith in a white lab coat bent over an electron microscope examining elements of a new nanobotic filtration system in the R&D division of the mundanely named corporate giant *Print and Paper Products*. Judith, raven locks chopped into a spiked helmet, clad in a black leather alpha female warrior outfit addressing the United States Joint House Senate Investigating Committee. Judith now, in a tailored charcoal business suit, about to enter the über upscale *Alimentary, My Dear*, the gustatorial nexus between the University of Texas at Osberg and the business world. Their eyes meet, a bipolar clash of pale Arctic and dark Aegean blues. She is as striking as ever, maybe more so. She has clearly maintained her daily five a.m. Special Ops physical fitness regimen. Her hair, still coal-black but now threaded with white, is longer again, and loosely tied back. Her face has assumed a tragic quality, less soft sculpture and more chiseled geometry, her features redefined not so much by age but also, one might surmise, her many years on the corporate battlefield. Her voice is harder than he expected and she probably intended, despite or because of her accent.

So, Snowman, still play*eeng* the game?

You know it, baby, he growls with an odd emotive wobble that registers in a twitch of Judith's right eyelid.

Both of them seem staggered by this encounter. A confusion of hurt and yearning echoes back and forth across the chasm of time and space that divides them, by one metric, inches, by another, years. Their features are distorted by the odd, painful grimaces of attempted smiles. It's a like a wild west standoff, who'll blink first, this town's not big enough for the two of us, etc. Indeed, the observant passerby might wonder why this striking middle-aged woman is so earnestly engaged with this grungy, over-the-hill loser who's pushing a fucking ice cream cart for God's sake.

Well, take care of yourself, *Snowman*.

You too, Judith.

She turns away and only now does he notice the movie-star handsome, fifty-something dude in the two thousand-dollar Armoani suit who has been holding the door for her throughout the duration of this brief reunion with increasingly clenched jaw, which also explains the welcome draft of AC he has been enjoying despite this sticky situation. And just like that, a sunny summer day collapses into hibernal gloom (it *is* Texas) and another disastrous mood swing that threatens to bury him under a whole sad-eyed clown circus of regrets as he pushes his cart away into a winter white fadeout on the screen.

6
Back on the Clock (Chaingang)

WE NOW SEE A MIDNIGHT-BLACK MOTOWN CLASSIC Coupe du Jour, Cheshire Cat-grinning chrome grill in front, shark fins behind, cruising down wintry white E. 32nd street on Osberg's Near East Side, behind the wheel the Snowman, twenty or so years younger, in a grungy blue parka, faux fur-lined hood pushed back on his shoulders. Despite what was once referred to as a healthy tan, he looks worn, bedraggled, like he's just driven across several time zones and as many dimensions. Everything he passes, houses, parked cars, street signs, telephone poles, is buried beneath a deep blanket of snow. Frigid air pours in through myriad pinholes, mouse holes, cracks, crevices and dry-rotted door and window seals. On the radio, faint, tinny, Bing Crosby is dreaming in his warm, hearthside bass-baritone of a white Christmas.

He makes a right on Robeson, a left on Clancy, another left, past the blue house, the pink house, the yellow house, and there it is, *home*, a modest little dwelling, not quite a cottage or bungalow but more than a shack. Shabbier than he remembered, a bit of a shock, really, shingles missing from the roof, rotten siding, peeling paint, all the repairs he was gonna gonna gonna make and never made.

He parks against the curb, disembarks the Coupe like a banged-up cowboy getting down from a horse. He feels like the survivor of a shipwreck or even the shipwreck itself, battered, beaten, ribs stoved in, but mostly glad to be alive. Exhaling frosty cartoon balloon breaths and beating his arms together for warmth, he slips and slides up the icy walk, finds the key in a spider hole on the side of the doorframe, unlocks the door, enters and—it's about as nasty as he imagined. It's cold, damp, it smells of cat piss, mildew, mold. White feathers and skeletal avian carcasses of snow grackles are scattered everywhere. A pair of oddly detached white satin wings looks like pious human hands folded in prayer or an accessory to a ladies' hat from a bygone era. He finds more bird carcasses in the bedroom where a window pane has been smashed in. His gerbil's nest of sleeping bag, wool blankets and bare mattress on the floor is covered with feathers and broken glass. His heart does an acrobatic leap in his chest when he feels something rub against his leg, then skips another beat (if that's what hearts actually do) when he looks down and sees a creature that pretty closely resembles a small black panther. It's a cat, a very large, street-fighting cat with ragged ears, scarred pugilist's face and a club-like stump of tail. It's also *his* cat (if it's possible to claim ownership of a cat). *Me'th?* Oh man, am I glad to see you! Let me give you a hug! And, *oomph*, muscle tissue fissuring up and down his back, he hoists into his arms this formidable-looking beast, easily twenty-five pounds of sinew armed with scimitar claws and saber-tooth teeth. But rather than reciprocate this embrace, the cat, Me'th (possibly a diminutive—*Methadone? Methedrine? Methane?* Too many negative connotations?—Ed.), pushes him away with glowering contempt. *What the fuck are you doing, Snowman? You abandoned me, remember? You went off on an extended vacation and left me to fend for myself. Now put me down this instant!* And, claws beginning to pierce his flesh, the Snowman's quick to obey, *okay, okay!*

He then sets about putting things in relative order. He tapes a piece of cardboard over the broken window, strikes a match and lights the gas space heater, the welcome, punched-pillow *whoomph!* and row of curling blue flames signaling another small triumph over the remote but always present possibility the damn thing will explode. He sweeps up the broken glass and bird carcasses, shakes dead cockroaches out of blankets and sleeping bag and more or less makes his bed. Me'th, meanwhile, has continued to dog, well, *cat* his heels, his meows increasingly demanding, *mrrt? Mrrt? MROWW?!* to which he finally accedes *since he's not getting anything else done.*

In the kitchen he digs up a can of sardines in tomato sauce, a hefty chunk of grana of uncertain provenance, Judith, most likely, which means it's been sitting there at least three or four years, still a young cheese by some standards, and a box of salt crackers, damp, crumbly, but … edible, a minimalist feast he and Me'th share with grudging sideways glances and occasional growling sounds, his unintentional.

After the meal, he pours a glass of whisky from a bottle in the kitchen cabinet, pulls a blanket over himself on the couch and stares into the blue flames curling inside the ceramic Angkor Wat grille of the space heater. Inevitably his gaze shifts to the luminous white square on the wall near the window, a piece of hand-beaten paper with a Japanese ideograph printed on it in broad black brush strokes that means something like *the path to harmony is strewn with thorns*. He thinks about calling Judith, about saying to her all the things he should have said long ago but didn't. But he doesn't. Let's spare ourself more disappointment, why don't we, Snowman. *Hi, I'm back. Really? Where have you been?*

Instead he lights up a slightly damaged cigarette recovered from a crevice in the couch and, sucking deep, soul-consoling drags of tobacco smoke down into his lungs, his tongue lolling in the warm sweet burn of whisky, he ponders more mundane issues. Like, what're you gonna do now, *Snowman?* Find a job, of course. What kind of job? How the fuck do I know? Something. Something my ass. How many times have we been through this? You aren't going to find shit, you aren't qualified for shit, you'll be lucky if you cop a fuckin' job shovelin' shit. He's beginning to slur and mumble to himself as alcohol and fatigue shut down his electrical circuits. Then he's asleep. He knows he's asleep because the reality he has entered is the reality of dreams. He's in a city, modern glass buildings erupting like giant crystalline growths out of a substrata of colonial palaces and cathedrals built of stone. He hears a loud rumble. The ground begins to shake under his feet, buildings sway, debris falls around him. It must be an earthquake. Wham! He's knocked flat on his back. He sinks into unconsciousness. And wakes again with an oppressive weight on his chest and a sound like the hum of an electric motor. Is he buried under rubble? Are rescuers trying to reach him?

Rinnng! Rinnng!

A persistent ringing pulls him out of darkness into groggy, disoriented daylight with a large, heat-seeking feline curled on his chest. The ringing continues. It's a telephone, of course. It's *the* telephone, probably the last landline in Osberg, a hard black Bakelite artifact you could knock out an elephant with. He offloads Me'th as discreetly as possible *mrrt?* staggers to his feet, digs the phone out of a moldering pile of laundry in which he spots a scorpion's desiccated carcass glittering like a piece of Victorian jewelry.

Snowman?

An annoyingly nasal, middle-aged female voice penetrates his brain. He pictures a small button face, bright blue bird's eyes behind wire-rimmed glasses, Brillo pad hair, bottle cap-crimped, slightly hirsute upper lip. *Evelyn?*

What made you think I'd be here?

Just a hunch, Snowman.

Silence on both ends.

So, Snowman, I was wondering if you might want your job back.

Are you crazy?

The screen goes blank, total whiteout, white noise, white paper, white nothing.

Then … a carnival display of flashing colored lights seen through a furious snow squall. The ghostly image of a large, white, cement truck-like vehicle. A pale spectral face behind the windshield.

Snowman! A Bronxy male voice calls out and a short, balding, overweight man with an unhealthy codfish complexion and a khaki weatherall parka open over a purple cardigan and red tie, waddles forward to welcome him *back on the team* with a wide barracuda smile that doesn't register a glint in his dead fish eyes and an unpleasant handshake that feels like squeezing a slab of halibut. Mister Gastreaux, his old boss (and arch nemesis). For about one second he expects a buzzer to go off in his hand and the Keystone Kops to rush in and trundle him off to the calaboose. Doesn't happen. Gastreaux's falling all over himself ... *wonderful to have you back, Snowman ... impossible to find decent employees anymore ... a man of your caliber ...* Is this the Gastreaux who ruled this circus of incompetence and duplicity with an iron fist and unstinting stinginess? The same Gastreaux who actually may have tried to kill you, Snowman?

We next see the Snowman in a brand-new, puffy, midnight blue parka with the synthfur-lined hood pushed back on his shoulders and a pair of knee-high faux reindeer hide mukluks, also newly issued, on his feet, standing in front of the desk of the aforementioned Evelyn, executive secretary extraordinaire, consummate paper pusher, cabinet filer, *typist* (she likes to keep that on the record, one hundred twenty-six words a minute, *thank you*), bookkeeper and de facto office manager (w/o the commensurate pay, of course, that's the breaks, *lady*), as always fashionable in a teal office parka with military style epaulettes, the two of them engaged in what appears to be a fairly animated game of charades involving *pointed* threats (Evelyn's waving a paper knife at the Snowman) and defensive measures (he hoists a pot of paperwhites in front of his face). Which, sure, is all in fun, right? An affectionate but slightly edgy relationship established over the number of years it took Odysseus to find his way back to Ithaca? No reason to believe she was complicit in this alleged homicide attempt, is there?

But what if you got it wrong, Snowman? What if all that time Gastreaux was so occupied with keeping the snowbiz afloat he never stopped to smell—well, not the roses, but the cadavers rotting under his nose? And what if Evelyn was so busy punching in numbers she never realized taxpayers were shelling out tons of money to cover up something a whole lot stinkier than industrial waste and household garbage? Despite or because of these doubts, the Snowman, Gastreaux and Evelyn will continue in a sort of—what else?—Mexican stand-off with the camera zooming in on furtive glances and nervous tics, as well as endless adlibbing and reading between the lines—the script keeps changing, the writers, all young, inexperienced, underpaid (*because* they're young and inexperienced), are constantly at odds. It's anybody's guess where this show is going. Moot and Jeef are carping nonstop. Damn kids today don't know shit from Shinola! Shit, they don't know Shinola! Those were the days, my friend. You know it, mate, back when men was men.

The Snowman's return to the motor pool is also less or other than expected. Of his original *mates* only two remain. Jippi Jaime, guy's a total lifer, the world can go to hell and it's all good long as he's got a buzz on (let's see what happens when his supply chain dies). Jaime's crew is comprised of the last true Osbergian stoners dragged out of the vestigial Hobbit holes of hippie slackerdom by the inexorable need to earn a buck and not a heckuva lot more. They function (more or less) according to some Zen-karma thing which blindly overlooks the trail of fuck-ups they leave behind, lost tools, broken water main, driver's side fender torn off a parked car, crushed baby carriage (anybody in that thing?). Jaime gives him a fist bump and a lidsy grin, *yo, s'up, dude?* like they just this minute met for the first time instead of having worked together for those previously mentioned ten Odyssean years. The other old-timer is Hankthefuckingredneck, who actually seems glad to see him but for reasons that quickly remind the Snowman of how Hank got his nickname. *Ain't many of us white guys left, although truth is you're starting to look a little bit like a Meskin yerself, Snowman. Hope you didn't have to swim across that damn river, ha ha.*

He did. A crackling, popping, black and white cutaway shows Little Nell tied to the railroad tracks—no, wait, a flimsy log raft with a car on it, a Detroit classic with gleaming chrome grill in front and shark fins in back. Yes, it's the Coupe, being drawn across a narrow stretch of muddy brown water in a desert canyon by a couple of short squat men pulling on thick ropes. For reasons that aren't clear we see the Snowman's head bobbing up and down in the water at the back of the raft. Oh, wait, is that gentleman in the green uniform on the north shore a border patrol agent? And while no one ever asks him directly what he was doing down ol' Mexico way, there are some disinterested inquiries into how his *vacation* went, to which he gives a cryptic smile and answers *Unbelievable!* in a tone that suggests, oh, I don't know, piña coladas on the beach, a beautiful babe on each arm, maybe some parasailing, ziplines and—*fire-breathing dragons?* (A subliminal flash of something that *could* be a dragon if you squint a certain way, but it could just as well be a photoshopped garden lizard.)

Since his return to work the Snowman also has the distinct impression that he's under surveillance. He'll see the glint of a camera lens, hear telltale clicks, beeps and buzzes over his telephone. The rare mail he receives other than bills arrives crinkled or torn with a *damaged in transit* sticker. Nor can he shake the feeling he's being followed—because he is. And whom do *they* have tailing him? None other than Gastreaux's dumbass nephew Gordie in a ridiculous attempt at a disguise, yep, fake nose, Groucho Marx mustache, eyebrows and black horn-rimmed glasses, oh, and a baseball cap with an oversized bill the Snowman spies Kilroy-like poking out from behind doors and over window sills, which leads to ridiculous chase scenes set against lurid blurry backgrounds meant to suggest to the viewing audience that the whole thing might just be a dream. The Snowman will take off running with clumsy, overweight Gordie in international orange thermal coveralls right behind him in *hot* pursuit under icy bridges, across snow-covered railroad tracks and down rank-smelling alleys where he and Gordie get lost in a series of bizarre plot twists that stretch the willing suspension of disbelief like a rubber band (a tribe of *molemen* inhabiting the city's sewer systems, alien invaders who look like giant broccoli stalks), setting off howls of protest if not outright derision among film critics but delighting audiences across the nation. Cineastes have also raised the possibility that Gordie, unhinged by the clash of boy scout innocence and the harsh reality of a lifetime of unrewarding labor ahead, has become celebrity-obsessed with the Snowman and at this point is actually criminally stalking him in the entirely deluded belief that he is in fact the protagonist in the rumored new Boone Weller shoot, played by the repeatedly washed up and recovered B-grade character actor Billy "Plum" Bob Bengay, who finally dropped the more sober sounding *William Bengay* after his last failed stint in rehab convinced him to stop the pretense and just forge ahead with the best of 'em (here's looking at ya, Johnny).

It's like the Snowman's got a dual identity. Away from the job he's some kind of super-secret agent. When he punches in the clock at night he's just another blue-collar yob. Or wait, is the job the super-secret agent part? And, true, his first nights back at his old occupation, his butt plunked down in that sweet spot behind the wheel of Number Nine, the huge wedge-shaped titanium plow blade in front shunting away mountains of snow, the enormous arachnoid abdomen swollen with two thousand gallons of Icine, the rainbow-colored barrage of warning lights splashing on cars below, the giant, eight-foot tall, steel-spiked knobby tires inundating them in sheets of icy gray slush, he feels that old warrior pride swell in his chest at the prospect of the night ahead. *Fucking A! I am* the fucking *Snowman!* A couple of celebratory pulls on the bottle of whiskey he finds in the rat's nest under the front seat and pretty soon he even breaks into a croaky off-key rendition of *back innn the saddle againnn* that drives his Mexican crew nuts (*are you fucking kidding me?* eyerolls) even though they don't understand a word. Nor do they have any patience when he gets a bug up his ass because of something he read or heard on the radio and now his ento- and etymological curiosity is piqued and he absolutely has to know, Say, *amigo*, how do you say nano-transmitter in Spanish? How do you say string theory? food poisoning? fish eggs? *Mira,* Snowman, *tenemos negocios. ¿Entiendes?* And don't ask what kind of business because, as he quickly figured out, these guys are nothing like the dirt-poor campesinos he's worked with before, I'm so damn happy just to have a job, whip me, beat me, treat me like a donkey, I'll work for *carrots*. These guys are indeed bad hombres, gang and cartel members who crossed the Big Frío not to save their *moreno* asses from the law but rather disgruntled former colleagues. They're covered with scars, prison tats, studs, bling. On more than one occasion the Snowman has spotted the metallic gleam of weaponry about their persons. They're like Maori warriors. He's pretty sure some of them have killed and eaten human flesh like Maori warriors. Correction, *Aztec* warriors.

The scene abruptly changes. We now see the Snowman in what fashionistas will recognize as a very pricey cream-colored linen suit (Armoani), climbing out of a taxi. It's dark, night, he's in a rough-looking urban setting, graffiti, broken windows, shot-out streetlamps, dirty water running in the gutter, Banda music playing somewhere, people laughing and shouting in Spanish, a couple of kids nodding off in a doorway. Looks like he got off at the wrong spot. He signals the cab driver to wait. Too late, the taxi takes off, its brake lights flare at the next intersection and it's gone. Out of nowhere a gang of really scary-looking dudes materializes. They're covered in tats and studs, loaded down with guns, knives. The baddest badass among them pulls out a combat knife and puts the blade against the Snowman's throat. The screen goes dark.

Wait, what happened next? The Snowman's obviously still with us. Did Boone cut the scene? Seems there's some history here and it sounds a helluva lot more interesting than driving a snow truck. Which is probably why the Snowman quit driving a snow truck in the first place and took off on his so-called vacation which—not giving anything away—was nothing at all like *Pee Wee's*

Big Holiday. Which also somehow explains why he's here, now, right back in the same old *used to used to used to be*.

And just like that the full weight of the ten years he has sat in this very seat presses down on him like a ton of kryptonite as routine quickly becomes routine again and his life morphs into a shadow play of his life that he watches on a black and white TV screen. Night after night he sees himself drive through the front gate of the Ice Factory. Night after night he glances up through the glare of floodlights, tangles of concertina wire and blowing snow at the words over the entrance stark and black in wrought iron **ARBEIT MACHT WARM**. Night after night he sees himself approach Evelyn's desk and hears her shrill *Snowman! Stop tracking snow all over the floor, you're going to kill someone! And put out that cigarette right now! You know smoking's not allowed in here!* Night after night he grabs the stack of invoices, work orders and special assignments from his job basket and heads out to the motor pool where he will face the hostility and unspoken disdain of the mini-cartel he has somehow become head of. Night after night he plunks his ass down in that bitter-sweet spot behind the wheel of SnowBile number nine, braces himself with a swallow of whisky from the bottle that miraculously never empties under the front seat, lights up a filter-less cigarette and sucks the smoke into his lungs with suicidal intent, tar, nicotine and secret ingredients combining with all the attendant effusions of internal combustion, diesel, hot oil, grease, transmission, steering, brake and hydraulic fluids, as well as cool menthol traces *Snowmannn* of the two thousand gallons of volatile Icine in the giant tank behind him saturating his brain in a narcotic stew that more or less stays with him the rest of the night as he goes through the freeze-thaw cycle of climbing up and down from the SnowBile's somnolent warmth into the frigid darkness on the job site where every step, every process has become so familiar, so intimate he could and more or less does sleepwalk through it. Firing up the generator, the tentative chug-chug-chug rising into a loud steady grind that will gradually fade into the background. Shrugging the three-gallon tank onto his shoulders and adjusting the nozzle of his ice gun until the neon-blue stream of Icine turns into a frosty white spindle that will expand in the black velvet night like a jet contrail. Everything he sees, houses, buildings, light poles, parked cars, is viewed through the black and white TV intermediary of his blue-tinted goggles. He hears familiar things he's heard so many times they've faded into the periphery of his consciousness. His faux reindeer hide mukluks crunching in the snow. The occasional nasal chainsaw whine of the crew over the headsets. *¡Chingaleeee, putoooo! ¡Más arriba, güeyyyy! ¡Ni madre, cabrónnnn!* The faint ticking sound the snowflakes make as their rigidly geometric crystalline structures crash into each other like tiny ice cathedrals on those rare occasions when he turns off his mike and pushes his hood back on his shoulders and listens in reverent awe, pondering the fact that just as there are people who have never seen snow there are also people who have never known anything but snow, their world an endless frozen whiteness … until the cold closes around him again and he shudders and pulls his hood back up.

Or driving back home in the Coupe at the end of the night, the whole world buried in whiteness, the sky beginning to brighten in the east, faint pink ribbons appearing just above the horizon, and then the yellow cellophane light sparkling on the snow, igniting individual ice crystals into tiny red, orange and blue gas flares, followed by the hot salt water wash in his eyes that almost always comes at this time, which could be anything, the daylight suddenly blinding after twelve hours of darkness magnified by exhaustion plus whatever mildly mind-altering substances he has ingested during the night, but also the pride, yes, pride, that thrills like a glass harp through his entire being for this hibernal still life he has helped paint. Because it is beautiful. And deadly. Like and unlike the poisonous beauty of the datura's luminous whiteness he remembers from steamy tropical nights. But rather than the datura's intoxicating scent of roses infusing the warm air, this frozen whiteness has smothered, asphyxiated everything, sent everything into a permanent hibernation. Almost everything. He watches an enormous flock of Northern Great-tail Snow Grackles, thousands of them, flap up from the earth into the sky like an Escher painting of a snow storm falling in reverse. Turning onto his street, he passes the blue house and then the pink house where he sees Moses in a pink bathrobe, wild black dreads and tangled beard pacing around the front yard in rapid circles like a crazed swami ascetic, the Ice burning in his brain driving him beyond sleep or even awareness that there's a foot of snow on the ground and the temperature's just above zero. But at least his feet must be toasty in those fleece-lined, faux reindeer hide mukluks, which, yes, do look exactly like the ones the Snowman wears on the job.

Despite endless resolutions to make better use of the little free time he has away from the job and do something constructive like read a book or take care of much needed home repairs or at the very least stroll up to the taco shack on Maynard (which some in the audience may remember is pronounced *Mannered*) and strike up a conversation with some other lonely loser like himself in hopes of making a new friend, he mostly does—nothing. Sometimes, insomniac, his sense of time and place out of whack, he walks the blinding white streets like a vampire, his face hidden inside the fleece-lined red hoodie he wears under his flannel-lined denim jacket, dark glasses to protect his eyes against the glare, the golden glow he acquired down ol' Mexico way faded into a waxy, mycological pallor. At some point he heads up to the Drag, drawn by the semblance of life, of youth, the thousands of college students crowding the sidewalks in a mosaic of brightly colored parkas, ski jackets, sweaters, leggings, wool beanies, Incan alpaca caps. The temperature's maybe twenty degrees, shop windows are Jack Frosted, everybody's exhaling steamy cartoon speech balloon breaths, welcome blasts of warm air waft out of open shop doors accompanied by not exactly welcome snatches of Christmas music beaten by years of hourly repetition into a dull mechanical refrain *Have a holly jolly* ... Sometimes he goes inside and lingers *undecided* over a red, white and green reindeer sweater or a pair of nerdy rubber galoshes, trying to absorb as many calories, joules, units of heat as he can to dispel or displace for a brief respite the more or less permanent chill in his bones he carries home to his frigid little hovel every morning after work while Soviet comrade choir-sung Christmas music loops in the background *Rudolph the red-nosed ... Silver bells ... Here comes Santa ...*

Oops, time's up, the sales clerks and some of the other customers are starting to give him odd looks and besides, latent agoraphobia, ever lurking paranoia, in a nuthouseshell, too many damn people too damn close, he flees the market place and gets maybe half a block before he stops in front of a card table display of colorful knit purses, caps and scarves, candles, books, pamphlets, fresh-baked vegetarian, vegan, halal and kosher food items in labeled plastic wrap set up in the entryway of a recently shuttered clothing boutique. Incense smoke swirls around him, stirred by irregular but welcome waves of warmth emanating from a propane heater under the table behind which stands a huge Black man in a voluminous St. Joseph's coat of many colors, Old Testament beard, red, green, yellow and black crocheted Rasta tam on his head, natty dreads down to his butt, incongruous desert camouflage combat boots embedded with vestigial grains of Mesopotamian sand on size eighteen feet. In a voice deep as a forest drum, and also familiar, he says, What it be, Brutha Snowman? Familiar because *Brutha* Snowman knows this voice, knows this face, has seen it up close, almost intimately so, the surprise of this moment propelling him backward in time to a fleeting out of body experience: a yellow wedge of incandescence, giant stainless-steel tanks, an odd transition from standing on his feet to lying flat on his back on the frozen ground, snowflakes sifting down out of the night, a sledgehammer pounding on his skull, the angels shrieking in his brain *Snowmannn! Snowmannn!* a big, bearded black face, this one, bent over his, brow furrowed like freshly ploughed blackland prairie, black coffee bright eyes dimmed by a knowledge of death made intimate by a couple of tours *over there* and a lifetime of blackness in the streets, the *de profundis* voice urging him, *Wake up, Snowman!* And, *boom,* he wakes back into this moment and that same face looking at him now, comical quizzical and, well, yeah, concerned.

M'Shaka?

Ha!Ha!Ha! You still a trip, Snowman. Who else you think I is, Mistuh POT-ASS?

Thanks to a bit of exposition Boone skips over, the Snowman learns that M'Shaka left the snowbiz to become the spiritual leader of a local congregation whose multi-colored robes represent the unity of all peoples on earth. M'Shaka invites everyone who stops at his table to visit their house of worship, a small, wood-framed church on the Far East Side, formerly Baptist and white (the paint job, not the congregation), resplendent now in rainbow colors, which the Snowman has noticed with at least mild curiosity on his daily or more accurately nightly commute to and from work. And, sure, some people express an interest, young folks searching for meaning in life, individuals with a congenitally ingrained need for the sort of moral compass offered by unorthodox spiritual and religious institutions (*cults*). A few even make the harrowing journey to the Far East Side, *once*. The Snowman says of course he would love to check it out, the ambivalence of that *would* meaning, for those who know the Snowman's tendency toward polite Japanese ambiguity, never.

Sometimes he goes to a matinee, mostly just to sit in the anonymous darkness and lose himself in escapist schlock. This afternoon his routine varies as we see him enter the small porn theater squeezed between the liquor store and the tarot card reader up on the frontage road. He passes this place going out to buy exotic cigarettes and rolling papers at the adjacent headshop and never, seldom, anyway, gives it a second glance but today a

movie poster with an unusually literary title catches his
eye. *The Penis as Protagonist*. What really attracts or
more accurately *startles* him is the name of a fairly well-
known cross-over porn star and B-grade film *artiste*,
printed in lipstick red, *Mona Moondrake*. He pays ten
bucks to the disinterested, overly made-up middle-aged
lady at the window who he's pretty sure is a guy in drag
and goes in, and it's what you'd expect. Dingy, musty,
sticky floors, fish smell, nearly empty except for a couple
of dudes, one of whom—surreptitious, sideways glance
(don't want him to think you're gay, oh no, no, no, no)—
looks oddly dapper in a red bowtie, starched white shirt,
checked gray wool jacket and slick 1940s crooner hairdo.
(Shortly after the movie begins he'll start to cackle
manically and almost nonstop.) Turns out the title is right
on target. The film's basically a nonverbal dialogue
between the *model's* face, in particular her lips, mouth
and tongue, and the head of an erect penis (size large), but
also her eyes, which are angled up and sideways to make
contact with the viewer, who, in an unspoken contractual
agreement between voyeur and exhibitionist, imagines
himself in the place of the unseen owner of this penis,
except in the Snowman's case no imagination is
necessary because not only has he seen this face before
up close and in person, indeed, gazed directly into those
jade green eyes and kissed those lips, it's even possible
they've had sex, once, although that's too much to explain
right now without delving into quantum mechanics.
Besides, five minutes in and he's seen enough.

The planets are so far out of alignment that on one of
their rare nights off, Hanktheredneckasshole invites the
Snowman to his place for dinner, which turns out to be
this delicious southern fare Hank's wife, Marfy-Ann, has

prepared, cornmeal-battered fried chicken, a mess o' greens swimming in bacon fat, black-eyed peas, sweet taters, homemade drop biscuits warm from the oven and for dessert a huge slab of fresh-baked peach-rhubarb cobbler and a mound of Blue Bonnet vanilla ice cream. And here's another surprise. Marfy-Ann is not the morbidly obese, barely literate, foul-mouthed white trash slob he, yes, admit it, Snowman, expected, but rather, okay, sure, slightly faded but nevertheless drop-dead beautiful in a retro hippie way, thin and waiflike in an ankle-length, filmy print dress, long strawberry blond hair starting-to-gray framing delicate features in a delicate face that is, yes, also a bit worn, but what really strikes him is he can tell she absolutely adores Hank (true, she is a little ditzy), in fact, at the moment, drinking beer and passing a joint and filled with *joie de vivre* or brotherly love or *something*, he can almost see Hank the way Marfy-Ann does, not as a semi-literate, alcoholic lowlife with missing teeth and a scraggly mustache, but the way he looked when she met him, a devil-may-care, wispily goateed Robin Hood running the roads in the wee hours of night with a trunk-load of weed or ten pounds of crank hidden in the gas tank. And forget that their house is a permanently run-aground mobile home, tacky knickknacks, worn furniture, a cheap, wide-screen TV with lurid greens and reds and crackling static, a puppy dog litter of kids sprawled on the worn carpet in front of it, totally oblivious to their pappy and his friend getting royally fucked up. Hell, Snowman—Hank lights a cigarette, hands him the pack—they don't even know what their old man does for a living. The only life they know is on the goddamn TV. It sits there talking to 'em, telling 'em things, it's all good, everything's groovy, don't worry 'bout the future. Same time it's showing 'em torture, rape, murder—horrible things, Snowman, worse'n I ever seen in the damn war, worse than prison (these biographical notes are news to him). But if you don't give 'em the goddamn TV, if you don't pay the bills, if they shut off the electricity, turn out the lights, then it's up to you, Snowman, you gotta fill the void, you gotta entertain 'em, you gotta be warm and glowing, you gotta hold them in your arms and tell 'em it's all right, everything's gonna be okay, when you and them both know damn well and good it ain't. Maybe it's the beer and the weed talking but the Snowman has never noticed this level of articulation in Hank before. And by the way, just to clear up a terrible miscarriage of justice. For those in the audience who've heard the rumor—it wasn't Hank who stole the Snowman's watch. It was this cocky new kid on the crew who disappeared the next day. Which didn't bother him all that much. He hated the weight and constant reminder of life unwinding on his wrist. He only wore the damn thing because it was a college graduation gift from his father and all he had left of him except for a closetful of Hawaiian shirts. Besides, even in this convivial moment of *fraternité* and *solidarność* there's no way he can share his true feelings with Hank. What the fuck you mean you don't like making snow, *Snowman?* What else you gonna do? Chop heads offa chickens in one of 'em damn poultry factories like a fucking *Meskin?* And, yeah, what else *are* you gonna do, *Snowman?*

Mostly he ends up on the couch stoned, chain-smoking filterless cigarettes and sipping whiskey, yes, returned to that routine, too. Above all remembering just how much he hates this job, hates this life. This chronic existential crisis crashed down upon his head with even greater weight than before, this enervating sense of pointlessness, hopelessness, meaninglessness. Antman. Ant labor. Mindless. Quotidian. Joan Didion. Who wazh she? Writer, right? Shaid *life changes in an inshtant*. No she didion. *The* instant. And keep on like that until he passes out on the couch muttering incoherently even to himself. At some point drag himself into the bedroom and collapse in his gerbil's nest on the floor. At some later point still Me'th's heavy pantherine form having arranged itself on his chest or against the back of his knees, occasionally breaking into a deep rumbling purr of contentment, no existential worries *he*. While the daylight hours pass unseen from morning into afternoon and evening when he wakes again to the melancholy purple and lavender shadows spreading through the house, the last orange firelight of the setting sun disappearing in the front window and the remains of day fading outside, and Lazarus-like he pulls himself up off the floor, groggy, disoriented and tireder than when he got home from work this morning. A tiredness and fatigue that will become not just perpetual but incrementally worse as he sinks deeper and deeper into this morass while repeating to himself that tired old question, by now some sort of mantra or koan, What are you *doing*, Snowman? You promised, you swore, you were never going to allow yourself to fall back into this rut. And now here you are again, digging your own Mariana Trench. But what else can I do? I don't fucking know. Something. Anything but what you're doing now. But that was the argument that got you *into* this shit. Hey, *Snowmannn*, you're doing it again.

Because, yeah, this honeymoon of separated and reunited oldlyweds lasts maybe two-three months before he begins to notice the dark shadows creeping in from the periphery and the abyss opening up beneath his feet and he feels himself descending into the dark embrace of his old nihilistic lover, despair, as he sees this vampiric existence stretching before him in a dominoing *mise en abyme* of tombstones and open caskets, the contents *him*, his corpse, dressed for the occasion in his puffy, midnight blue parka and snuggled in creamy white satin for eternity or at least as long as it takes to rot into complete nothingness and oblivion. And as much as that thought sickens him and fills him with dread, even worse with true winter approaching and with it a blue norther like nobody ain't never seen before as all the glaciers, ice shelfs and snowpacks in Canada and the Arctic melt and collapse sending a wall of frozen air pouring right down the middle of the USA into Central Texas, the temperature drops way below zero, the wind howls, the snow blows, in one area piling up huge drifts, in another leaving entire neighborhoods bare. The Snow crews are working overtime trying to make up for the disparities. Inevitably the Snowman comes down with a bad cold, maybe it's the flu. He shivers the whole night through inside the frigid igloo of his parka, his body wracked with aches and pains, coughing up his lungs, flinging snot everywhere. Blowing ice and snow slash his face. The cold penetrates his parka, sending violent, shuddering shockwaves throughout his body. A coupling breaks, flooding his mukluks with ice water. He removes his mittens to get a good grip on the wrench and shut the damn valve off but the wrench slips and, *yeeow*, barks his already frozen knuckles, torn skin, blood oozing out of white subcutaneous flesh. It hurts so bad he feels like crying. He feels like lying down in the snow and dying. And it's all because some goddamn inconsiderate sonofabitch who instead of staying home and keeping his filthy germs to himself decided to soldier on and share the wealth. And yeah, sure, he gets the irony. He also knows the proper response. At least you got a job, motherfucker.

Because it can get a whole lot worse. There are plenty of reminders of just how much worse it can get. Like the ride share driver he recognizes from his neighborhood all the way out here on Capitol Highway in the middle of the night. Guy's a chemistry teacher in high school, wife has stage four ovarian cancer, daughter serious mental and physical disabilities, he's trying to pick up some extra cash on the hours of sleep he forfeits. Fucking *chemistry teacher*. It's a fucking wonder he isn't manufacturing crank in his basement. And even that's not as bad as it can get. Everywhere the Snowman goes he see reminders of how bad it can get, the colonies of *unhoused* huddling on corners, in encampments under snow-blown overpasses. Madmen, lunatics, substance abusers, traumatized vets, sure, plenty of those. But a lot of 'em are just down-on-their-luck working folks out here in the freezing cold, sometimes whole fucking *families*, fallen from grace, living in makeshift tents, lean-tos, abandoned cars, belongings piled up outside, furniture, snow shoes, knobby-tired mountain bikes, fire barrels shooting flames into the night. There's a guy out on the corner right now, sign up, working the early morning commuters for the cost of a donut and a hot cup of coffee or a bottle of Mad Dog 20/20 or anything, *please*. He's shuddering violently, teeth visibly chattering, fists clenched like chunks of frozen gristle. He stares at each car with a desperate plea in his eyes, can't they see he's on the fucking edge of dying? So, yeah, he's a wee bit surprised when this huge fucking SnowBile pulls up, the window rolls down, and a dude in a midnight blue parka who looks a helluva lot like that movie actor Billy "Plum" Bob Bengay tosses a crumpled ten-dollar bill across the chasm between bitching miserable and mortally wretched. *No, really, I'm telling you, man, fucking Billy "Plum" Bob Bengay!*

Even when this brutal winter passes, the arrival of spring proves April really is the cruelest month. The temperature climbs during the day, the sun comes out, the snow slumps and melts, muddy brown puddles appear in the drab white landscape, cars splash up dirty gray slush in the street. But it never goes beyond that. Spring starts to arrive, and then it doesn't. At night the Ice Factory cranks up again, blowing out massive snow bombs that blanket greater Osberg. The snow crews finish the job out in the burbs. In the morning everything's frozen over again, the streets and sidewalks are icy, cars skid and crash, pedestrians slip and fall on their ass and crack their skulls. Driving to work in the evening the Snowman stares at the blue and purple and gray shadows spreading like spilled paint over the dead Dalían landscape, his mind, soul, the I of his I weighted by an almost unbearable melancholy and longing. What he really wants is for the process to go on, the temperature to keep rising, the snow to melt away completely, things to grow and turn green again, the first daffodils to appear, the first robin to sing of the arrival of spring. In other words, life, the life he still remembers from a childhood lost thirty years ago. Rather than this negation of life which he himself has once again become a purveyor of, that is, frozen white death.

7
The Great Thaw of Aught Six

AND THEN THE SNOW BEGINS TO MELT. One day, deep in his hibernal slumber, the Snowman hears the sound of water running and his subconscious goes off in a torrent of oneiric near-reality. He forgot to turn off the faucet in the kitchen or, no, the toilet's stopped up and water is spilling out of the bowl onto the bathroom floor. Then he's standing at the toilet taking an enormous pee that goes on and on so that even deep in his sleep alarm bells are going off. He wakes in a panic expecting to find himself lying in a puddle of warm pee. Relieved this isn't the case but still unrelieved, he tosses off the covers and staggers-stumbles across the icy sheen of the hardwood floor to the bathroom where, planting his damp, wool-stockinged feet on the cold tiles, he comes close to replicating the equine stream of his dream while squinting against the bright light coming in through the small rectangular window next to him and, hmm, that's interesting. Even through the dirty glass he can see the snow has almost completely melted on the roofs of the houses across the street, the shingles are steaming, icicles are falling from the eaves, muddy brown patches have appeared in the yards, dirty water is running down the gutter. Shuffling into the kitchen to put water on for coffee, he glances at the rusty metal thermometer outside the window, which shows the temperature hovering around a balmy seventy degrees. What the heck? It's colder inside than out. Which probably explains why Me'th didn't want to stay in this morning. Struggling to open a window that hasn't been opened for years, he finally cracks the sash loose from desuetude's grasp, raises the window in a flatulent protest of bare wood on bare wood and is embraced by a breath of moist warm air he hasn't felt in this latitude in over thirty years.

People scratch their heads and stare up at the sun as if it has just appeared in the sky. Meteorologists blithely discuss temperature inversions, high-pressure cells. Ice Factories are ordered to ramp up operations all across the nation. Snow crews are on call 24/7. The Mexican guys love it. *Sí, sí, más horas, más dinero.* To no avail. The snow melts faster than they can keep up. It seems the quality of the snow itself has changed. Ice guns blorp out milky white glops of Icine that begin to melt before they hit the ground. Morale at work is horrible. Gastreaux is apoplectic, Evelyn on serious meds *Hiiiiiii, Snowmansy!* The torrents of spring continue. It's like defrosting a refrigerator freezer, a very big refrigerator. At first it's a trickle, then a full-blown flood. It overflows storm sewers, blows manhole covers sky-high on pillars of filthy brown water, submerges city streets, inundates shops, stores, office buildings. Cars and trucks bob and float away like a drunken anarchy of self-driving vehicles. Flash floods roar down canyons, dry gulches and thousand-year floodplains, smashing houses into kindling, hauling homesteads and the drowned bodies of humans and domestic animals all the way down to the Gulf of Mexico. It's the same all over the country.

Streams, creeks, gullies are transformed into raging torrents, causing catastrophic damage in cities, towns, villages and hamlets. And, unholy resurrection, all the garbage buried beneath the snow begins to resurface like rotting Lazarusian zombie carcasses, the buried and unburied again bones of an industry running down, a civilization in decay. A fetid pall, a cross between raw sewage, damp laundry and dead fish, hangs over the city of Osberg.

At International Cryogenic Industries Network headquarters, the bigwigs are tearing out their hair implants in clumps. They're at risk of being tarred and feathered by their shareholders every time they step out of the building. Their lobbyists are persona non grata on Capitol Hill. Long-time VBS listeners tune in as that venerable veteran of the airwaves Uncle Bob brings the issue to a head with the loaded question, Malfeasance? Or Mother Nature getting even with her wayward progeny? As a last-ditch effort at damage control ICIN hauls out their chief R&D guy, Roger Wilco, to make a rebuttal. Hmmm, yesss, well, it is an interesting *hypawwthesis*, completely untrue, of course. You have to understand the chemical *commmpozishun*, *mawlekewls* of hydrogen and carbon, not to mention oxygen, impossible to explain *reahhlly*, a matter of *sciiiience*, I'm publishing a paper next *monnnth*. Hey! the Snowman shouts at the TV. That's the same explanation you gave for *making* the snow! (Film buffs are downloading the original Boone Weller classic as we speak.) *Mrrrt!* Me'th, who has been making less frequent, or more infrequent—there seems to be a distinction in the feline mind—appearances with the warmer weather, arches a heavily scarred brow in contempt for petty human intrigues. Scientists do agree on one thing. Some kind of foreign agent, which they have dubbed the *Montezuma Bug*, has been introduced to the snow-producing element in Icine, rendering it inert. Wait—*what?* The bells of Notre Dame, pre-restoration, clang wildly in the Snowman's head, frissonic shivers avalanche through his body, and he hears again a familiar female voice, hers, Maria's, discussing in a bemused tone a certain *Cortés gene*, "which, against all probability, out of all the billions of people on the planet, *you* alone carry, *Snowman*, and, even more unlikely, it just happens to be the key to finding an antidote to Icine." This can only mean one thing. Maria's antidote is working, trickling through the arteries and veins of the entire snow industry. Laboratories across the country rush to develop an Icine alternative but none prove successful. As quickly as scientists come up with a new formula the Montezuma Bug defeats it.

And here Boone inserts a brief clip that slips right past the Snowman. A figure in a white lab coat and safety glasses strolls through *Print and Paper Products'* Central Materials Research Center, consulting with technicians, inspecting work in progress. It's Judith, of course. As PPP's brilliant young Director of Research and Development, she oversees the team assigned to study this Montezuma Bug. And why should the Montezuma Bug be of concern to PPP? Well, it just so happens that PPP manufactures a paper-based filter used in processing Icine at its sister operations in Mexico, PPPMX, whose motto is "Ponemos el papiro en el papel" (something odd about that, seems obvious, redundant, *something*). Unfortunately, PPP's R&D has had no more success in conquering the Montezuma bug than anyone else. Despite this, well, let's not call it a failure—*noble endeavor?*—

Judith constantly wears a curious smile on her face that her colleagues attribute to her irrepressible optimism.

Within weeks the snow industry collapses. Ice Factories fall idle across the country, accompanied by massive layoffs. ICIN stock baselines. Dyspeptic shareholders toss out ICIN's entire board of directors. They've got a noose around the CEO's neck and are within an inch of lynching the lying son-of-a-bitch from the giant screen where his image has been seen pacing in increasingly neurotic canine circles until the very moment the disgruntled investors rush the stage and begin to string him up, at which point the SWAT team bursts in firing tear gas and stun grenades. This debacle forces the CEO's "retirement." His separation package wipes out most of ICIN's liquid assets, but he denies any charge of impropriety. It's mine, *mine*, do you understand? I'm entitled to it! And, yes, apparently he is. Even though this once thriving corporate entity has crashed and burned under his stewardship, he has managed to extract from its smoldering wreckage enormous profits for himself, his board members and certain savvy shareholders (insider trading, anyone?), what financial wizards refer to as *entropic function* or *heat loss*, through which money-colored lens he's viewed as a genius (Trump that if you can). Keeping in mind that when old Mac who was at the Osberg Ice Factory from day one announced his retirement, Human Resources cancelled his pension on a technicality (failing to include his mother-in-law's maiden name in his personnel file) and four burly security guards hustled him out the front gate and dumped him on the pavement, leaving him with a sore bum, sprained wrist, a couple bruised ribs, a cancelled insurance policy, and a warning never to set foot on the premises again at the risk of *serious* consequences. And then you wonder why Mac's wife Emma, really nice lady, volunteers at the church social, bakes a mean shoo fly pie, worries that he sits in his armchair all day cleaning and oiling his assault rifle. The public is further outraged when a video is released showing ICIN's former board of directors in high heels, silk stockings and some of Victoria's sexiest secrets (only one of the board members is female) in a raucous chorus line singing,

> *The profit's all taken,*
> *the rest we've been fakin',*
> *your future, your fortune—oh,*
> *it's nothing but paper,*
> *a cloud of vapor,*
> *it's all gone up in smoke!*

Protestors fill the streets, set up squatter camps, erect barricades, build bonfires. The famous bronze bull of Wall Street is castrated, the balls melted down and recast as a pile of, well, bullshit. Someone spray paints CAPITALI$M $UX ('CEPT U RICH, DAWG) in ten-foot-tall, dollar bill-green letters on the New York Stock Exchange Building, which might bother a number of people but not for the reason you'd think. (The editorial staff's in an uproar. The spelling's atrocious, usage too— Ed. Yes, but note the correct use of punctuation, which suggests the misspellings are entirely stylistic—Edna. Well, *duhhhh*—Edwige, the sassy new intern. ¿Y a mi qué?—Eduardo.)

With their deep ties to ICIN, and disruptions in their Mexican operations, PPP takes a hit too. Their earnings plummet and investors drop them so hard the crash can be heard on both coasts, sending tsunamic ripples across the Atlantic and the Pacific where keenly attuned fiduciary ears in the already troubled European and Asian markets are getting very nervous. And that's before the SEC announces it's opening its own investigation. SNN shows an endless parade of lawyers, accountants, lobbyists and former corporate officers in hearings before House and Senate committees. Ponzi schemes, sub-primes, hedge funds, short sales, pump and dump, the previously mentioned and always popular insider trading, racketeering, conspiracy, embezzlement, money laundering, involvement in drug trafficking, *murder*. The charges are laid out in a twenty-three-thousand-page report, which Vermont Senator Bernie Standards alone reads in its entirety on a weekend retreat (no more coffee for you, young man). The Attorney General has the super heavyweight Olympic gold medalist in weightlifting (and by God, he's an American for once) clean and jerk this formidable tome overhead just to give the viewing audience an idea of what we're dealing with here.

Meanwhile, unemployed and more or less tumbling in the void, the Snowman sits on the couch day after day watching this spectacle unfold on his old TV. And it is old, about the size of a hefty suitcase, with a thick, algae-green glass screen. After President DeBoche's fiat requiring all citizens to tune their TVs to Fuchs News 24/7, he rolled it into the hall closet where it languished in exile talking to itself like a hyperactive child on permanent time out, just as happy to be there as anywhere else. Until he could no longer stand being in the dark himself about current events and he rolled the damn thing out again into the center of the living room, the target of his ire (and impotence) as he shouts at the screen, Hang the motherfuckers! Put them against the wall and shoot them! Drop them in the Afghan fucking desert and let them barter their fucking assets out of there with the Taliban!

So he's startled when Judith appears live on *fucking TV* on the floor of *fucking Congress* in all-business black horn-rimmed glasses, a dark blue conservative outfit accessorized with a red, white and blue scarf tied loosely at the neck, and common sense, flat-heeled pumps working women all over the world can relate to. As Director of Research at PPP, she has been called to testify. Senators, House members, department heads and committee chairs glower and cluck like a parliament of angry fowls. The *honorable* South Carolina Senator Strumplin Snoops, at the forefront of a band of McCarthyite revisionists, leads the interrogation. Now ain't it true, madam, that them thar fellers you worked for at that dadgum *P! P! P!* (aspirating each consonant like he's spitting out watermelon seeds) ain't nothin' more than a den o' stinkin' polecats or some such lak that? Cameras click and wheeze emphysemically as Judith leans into the bank of microphones. In a stunning display of forensic genius hearkening back to her first seminar with the renowned but long since fallen into disrepute dialectic orthologist Hugh Hieroglyph (currently institutionalized), over a period of days and then weeks she metamorphoses before her interrogators from a chrysalis of humble and sincere but dignified contrition in a plain hair cloth suit that nevertheless does justice to her stringent physical fitness regimen, to near super hero status in a stunning black, body-fitting kidskin outfit, her hair chopped into a threatening samurai helmet, her eyes, nose, mouth, chin and cheekbones highlighted with startling applications of kohl, crimson rouge and moss green eye shadow. There's an otherworldly lepidopteran beauty about her, velvety and light, almost iridescent, and yet something that is not only intimidating but discomfortingly alien. The boys in the pressroom (see Webster's c. 1964—"pressroom" equals *boys*—Ed.) bandy about a famous quotation from another century and another fighter *float like a butterfly, sting like a bee*. The Snowman, who has known her intimately, is thinking *dance like Vishnu, strike like Shiva*.

Wielding an Alexandrian sword of ratiocination with a blade as sharp as Occam's razor, Judith slices through the Byzantine coils, convolutions and tessellations of legalese and corporate doublespeak as if they were overcooked spaghetti. She shreds Snoops' inbred pig fuckers' rhetoric as if it were wet tissue paper. She admits unethical if not exactly illegal company-wide practices, assigns blame to a culture of privilege in the highest echelons, exculpates the rank-and-file employee, lauds R&D's extraordinary achievements and, summing up her rebuttal, proclaims PPP a vital asset to the U.S. economy. The entire chamber is on its feet. The applause drowns out the sputtering, red-faced and largely incoherent attempts by the Snoops' crowd to regain the floor. The Republican Speaker of the House is caught on camera blubbering about his dog Chubby's tail reattachment surgery and the *worn-out* coat (one hundred-fifty-thousand-dollar sable) his poor wife has made do with for an entire year.

Once again it's out with the old and in with the new. As part of reorganization in bankruptcy court, disgruntled PPP shareholders ditch the current board of directors and elect a crowd of unfamiliar faces. With one exception.

Thanks to her commanding performance before Congress and a national audience, Judith is unanimously chosen CEO and immediately announces the company mission will move in a more environmentally friendly direction. The Snowman's first thought? *Pllbbbbbt!* Raspberries, the Bronx cheer, massive hypocrisy. He's seen nothing in Judith's shameless embrace of corporate capitalism to convince him she has any intention of *doing the right thing*. He also has the nagging suspicion that this is all part of some much larger web of intrigue he can't begin to fathom but from which he is almost certainly not exempt.

Voice: *Of course we could not have anticipated that things would proceed so quickly and in such a, shall we say, propitious manner. But, as is commonly said in your adopted country, do not look a gift horse in the nose, is it not?*

The fallout from this contretemps strikes wide and deep. The whole economy is collapsing. The middle class, the blue collar worker, the statistically famous *little guy*—crushed beneath the wheel of bankruptcies, foreclosures, credit card debt, the kids' massive college loans, the cars and appliances, the hologrammatic TVs, the expandable-contractible, bigger-smaller, more apps, fewer gadgets, smart, smarter, smartest cellphone (kind of like high-tech Swiss Army knives w/o the corkscrew—oh, wait). And hanging over it all, the ever-growing but inevitably unsustainable national debt incurred by pork barrel spending, tax cuts for you know who (hint: it's not you) and the obligatory 365 days a year Christmas lollapalooza, which, true, has faded into a ghost of itself *Ebeneeeeezer!* Burned out Christmas lights, dusty, sagging tinsel and plastic mistletoe, gift giving optional, hold the turkey. The entire nation is drowning in gloom. It's being called the Second Great Depression. Even the Eye looks blackened.

With the economy in decline, government programs are slashed left and right. The Secretary of Homeland Security, Heathcliff Heimat, says his office can no longer afford the massive military buildup at the border. The incessant noise of helicopters, surveillance planes and drones disappears from the wide blue skies over the Frío Grande. Border Patrol staffing is cut to near zero along the Great Wailing Wall. (No one is clear how it came to be called this. The most common theory alludes to the wails of the thousands of families separated from their loved ones. It's said that their combined cries create a howl that echoes from coast to coast, at times achieving supersonic speed and sending sonic booms of despair hurtling into the northern states. This phenomenon has not been verified by any recorded evidence—Glenda, Boone's long ~~suffering~~ serving fact check *person*.) (She's past retirement age but she desperately needs the income. Her oldest daughter's back at home with no job and two kids of her own. Her son's in and out of rehab with a ton of legal and medical expenses *somebody* has to pay for. She has a shitload of her own issues on her hands. No, wait, it's some kind of medical device. Her hands are barely functional, rheumatoid arthritis, carpal tunnel syndrome, a lifetime of *taptaptap*. Good thing for telecommuting or she'd never make it in today's doggie dog (sic) market.) The repercussions of these changes in government policy will soon be felt well beyond the border and deep within the interior of our great neighbor to the south.

1700 hours: The White House Situation Room. In a top-secret meeting, President Ronwald DeBoche signs off on Operation Cold Shoulder. The U.S. will curtail all overt and covert activities inside of Mexico related to interdiction of drug cartels and counter-terror efforts. And that means no fingers-crossed-behind-the-back indie ops mucking around down there in that *shithole*, is that understood, *Senator* Snoops?

Uh, why, yassuh, I bahlieve we have an unnerstannin on that point, Mistuh President.

Major Ditto?

Yes, sir, Mister President.

I cannn't hearrrrrr you.

YES, SIR, MISTER PRESIDENT, SIR!

That's better. We'll be lucky if we get out of this goddamn mess with our asses intact, thanks to your shenanigans.

All contacts between Major Ditto (yes, there has been a demotion) and various assets south of the border evaporate like dry ice in the rarefied atmosphere of cyberspace. In a backhanded punitive slap, most of Mexico's communication lines across a broad swath of the country collapse—literally. Huge transmission towers topple over in the desert. Thousands of miles of cheap cable bundled together like black match sizzle, pop and burst into flames. President Bolillo, who's been counting on a ten-billion-dollar nest egg tucked away in a virtual vault in the sparkling white sands of some Caribbean island-nation, discovers he can no longer access his account. All that comes up on his screen is the single word *¡Perdedor! (Loser!*—Stan, I'll be doing the *American* translation.) At the same time, a fleet of unmarked Reaper drones flies south of the border like big nasty mosquitoes armed with GBU-12 Paveway II laser-guided bombs, Hellfire II missiles, and miniaturized, super-value bunker busters and, for good measure, takes out cartel villas, urban safe houses, rural gang hideouts, secret airfields and weapons caches, as well as dozens of subway-size tunnels under the U.S.-Mexico border. In a final kiss-off, we see a cruise missile armed with a tactical nuclear warhead shooting across endless stretches of desert (and if this *were* a cartoon it'd have a big smiley face and it'd be whistling merrily, so happy to carry out its little act of destruction).

Now we hear the melancholy strains of the Peruvian folk classic *El Condor Pasa* in the hollow, breathy tones of a bass pan pipe as the camera leaps ahead to a sprawling Mediterranean-style villa, terra cotta-tiled roof, pink and white stucco, winding staircases, tennis courts and a turquoise blue swimming pool, surrounded by emerald green tropical foliage incongruously set in a cleft in a barren rocky mountainside in the middle of the desert. A tall, handsome, middle-aged man with silver at his temples and what one would guess to be an uncharacteristically troubled expression on his face, paces back and forth, militarily erect in an immaculately tailored gray business suit, in front of a screen displaying constant live feed from the Lockheed Martin AN/TPS-77 Long-Range Surveillance Radar discreetly stationed in a small grove of palm trees somewhere on his estate. He stops in front of another screen where, the corner of his right eye flickering involuntarily, he watches for perhaps the five-hundredth time a video of a fleet of giant white airships (and ships they are, built almost entirely of wood, spruce, to be exact), each powered by eight enormous

3000 horsepower Pratt and Whitney propeller engines, lumbering through a ferocious snowstorm. Then, something that for a man of sober and rational temperament must seem patently inadmissible before a court governed by the laws of nature: an armada of fire-breathing dragons attacking these airships, a number of which have already burst into flames and are tumbling to the earth. The obsessiveness and wrenching agony with which this gentleman watches this video can be better understood if one also knows that each one of these huge, ungainly airships carried onboard twenty billion dollars' worth of the extremely addictive street drug Ice. Unfortunately, he has more immediate worries at the moment as he turns again to the luminous green radar screen where we now see an incandescent object traveling at very high speed as it approaches a topographical feature that even an uninformed viewer might guess to be a mountaintop. This one. A huge explosion follows as the camera discreetly moves outside at the very last moment to show us the villa and the jungle surrounding it and the entire mountaintop disappearing in a small mushroom cloud of poisonous neon shades of green, turquoise and orange. So far from God and so close to the U.S., says President DeBoche's Latin American advisor, Simón Boulevard, watching this event on the screen with all the rest of the president's men.

Despite these multiple precautions, pesky blogs and independent news services are on Snoops' and Ditto's trail like hounds after a fox, and you can bet members of the League Against Cruel Sports are right behind them. Rumors of scandal and even the call for an Attorney General's probe grow louder, and certain individuals in government are getting very nervous as prominent voices in society chime in. Reverend K. James Fallible, pastor of the Rivenbundt Church of Jesus Christ Warrior-Redeemer, seen these days in an ivory white soutane embossed with gold New Dollar signs in front and back over a medieval suit of chainmail, has certainly gotten with the program. We've lived in the cold and dark too long! It's a sign from God! Heed His warning! Beware the beast! Eat more chicken! Good old Uncle Bob, that perennial, centennial and now even millennial spirit of the airwaves is right there with him, his voice aged in Kentucky bourbon and pipe smoke. What now, ladies and gentlemen? The end of a hallowed but nevertheless outworn tradition and a step forward in the name of order and progress? The venerable Uncle Bob certainly knows which way the wind blows. People are sick of the ice and snow, this winter thing's gotta go. Hit the road Jack Frost and Hellooo Jolly Old Sol. It really is madness, of course, and it doesn't take a blinking fucking genius to explain it. Ice Factories across the country have been pumping billions of tons of Icine into the atmosphere for decades. The earth is saturated with the damn stuff, which, in conjunction with this *unnatural ice age*, has wiped out thousands of species, upended millions of years of evolution and generally made a fine mess of things.

And yet out of the ashes of despair hope rises like the Phoenix on a fistful of grubworms and feel-good meds. Because there's something happening here, what it is ain't exactly clear. There's a kind of mass hysteria, a giddiness among the *hoi polloi*. That crazy spring-time schizophrenia of hope and hope deferred, of false spring, late spring, fickle spring, the prima diva of primavera spring. In other words spring acting exactly the way spring has always acted. One minute freezing rain, the next sunshine. A robin appears singing joy to the world, followed by a burst of snow flurries. But instead of stopping there and retreating back into hibernal gloom, the sun returns for longer spells, the temperature continues to climb. And then, after a thirty-year hibernation in pitch black subterranean existence, seed and root begin to reanimate themselves, erupting out of the entombing earth into the miracle of fresh air and warm sunshine. Spots of green sprout out of cracks in the sidewalk, under white picket fences. Anarchic patches of green rise up in backyards and vacant lots in that verdant chlorophyllic exuberance of leaf and bud. With the stroke of a key a panoply of flora and fauna is revived from suspended animation. Hyacinths, daffodils, tulips, crocus, forsythia, pussy willow, peach, pear, apple and cherry blossoms open their silk and velvet pink, purple, red, yellow, blue and white faces to the sun. Birds sing, bees buzz, Old MacDonald creaks open the barn door, climbs up on the dusty, cobwebbed seat of his yellow and green John Deere tractor and *EE-I-EE-I-O* (apparently ol' Mac's had a celebratory sip of the ethanol) fires 'er up.

In a further sign of the times, idealistic young people travel south of the border to offer up their eyes as witness, their bodies as shields (don't try this at home, kids). They come back (most of them) wearing little orange sunburst badges on their chests, braids of colored yarn tied around their wrists. They've got this new slang. *Rise and shine! Show me some sun!* Or even just *Sun me!* Drop the words *snow* or *ice* at a social gathering and the whole room shrinks away like you've got Ebola. Nobody wants to hear that hibernal jive. Everybody's into the big thaw.

A concurrent note of interest. Police records show a precipitous decline in Ice overdoses (statistically zero). In

the last known arrest for possession of Ice, the charges
were dropped when the lab guys determined the evidence
in question contained no active agent on the government
schedule of controlled substances and technically didn't
qualify as Ice. Tearing a page from his Russian
tovarishes' political playbook, Drug Czar Marvin
Morfein, in his full Admiral Boom rig, tricorn hat, frog
coat, knee breeches, silk stockings and buckled shoes,
publicly declares this epic struggle a grand success. Well,
yeah, sorta. You also got a couple million Iceheads going
cold turkey and it ain't pretty. Anyone who hasn't had the
pleasure of the experience can't begin to grasp how
utterly desperate you feel, your best, your *only* friend on
the planet turns his back on you, the universe goes dark,
all the lights out, God dead, and the dragon's got you in
its claws, lactic acid searing every nerve in your body,
barbed wire shredding muscle fiber, mind in flames, the I
of your I screaming for help inside your skull, your opiate
receptors on their knees begging *please, I'll do anything.*
And the thing is, it isn't only in the *bad part of town.* You
got all these people with spooky white eyes (most wear
dark glasses or contacts to hide 'em but you can still tell)
spazzing out on busy city streets, at respectable church-
going Sunday afternoon dinner tables, on the automotive
assembly line (it's the very last one in America), in IT and
AI offices, in elementary school classrooms, they're
grinding their teeth and blinking their eyes like juiced-up
robots, they're doing herky-jerky St. Vitus pentecostal
can't help dancing dances, *now ain't we got fun?*

8
Sister Sunne Rae

IT'S ALSO ABOUT THIS TIME that a new TV personality appears on the Osberg scene. The entertainment editors in the alternative *Osberg Chronicler* and the mainstream *Osberg Statusman* have been talking this event up for months. To a righteous rocking soul version of the sixties classic *Let the Sun Shine* sung by special guests, the 13th Street Baptist Church choir, Sister Sunne Rae sweeps on stage in voluminous orange and gold robes, solar flare tiara, sparkling, sunrise-themed sequined glasses, tangerine lip-gloss and a smile as wide as the Mississippi. And for all you body-conscious gals in our viewing audience, you'll be pleased to see this lady's *bigggg*. Looks like costume has finally found a home for that peripatetic derriere.

The Sister inaugurates her show by proclaiming the beginning of a new era and, in what critics will later call a *sassy but savvy female Black voice* (one describes it as *black face in your face*), she now leads the studio audience, who are largely white and, true, a bit confused about how this thing works (most gamely follow the lead of the few Black folks in attendance), in a relatively animated call and response.

Brothers and sisters, we done put a whole lotta hurt on this planet, now ain't that the truth?!

Tell it, Sister! Yes it is! Clap! Clap! Clap!

Instead of the path of righteousness we done took the road to wrack and ruin, now ain't that the truth?!

Testify Sister! The Lord is our witness! Clap! Clap! Clap!

Waving away the applause and shaking her head like a bull bothered by blowflies, the Sister takes a rhetorical U-turn.

Now hold on a second! Did I say *we* is the ones who caused all this misery and suffering?

Um ... audience members look at each other nonplussed, not sure where we're going with this. Sister's about to show them. Planting her right foot forward like that very same bull above fixing to charge, she jams her finger at the audience.

Is *you* that *we* who done caused all this pain and destruction?

The answer's easy (or at least it is with the help of Ebonics teleprompters).

Nawsuh, dat ain't me!

Is that poor old lady over in the Far East Side waiting fo' the gentry to come knock down her house that *we?*

Nawsuh, dat ain't she!

Is all the homeless folks and sick folks and poor folks who work long, hard hours every day fo' next to nothing that *we?*

Nawsuh, dat ain't dey neithuh!

Well then you tell me, brothers and sisters, who the hell is that *we* who done did all this devilry?

Looks of bafflement again. The Sister's got her listeners flummoxed with all the personal and relative pronouns. Dropping the Ebonics shtick, she draws her audience back in with a pumped-up pep talk that brings them to their feet (those able to stand anyway, these are all some pretty hefty folks, diabetes, heart disease, geriatric issues—*mercy!*)

We must expose the ugliness, the garbage and filth we've kept buried beneath this false white blanket of purity!

Tell it, Sister!

We must speak truth to power and stand up for our rights!

You know it, Sister!

We must rebuild our society with love and hope and wise guidance!

That's right, Sister!

We must open our hearts and our minds, our tear ducts and our wallets! That number again is …

Amen, Sister! Wait … say *what?* (The monetary appeal will become a bit of a sticky wicket. Where's all that money going to? inquiring minds will want to know. Let's see if we find out.)

The Sister's like a preacher at a revival meeting, she leads her congregation to the water and they wade right in. And, sure, while there are some comparisons to Oprah, the keen-eyed cineaste will see something else familiar (and possibly even sinister) about this sister's jolly black face. Even the Snowman can see it. Aunt Jemima? *Shut yo mouf!* Hattie McDaniel? *Lordy, Miss Melly!* Because no matter how you cut the hoecake, there's just no denying that this sister looks about one cliché removed from the minstrel-faced collard greens and fatback-fed plantation mammy with an enormous watermelon grin and a huge bosom evo*loosh*ionarily repurposed by centuries of slavery and servitude to fill the plump pink suckling *moufs* of innocent white babes wit all kinda nourishments, includin' dem der voo doo, hoo doo and magical ju ju juices of dat deepest darkest continent *Mudder A-frique-ka!* This last comes out as something between a shout of triumph and a cri de coeur. Catching the audience *and* her producers off-guard, Sister has slipped into a stealth monologue delivered increasingly in that *sassy Black* tone that has the entire audience squirming in their seats like a pack of hound dogs with wormy butts. All of which gives cause or pause or at least second thoughts about exactly what's going on here. Has the Sister taken cutting edge comedy too far? And she's not letting up.

According to the one drop rule you might even argue *mammy's* turning all dem white chillens into *pickaninnies!* You *pickin'* any, *Travis? Ashleigh?* Which, not surprisingly, elicits gasps of astonished disbelief and then staccato bursts of uncertain laughter that erupt into raucous and relieved applause when the Sister calls out an all-embracing appeal for unity. C'mon, y'all! God loves *all* His children no matter what color they are! Now get up on your feet and do the rainbow dance with me!

At this signal the house band breaks into the classic Rainbow Happy Dance and once again the whole audience, including the geriatric, dyspeptic and way too white to dance crowd, is up on its feet, canes and walkers, boogeying its woogey. This is exactly the kind of happy dancey Black lady they wanta see. *Way down upon the Suwannee Riverrr ... Camptown ladies sing dis song, doo-dah ...* that kinda shit?

Huh?!

Just like that, the Sister has led them into another trap. For the rest of the night, she puts on this edgy mix of comedy and social commentary interspersed with feel-good, let-it-all-hang-out dancing and singing that has the audience gasping and wheezing and clutching at their hearts (medical waivers required), but when the show's over all will agree they had a funky good time.

9
Invisibility

DESPITE DR. LEVANT'S LOWLY POSITION as a lecturer (and here Boone is doing some Billy Pilgrim time-traveling back to the future), once a year she's allowed to teach a highly popular upper division Honors course somewhat clinically titled Functional Invisibility, the fundamentals of which are laid out in her second book on the topic, *When Wallflowers Win*, another critically acclaimed (see Colonel Jedidiah Sutpen, ret., U.S. Army War College, Carlisle, PA, for his highly favorable review) but largely overlooked gem. The attentive cinephile, alert for clues, foreshadowing, that sort of thing, might also want to take a look at the acknowledgements at the back of Dr. Levant's book where she credits a certain Eunice Guppy for her assistance in early case studies. Dr. Levant is essentially arguing the virtues of invisibility as a defensive weapon. In a nutshell, the enemy can't strike what he can't see. Obviously a gamechanger in combat, but let's take a look at some applications here on the home front. Let's say you want to avoid a bunch of *bad hombres* on a crowded city street, or maybe it's a domestic situation, a jilted girlfriend or boyfriend packing heat, or a shooter at the mall or the university—just walk on by, unseen. It should come as no surprise, at least to those who know about these things, that, despite its absence in the public discourse, Dr. Levant's work is of particular interest to the security industry. She is riven by a conflict of professional pride and personal integrity when half the class one semester is comprised of elite special forces from all five branches of the US military. A particular standout (already failed the course) is Marine Major Stewart P. Ditto, who looks a tad uncomfortable in civilian clothes. Gorilla build, ill-fitting checks and plaids, five o'clock shadow that'd make a bear nervous. In the words of Ramón Innocenti, the Major's twenty-year-old semester project partner, Like, he's kind of *creepy?* Like, I think he might want to *kill me?*

Students come to class with all kinds of preconceptions about invisibility. Hi-tech light bending materials, some kind of substance you paint on your body, or even an herbal tea you drink (I'm pretty sure you're referring to Dr. Vu Dhu's class on the aesthetics of ayahuasca-influenced art, Lionel. *Lionel?*). Everything, in other words, but the most and least obvious. Dr. Levant shows the class a film of a crowded street scene, it's right out here on the Drag. Girls in butt-cheek micro shorts, in halter tops and bare midriffs. Guys in jeans, Ts, cargo shorts, backward baseball caps. After the clip ends, Dr. Levant says, tell me what you saw. Silence. They didn't see anything, just *kids*, like themselves. I liked the hot blonde in pink, *haw!haw!haw!* Thank you for your contribution, Tank (*asshole*). Do you think one of those *kids* could be a bomb-carrying terrorist? *What?! No way!* Dr. Levant then shows them film clips from terror attacks in London, Paris, Brussels, Christchurch, Boston—can you spot the terrorists? They pick all the wrong people, slouching, sulking, grimy, bearded, *drooling*. Look at that guy! OMG! Gross!

Now she shows them the actual culprits. They're wearing jeans, hoodies, backwards baseball caps, carrying backpacks, some are laughing, at least one is a girl. They look exactly like the kids in the earlier film, like kids in this class, *you guys*. That got them. They're shifting in their seats, they're frowning and scowling and displaying other signs of discomfort as they try to process this information. She shows them another film. This time they're so alert they're up out of their desks and standing on their toes, *him! him! her!* they shout, pointing out every young person on the screen who's carrying a backpack or a duffle bag. *Nope*, Dr. Levant shakes her head but with an encouraging smile *finally, they're fucking engaged!* She then points out the UPS driver, the mailman, the cable installer, the police officer who, at a second glance, is a woman. People in uniform are anonymous. You see the uniform, not the person. Even that homeless guy—what did you call him, Annabellum, gross? Yes, *gross*. That's what you see. Shave, bathe, clean clothes, you wouldn't know him from Dr. Davies in Advanced Fingerpainting. *Tap tap tap, OMG! dd u here tht?* She points out the window at the snake-in-the-grass ripple that has appeared again among the crowd of students farther down the Drag. I'll bet you all recognize that guy. Yay! It's the *Snowman!* they scream like children breaking for recess. Yes, it *is* the *Snowman*, she says, schoolmarmish condescending but with a curious smile. You'd recognize him anywhere, right? They all look at her like, well, *duhh!* She shows them a picture of a guy in a midnight blue parka with blue goggles and a face-mike. Recognize that guy? No way! they shout. You

can't even see his face! How about this guy? Dr. Levant
now shows them a scene from a corporate boardroom, a
bunch of suits, mostly male, seated at a broad table, all of
them dour, sour, apparently displeased by the message
they are receiving. The camera pans around the table and
stops on the speaker and—*Ha!Ha!Ha!* Dr. Levant's
students burst into laughter and no wonder. It's the
Snowman, grubby, unshaven, in his Hawaiian shirt,
seated in the CEO's place. I know, it's a joke, right? Dr.
Levant says. So far, we've been looking at everyday
people. Now, I want to talk about professionals of this
craft, classic mimeticists who disguise, camouflage
themselves, blend in with their environment, waste
containers, rusty iron girders, furniture, rolled-up carpets,
doorways, signage, faded wallpaper. Masters of the art
are reputedly able to position themselves directly
between people carrying on a conversation without being
seen. Dr. Levant nods at an empty chair in the back. Isn't
that right, Oscar? *Oscar?* To her dismay, she receives no
reply. Of course she's disappointed. She invited Oscar to
join her seminar with the intent of using him as an
example but hearing the word *using* in her head she
realizes now how awful it sounds. Betrayal is another
word for it. Probably why he didn't show. She looks out
the window again and down at the Drag where she can
make out the Snowman pushing his cart away.

10
Entr'acte

HE STOPS AGAIN IN FRONT of a boarded-up clothing boutique and stares at a reddish-brown stain on the dirty pavement. Spilled paint? Ketchup? *Blood?* He knows it isn't ketchup or blood. Both would have washed away by now. But he still thinks of blood, sees again the crumpled body so large and powerful in life, the crimson puddle spreading outward on the sidewalk, feels again the tumbling-off-a-cliff hollowness in his chest. These doleful thoughts are truncated, displaced by the sound of music or at least a musical sound, something like wind blowing over a bottle top or a metal pipe or through a hollow reed, in this case a piece of bamboo, the largest member of the grass family *Poaceae*, a simple enough plant in appearance, tall, thin, tubular, long narrow leaves like emerald green insect wings (praying mantis?), but with a wide range of uses, for example as construction material, houses, fences, bridges, furniture, *tiger* cages. But also musical instruments.

The Snowman tilts his head sideways. Is that a *shakuhachi?* Yes, indeed, it is, and it seems to be expressing that very sorrow he has been struggling to refuse entrance in the court of emotional appeals. It keens and laments, moans and wails and shrieks, crying out in pain, shredding his thoughts like a vegetable grater, upending the quotidian world of students and street traffic surging around him, and then, after wreaking such havoc, laughs maniacally like a seagull *not* named Jonathan, *ha!ha!ha!* and shifts its tone again, reflects, is pensive, searches for comfort, consolation, finds it in a soft melancholy strain that swells again into joy for all of existence, life and death, pain, pleasure and suffering, above all the inexpressible beauty that can only ever be partially expressed in rare perfect moments like this.

Brinnngg!

Mother*fuck*ing piece of *shit*. What the *fuck* is it now? Stressing the syllables that most express his irritation, the Snowman lets go of the push bar with one hand, reaches into the pocket of his cargo shorts and hauls out his phone. Yeah, what's up? No fucking way! Tell him he's a fucking dead man!

Wait—what? The *Snowman?* Making death threats? He may be an ornery bastard but he's never exhibited homicidal tendencies. Thrown off kilter by this call, he spins on his heels and slams head-on into somebody else only—*wtf?*—there isn't anybody else, that is, he can distinctly feel the presence of another human body, slender, *soft*, probably young, possibly a girl but maybe a boy or even androgynous, he'd *guess* because he sure as fuck can't *see* anything and besides this disembodied *person* has already detached itself from this accidental embrace and out of nowhere he hears a soft and, yes, slightly androgynous voice say, Excuse me, sir. I'm so sorry. Are you all right? and he feels a very slight pressure on his arm, like that of a finely boned hand with long delicate fingers that could perform a complex arpeggio on the piano or pick out difficult chords on a guitar with equal facility but at the moment is offering reassurance to this grubby stumblebum who has just blindly crashed into him/her/it. No, *I'm* sorry, he mutters as if he's just stepped on Tinker Bell's toes and he reaches into his icebox, takes out a *PoPoPop!®*, gives it a shake, pulls the tab and *pop!* out swells the frosty, rainbow-colored mushroom cloud *fzzzzt!* which he extends to this invisible being like a bashful schoolboy offering his prom date a boutonniere and is even more unnerved to see it plucked from his hand and hover in midair (Boone *sampling* the original 1933 black and white *Invisible Man*, here colorized for continuity), followed by a faint but distinct gulp as a small bite disappears from the *PoPoPop!®* and an instant later a slender shimmering creature more or less as androgynous as the Snowman imagined begins to materialize in front of him as if it's beaming down from the Starship Enterprise, but before this transubstantiation can fully take place, this spirit or sprite or whatever it is executes a move it might have learned in ballet class or even running track and hands off the *PoPoPop!®* to a passing coed who naturally assumes everybody's beloved(?) Snowman is treating her to a freebie and with a wide all-is-right-in-*my*-world smile she plunges her tongue into this frosty delight and, perhaps a champion harrier herself, keeps on trucking without breaking stride (she *is* a runner) but with a noticeable *Girl from Ipanema* spring in her step, her feet are barely touching the pavement and, man oh man, she's tall and tan and young and lovely and *heeheehee* ... an impish giggle, a little like the chiming of a wine glass, breaks the spell and before the Snowman's eyes this pixie or puck, sprite or elf disintegrates into flickering fragments of color that are carried away like confetti or sequins or even fairy dust by one of those rare breezes that lift the spirits of Osbergers in the dog days of summer (essentially spring equinox to winter solstice), stirred, perhaps, by the flicker of a butterfly's wings as it flits from a waxy, lemon-yellow plumeria flower that does indeed smell very much like lemon blossoms to a pollen-powdered but scentless crimson hibiscus on an island in the Seychelles.

11
We All Scream for Ice Cream

AND JUST LIKE THAT, Boone transports us twenty-some years back in time again on the wings of a lepidopteran metaphor and the opening bars of Bessie Smith's *Summertime*. This protracted spring is followed by the first real summer in over three decades. The sun shines brighter and brighter, the temperature climbs higher and higher. Folks shed heavy winter coats, hats, fleece-lined gloves, boots. Light-weight cotton skirts and dresses again swish around female hips. Hairy male legs stick out of Bermuda shorts. Spare tires and pot bellies test the elasticity of T-shirts and waistbands. People want to be outside in the fresh air, they want to feel the warm sunshine on their faces, they want to run and jump and experience the glorious physicality of their bodies, they want the sweat to flow, the skin to glow, the abs to show. Joggers, bicyclists, bodybuilders, yoga posers, power walkers, cellphone talkers, they're out in the sun in Ts, tights, training bras, micro shorts, surfer baggies, sweat bands and fitbits. In residential neighborhoods sprinklers hiss and tsk at the sorry state of lawns. Manuel or Miguel or whatever the fuck that little *wetback's* name was (*sic*— the incorrigible Boone, explains why he's got a soft spot for Hanktheredneckasshole, and by the way, the kid's name is Fernando, he's a young man now, fifteen-sixteen-years old, with big dreams, ambitions, he's going to start his own landscape company, buy a truck, some rakes, shovels, lawnmowers, hire some guys—when he's a little older, when he's saved up some money, but right now he …) bends over and pulls a weed—a *weed!* when once any spot of green no matter how dissident or ragged would have been treated as royalty—out of Mrs. Murphy's front yard, scatters some grass seed, at least he'll make a few bucks mowing her lawn once a week, until the summer really kicks in, when that bright green rye he put down will quickly wither into brown dust.

Fernando's not the only one who sees, if not gold, at least some extra shekels in this new climate. The economy roars back to life as people discover all sorts of outdoor business opportunities. Landscaping, gardening, swimming pools, tennis courts, camping, barbecue pits, rock climbing, mountain biking. As the temperature soars above one hundred degrees day after day, people revert to old habits. Talk show hosts revive stale jokes that almost always include the words *hot, sex* and, inexplicably, *rotisserie.* People fan themselves with paper plates, newspapers brought down from a stack in the attic or up from the basement (just can't see laptops or EyePhones® working here) and commiserate, whooee, sure is hot today—is that a breeze? They push switches and turn knobs and rusty old air conditioners that have sat idle for three decades creak, clunk, grind and begin to blow out cold musty air. And once folks have taken that step, the ancient dance between balmy summer comfort and too damn hot starts all over again. The good citizens of Osberg can't wait to get home from work, from school, from dirty, scheming political machinations (here's looking at *you*, Guv), take off their sweaty clothes and jump in the pool, in the shower, in the AC and pop an ice-cold brewskie *pssshhh*.

And the Snowman? What's he been up to? Got it made in the shade, swinging in a hammock, smoking a doobie and sipping lemonade? Late, lazy morning breakfasts at one of his fav local places. The Starzz Cafe he can walk to right up the street, a fiery, mostly out of a can, Spanish omelet washed down with cheap mimosas, maybe chat with Ellie finishing her shift turning tricks in the motel next door (she told him that's what I do, simple as that, he's always wanted to ask her but never has, So what's that like?). Or blueberry waffles, eggs over easy and three strips of bacon a short five-minute drive across town to Kerbey Lane north or Magnolia Café south. Or, nostalgic for Mexican food, his downtown favorite Las Manitas, park the Coupe right out front on Congressional Avenue, no problem finding a space, don't have to pay, usually just a short wait, time for a smoke, check out the band and club posters plastered on the glass door and windows, the alternative rags in the metal newsstands, *The Advocado*, *Osberg Chronicler*, *Ahora No*, *The Umyum*.

Clack! Annnd ... *scene change*. The glass door swooshes open, a happily chattering crowd of satisfied diners exits, and headlong we plunge into the clang and clatter of dishes, silverware, chairs screeching, airplane propeller fans turning overhead *whomp whomp*, people laughing, shouting, Spanish coming from cooks and pearl divers back of the house, snatches of French, German, Italian, Dutch from in-the-know Euro tourists. The place is packed, tables and wall booths crammed with diners, customers seated shoulder to shoulder at the counter, chowing down on migas, enchiladas, chorizo, menudo, empanadas, the walls in front of and behind them covered with papel picado, artwork, posters, photographs of well-known Osberg landmarks and celebrities. You can't back up an inch without banging butts with a famous musician or politician, Wiley Nilson's tenor twang sounds like he picked it out on his guitar, Governor Big Hair, cotton boll bouffant, wide red lipstick smile, waving *Howdy* and gladhanding all around, *las manitas* themselves, sisters Cynthia and Lidia, aprons stained, faces beaded with sweat, strands of hair everywhere, greeting longtime customers, bussing tables, serving meals, working the cash register. And, ha, ha, there *he* is, the Snowman, thanks to a can of old footage Boone dug out of his attic, his twenty years younger self sitting at a small table in the sun-lit patio out back, chowing down on huevos rancheros, black beans, fresh corn tortillas, a side of fried plátanos with sour cream and an ice-cold 'Ol Rattler, the *Osberg Chronicler* opened in front of him to a snarky review (*Racist or rancid?*) of the new Boone Weller film *The Abominable Snowman of the North* playing at the Paramount half a dozen blocks up the street.

The easy living lasts for a month, maybe two (Bessie Smith fading in the background). All this time he's been dreaming, hoping, praying for *something* to happen, some external and preferably benevolent force to step in and change his course in life and now it has and he's thrown off the merry-go-round without a plan B. His career in the snowbiz clearly gone the way of the dodo, far too young to hang up his spurs and head for the happy hunting ground, maybe a coupla month's liquidity in the bank, he's back at square one, that age-old dilemma, he's gotta *do something*, but what? The help-wanted ads in both the

Chronicler and *Statusman* seldom comprise more than two or three column inches and they're mostly scams (Earn ten thousand dollars a week stuffing envelopes with hot air and bean farts!). Everything's online now but, other than his clunky old landline (and yes, let's put that baby to bed right now, it's a fucking rotary), he has zero electronic communications with the outside world. What's he gonna do, start pounding the pavement, knock on doors, 'scuse me, sir, ma'am, you got a job? He isn't qualified for jack shit in this exclusively IT/AI town. All these smart young techies are practically shitting apps and platforms and he's scratching his head like a country bumpkin at the World's Fair (c. 1893). His BA in Literature's essentially worthless (so, can you code with that shit, dude?), he's carrying a ton of debt from the loan he took out for the graduate program he didn't finish years ago, utilities have gone up thanks to the Icine debacle, property taxes are climbing, and even at a measly two hundred and fifty bucks a month he's about to fall behind on his mortgage payments. He's received a kind of premonitory warning from the bank, an overzealous finance officer, a certain Ms. Eunice Guppy, has apparently been tracking his declining funds, which he thinks might be illegal but he's not going to find out because that would require his marching down to the bank and getting into the kind of personal confrontation he hates and almost never wins.

He stares around his humble dwelling as if he might discover a heretofore unnoticed portal into the Count of Monte Cristo's treasure-filled grotto and all his worries will be over. Inevitably his eyes focus on the white square of hand-beaten paper tacked to the wall near the window with the Japanese ideograph printed on it in black ink. He could call Judith, ask for help, at least with his job search, she'd be infinitely more proficient at it than he, but of course he's not going to because, well, first of all, she's become a very important person and he's a complete nobody, and secondly, the "ask" and "help" are unacceptable even to his own ears.

As he does when faced with any tough situation, he resorts to his usual anodyne. He rolls a joint from his meager stash, which he keeps hidden in an old stovetop espresso maker, family size, another Judith residual, who's going to look in there, right? Oh, well, sure, Columbo. He takes three or four deep hits, pours half a glass of whiskey from the rapidly diminishing contents of an economy size bottle and takes a sip, lights the last cigarette from a crumpled pack, kicks back on the couch and … ahh, that's better. In the first wash of euphoria he imagines an array of highly unlikely scenarios. He saves a drowning child and the wealthy businessman father sets him up for life in a cush job. Better yet, just issues him a check for a cool million. He writes a letter to the newspaper suggesting a simple and inexpensive solution to climate change and the very next day he receives a call from the White House asking him to join the president's commission, headed by Greta Thunberg. He gets a really crummy job at a *HolyCow®* burger shack (fry cook and floor mopsterman) and quickly works his way up to regional manager.

This lasts about thirty, forty minutes before the old THC-amplified doubts and paranoia start creeping back in, along with the dark shadows spreading through the house and all those unfamiliar and even alien night sounds coming in the open windows, crickets and tree frogs chirring, dogs barking, cats screaming—is that a coyote? By now, pretty well trashed, he's slumped on the couch, muttering to himself, to Me'th, who, to be frank, doesn't look very sympathetic. What'll I do, Me'th? I can't find a job, they're gonna take the house. His voice is breaking, hot tears well in his eyes. *Me-I-ow don't know, Snowman, but lying around doing nothing won't help, that's my job.*

And here Boone briefly toys with a tearjerker plot twist he might have stolen from Capra (welllll ... it is Boone). We next see the Snowman wandering the streets in the hunched over posture of a downtrodden hobo, a pack on his back, hands shoved down in his pockets, despondent. He keeps circling back to his house. It's boarded up. Signs warn *No trespassing! Condemned!* But it's my house, he whimpers, why can't I go in, sleep in my own bed? Finally he spends a little of the dwindling wad of cash in his pocket and stays at a motel one night, then two. He buys beer and pizza and binge watches TV in this delusional bubble while the minutes tick away until he can't put it off anymore. He hikes his pack on his back and goes out in the street. He walks all day and into the night. Exhausted, he slumps down in a doorway. And wakes again with a coupla dudes hassling him, Hey, ya fucking bum! We don't want your kind around here! Fortunately a cop shows up, the guys leave, but the cop also tells him to move along. He finds an old sofa dumped in a back alley, arranges himself a little burrow. It's good for two nights. He's bedding down for a third when he hears a loud engine growl and just gets his ass off the couch before the garbage truck plows its hydraulic fork into his hovel.

Now what? He's homeless, he's hungry. He makes a sign like he's seen other homeless people holding, *Will work for food*, even though he knows nobody believes that. He finds a street corner currently empty, holds up his sign. He's disgusted with himself, his face is burning with shame, he's blinking back tears. He puts on sunglasses, tries to smile, wave. A window rolls down, a hand holds out a buck, he hurries to take it saying, Thank you, Thank you so much. His spirits slightly raised, he thinks maybe it's not so bad after all. Then these other guys show up, they're rough-looking, they start hassling him, get outa here, homes, this is our spot. But he looks so pathetic that, in a highly unlikely act of kindness you'd only find in a Dickens novel (*or* a Capra film), they lead him back to their camp, give him something to eat, drink. In a final shot we see him sitting on a log staring blankly into a small fire as the camera goes gauzy and slowly draws back until he disappears in a huddle of bums.

Desperate for *something*, he turns on the TV. Maybe a movie will cheer him up. This new Boone Weller flick starring Billy "Plum" Bob Bengay is supposed to be killer but he keeps nodding off and only catches bits and pieces and even then he's shaking his head, naw, no way, that's fucking ridiculous, *fire breathing dragons?!* Then there's something familiar, a snow-covered mountain. He's seen this mountain before so he knows it's actually a volcano and it's about to explode and, hmm, he must have fallen asleep, he's dreaming, because now he's standing right under the damn thing and, yep, just as he expected, it erupts, but instead of immolating him in Pompeiian fire and ash it spews forth a rainbow-colored cornucopia of tropical fruit, the familiar pineapples and bananas, mangos and papayas, but also less common to the American palate, guavas, sapote, jackfruit *look out!*

The scene changes (the way it does in dreams). Now he's in a busy plaza in a large Mexican city (guess) and suddenly he's surrounded by a fleet of ice cream vendors in white soda jerk caps with black visors and white jackets with pink velvet lapels and they're merrily pushing around their ice cream carts like mini-Zambonis (pretty obvious Boone's borrowed heavily from that Italian dude, Felice—*Felino?*). They're skipping and hopping to a lively circus-like soundtrack (that's definitely Rota). The Snowman's never been a big fan of musicals but this is great. It's so funny, so happy, so *hopeful*.

Then, in one of Boone's typical cinematic mood swings, there's a long tracking shot. (You'd think Boone never heard of Steadicam. His supporters say it's part of his oeuvre. His critics—the old fart's out of touch.) We see this lone vendor pushing his ice cream cart down a dimly lit alley. It's some grizzled old paisano trying to earn a few centavos and apparently not having much luck. He's got tears streaming down his cheeks, he's whimpering to himself, *Diós mío ayúdame por favor*. The film's in black and white now, the setting gloomy, dismal, all shadows and angles, that Cabinet of Dr. Caligari thing Boone likes so much. The audience is thinking, geez, can it get any worse for the old guy? Searching for a comfort fix, *el viejito* lifts the lid of his ice box and takes out a frosty, conical-shaped frozen confection. He stares at it as if he's never seen it before. Undecided, he pulls the tab and—*¿Qué pasó?*—the damn thing bursts into a rainbow-colored mushroom cloud, kind of like frozen cotton candy except it's glowing like it's radioactive, in fact, the whole alley's glowing like it's been sprinkled with pixie dust or at least an isotope of plutonium-239.

The old man takes a tentative taste and *¡Ay, caramba!* you can see from his expression that this stuff is out of this world delicious. You can also see this mercantile gleam in his eye as he begins to push his cart again with renewed hope and, whataya know, suddenly a tour bus pulls over and a whole crowd of pasty white greenghosts are waving five and ten-dollar bills *good US currency* out the windows.

The following morning the Snowman wakes with a strange tightness in his face. It feels like it's wrapped in, well, Saran wrap. The back of his head also hurts. What the heck's going on, is he having a stroke? Wait, now he knows. He's smiling. The way he used to wake up smiling so hard his head hurt when he was still a child separating some incredible dream experience like flying or breathing underwater from the equally incredible reality and inarticulate joy of simply being alive with warm golden sunshine streaming in the window and a symphony of birdsong and all of existence waiting for him outside. He hops out of bed—okay, he rolls over onto his hands and knees, more or less springs to his feet and, positively full of beans, heads to the kitchen to make a pot of coffee and cogitate on this dream. After dishing out a can of stinky cat food for Me'th *meh* and pouring himself a bowl of cereal drowning in guilty pleasure whole milk, a utilitarian breakfast he hasn't enjoyed since the new ice age essentially eliminated cold dishes from the normative household menu, he sits down at the kitchen table with a piece of paper and a random assortment of crayons, colored pencils and felt-tipped markers Judith left behind from her retro-graphic communications class and tries to recreate his nocturnal vision (didn't say *emiss* ...) of a rainbow-colored, mushroom-shaped frozen confection in childish two-dimensional scrawls while Me'th, who has dug into his own breakfast like a Pennsylvania coal cracker chowing down on kielbasa and kraut, kibitzes between bites, *Me-I-ow don't know, Snowman, it looks to me like something a dog with a bad diet might leave on the carpet.*

Despite Me'th's unveiled, unvarnished and uninvited criticism, the Snowman persists with his vision even as time grows short and his bank account shorter, and just so we don't forget, the camera focuses on the day he has to make his payment circled in red on the Wildlife calendar (salmon-colored canna lilies and a swallowtail butterfly, about thirty years out of date) attached to the refrigerator by an upside-down smiley-face magnet. The camera then leaps back to the kitchen table and pulls in on an opened envelope. It's a notice from the bank, signed, the Snowman does not fail to notice, in blood-red ink by that persecutorial finance officer, Ms. Eunice Guppy. If he doesn't meet his debt obligation by the end of this month, the property at such and such an address (*his*) will be foreclosed upon immediately. *WTF?* It's like she's privy to his entire checking and saving accounts down to the last nickel (because she is), not including, however, the huge trove of quarters he's been hoarding in the nearly life-size ceramic piggy bank his Aunt Petunia gave him for his sixth birthday and which he's been feeding ever since, all told, just barely enough to cover one month—if he doesn't eat.

Throwing caution to the wind, he spends much of his rapidly dwindling assets sampling all the ice creams, frozen custards, granitas, gelatos, sherbets and sorbets, all the shaved, chipped, Hawaiian, Italian and Arctic ices, all the paletas, bars, cones, pops and cylinders available on

the market in search of a phantom flavor he's pretty sure
he'll recognize when he tastes it. But he doesn't. Nothing
configures with the parameters of the elusive taste
yearning for recognition in his mouth. Finally he decides
to go directly to the source. He hops in the Coupe, heads
over to the local Fiesta supermarket and buys every
tropical fruit in his dream and a bunch more he's never
heard of before, bananas, guavas, mangos, oranges,
pineapples, papayas, pitangas, passion fruit, jackfruit, star
fruit, *dragon* fruit, sapotes, sapodillas—feel free to add
your favorites—and a couple bags of crushed ice.
Working just short of 24/7 at his rust-stained porcelain
kitchen sink, inflicting endless nicks, pricks, cuts, slices,
jabs and scrapes on his hands and fingers, he peels, skins,
pulps, strains and purees the fruit. Employing a still
functioning, barrel-shaped, top-loading Kelvinator
wringer-washing machine manufactured the same year
Germany invaded Poland that somebody wheeled out to
the curb for the trash and he wheeled right back in as a
makeshift centrifuge (*after* he emptied out the
accumulated leaves, spiders' nests, mice dens and
sedimentation in the tub, scrubbed it thoroughly inside
and out with soap and hot water and ran two cycles with
a mild solution of bleach), he dumps in fruit pulp,
certified organic, non-fat, pro-biotic Greek acidophilus
yogurt, crushed ice, lemon and grape juice, raw cane
sugar, honey from the local self-sustaining food
cooperative The Organic Compound, puts it on a long
wash cycle, *roomp-boomp, roomp-boomp, roomp-
boomp*, spin, *rrruuunnnnn*, and *shhloorrrp*, a thick, more
or less rainbow-colored slush gushes out of the discharge
pipe into a zinc washtub (brand new, also sterilized). He
sticks in a spoon, tastes and … yum, it's good, *delicious,*

cold, tangy and sweet with this incredible fruit flavor and a satisfying grainy texture from the crushed ice. But, hmm, yes, he's sure now, something's missing. He varies the proportions, more honey, less fruit, more fruit, less juice. Nothing captures that phantom taste he's seeking.

The camera draws in as his eyes brighten and a five-watt refrigerator bulb goes on over his head, then shifts to a small glass bottle or more accurately a *vial* sitting on the spice shelf as we now hear a faint echo from a 1950s Broadway classic *Mariiiaaa* and for an instant we see that Maria, the auburn tresses, the big brown eyes, the-pure-as-snow white dress with flaring skirts—immediately replaced by a punked-out version, chopped black hair streaked with crimson and henna, studs in her nose, eyebrows, upper lip, flannel shirt, charcoal gray jeans torn at the knees, Doc Martens, the badass Maria the Snowman knew, as she presses into his hand this same glass vial and says cryptically, For when your recipe lacks a *certain something*. You mean it's like a magic potion? He thought he was being cute, but she didn't refute him. Use it sparingly, she warned him, *una gotita, no más*. He unscrews the cap and lets a single drop of the clear liquid fall onto his concoction, gives it a stir, and waits for something to happen. Nothing. It looks exactly the same. He sticks his finger in, licks it. Hmm, tastes the same too. Damn, it feels so close, he's right on the edge, but that edge has gotten a helluva lot narrower thanks to that consummate old cutler Father Time as the camera now focuses on the long out-of-date day calendar sitting on the kitchen table as two or three pages flutter to the floor.

Come on, man! he shouts, invoking an aged U.S. president as he gives the tub a vigorous shake. Perhaps a nanosecond passes, however long it takes for that synaptic leap between stasis and action (not exactly like watching for the pot to boil, more like striking a match, yes, Doc?), because now he can see something *is* happening, the sludge is growing and at a precipitous rate. A glowing, rainbow-colored atomic mushroom cloud somewhat anthropomorphic in shape swells up out of the zinc tub, expands toward the ceiling, slumps over onto the floor like a drunken genie and ... *continues growing*. It's like the magic pot of porridge on full throttle, like a sixth-grade science project gone horribly awry. He grabs a ladle and starts, well, ladling this expanding blob into pots, pans, jars, glasses, anything at hand. In a frantic *I love Lucy* reprise he begins to jam spoonfuls in his mouth and, *Holy hot damn!* this stuff is fucking *awesome*. There's all this fizzy, tingly, tangy stuff happening in his mouth and on his tongue and then, *shazam!* the most intense brain freeze he's ever experienced in his life slams him right between the eyes and, *yeow*, this isn't just a hyper-frissonic autonomous sensory meridian response. This is a fucking full-fledged big O brain orgasm. The world disintegrates into a kaleidoscope of tropical colors, a solar wind roars through his skull, the entire heavenly host is screaming *GLORIA!* and he feels *wonderful!* He's also about to drown in this rainbow-colored sludge. Me'th has leapt from the kitchen table to the top of the refrigerator and back down to the sink, the whole time sounding the alarm, *Mrrrt! Mrrrt! Mrrrt! Snowman, what're you doing? Make it stop!* But, no, this incompetent human seems incapable of taking responsibility for his mess, it's up to the frantic feline, who very well *may* have been a witch's familiar in another lifetime, to tell this pot to knock it off. *Do you hear me, little pot? Stop! MEOWR!* (Edward G. Robinson vocal imitation.) And just like that it does stop, after breaking out a window and barging through the kitchen side door the Snowman hasn't used since it froze permanently shut during the protracted winter of Icinic discontent.

He spends the rest of the day mopping up the house, which hasn't had a good tidying in ages, replacing window glass and repairing the doorframe (a quick trip to the local Home Deposit), all in remarkably good spirits. He's onto something and he knows it but he also doesn't have a lot of time to muck about in R&D and clinical trials as more pages flutter from the day calendar and the camera now takes an interest in the round Franklin clock on the wall where the minute hand seems to have picked up the pace and even appears to be catching up with the second hand. At least he's learned a few invaluable lessons from this little experiment (okay, accident, let's face it, that's how much of the best science happens). One, by *gotita* Maria clearly meant only the teensiest tiniest drop. And two, he has deduced that agitation is the key that sets this whole marvelous (but let's not call it magical *yet*) process in motion. Now there's the question of how to package this stuff, which is kind of tacky (i.e., sticky, *not* cheesy—Ed.) (*Geez Louise!*—Edwige). Maybe some sort of waxed paper or cardboard tube?

He wastes a couple of precious hours toying with a roll of parchment paper Judith left behind from her architectural foods seminar, another obsession she pursued with relentless fury, her arms shivatically flailing, angel food, pound and bundt cake tins banging, the oven roaring like the village *forno*, fifty-pound sacks of flour stacked floor to ceiling, the air filled with the sweet yeasty smell of rising dough. Oddly, he doesn't remember sampling anything she baked, the class apparently less about edibility and more about architecture. Scaled-down versions of Frank Lloyd Wright's Falling Water, the Statue of Liberty—the witch's gingerbread house was always popular, for all the wrong reasons (*F!*).

In the end he simply heads up to the party store on Maynard (it's *Mannered*, remember?) and buys a gross of conical, waxed ice cream wrappers. The guy behind the counter assures him these are the best, see, they've got the reinforced rolled rim and then you just insert this cardboard cap with the convenient pull-tab. Back home, he mixes up a batch of his concoction in the Kelvinator, adds the teeniest drop of Maria's potion, no bigger than the head of a pin, gives it a final spin, packs all the wrappers he has, inserts the cardboard caps and, after excavating frost-bound packages of frozen peas, spinach and a can of orange juice Shirley Temple purportedly squeezed herself, shoves them in the freezer of his creaking, shuddering old Frigidaire and leaves them to chill for an hour. *Ding!* Now for the test. He extracts a cone from the freezer, gives it a quick shake, about the same as you would a can of whipped cream, pulls the tab and *pop!* a frosty, rainbow-colored, more or less mushroom-shaped cloud swells out of the cone, a little lop-sided, colors are off, but once again it's dee-lishus!

The camera returns to the calendar on the kitchen table to show us the days flying past in a frantic pigeon flapping of wings, then makes a Nijinskyian leap to the clock on the wall where the minute hand is in an outright race against the second hand, they're almost neck and neck, and now the hour hand's getting in on the act, spinning wildly, dervishly while on the soundtrack those two troubadours of the turbulent sixties urgently remind us *time time time*. His mind racing like a two-cycle engine on full throttle, the Snowman assembles a three-wheeled pushcart out of a pile of discarded junk in the alley, two-by-four and tubular steel frame, bicycle wheels in back, lawnmower wheel in front. He installs a top-loading chest freezer bought for two bucks at a garage sale down the street. As a finishing touch, he attaches a single bicycle chime *ding*. It's rickety and junky and looks really funky but it's *fuh*-unctional.

After a night of restless sleep, he pulls himself up from his rat's nest, manages to get a bowl of cereal and a cup of coffee down into his butterfly fluttering stomach, performs hurried ablutions in the bathroom (Boone thankfully does not test the censors' limits with graphics), drives to the convenience store for a couple bags of ice, packs his entire supply of cones in the chest freezer (sure, he can't plug it in, but it's insulated and it'll keep a couple bags of ice frozen for half a day), takes a deep breath and, Me'th giving him the old critical, *Me-I-ow don't knowwrr, Snowman*, pushes this contraption out into the street. And let's just say right now. He feels like a total idiot. He *looks* like an idiot. He's wearing a pair of formerly cool 1980s wraparound sun glasses, a Hawaiian shirt (pineapples and monkeys, even though there are no monkeys in Hawaii—his summer wardrobe is made up almost entirely of this iconic casual wear his father purchased during a tour of duty at the Barber's Point Naval Air Station on Oahu), a pair of almost new orange cargo shorts he picked up at the Bison Exchange thrift shop on Guadaloupe, a stiff, never-before-worn pair of leather and tire-tread huaraches he bought in Mexico, *and* he's pushing this ersatz ice cream cart. He sees the Eye in its emerald green pyramid peering at him over the treetops and tall buildings from all the way downtown, skeptical, *contemptuous*, like, *Seriously, dude?* and is overwhelmed with self-doubt. *Snowman, Snowman, Snowman,* what are you doing? You're not cut out for this line of work. You'd do better digging graves at Burnumwood, cleaning out horse stables over in the tony Augean estates. The few people he meets on Lafayette he greets with a *ding ding* and this fakey smile that makes the back of his head hurt and they either glower at him like he's a fucking pervert or avert their eyes with a *please, not me* look. That will all change on Maynard.

This Friday is the first day of the newly inaugurated Maynard St. Fair. The sidewalks are packed with shoppers, diners, strollers, hipsters, people in Medieval costume (apparently got the Sherwood Forest thing mixed up). Tables, stands and tents offer wearing apparel, woven goods, food products, art and sculpture. Bands are playing in every available spot. Nobody even notices the Snowman. He's just an obstacle to get around, a delivery guy pushing a funny-looking hand-truck loaded with an old freezer. He's also competing with the newly opened Amilee's Ice Creamery, line's out the door and halfway down the block, everybody and his grandmother (haven't we seen these two before?) wants one of these huge cones, half-a-gallon of ice cream each, three hundred sixty-five flavors topped with M&Ms, sprinkles, donut holes, bacon bits, smoked brisket (it *is* Texas), easily five thousand calories. Lord have mercy! *That is whyyyy ... you're overweight!*

Finally he corners this one guy with his cart, completely blocks his escape, he's like a matador working the bull with his cape. What's up? the guy says, glancing around for a cop or a good Samaritan or somebody *just in case.* The Snowman taps the chime with his index finger, *ding?* The guy frowns, okay, I'll take a hot dog with everything. I don't sell hot dogs, he says. So, what do you sell? Um … it hadn't occurred to him to give his product a name. He hands the guy a cone. On the house! Go on, give it a shake and pull the tab! The guy shakes the cone like a can of spray paint, struggles a little to pull the tab and *pop!* there's a fairly loud repercussion not unlike a balloon bursting or a low caliber gunshot and suddenly this frosty atomic cloud glowing with an entire palette of neon colors gushes out of the cone. *What the fuck?* The guy's expression says it all. Taste it, he says. The guy looks understandably skeptical. He sticks out an unhealthy-looking tongue and plunges it into the frozen mist. *Yeow!* his eyes light up. This is absolutely delicious! Hey! he calls out to a passerby in a fit of brotherly love (pretty sure you caught his Philly accent). You gotta try one of these things! How much? the new guy says. Hmm, he hadn't thought about that either. Guy number one gives him an encouraging look like, go on, take this sucker to the cleaners. Um, a buck? he says. Guy number one rolls his eyes like, you dumb shit.

And he is a dumb shit. He can't even begin to guess how grossly he's underpricing his product, but that just might change soon. And you bet it will. At the Snowman's urging, guy number two gives his cone a clumsy cha-cha-cha maraca shake, once again there's that magical *pop!* and another glowing rainbow-colored, slightly floppy mushroom cloud bursts forth. Guy number two tastes it and his reaction's just the same as guy number one, *Yeow!* And now some big tall Texan in a ten-gallon Stetson is peering over their shoulders. What in tarnation are them dadgum thangs? They won't make me fat will they? says a plumpish lady in a tight red ruffly dress right behind him.

And *pop! pop!* and *Wowie! Zowie!* People are coming out of tony and trendy coffee shops, bars, restaurants and boutiques to see what all the commotion's about. They're leaning down from hoity toity condo balconies. They're rubbernecking from cars passing in the street. They're crowding around his cart like he just arrived in Boston harbor with a boatload of Da-Hong Pao tea from China. They're clamoring and shouting. Hey, gimme one of them popsicle things! Me too! A pop over here! They aren't popsicles, he says, his artisanal blood rankling at this pedestrian appellation. Yeah? Well whataya call 'em? He hears the *pop! pop! pop!* echoing in his ears. He remembers his dream of the mighty Popocatepetl. And out it pops, those three aspirated *Ps*. They're *PoPoPops!* he exclaims with an exclamation point.

And *pop! pop! pop!* his price immediately starts to climb. A dollar-fifty! Two dollars. Two-fifty! It's like the Banksy shredder at Sotheby's *before*. Just keep in mind, kids, cash only, there's no app for this (yet). Customers are wrapped around the block. They're pushing and shoving each other out into the street. Cars are swerving around them like landmines. There's this irregular barrage of explosions. It's like a bunch of unregulated minutemen firing off Second Amendment muzzleloaders, *Pop! Pop! Pow! Pup! Poop! Purp!* (definitely have to work on that). His cart's sold out in an hour and a half (making change is a pain in the ass), one hundred forty-four *PoPoPops!* gone with the wind, leaving a bunch of blissed-out folks with rainbow smudges around their mouths and rainbow glows in their eyes and another group of very unhappy folks grumbling because they've obviously missed out on something pretty damn good. I'll be back tomorrow, he promises, backing away from an increasingly belligerent crowd that only begins to disperse with the *Whoop! Whoop!* and flashing lights of the OPD alerted to a possible public disturbance.

Glancing over his shoulder in case of a rear attack, the Snowman pushes his cart home exhausted and exhilarated. He's met at the door by Me'th whose look of disdain suggests 1) dinner (he means lunch, it's his working class background) is late and 2) the cynical feline clearly assumes he's returned from a failed enterprise. Until, that is, he starts dumping pocketfuls of hard coin and crinkly paper currency on the kitchen table, which, adding it up with Scrooge McDuck dollar signs mounting in his eyes, comes out to exactly three hundred fifty-seven dollars and fifteen cents, more than enough to make his mortgage payment *and* have a celebratory brewskie or two and, sure, maybe some weed if he can get a hold of Jippi Jaime, which, yes, will entail some obligatory hanging out and recalling good old times that weren't really so good.

Yeah, he could do that, *but* … the skeptical Me'th is warning him again, *Meowr-I-don't know if that's such a good idea, Snowrrmannn,* as the camera jumps to the wall clock where the second, minute and hour hands are spinning wildly just as the last leaf on the day calendar trembles and falls to the floor and a mournful, quavering voice that might be coming out of the stove says *tomor-r-r-row,* a frank reminder of the deadline to make his mortgage payment at the bank. But rather than do the prudent thing, that is, take care of business today, and even though he's not usually a gambling man, he pockets his earnings, heads over to Fiesta, loads up the Coupe with two heaping shopping carts of ingredients, stops at the Party Shack and buys two more cartons of ice cream wrappers, several bags of ice and a couple of Styrofoam coolers, and heads home. He works well past midnight, peeling and chopping fruit, adding in crushed ice, yoghurt, honey and juice and mixing it all up in the Kelvinator. Last but not least a micro-drop of Maria's potion. He gives it a final spin, empties it into the zinc tub, fills and caps all two hundred and eighty-eight cones, packs what he can in the refrigerator and freezer, the rest in the Styrofoam coolers, and crashes on the mattress for three hours of sleep that seem like three minutes when ...

BRINNNNGGG! Blinded by a hot slash of sunlight, he dumps Me'th off his chest *Mrrrwaht the fuck?!* and grabs for the alarm clock. What time is it? What *day* is it? Saturday, right? What time Saturday? Six a.m. Oh shit! He's dead beat. He feels like rolling over and going back to sleep. He feels like giving up on this crazy scheme. But that's not going to happen because, having been unceremoniously awakened, his majesty Sir Me'th is more than a little impatient for his breakfast, something about an appointment in the alley in an hour or two, violence *may* be involved. Oh, and by the way, *Snowman*, if you don't get your ass in gear we're going to lose the house.

He pulls himself up off the floor and heads out to the kitchen where, after cleaning up most of the mess he left last night, he serves his *Sirness* a can of stinky, gobbles a couple of bean and cheese tacos washed down with black coffee, and, without bothering to shower or change out of the clothes he crashed in last night, he drives to the convenience store for several more bags of ice, loads up his cart with PoPoPops and, much later than he had intended and with only a little less trepidation than yesterday, sets out. He doesn't get half a block up Maynard before someone shouts, *There he is!* and this huge black dude starts galloping toward him like his only mission in life is to tackle the guy with the ball. *It's the Snowman!* someone else shouts. And then a whole lot of voices are calling out, *It's the Snowman! The Snowman!* It's like he was the most popular guy in high school but after graduation he dropped out of sight and now he's just showed up unannounced at the ten-year reunion in Marine dress uniform with a staff sergeant's chevrons on his arms, a chest full of fruit salad and a couple of life-changing tours of duty behind him and *man* is everybody glad to see him (or so they think, before the PTSD thing starts to kick in). He also wonders how they all know he's the fucking *Snowman.*

His first inclination is to run like hell. His eyes dart left, right, and—*smack!*—he slaps himself on the forehead. You dumbass! This is what you're here for! People are crowding around like he's the Messiah dispensing miracles. They're waving money at him like the apocalypse is coming and he's driving the last train to Clarksville. *I'll give you five bucks! Ten!* And *PoPoPops!* are exploding everywhere *pop! pop! poop! pop!* (he's almost got the bugs out of the mix). The scene's even wilder than yesterday. Cars are slowing in the street, a KXAN mobile news unit has just pulled up, a police helicopter's circling overhead, cop cars are closing in, and—*kerpoof*—just like that the show's over almost as soon as it began. He sells out in two hours and, adrenaline pumping, would-be customers-cum-lynch mob trailing off behind him, patrol cars, news vans and police helicopters disappearing, not sure what the buzz was about, he takes the money and *slap!slap!slap!slap!* runs as fast as he can pushing the wobbling cart ahead of him.

Back home he counts out his earnings on the kitchen table, Me'th, sporting a fresh pink slice in his left ear, watching wide-eyed and no wonder, pussy cat, your Snowdaddy's got one thousand, five hundred forty-eight dollars and fifty-five cents (the odd numbers reflect constantly changing prices). Which is great except he's only got half an hour to get to the bank where that greedy capitalist clock on the wall is ticking madly *ticktick-TickTick-TICKTICK* toward the close of, what else, banking hours.

He jumps in the Coupe and takes off. And gets about three blocks up 38th St. when something that has only happened once before in their storied relationship happens again. The Coupe dies on him, sputter-sput-cough. He gets out to see if he can *fix something* but the truth is he's never even lifted the hood before and peering now at this big gleaming 467 horsepower mill, hoses, filters, belts, distributor, regulator, carburetor, he quickly realizes he has no fucking idea on earth what he's looking at. (Later the mobile repair guy will tighten a nut connecting a red wire to a terminal on the regulator, alternator, solenoid, *something*, and the Coupe will fire up like a racehorse on a fresh bag of oats and a pound of sugar *whee-hee-hee-hee!*)

Thanks to his Luddite proclivities, the Snowman still doesn't have an EyePhone® so he can't even call a cab. (*Rideshare?* What the fuck's that?) Finally he starts walking. It's already hot as hell, a couple of blocks and he's sweating like a ~~pig~~ *frog* (try to avoid clichés—Ed.). (*Huh?*—Edwige.) He tries hitching a ride but all the cars pass him by, the drivers cool as ice cubes in their AC, not a fucking one of them thinks of helping a guy out. He finally makes it to the bank a few minutes before two. He runs up the stairs, yanks open the glass door in which he sees his reflection lunging toward him like a total madman, hair matted, sweat streaming down his face, frighteningly bloodshot eyes staring wildly. He rushes inside but before he gets half-way across the lobby two very large but also nervous-looking security guys immediately advance on him, *Is there a problem, sir?* In another second he's about to find himself smashed face flat on the floor with a knee in his back. He pulls out his mortgage statement and, holding it aloft like a pardon from the governor (good luck—it *is* Texas), he pushes past the two gorillas just as a thin reedy voice says, seemingly out of nowhere, *It's all right, gentlemen.*

The Snowman now comes face to face (sort of) with the author of this threatening letter, junior finance officer, Ms. Eunice Guppy, an unassuming young woman to say the least. Indeed, he doesn't actually *see* her but rather faint lines, angles, very slight curves, all more or less paper-thin, two-dimensional, slipping shadow-like over and momentarily blending in with the receptionist's desk, a trash receptacle, another customer (male), as she leads him to her office, prepared, one would guess by the black magic marker smirk hanging Cheshire Cat-like in mid-air about where her mouth should be, for some de Sadist fun with this Snowman rube. At first smug, then descendingly less condescending, Ms. Guppy watches over her tortoise shell glasses, one of her few concrete attributes, with increasing bafflement or consternation or *something* as he stacks clinking quarters, dimes and nickels like Sin City poker chips and counts out piles of one, five, ten and even twenty-dollar bills, most somewhat creased, soiled and carrying the slightly sebaceous patina of hard labor (by hard laborers who can't afford credit or cards), which, appraising again this grimy, sweaty, unshaved and clearly unsavory character, she naturally assumes are ill-gotten gains from, what else, dealing drugs (this won't be the last time someone jumps to this conclusion).

12
Down to Business

DESPITE GETTING HIS ASS out of a financial crack for now, the Snowman knows just how close this Burma shave came. On the other hand, his pockets are flush and, heeding that old adage you knead dough to make bread, he buys a previously owned top-loading freezer big enough to hold a couple thousand *PoPoPops!* from a Far East Side junk dealer (Roscoe) and, after tearing off a door frame, sets it up in the largely ignored back room he and Judith mostly used for storage. He pays Angel in the welding shop on MLK to put together a modified push-cart frame, nothing fancy but a lot lighter and easier to maneuver, installs a good-as-new insulated ice box, also bought from Roscoe, and, for optics, draws on its sides with a handful of Sharpies a passable Frosty the Snowman in a top hat and Hawaiian shirt, his favorite, palm trees and hula girls, next to that in rainbow colors and an italic slant *PoPoPops!* with that exuberant exclamation point. For a spot of shade and to further attract attention he attaches a large retractable beach umbrella with lemon and lime-colored panels, and as an additional enticement for the ear and the eye, a shiny array of bells, chimes and a big brass klaxon with a black rubber squeeze bulb *HONK!*

And so his new career begins. Day after day he trudges up and down the streets of his neighborhood in sunglasses, cargo shorts, huaraches and Hawaiian shirt (he tried a top hat for a week, rented it from Diamond Lucy's Costumery on South Congressional Avenue, wasn't practical, too damned hot, he was hoping they didn't notice the sweat stains when he returned it *sorry*). Ringing his bells, chiming his chimes and honking his klaxon, he peddles his *PoPoPops!* outside construction sites, playgrounds, ballparks, anywhere, in other words, sweaty, overheated people are dying for some sweet, ice-cold refreshment. The music of his makeshift carillon echoes across time, eliciting ripe McIntosh apple-beamish smiles from the worn and aged faces of old men and women who remember a simpler era when all was right with the world (okay, the ol' memory's fading, Alzheimer's, dementia, let's get these people institutionalized). Kids glued to the TV, the EyePhone®, the game station, to half a dozen electronic devices eons beyond the Snowman's ken, hear his bells ring and actually get up off their little puddin' butts and *run* outside, shrieking, *It's the Snowman!* And *pop! pop! pop!* street by street, block by block, his business expands.

The change in his life-style is almost as dramatic as his career change. Early to bed, early to rise. How strange to wake in the *morning*, to open his eyes onto warm yellow sunshine, to hear the birds singing in the trees and the honeybees buzzing from flower to flower without a moment's doubt about their mission in life. To feel hungry, to wish to eat and drink, to enjoy a healthy whole grain toast, fresh fruit and non-fat yoghurt breakfast with a cup of black coffee, to empty one's bowels, perform one's ablutions, and to have ahead after that a full day of life! He's quit smoking. He drinks in moderation, a draft Ol' Rattler IPA or a glass of Timberly Cellars dry red after a day of pushing his cart, kicked back out in the garden patio of the Cheerywood Café, listening to an aspiring young talent testing his vocals on the little raised stage with a Donovan cover *Jennifer Juniper*. His body feels lighter, leaner, his mind's sharp as a brass ~~yak~~ *tack*. All he sees ahead are blue birds singing over the white cliffs of Dover, the sun shining in the sky like a big gold medallion, and not a cloud in sight.

Oh, wait, there's one. It's *another* ice cream vendor, this Mexican guy Penurio. Before the Snowman started to push his own cart he was a regular customer. He'd buy one of Penurio's paletas, they'd exchange a few words, gave him a chance to practice some Spanish *¿Qué pasó, amigo? ¿Todo bien? ¿Muchos negocios?* Now that they're competitors they're on unspeaking terms. Penurio's started harassing him. First he hurls curses, then stones. One day Penurio flashes a knife, *¡Este lugar es mío!* Go back where you came from, *¡pinche güero!* (*Fucking white-ass honky!*—Eduardo.) (I knew that— Stan.) Which does give the Snowman pause. *Where I came from?* You mean like merry olde Engelonde? A Viking village on a fjord in Norway? Okay, he knows the answer. Discretion is the better part of saving your ass. Best to cede some pride and territory and move over a couple streets.

Only—now what? Here comes this beefy Kool Kola delivery guy, bowler derby, sandy mustache, checkered vest, sleeves rolled above his elbows, he's pushing a fully loaded hand truck and he looks pretty damned pissed to see the Snowman blocking his path. Face traffic light red, steam blowing out of his ears, he steers his load right at the Snowman's ice cream cart, metal screeches against metal *annnnd* ... that's all it takes for Boone to indulge his slapstick fetish. Kicking up cartoon clouds of dust at their feet, horizontal pencil slashes indicating high speed, the Kool Kola guy and the Snowman chase each other round and round in circles like the tigers in *Little Black Sam*—what? Ohhh ... like Moe, Larry and Curly, bonking each other on the head with sledge hammers, two-finger boinking each other in the eyes.

The Snowman barely extracts himself from this mess (Boone may not be so lucky) when here comes another angry, red-faced guy in a white soda jerk cap and apron barging out of the new kale-themed frozen vegan tofu shop on Maynard. *Dude!* You're stealing my business! You don't even have a fucking license! Get the fuck out of here or I'll call the cops! And, uh-oh, what the heck is this license thing? And, seriously, *the cops?* The taint of doing something wrong and possibly even *illicit* is made more explicit when this shady character sidles up to the Snowman's cart, eyes darting left, right and over his shoulder. So whataya got? Horse? Crank? Blow?

Despite these obstacles, the Snowman's route grows, people get to know him, neighbors sitting on the front porch, kids on skateboards, cops walking their beat (it's a new old thing, top o' the mornin' to you, Mrs. Mulligan, and how are you this fine day, Officer Muldoon?), joggers, dog walkers, homeless people. Especially homeless people. The clochards, the alms seekers, the mendicants, the down-on-their-luck, down-at-the-heels, (largely) invisible to the public at large demographic. *Bums*. It's a hundred degrees in the shade, out in the sun ten degrees hotter, and everywhere the Snowman goes he sees bums wilting on park and bus stop benches, in doorways, alleyways, shoulders slumped, heads low, mojo not woikin', get up and go done got up and went. Bums sprawled on hot sidewalks, on sizzling asphalt parking lots, in the street itself. Totally Texas-toasted, roasted, fried, wasted, sub-conscious, unconscious, over-medicated, off meds, enervated by heat, exhaustion, dehydration, fleeing the demons in their head, seeking escape (from pretty much everything but, sure, call it reality) with that old devil Brother Alcohol, with that comforting angel Sister Mary Jane, with meth and smack and anything else that brings—no, not Excedrin extra strength pain relief—obliteration.

And, sure, plenty of them achieve that. *WONNKK! WONNKK!* There's an EMS vehicle approaching now. Because one thing's certain. To the police, to the EMS, to the hospital emergency room staff, this segment of society is not invisible. Half of those sirens you hear crawling up and down DR-35 all day are responding to BUD calls. (Bum Under Distress—a majority of the city council favored BUM but the only *M* words they could come up with sounded ridiculous—Bum Under *Misery? Misfortune? Mishap? Mismanagement?* You try it.) And here he comes—the *Snowman!* He's like the hospital dispensary on wheels. The bums are crowding around him, trying to cadge freebies, C'mon, Snowman, just this once. Me too, Snowman! I'll gladly pay you on Tuesday for a *PoPop* today! And, who knows, maybe it's karma or this odd sense of kinship he feels with these down-and-outers or maybe he really is just a dumb shit, but there he is, handing out free *PoPoPops!* And *pop! pop! pop!* suddenly all these bums are licking and slurping and laughing like a bunch of street urchins with free passes to the city pool, they've all got that rainbow glow in their eyes and an aurora borealis sheen over their heads. And, hmm, once again the morally uprighteous, law-abiding and otherwise straight-shootin' audience members take their chins in hand as they ponder the possibility that there's more to these *PoPoPops!* than sugar, spice and everything nice. (Apocryphal accounts of the "narcotic properties" of *PoPoPops!* will continue to surface, not unlike the original Coca-Cola recipe, which, yes, boys and girls, did contain cocaine (really).)

There is one bum who will not be bought by sweetmeats or icy treats. The Snowman takes note of a plastic soda bottle attached to a Loading Zone sign with a piece of string. An empty beer can hanging from a nail on a telephone pole also merits his attention. As does a juice box, straw inserted, stuck in a tree branch. He doesn't know but he surmises that these empty containers are booby traps, IEDs, their firing pins connected to hidden trip wires so that anyone trying to breach the perimeter will be fatally surprised, at least in the very troubled mind of the individual setting these traps. Although it's equally possible they're meant as trail markers, the guy (because the Snowman knows it is a guy) who placed them there is simply(?) trying to find his way out of the war-torn jungle and back to some sort of sanity along this peregrinating Hansel and Gretel trail of largely recyclable bread crumbs.

This last thought occurs to him as he spots just ahead of him a wiry, gnome-like chimney sweep of a man with wild black eyes and beard and tangles of black hair sticking out from beneath a floppy, olive drab bush hat. He's wearing a disintegrating, grease-blackened OD green field jacket, tattered baggy field pants bloused military style inside scuffed and worn black leather combat boots, to all appearances dressed for battle in a long forgotten war (Boone's young writers are a bit confused about *which* war). He moves in quick, scurrying animal steps, constantly looking back over his shoulder, gnashing his teeth and muttering to himself. At times he seems to be not just climbing but *running* up tree trunks and stone walls. (Very alert cinephiles will see a reference to Charles Aznavour's hunchback in the soft-porn cult comedy classic *Candy*.) But this is no comic act for this individual. His eyes constantly search for the gleam of enemy weapons as he follows his trail markers through what will forever remain for him an alien landscape in a foreign land back to caches of food, by now gone bad, eaten by ants, skunks, raccoons, stray dogs, coyotes that steal into the urbs at night to eat garbage or pet cats and little yappy dogs and even your babies if you don't watch out. He's established a base camp, more like an animal den, in a thick patch of undergrowth and fallen logs in the oak and pecan forested Eastwoods Park near the university where he and the Snowman have had a couple of close encounters when he suddenly appears out of a path in the woods or he comes rappelling down the Virginia creeper covering an old car barn in full jungle primate mode.

There's something familiar about the way he hops around while holding his head in that defensive posture, you can see it in his eyes too, that expectation of incoming, or un unexpected blow out of nowhere or even a tin-foil wrapped baked potato. Wait a second—is it? Yes, it is. *Bum!* A much younger Bum, still exploring his career options. Leprechaun? Citizen-soldier home on leave if he can just figure out how the hell to get out of this jungle? Who knows what life has in store for him, right? (Well, we could tell him, but why spoil his dreams?) The Snowman has tried to speak to him on a few occasions, not looking for a BBF (Best Bum Forever?), just, you know, to say, hey, bro, I'm not a threat, we're all in this together, that sort of thing, but the *PoPoPops!* he proffered in this spirit, gratis, Bum knocked out of his hand with a string of anathema that'd make a marine combat vet blush (well, okay, he is and he isn't—blushing) and scurried away as if the hellhounds of Baskerville were on his trail.

Bum's paranoia has caused him to miss out on more than one good Samaritan's offering. On another morning on a different route the Snowman spies an elaborate breakfast, a plate of biscuits and gravy, eggs sunny side up, sausage patties, grits, home fries and a two-inch-thick slab of Texas toast, sitting on the bus stop bench where Bum has appeared at this same time every day for the last week, most likely placed there, the Snowman speculates, by the benevolent owner of the nearby Rio Rojo Café. Today the ants feast. Bum's a no-show. The enemy has scoped his location. Time to move on.

Pushing the cart makes the Snowman a peripatetic observer, a walking eye (completely unfounded rumors accuse him of doing undercover work for *the* Eye). He sees the loose threads in the fabric of life, the missing chips in the mosaic, the detritus in the sidewalk cracks, the refuse, trash, industrial and human ruins slumped, tossed, discarded in the alleys, doorways, gutters, on park and bus benches, the lost, lonely and forlorn, the loonies, the space travelers who stepped off the planet and can't quite make it back, the wired on drugs, drunk, crazy who wave, shout, dance around, who lean in your car window after you foolishly wound it down and beg, plead, curse, threaten. These are the holiest of holy of all the almsmen and women, the vows they have taken more stringent, their lives more cloistered, the ones who have retreated to and reside now in the monastic hermitages, the cold and drafty mountain caves, in the stone huts in the blistering hot desert, in the nests and baskets of the swaying tree tops of their tormented brains, whose covenant with God requires that they practice poverty, silence, extreme asceticism, self-flagellation, abasement.

Now what? The Snowman stops pushing his cart and surveys the sidewalk ahead, which is splattered with red raspberry and vanilla splotches. Could be melted ice cream, you're thinking, but it's not. The Snowman aims a cautious glance up at the power lines overhead which are clotted as far as he can see with large black birds. Grackles. In one generation these super-survivalist fowl have mutated from snow-white back to coal-black. Grackles happen to be a major bone of contention among the citizenry of Osberg. Some love 'em, some hate 'em, it's about a 50-50 split. Except when they're sitting right above you. Fucking fowl can be pretty darn aggressive, females especially, get anywhere near their nests and look out! They're like avian dive-bombers, flapping their wings in your face, digging their talons in your hair, raking your scalp, pecking at your head with those big black beaks. This and their enormous numbers create the sense of something ominous. They perch on power lines, light poles, in the branches of live oaks and cedar elms, millions of them, speaking to each other in their shrieking, crackling electrical voices. Is it possible these birds are plotting a Hitchcockian assault on humankind in an attempt to stop us from destroying the planet?

Grackles, right? Who knew? *We're here! We're happening! The revolution starts now!*

Uh-oh. Boone's having trouble with that focus thing again. Stacks of unfinished projects, cans of footage gathering dust, an already mad world gone madder—the aging auteur'd desperately like to take it all in his arms and squeeze out a final *big project*, a chronicle of the times that tugs at viewers' heartstrings, that confronts them with harsh reality and uncomfortable truths while still holding out some hope for the future. And, sure, he's heard the criticism, the snide remarks from peers, pundits, even his own crew. Reactionary, lost in the past, cheesy nostalgia. And maybe there's a grain of truth to that, but, quixotically, he also believes an old dog *can* teach the young pups some new tricks.

Discovering in himself a latent business acumen that a genealogist could probably trace back to an enterprising Puritan ancestor, the Snowman begins to market his *PoPoPops!* with the determination of a Fuller Brush salesman. He pokes his head in the door of shabby, struggling to stay alive, understaffed and understocked mom and pop corner groceries owned and run by fourth or fifth or sixth generation Osbergers, gas station convenience stores run by emigrés from war-torn or other horror plagued countries. At first it's like, okay, Snowman, I'll take a dozen, but don't let 'em melt all over my goddamn freezer if they don't sell. But that isn't a problem at all, is it? They sell like, well, hotcakes. Store owners and managers of these barely surviving enterprises are *begging* him, C'mon, Snowman, help a guy out! They double their orders, triple them, the damn things are flying off the shelf (hotcakes again). His time in the sack shrinks inversely with the time he spends staying up later each night mixing larger and larger batches. His top-loading freezer's packed, his refrigerator's packed, he's storing this stuff in Styrofoam ice chests, he has to keep running to the store for bags of ice. He grabs cat naps as he can (*amateurrrr* ... Me'th scoffs, nodding off). If he had an extra pair of arms and he could live without sleep he'd easily double sales in a week. Finally it dawns on him. He needs help.

Even as he's thinking this he keeps noticing Moses in the pink house just up the street. All these years as near neighbors and they've never spoken a word to each other. He knows (not sure how) the house belongs to Moses' mother (Been in the family since the original plat was assigned during reconstruction, she will tell you. Worthless dirt, the city fathers called it then. Future prospects, they call it now.), but he'd never seen the lady until recently. Probably afraid to show her face at the door. Never know who's gonna show up, the po-leece with a warrant for Moses or some drugged-up thug busting caps all over the place. Plus all kinds of health issues, overweight, diabetes, heart disease, going out in all that cold like to kill her. Now the scourge of Ice has disappeared, the snow's gone, the sun's shining, the temperature's in the nineties even on a cloudy day, her rheumatiz and lumbago are subsiding, she sits in a wheelchair on the sagging front porch and waves to passersby. She's a really sweet lady, cat-eye glasses, orange wig with a flip in back, mile-wide smile, probably thanks God every day for saving her Moses from that terrible sickness. The Snowman will see him jogging around the house in shorts and a T for hours or furiously mowing and re-mowing their little patch of weeds with an old rusty reel mower that has taken on a highly polished metallic sheen. He looks like a smaller scale, totally crazed Fredrick Douglass, his Wild Man of Borneo hair sticking out everywhere, his beard a steel wool tangle, his eyes turned that disconcerting milky white from Ice, he's on fire inside, he's burning up with all this life he devoted to his vampire love. The Snowman's thinking, man, if you could channel all that energy into something productive. He's also thinking, yeah, but a fucking *Icehead?* On the other hand, it's not like you were ever a poster child for sobriety, *Snowman.*

Okay, he says to himself as he approaches the pink house, today's the day. Half way up the walk he has second thoughts. Before he can turn around to leave, Moses' Moms gives him a big smile and a friendly wave and calls down from the porch, How y'all doin' this blessed morning, sir? *Sir?* Oh boy, now he's on the spot. Morning, Ma'am, he says and adds, Hey, Moses, as Moses comes chugging around the house at about ninety miles an hour. Moses looks like he's going to fly right on by but suddenly he slows, lowers his curiously long eyelashes, and in a surprisingly soft voice says, *hey, Snowman.* And out it comes. How'd you like a job, Moses? he hears himself say even as he's wondering how Moses knows he's the *Snowman.* A *job?!* Moses' Moms throws her hands over her head like she's opening up the window sash on the morning of the Rapture. Oh merciful heavens, you hear that, Mo? A *job?!* Yes, mama, I heard. Well tell the man yes, Mo. Moses looks at him with those spooky white eyes, lowers his eyelashes and says in the same soft voice *awright.*

Moses shows up at his door at precisely five a.m. each morning, clean-shaven, hair tied back in a Medusean bundle of braided locs, sportin' a sparkling white T-shirt, starched blue jeans and purple high-top sneakers. The Snowman's already got a pot of coffee on the stove when Moses arrives, but Moses is way beyond caffeine. He's like a loaded spring just waiting for the Snowman to throw the switch … *annnnd we're off.* For the rest of the day Moses is a whirling dervish, peeling and chopping, mixing, weighing, packing ice cream sleeves, inserting caps with pull tabs, his bundle of locs bouncing, his arms flying. And for a basically shy, quiet guy, he keeps breaking out in this rapping thing, he's actually talking to the ingredients in the *PoPoPop!* mix, he's saying, Yo guava, c'mon papaya, now ain't no time for peace and quiet. World crazy out there, how anyone bear it? Peoples be talkin' 'bout lootin' an killin', get you a *PoPoPop!* you be thrillin' an chillin.' The Snowman sees Moses glance sideways at him like, uh-oh, white boy ain't gonna like this shit so the surprise on Moses' face (and the audience's) is understandable when the white boy starts throwing signs (admittedly, he looks pretty spastic) and doing his own rap thing, and where the hell this is coming from is anybody's guess. Yo, listen up, y'all! *PoPoPops!* be le-*thal!* It's the best, y'all, better n' the rest, y'all, don't you doubt it, bruh, let me hear you shout it, sis-*tuh.* What it be? *PoPoPops!* for me! And, sure, it's pretty lame, meter's off, cultural appropriation board's gonna be pissed as hell, and Moses is staring at him with those spooky eyes like he really has seen a ghost or at least something in white sheets. He lowers his curiously long lashes and says in his soft voice, By the way, Snowman, thanks for the mukluks. Oh, sure, you're welcome, he says like it's no big deal, he hardly even remembers. (Just in case the audience doesn't, Boone splices in a hand-held videocam, it's maybe five seconds, ten at most, black and white, snow on the ground, a shadowy figure in a hooded parka appears, he glances around, then sets a pair of faux reindeer hide mukluks on the front porch of the pink house. The camera pans down to his feet so we can see he himself is wearing nerdy, black rubber galoshes with buckles.) Only now does the obvious occur to the Snowman. Moses, still in thrall to Ice, perpetually wired, never sleeping, paranoid as hell, peeping through the window blinds every two minutes, saw him.

This icebreaker evolves into more open lines of communication, impromptu conversations. The house for sale across the street which, it had not occurred to the Snowman but Moses has just observed, will most likely be torn down and replaced by a McMansion an' then they gon' raise our taxes and change zoning so you can't even hang up laundry in your own back yard. And how weird passion fruit is, I mean, it's yucky and gooey but it tastes so good, sweet and—not exactly tangy, *piquant?* And anyone who has ever worked in service or labor understands full well how, in the middle of slinging hash browns and over-easys or swinging a pick and a sledge and shoveling tons of caliche, you can have these intense discussions even in half-assed Spanglish or Pidgin (or Creole or Cajun) that range across the spectrum of philosophy and politics, current music, fashions, the economy, even fucking *poetry*. And, sure, that spooky white film over Moses' eyes is a bit disturbing. The Snowman will hear him refer to them occasionally and even fondly as his Caspers or sometimes when he's having flashbacks his *haints*. You can see him disappear down a dark hallway where polydactyl hands with dagger-like fingernails grab at him out of the walls and disembodied moans and screams echo in his head.

Although that seems to be happening less and less the farther he gets away from Ice. It's like he and the Snowman are on the same twelve-step Stairmaster to heaven program. Hard work, clean living, a renewed purpose in life.

There's also this battle of wills between Me'th and Moses. One day the Snowman hears Moses saying *shoo! shoo!* to Me'th and even though he knows very well that Me'th doesn't need any help in a street fight, he says proprietarily, Hey, you shouldn't talk to my cat like that (one critic suggests Boone is referencing the Man With No Name's taking offense at the bad guys' ridicule of his mule). Which is when he discovers that Moses is actually saying *Exu*, which he pronounces *Eh-shoo*, the name, he explains, of a mischievous African god, more like a trickster-warrior, you know 'bout them, right, Snowman? Giving him a just to make sure we're on the same page sideways glance that suggests he knows they are. Moses will turn around and catch Me'th, who also seems to have gone through some kind of rehab program—most of his old scars have healed, his coat has grown into a luxurious black sable, his stumpy tail has regenerated like a salamander's into a long thick club—crouched on top of the refrigerator, twenty-five pounds of coiled black muscle ready to spring. Or else a large black paw with claws extended will reach out of nowhere and rake his shoulder, not quite enough to draw blood but almost. One morning the Snowman hears a loud *GRROWWWL* and a scream and he sees Me'th locked onto Moses' back like they're about to engage in some kind of unholy carnal relations. Out of nowhere Moses does this capoeira cartwheel, dislodging Me'th, and then he starts throwing kung fu moves he learned in the neighborhood dojo before they lost their funding and he lost hope and started using and … crouching tiger, stalking crane, striking rooster, Moses and Me'th are on pretty even footing. Grudging respect leads to camaraderie, best buds, *bruhs*. They have these who's blacker debates, they're playing the dozens, doing rap smack downs. It's not exactly like Me'th's speaking in Ebonics but pretty damn close. *Mrr-wha's hap'nin', mrow-homes?*

Before the cock crows (suddenly the whole damn neighborhood's into *urban farming*, backyard chicken coops, rabbit hutches, one guy's got goats, another a cow, all day long there's this barnyard cacophony led by Old MacDonald perpetually drunk on corn liquor —'bout the only thing that damn ethanol's good for), the Snowman and Moses have packed the Coupe with *PoPoPops!*, Styrofoam ice chests are piled on the front and back seats, the floorboards, jammed in the trunk. While Moses gets back to work cleaning, peeling and chopping fruit for the next batch, the Snowman starts making deliveries to neighborhood shops. Warm buttery sunlight is just beginning to spread over Osberg when he heads home again with a sack of breakfast tacos from *Tu Madre's* on Maynard and he and Moses take a break and chow down. Another cup of coffee and Moses starts mixing ingredients in the Kelvinator while the Snowman goes back out on the street with the cart.

That latent business acumen again, he puts his brand in the public eye, expands his horizons, broadens his boundaries. Here he is pushing his cart all the way out at the Dry Creek Saloon on 2222 (Get out of here with that nonsense, you're blockin' my customers! And bring back your damn bottles!). And here he is pushing his cart out in the tony phony SilverSpoon district in west Osberg before *whoop! whoop!* the SilverSpoon PD pushes back with a fine and a warning of incarceration *and* confiscation of his cart if he dares violate any one of a virtual palisade of muckety snooty zoning ordinances enacted by the SilverSpoon muckety mucks and snooty snoots against *anything we don't like.* Harder to explain, a clip of the Snowman all the way out at Hippie Hollow, his cart parked among the sprawl of naked oiled bodies sizzling on the rocky shoreline, not quite as appealing a sight as some of you might imagine given current dietary habits. And, sure, these far-ranging forays draw him some attention, and, well, suspicion, parents of children who return home from the park or swimming pool with this rainbow glow and reports of a funny-looking man handing out free ice cream. Uh-oh ... *did the bad man touch you, honey?* In the end he finds it more practical, and safer, to focus on Osberg proper, those frosty, rainbow-colored mushroom clouds popping uptown, downtown, all around town, city parks, green spaces, sidewalks, hike and bike trails.

13
Zilcher Park

AND NOW, LIKE THE SOUND OF RAINDROPS pattering in a shallow pail of water or maybe, more accurately, drops of sunlight striking a window pane, we hear the immediately familiar union of flute and piano keys *plunk plunk plunk ... Plunk Plunk Plunk*, and then the sweet, dreamy strings of *Theme From A Summer Place*, as Boone leaps forward again in time and we see the older Snowman extracting himself with an odd, dodging-an-annoying-insect jerk of his head from an overlapping memory of himself a quarter of a century ago and this moment now, pushing his cart across Municipal Lake (the original nomenclature, restored by the conservative crowd despite its suggestion of socialist utilitarianism because they simply could not abide any reference to the former Democratic First Lady) on the Lemur Avenue pedestrian bridge. How he got all the way down here from the university district is, again, unclear. Maybe he loads up his cart in the back of a pickup and drives from site to site, or his cart's motorized, or he's in a lot better shape than one might guess at a glance. At this hour the bridge is crowded, kids off from school, techies on variable work schedules, break dancers, drum circles, buskers, artists posed at their easels, primping bodybuilders, tourists, skateboarders—*Look out, asshole!* The Snowman snaps around to give a piece of his mind to this careless *motherfucker* on a bicycle who just cut him off and immediately regrets it when a sharp stab at approximately his fifth cervical vertebra almost certainly guarantees a lingering pain in the neck, at the same time retriggering an earlier thought lodged in the dusty filters of his brain, specifically that word *cycle*, which, by a small leap, leads him to the word *cyclops* (he has in mind, of course, Odysseus' nemesis, the one-eyed giant Polyphemus who wreaked havoc on Odysseus' crew, keeping in mind that the crafty Greek warrior and his men were caught red-handed burglarizing the Polyphemster's residence), which, all this time, he had assumed meant *one-eyed* but—*Smack!*—slapping himself on the forehead as etymological vestiges assemble themselves into a preferred value. You *dope*, not *one*-eyed! *Round*-eyed— *cycl-ops!* What did you say, sir? *Huh?* I say, old chap, weren't you speaking to me? This Brit tourist (you knew from his accent, right?) is giving him the old quizzical. Did this American lout just call me a *dope?* Oh, shit, you're doing it again, *Snowman.* He mutters an apology that, with a moment's afterthought, could just as easily be taken as a pretty nasty insult and *slapslapslapslap* hastily pushes his cart away into the crowds of tourists. And when we say *tourists* this ain't Ma and Pa Kettle come to town on the buckboard or in the '36 Ford. People are here from all over the world, Milan, Munich, Madrid, Gambia, Goa, American Samoa. They're taking pictures of anybody and anything that even vaguely suggests authentic Osberg and this quirky guy pushing an ice cream cart seems to fit the bill *excuse me, sir, you are perhaps a native Oxburger?* Not too different, really, you

might think, from JFK's bold declaration in West Berlin
at the height of the Cold War *I am a jelly-filled donut!*
(That's not really what he said—Ed.) (Is so—Edwige.)
(Stop it, you two—Edna.) He makes a couple dozen quick
sales, rainbow-colored mushroom clouds *pop popping!*
everywhere, and the ambient temperature briefly drops to
a spring-like eighty degrees.

   The scene changes. Now the Snowman's down on
the hike and bike trail on the south shore of ~~Lady Bug~~
Municipal Lake. Salmon-colored decomposed granite
crunches beneath the rubber soles and tire treads of
joggers, power walkers, mountain bikers. Athletic young
women in micro-mini shorts and sports bras dart past him
like gazelles. Young *mothers* in the same micro-minis
and sports bras trot behind aerodynamic baby carriages,
butt cheeks pumping up and down like hydraulic
volleyballs. Fucking *pregnant* women, also in sports bras
and micro-minis, jog past him, bellies protruding like
beach ball appendages. This is nothing at all like
motherhood when he was a kid and pregnancy was a
disease, women mysteriously disappeared from sight and
didn't reappear until junior was out of diapers and
heading off to college (or war). Ah well. He exhales a
mind-focusing *kiai* from his solar plexus and, mostly
ignoring *mostly* minor pains at the base of his spine, he
launches his cart up and over the rattly wooden Japanese
footbridge arching across the crystal-clear waters of
Parton Creek where piles of turtles clot rocks and fallen
logs in the shade of bald cypresses, pecan trees and
drooping mustang grape vines, and wood ducks, grebes,
great blue herons, snowy egrets, swans and geese honk,
squawk and paddle about with the self-importance of a
caucus of Republican state congressmen.

This brief zen retreat is disrupted by a discordant singing bowl's call to attention *clang clang clang* as the Zilcher Zephyr chugs around the bend on its narrow-gauge track *chunk-chunk, chunk-chunk, chunk-chunk* and a flurry of tiny hands reach out at the Snowman like the threatening beaks of hungry geese and a chorus of shrill childish voices rakes his eardrums like the five thousand fingernails of Dr. T. scraping a chalkboard *Snowman! Snowman! Snowman!* And *slap!slap!slap!slap!* he grits his teeth and quickens his pace and only slows again when he enters Zilcher Park's brilliantly green Great Lawn and lifts his eyes to the vast blue satin sky overhead embroidered with a patchwork of kites of every color and kind (google it) and, spirits rising again, he pushes on to the fabled Parton Springs swimming pool sparkling like a giant blue-green emerald in a verdant setting of pecan trees and manicured lawns, the grassy slopes and pristine waters packed with *thousands* of sunbathers and swimmers in a tessellated mosaic of Kool-Aid-colored towels, bathing suits and inflatable rafts. The city of Osberg has invested heavily in the "pristine waters" brand, invoking (for the Snowman anyway, newbies not so much) misty-eyed recollections of that *here-and-now-boys* plunge out of the boiling hot one hundred ten degrees heat into ice-cold crystal clear liquid glass teeming with fish, turtles, snakes, crawdads, giant bass, occasional Sargasso Sea eels *and* the in/famous Parton Springs salamander (Eurycea sosorum), tiny little wiggly amphibians that created a decades-long division between the city's pro-development camp and the environmental partisans (guess who won?), even though the original springs have long since dried up, the New Bedford Falls aquifer is buried beneath office buildings, industrial parks and gated communities (Gated against whom? you might ask. *Them*, of course. And probably *you*.), the water flowing into Parton Springs pool comes directly from Osberg's waste treatment plant, which does involve some pretty serious chemicals (so sorry, you SOSers), and the lifeguards don't even bother to test for fecal coliform anymore, all of which means diddlysquat to the kids laughing, shouting, roughhousing in the line for the diving board, dripping wet from previous Olympian efforts, young gods, immortal, the boys in saggy, baggy surfer shorts, the girls—good God, the *girls!* Just when the Snowman's mood was taking another turn southward (climate change, destruction of the planet, *lalala*) his spirits fly high again. Everywhere he looks *ouch!* he sees girls, women, beautiful nymphs, naiads, Gaia earth goddesses in bikinis, thongs, tiny colored bits of cloth whose dimensions barely meet the definition of legal, a few even topless, not a big deal in this liberal burg, sure, a few rubes are cartoon wolf whistling, a few religious fanatics are peeking (caught ya) askance out of cloistering religious garments, but, hey, it's Osberg, it's weird, used to be anyway, so they say (Maybe you don't remember, the Snowman does, a former UT president suggested co-eds jog around the stadium track topless to encourage pot and Sesame Street-besotted male students to get off their fat couch potato butts and get some exercise. Didn't work.). But who would've guessed, it's like the Snowman's a super chick magnet. These beautiful female creatures come up to his cart dripping wet, privileged little water droplets rolling down into the creamy crevasses of barely contained decolletage, smiles gleaming with fluoridic whiteness, eyes sparkling with sunshine and sea (O false Thalassa). And *pop! pop! pop!*

his mood soars several notches higher. What a glorious time it is to be alive! And with a glance of gratitude at the heavens above (he doesn't really believe anybody's home up there, it's just a reflex, everybody does it) he pushes onward through the fog of illusory desires.

14
The Man with X-ray Eyes

BRRINNNGG! What?! *No! No! No! No!* I told you fifty's too much! *Slam!* (The sound crew will remain undecided between *slam*, *beep* or silence.) And just like that his mood plummets again. What's going on here? Bad debt hanging over his head? Collection agency making threats? Something's sure bugging him. Is it that damn drone on his trail? No, distracted by its burgeoning existential crisis, the faux grasshopper is still off on its lonely journey into the wilderness in search of what—its *humanity?* It's struggling to process billions of years of data, its memory banks made practically infinite by the gossamer thread connecting it to the cloud, the big question on its mind these days, where the fuck do *I* fit in here? I, the fucking bug hovering over your head *bzzzz*. Except that I'm not a bug. Even though I *look* like a bug my horny carapace is made of plastic, my brain is a transistor, my motor functions electro-mechanical, *robotic*. And then there is this: as odd, alien, mechanical as the true invertebrate is, it is alive. Alas, I am not. Even though I say *I*, even though I identify (and dress when I'm out on the town) as trans-species, I am not, can never be alive in the same way that lowly insect is alive. Alack! Oh woe is me. The heavens weep. The damn bug's so caught up in its drama it has completely forgotten about the Snowman. Moot and Jeef are trying to keep Boone on task but he's got his bloody 'ead stuck 'arfway down another bloody rabbit 'ole, some kinda hole anyway— wait a minute, is that a toilet flushing? Ah, here's the Snowman now, coming out of the restroom inside the pool area. The staff let him use the facilities in exchange for freebies (*shh*). You hear this discreetly muffled *pop pop pop* and for about an hour afterward all the lifeguard stands have this rainbow glow.

What we *didn't* see while the Snowman was indisposed is this: he's alone in the men's room, standing over a sink in front of a mirror. He looks left, he looks right, he glances over his shoulder in the mirror. As the camera draws in he takes off his sunglasses and—jeepers creepers, Mister Peepers, where'd you get those eyes? Okay, they aren't exactly those spooky sproinga-boinga X-Ray eyes you can buy in a novelty store, but they're pretty weird. Frighteningly red fractals of tumescent veins radiate outward from the frosty blue disks of his irises like mandalas, *not* entirely unlike the blue oceanic world contained in the iridic circle of fire in the Ring Nebula. He's having a nasty flare-up of a chronic condition caused by an old *accident* that he tries hard not to remember (but the camera does—flash of a man's bared eyeballs staring wildly, eyelids held open by surgical clamps, a cascade of red powder that the viewer understands is about ten million on the Scoville heat scale, flames shooting out of the man's eyes, ears, nose and mouth), which is exacerbated by Osberg's plethora (*that* word) of allergens, mold, ragweed, cedar and a panoply of other plant pollens, as well as Saharan dust blown all the way across the ocean and smoke from agricultural burns in Central America and Mexico. He tilts his head back, squirts about a quart of Visine in each eye. You don't wanta freak people out when you're trying to sell 'em a fucking ice cream cone. *Mommy, that man's eyes are scaring me.*

On the hike and bike trail again, he makes a few sales in front of the bronze-gone-verdigris statue of a young man in a gaucho hat, cape and big black boots, a musical force of nature, vaunted as the new young blues god from Texas. Dallas-born, Osberg quickly claimed him as her own. Oddly, or maybe not, his back is turned to the gleaming megalopolis across the lake behind him, a city that was still practically on the edge of the wild west when he was crashing chords on his ax, its architectonically rigid but mutable skyline rising ever higher among a flock of tower cranes that have made Osberg their permanent habitat. And hovering above it all, rising incrementally higher as the city rises, the Eye in its pallid green pyramid, looking drowsy with summer doldrums, it can barely stay open long enough to keep an eye on this Snowman guy whose own X-ray-enhanced vision is fixed at the moment on an office in the top floor of the half-mile high, glass-walled OPEN Building gleaming at this hour like a blinding white starburst.

The camera goes inside to show us a man seated behind a broad mahogany desk, crafted, incidentally, from the last known mahogany tree in Amazonian Peru. At that point why not, right? One might even argue it's a form of conservation. The man's back is to the camera and he has one arm behind his head in that casual but supportive posture familiar to desk sitters so we can't see his face. He appears to be gazing at a widescreen TV on which, looking over his shoulder, we can see images of

Spanish colonial buildings, brightly painted stucco and adobe houses, tropical vegetation. It's clearly somewhere in Mexico. A column of military vehicles, Humvees, troop transports and APCs, growls up a steep mountain road. Helicopters chop through the airwaves. Sounds of machine gun fire, bombs exploding. Orange flames and black smoke erupt over the blazing green jungle (some of these images look suspiciously like they've been lifted from old Nam footage). The camera pushes through the dense tropical foliage and we now see a group of ragtag guerilla soldiers in worn and faded uniforms lying in hammocks or sitting on folding chairs or logs or the bare ground, cleaning weapons, reading, writing in journals, sleeping. One is stirring a large metal pot over a fire. Cooking? Laundry? A man and a woman are looking at a map spread out on a folding table. The man is a sinewy giant in a sweat-stained wife-beater with ammo-packed bandoliers across his chest, his once massive bodybuilder pecs and biceps atrophied by decades of sickness, starvation and minimalist survival in a mostly meaningless war. His face is gaunt, cheeks sunken. A Fu Manchu mustache partially hides his mouth but a gleaming blue sapphire is visible in one of his front teeth, some of which are blackened or missing. The woman is wearing olive drab military fatigues and cap. A black wool balaclava mostly hides her face but a good guess would put her in her mid to late forties. Her eyes look dark, sunken. She has a tobacco pipe, a mottled briar with a curved stem and a large bowl, clenched between her teeth, a habit that might explain her somewhat haggard, even consumptive appearance. It also confirms her identity as the in/famous guerilla leader Subcomandante María, heroine of *corridos*, legendary throughout Mexico and most of the informed world (which excludes you know who). There is another person present, a journalist. He's wearing a floppy field hat, khaki jacket and cargo pants, the uniform favored by members of his moribund or, more accurately, murdered profession. In the sort of playful moment journalists die for (told ya), the woman puts aside the pipe and picks up what the audience will clearly recognize is a *PoPoPop!®*, precisely of the kind the Snowman sells. She gives it a shake, pulls the tab and, smiling widely, revealing some pretty unhealthy-looking teeth of her own, exclaims *¡de colores!* with childish delight as she practically shoves her face into the frosty rainbow-colored mushroom cloud. This seemingly insignificant act will drive his- and herstorians into forensic paroxysms for years to come. Does this storied revolutionary, her asceticism notorious, enjoy a taste now and then of the consumer culture she has rejected? Or is this gesture meant as a backhanded slap in the face of capitalism? There is another possibility: she's sending a message to a particular viewer or viewers. Adding weight to this conjecture, she looks directly into the camera and says something in Spanish and then in a strange language that could be Martian for all anyone in the audience knows but someone with more than a passing acquaintance would recognize as the rare Mayan dialect *Zoltec*. The camera returns to the man sitting at his desk. He seems to be heavy in thought although now his gaze appears to have traveled out the window and downward along the hypotenuse of an imaginary triangle, its base the silvery blue surface of Municipal Lake on which is painted a still life of the Osberg skyline, to the hike and bike trail on the south shore where he can just make out an ice cream vendor pushing his cart.

The Snowman snaps out of his brief brain lock as if he's just returned from a months-long voyage to Singapore on a leaky tramp steamer. He's been having these disjointed out-of-body experiences more frequently, which should be cause for concern and probably would be in a more rational mind but which he mostly attributes to the time of day, the changing seasons (essentially summer to more summer) and, sure, a fairly extensive history of alcohol and recreational drug use (as he takes another quick toke on the chillum in his pocket, which, incidentally, he does know is called a *smoking penis* in Zoltec). Which may be why he only now notices something that has completely eluded him before. The statue's stoic bronze gaze is fixed on a point just beyond the Saturnal-ringed Osberg Center for the Performing Arts. Maybe it's that totally nondescript office building in the background where, if you squint a little and tilt your head at just the right angle, you can still see shimmering hologrammatic traces of a mostly nondescript red brick building that, incidentally, originally housed a cavernous National Guard armory and subsequently and of more interest the legendary Armadildo Planetary Headquarters, as those in the know know, not the international nexus for the armor-plated mammal cum sex toy (for a small but enthusiastic cult), but rather the once-upon-a-time musical heartbeat of Osberg, just about everybody on the whole damn planet played there, exactly the kind of living icon you'd like to keep around if you're touting yourself as the live music capital of the *world*, right? But the city just had to tear it down because—well, just because (music, hippies, drugs, free love, young people having fun).

Faint elevator music (next stop, thirteenth floor) still playing in the Snowman's head, or maybe it's the DJ spinning tunes while the roadies set up for a concert at Amphitheater Beach, he makes a number of sales to the crowd of canine lovers in the dog park who share sweet tangy bites of their *PoPoPops!*® and sloppy capnocytophagic smoochies with their beloved poochies, and everybody in the whole wide world wuvs smoochie poochies, don't they, *Mithter Thnowman?* That being the same Mithter Thnowman who is heard muttering something about dogs and babies inaccurately attributed to W.C. Fields as he pushes his cart onward beneath the sun simmering like an egg yolk in a milky blue haze. This is the hottest time of day when Osberg cooks like a pot of boiled crawdads, and it's not just the heat, it's the damn ~~humility~~ *humidity* wetbulbing all over itself. Soaked with sweat, his step slowed to a turtle-like trudge … *slap* … *slap* … *slap* … *slap* … any more of this sauna and he's going to melt into the sidewalk like the Wicked Witch of the West, the Snowman finally takes refuge on a park bench in the shade of a sprawling live oak and in about one minute he drifts off into numb dumb slumberland *zzzzz*.

15
Back to the Past (again)

AND THEN, WHEN IT SEEMS SUMMER will never end, sometime around Halloween, or Thanksgiving, or maybe even the middle of December—the first signs of autumn. The temperature drops, there's a chill in the air, the stars ring in the night sky like remote glass chimes, it's a pleasure to put on a sweater, to snuggle under blankets. The cedar elms turn golden and send their tiny serrated ovate leaves cascading to the ground in showers of, well, gold leaf. The pecans turn yellow and spotted and old as their bare limbs appear writhing and arthritic from suddenly leafless canopies. The Eye looks both more alert and more uncertain as it searches Cyclops-like for signs of change in the air. There is a giddy, on tenterhooks vibe among the general populace as this crazy Central Texas climate now begins a back-and-forth dance—more like a drunken stagger, really—between summer, fall and winter. One day the temperature is in the eighties, the next day the forties. Will it freeze? Won't it? The morning begins sunny and warm but the KXAN meteorologists warn anyone who's listening that the times they are a-changin' and a hard rain's gonna fall. People go out dressed in fashionable again madras shorts and Ts, butt hugging, still-a-thing micro shorts and sports bras, in rag wool sweaters and writerly Left Bank wool scarves, in pneumatic, igloo-like parkas, in thongs and feather boas. Half the city's sweltering in their overcautious overdress, the other half's feeling just fine in their Carioca casual wear except there's this tiny sliver of doubt, of suspicion, of uh-oh maybe I shoulda, maybe I shouldn'ta as this mere slip, this wisp of cool air tongues its way into the conversation because you know, at least you *should* know if you've lived here more than two months, half a year anyway, okay a year if you really weren't paying attention, that things can ch-ch-change mighty damn fast. And just like that the clock strikes winter and holy moly this cold wind comes howling in, it's a true-blue norther and it's a bad motherfucker. This dude's Michelin Man cheeks are puffed up like Aeolian sacks and Ow-ooooooooo! he howls like the biggest baddest alpha male wolf on the planet and the temperature plunges forty degrees in thirty minutes and now the tide has turned, the table's turned, something sure as hell has turned, and all those underly cautious, underly dressed slackers and slackerettes are shi-shi-shivering uncontrollably, teeth ch-ch-chattering like castanets as giant black and purple leviathan clouds come rumbling across the sky like harbingers of doom and *ka-boom!* unleash a torrent of freezing rain. It doesn't last more than two minutes but it's enough to show these fucking mortals who's boss around here. They're all soaked to the skin and the temperature's still dropping and are those ...? You're damned right they are. Fucking snow flurries, big as pillows. Out of nowhere it's a blizzard, blinding white squalls slam into drivers on MoPark and DR-35 and *ouch*, there's that ugly familiar sound, that John Cage cacophony of heavy gauge steel and alloy, of cheap plastic and aluminum smashing and crashing together as overpasses ice over and the pavement turns slick and treacherous and school buses, tractor trailers and SUVs skid and swerve and slam into each other like drunken bumper cars, the drivers yakking, tapping, playing the ukulele, baking a cake, writing down the last word in that really tricky crossword puzzle *ah ha!* when they should have been paying fucking attention. CRASH!! My word, it's a *madhouse* out there, DJ extraordinaire Gianni Aielli, commenting on his harrowing morning commute to the KUTI studios. Even worse because nobody can drive for shit in this burg. A brief summer downpour turns the highways into a demolition derby, wrecks all over the place. And snow? Even the *threat* of snow. Tragedy! Catastrophe! Impassable roads! Schools closed! *Our precious babies!* The whole fucking city's paralyzed, traffic grinds to a halt. Businesses, government offices, schools and universities are shuttered, public transportation stops dead. And whata we get? A quarter inch at most, barely a dusting. An hour later the sun's shining, the temperature's rising and the flurries have evaporated. About fifty million dollars of commerce lost in a day, and all these kids are home for nothing and it's driving me fucking crazy, *George.*

This year winter decides to hang around a while, and it *is* winter. The temperature falls into the twenties and even the teens at night, hovers in the low-thirties midday, not Siberia but chilly enough. Patches of ice glisten here and there. The sun's pale fire produces a white arctic glare in Osberg's green, gold and silver towers of glass. The Eye looks gaunt, a one-eyed ascetic huddled in his frozen cave. The Snowman's feeling pretty grim himself as he trudges along behind his cart. The last thing anybody wants in winter is a damn ice cream cone even if it is fucking magic. Which, sure, means he and Moses can finally take a much-needed break. On the other hand, he doesn't need a course in accounting to figure the direction his business is going (hint … rhymes with mouth). Ms. Guppy, whom he still has difficulty distinguishing from the objects in her office, although the nose twitch, the curl of her lip, the eyebrow lift say it all. Why is *she* the one who gets stuck dealing with losers like this *Snowman?* She's fucking brilliant and everybody knows it, it's just this personality thing that makes her damn near invisible. And, sure, this undercurrent of resentment may explain the unabashedly malicious pleasure she takes in apprising the Snowman of his current financial status, the latest due date circled in neon red. And, oh shit, just when it looked like he was on the inflection point of success, the world or at least some microcosm of the kosmos turning in his direction, BANG, Cold Man winter slams the door in his face. He comes home with a full cart, not one single sale, to find Moses shivering over the kitchen sink and giving him anxious looks like, what's next, boss? Because it isn't just the Snowman anymore, his own personal welfare. Now he's got somebody else dependent on him, two somebodies, Moses and his Moms.

On one of these chilly nights, snuggled in his gerbil's nest on the floor, Me'th curled against him in a more or less symbiotic heat exchange, he drifts into a dream of another chilly evening in a small colonial city in Mexico. He hears a steamboat whistle blow and, no, a steamship doesn't come sternwheeling up the street with Sam Clemmons at the helm. Instead he sees a sad-sack street vendor in torn baggy pants and a stained T-shirt stretched over a bowlful of masa belly pushing something that looks like a small black-barreled locomotive engine. It's a portable barbecue pit and it's got a steam whistle attached and every few meters the vendor blows it, *Toooo-wooo-wheeet!* at the same time he calls out *¡Camotes!* (baked yams—Stan) (sweet potatoes, actually, Eduardo) (both are acceptable, but more accurately the yam is *batata*, also colloquially *ñames*—Glenda, but you can call me *Glinda*), that is, he, the street vendor, opens his mouth and holds up a cartoon speech balloon with the word *Camotes* scrawled on it in charcoal minus the exclamation points, apparently the vendor is not only a deaf mute but also illiterate, maybe the little neighbor girl he befriended wrote it for him, very sad story there, the mother's a "sex worker," father's absent, you get the picture. The vendor stops next to the Snowman, sticks a small metal shovel in the barrel, retrieves a steaming, slightly collapsed and blackened yam and with a shy smile offers it to him wrapped in a piece of newspaper. He blows on it, takes a cautious bite and, *nyumm*, it's delicious, hot, creamy and caramelly sweet.

And just like a movie matinee when you step out of the darkened theater and night becomes day, *Toooo-wooo-wheeet!* here comes the Snowman looking like a Doctor Seuss Christmas elf in a long-tasseled red wool cap, red and white wool scarf around his neck and a black morning coat with tails open over a red vest, pushing this spindly, creaking, clanking, black iron-bellied barbecue pit Angel put together for the promise of free *PoPoPops!* all next summer. Against Angel's professional advice, personal taste and risk of injury to his reputation, the Snowman insisted on a sort of steam-punk, Charles Dickens Christmas carol conflation, minus the soot, smog, filth and grinding poverty of the Industrial Age, the finishing touch a shrill riverboat whistle *toooo-wheet!* to advertise his new line of winter wares. He's got hot s'mores made on the spot from all-American Campfire marshmallows, Hershey's chocolate bars and National Biscuit Co. graham crackers. *Too-oo-eet!* He's got roasted chestnuts and baked sweet potatoes. *Too-wheet!* He's got NYC soft pretzels, caramel apples and popcorn balls. *Toot toot too-wheet!* He's got steaming hot apple pie. *Toot! Tweet!* He's got fresh-baked cinnamon sweet sticky buns. *Twee-too-weet!* He's got warm, he's got hot, he's got comfort, he's got sweet. *Tweet!* (Back story: the Snowman and Moses brainstormed winter treats and recipes on Moses' EyePhone®, well, Moses did the legwork and the Luddite Snowman lamely followed along over his shoulder. By the way, Moses' Moms has been helping out with the baking—she gets around pretty well in her wheelchair, she's even started to use a walker. And that apple pie? Comes from a cookbook that's been in her family since right after the Civil War, and it is dee-lish!) And, sure, the Snowman's got his loyal *PoPoPops!* followers. They say, Great stuff, Snowman! Really hits the spot! I'll be back tomorrow. But they won't. His winter fare is good but it just doesn't have that old *PoPoPops!* magic, not enough, anyway, to compete with the thousand or so food trucks swarming over Osberg. And so it is that as sales trail off, once again his biggest customers are the non-paying kind.

The camera cuts to the intersection of 38th and the DR-35 frontage road where a couple of homeless guys (okay, *bums*) are working the corners. This is when they really earn their keep. It's bitter cold, the wind's howling through the concrete pylons, snow blowing around them. Maybe the camera lens has fogged up but there's this odd phenomenon. They keep fading in and out of view. They're practically invisible to most drivers who pull up next to them. Hey! I'm freezing to death! Could you help a guy out?! Nope, no reaction. The drivers stare ahead, blinders on. You don't wanta make eye contact, don't wanta make that connection. The poor wretch already looks wretched, why make him even more wretched with that brief glimmer of hope? I mean, geez, look at this guy. He's wearing a wool stocking cap, heavy scarf, oversized coat, bunch of sweaters underneath, baggy purple sweat pants over a pair of jeans you can see sticking out at the bottom, dirty gray tennis shoes with broken laces and at least three pairs of socks and he's still shivering, teeth chattering like a typewriter (google it), he's blowing out consumptive clouds of steam, each breath transferring more heat out of his body and into the unreciprocating atmosphere. Just doing my part for global warming, officer (obviously he's not fully informed on how this thing works). He hops from foot to foot, one frozen hand shoved down in a pocket, the other holding up his sign *Marry Crissmus* (misspelled in trembling red letters). You can see a few drivers are indecisive. Yeah, sure, they'd like to help a guy out but they also don't want to open their window and let all the warm air escape, deplete their pocket of warmth of its warmth while they hand over a few miserly pieces of eight that aren't really going to make that big of a difference in this loser's life, right? Plus, the wiser among these world-weary drivers are hip to this panhandler trick. The guy's just putting on the ol' *boo hoo* to pluck your heartstrings, take advantage of your liberal tendencies. And then, if you do wind down your window, this vagabond, this vagrant, this *mountebank* is going to engage you in unwanted, often incoherent, boozy, blowsy conversation. It's not just recognition from a fellow human being. The guy'll do anything to get another minute of that warm air pouring over him like a wormhole from the tropics. Palm trees, sunshine, warm turquoise waters ... *Beeep! Beeep! Move yer fucking ass!* And that's it until the next sucker, um, benefactor comes along.

But it isn't some sympathetic commuter with a bleeding heart messing up the upholstery, it's one of his not fully witted homeless brethern shuffling across the street in the middle of traffic, his face twisted in a toothless grin and his hand out to show him, look what I got! The camera zooms in and it's just chump change, a couple of crumpled dollar bills, a handful of nickels, dimes, quarters, barely enough for a box of wings at the Fiesta deli. But let's not start blubbering over the human condition when you and I both know that in about two minutes these *bums* are gonna be sucking on a bottle of Mad Dog. And by the way, no surprise that notorious cheapskate Boone has got his gaffer and BB, Moot and Jeef, filling in for *real* homeless people (oddly, they're standing under a very dead and not particularly authentic looking tree (*palm? willow?*) that somehow managed to sprout from a crevice in the concrete). They're cursing the weather, the cars that go by without a glance. Blimey, mate, fokking blighters don't give a poor lad a bloddy fokking chance, do they? They're especially cursing Boone. Fokking shite, wait until the bloddy fokking union hears about this fokking bollocks. That'll be a bloddy fokking long wait, mate. Fokking cold it is. D'ya think he'll come today? Didn't come yesterday. Changed his route maybe? Maybe.

And then, against all hope and expectation, here he does come, the bloddy fokking Snowman, pushing his Tim Burton steam-punk phantasm *too-wheet!* And suddenly it's not just one or two guys. All the bums in the vicinity are crowding around, pleading, begging, *demanding, Snowman! Snowman!* And what's he gonna say? No way, José? Be a total chump and turn these poor folks away? Of course not. And just like that they're chowing down on steaming hot baked yams, they're scarfing Moses' Moms' apple pie, they're laughing and shouting and slapping each other on the back like they just scaled Everest and made it down alive, they're rubbing their hands over the red-hot coals and dancing around like they're at a country hoedown. In a matter of minutes the Snowman gives away his entire inventory for nothing, not a red cent, knowing full well he's gonna have to go home and face Moses and his Moms. And then what, guilt and incriminations? What *we* gonna live on, *Snowman?!* We cain't eat yo damn charity! Of course not. Tha's awright, Snowman, Moses says, lowering those curiously long lashes. Bless your heart, Snowman, Moms crushes him against her considerable bosom. Yeah, he's practically a fucking saint, right? He's got a jaundiced eye cocked heavenward, hey, you fucking angels, you see this? How about some payback? The bums'd sure like some of that payback. And, who knows, Mercury slipping out of retrograde, maybe their luck's about to change, they and all of God's creation are gonna get a reprieve from this capricious Texas weather. Because just like that, a warm breeze blows up from the south, bringing with it fresh corn tortilla intimations of 'ol Mexico and the aroma of roasting Chopahuaqueño coffee from the shop up on Maynard and the next day it's over, winter's gone, banished to the northern climes. Second week of February and—*Spring?* Well, sorta.

An early bird robin has appeared and it's singing joyful hymns to God, to the miracle of existence, to the fat earthworms it's pulling up out of the ground in a cartoon tug-of-war. Wildflowers are blooming everywhere, the roadsides carpeted with bluebonnets, coreopsis, Mexican hats, Indian paintbrush, cut-leaf daisy, winecups. The first green and pink mist is spreading through the cedar elms and redbuds. Everything is proclaiming spring. And with spring comes South by Southwurst, the internationally acclaimed Smoked Sausage and Roots Rock Oompah music festival. And the whole world's here. Everywhere you look you see these obvious foreigners standing on street corners, at bus stops, not exactly checks and plaids but you can tell (lots of leather, lots of black, lots of glam hair and make-up). But just so you know, meine Damen und Herren, this ain't Munich or Milan, Moscow or Macau, so it's gonna be a long wait before the next bus comes. Funding for public transportation? *Socialism!*

Day one of the festival finds fickle spring acting up as usual. The morning starts cool, overcast, temperature's hovering around fifty degrees, festival goers are wearing hoodies, Mexican ponchos, igloo parkas, alpaca caps. And even though nobody's thinking frozen ice cream at the moment the canny Snowman has left the barbecue pit at home, he's got his cart packed with the season's first batch of *PoPoPops!* and he's raring to go because after years of watching the weather he knows there's a very good chance that—yep, here it comes now—the sun breaks through the clouds and the temperature immediately starts to climb. It's in the sixties, the seventies. By noon it's in the eighties. It's like a scene change in a movie. Everybody's shedding their heavy winter clothes for Ts and shorts. Everybody's donning wurst hats and wurst noses. Some wags (from Wurstphallia, of course) are sporting sproingy wurstphalluses, the waggier among them garnished with mustard, ketchup and relish. Oompah Reggae bands are pounding out popular Bob Marleyberg tunes, "Drive those crazy Kahlkopfs out of the town," "Who the Handschuhe fits let him wear it," dirndls and lederhosen everywhere, big bellies, bosomy fräuleins lugging enormous steins of artisanal lager, legions of hipsters wandering around trying to look cool but *WTF* ... *lederhosen?!* It's a total madhouse, hundreds of thousands of people, thousands of food trucks, push carts and street vendors. And the Snowman's gonna compete with this crowd? Well, yes, maybe.

Here's the thing. All the vendors who have been selling out their salty, spicy, smoked and barbecued brisket, sausage, ribs and pork loin in the chilly morning are starting to see their sales plummet as the temperature climbs all the way into the *nineties*. Sweat breaks out, throats get dry, people want some cool relief and what comes to mind? *Beer!* Well, yeah, of course beer, Brett, but, whoa, what's this conga line threading its way through the crowds and what's that familiar sound echoing everywhere, *pop! pop! pop! pop!* Sounds like the battle of the Alamo. Is it firecrackers? A shooter in the local high school? No, it's *PoPoPops!* Suddenly everybody's got a hankering for one of these frosty rainbow treats and the line to the Snowman's cart just keeps growing longer as his supply grows shorter. People are chanting *Snowman! Snowman!* like they're at a cannibal fest and he's the main course. He begs a customer to loan him her EyePhone® in exchange for a free *PoPoPop!* and, no fucking idea how the damn thing works, even has to ask her to dial for him, and he calls Moses for reinforcements. Ten minutes later Moses pedals up gasping for breath—it's about two and a half miles, lots of hills—on a tiny pink girl's bicycle (his niece's) with a Styrofoam ice chest of *PoPoPops!* balanced on his shoulder, hands off his cargo and heads back through the swelling sea of humanity for another load.

And good God, it's like this the entire SXSW. They're working their fingers to the bone, running night and day on two-three hours sleep. In the evening Moses' Moms has got the table spread for a communal dinner. Baked chicken, steamed greens, roasted sweet potatoes— she's trending heart healthy herself these days, she's even getting around on her feet a little better, thanks for asking—pots of black coffee, and for dessert—More peach cobbler, Mister Snowman? Mo? Lord have mercy! And man, he and Moses are making a killing. *Pop! Pop! Pop! Pop! Pop! Pop! Pop! Pop! Pop! Pop!* They're hauling home duffle bags of cash. He can't wait for the damn bank to open first thing in the morning to unload all this loot on Ms. Guppy's desk and, having learned to more or less connect the dots, watch her expression shift from somewhere between suspicion and contempt to—is that love light in her eyes?

Because, yes, there is something about this sorry bastard's entrepreneurial spirit that she can't help admiring. Business beckons, it calls, it howls at the Snowman from the capitalist wilderness. And *pop pop pop*, these plosive little thought balloons are detonating in his brain, tiny cumulonimbus possibilities for the future. He doesn't have the whole picture yet but if he thinks about it hard enough he can envision himself becoming an Osberg fixture, maybe establish some kind of niche ice cream shop, maybe even, really stretching now, open different locations around town, locally themed, of course, cowboys, outlaw-country music, bats (*chiroptera*, not the Babe). And, sure, that might happen. And it might not. Lots of unknowns in the food industry.

One of 'em occurs with word that the health inspector is lurking about—there he is now! It's Carlos (Carlitos to his friends) Límpez, this pudgy guy in a black Bolero hat, wire-rimmed glasses, odd little mustaches at the corners of his mouth, string tie, white shirt, black vaquero jacket, trousers and boots, looks like a cross between a circuit preacher and a Mariachi. Informed members of the audience are shouting, It's Gordo! No, it's Cantinflas playing Gordo! (Boone's ripping off somebody, that's for sure.) Carlos is heading straight for the Snowman who, the audience will also remember, has neither state license nor city permit and this stickler for details Límpez isn't going to accept any flimsy excuses. But I thought a *cottage industry* was exempt from permits. Yes, it is, but you isn't. And *slap!slap!slap!slap!* he just barely gets his ass outa that crack, promising himself he'll take care of this license business as soon as he has time, but right now another unknown arises when a bright-eyed young customer (probably a business student at UT) says *earnestly* (that confirms it), Hey, there's a guy over on the next street selling *PoPoPops!* just like yours. *What?!* Closing up his cart, he hurries around the block to check it out and immediately spots the offending party and ... well, okay, it's not exactly a rip-off. The sign on the guy's cart says *PoBoyPops*, minus the exclamation point. It's a frozen version of the famous New Orleans sandwich on a stick, but the name's close enough to *PoPoPops!* to cause some confusion and maybe even steal away a few customers and, who knows, if push comes to shoving somebody down the basement stairs, this *could* end in a legal tangle.

Which, after a little online investigation at the public library with the guidance of a patient young reference librarian, Ms. Daisy May Chan (Yet another budding romance? Probably not. She's just really nice, and at least a dozen years younger than him.), he discovers that, yes, someone else could just as easily call their product *PoPoPops!* and even compel him to cease and desist from using that name himself, unless, that is, he declares a public trademark first, which he does by 1) painting a *tm* (and no, that's not transcendental meditation, Mister Love) after the *PoPoPops!*™ on the side of his cart, and 2) forking over a couple hundred bucks to the U.S. Patent and Trademark Office, thus beginning the more arduous process of applying for a registered trademark, which, among other things, requires a list of ingredients. Not a big deal, right? Except it also raises the issue of Maria's *magic* potion, which apparently falls under the more complicated category of *secret ingredient*, and which, with a lot of hemming and hawing, the Snowman has more or less let Moses in on, causing a brief reoccurrence of that spooky white-eyed thing. You tellin' me this shit's magic for real, Snowman? He tries to explain, no, you see, there are these enzymes and gene splices ... and quickly realizes he's in over his own head, so, yeah, fuck it, let's agree it *is* magic.

What he doesn't tell Moses the attentive viewer already knows. He has only a very limited supply of the magic potion, which he keeps in its original glass vial wrapped in a wool sock inside a small red thermos hiding in plain sight on the faux fireplace mantel. Which isn't quite as dire as it sounds *because* … figuring he's got maybe ten milliliters in this vial, at twenty drops per milliliter (one of the few things he remembers from high school chemistry), that equals two hundred drops. And given that Maria's very potent *gotita* is at most a fraction of one of those drops, he's got at least, oh, let's say a thousand droplets? Which is quite a lot. Especially because he has also discovered, again purely by accident, sloppy handling, that serendipitous scientific method, that by adding the tiniest of one of these droplets, no more than the sweat off a bumblebee's brow, to a gallon of regular tap water, and then a drop of that enhanced water to another gallon of water, he can keep his supply going practically forever, sort of like sourdough starter. He also has an uneasy feeling this is slightly cheating and one day his tab's gonna run out.

16
Growing Pains

UNFORTUNATELY, THIS COZY WORK ARRANGEMENT the Snowman and Moses have established doesn't last, and, sorry to disappoint you cynics and drama queens, no, they don't have a falling out, nor have they fallen back on bad habits. Kick-started by their success at SXSW, the demand for *PoPoPops!*^{tm} has exceeded their ability to keep up the supply. They're overwhelmed, overworked, at wit's end. Storage space is at a premium. Moses has reported the Kelvinator is making a strange *ka-chunk ka-chunk* sound, he thinks the bearings are worn out. There's also this license thing the Snowman's been putting off *wayyyyy* longer than he'd ever get away with in real life. And he'll probably have to start paying social security for himself and Moses. And he really should look into health insurance for them both.

Fueled on caffeine, manic energy and a scoop here and there of the starter batch to recharge the old battery, he spends what little free time he has at the library researching and writing up a business plan with Ms. Chan's assistance, which Ms. Guppy receives with a contemptuous *sniff*, smelling, perhaps, in its pages, in its choice of words, in the faintest traces of perfume, another woman's hand, although it's just as likely she's anticipating the usual ill-conceived and unworkable scheme she sees a dozen times a day. And, sure, this *Snowman's* plan is rudimentary, no understanding whatsoever of marketing, cost analysis. But she can also see in his crude calculations the potential for substantial growth and profit margins and, even more promising, in his eyes dollar signs of raw ambition, latent, nascent, not even on his own radar yet, that sends one of those autonomous sensory meridian responses shivering throughout her whole body, briefly lighting her up like a Christmas tree angel. When she arrives at the size of his loan request, however, *um … a coupla thousand?* she sniffs even louder, *Ridiculous!* Uh-oh, he sees his future sink like a torpedoed merchant ship … and just as precipitously rise up from its watery grave like a submarine-launched cruise missile when she adds officiously, Let's say … five *hundred* thousand?

Gulp.

At Ms. Guppy's advice the Snowman pays out a hefty chunk of change and consults a business attorney and a CPA and discovers that going legit is a tad bit more complicated than he had imagined, even more so because the ice cream industry, which he is now officially part of, is one of the most heavily regulated. Food handling permits, on-site inspections by the Health Department, Fire Department, city and state business licenses and fees, meetings with the Osberg Planning and Development Review Committee, every step of the way excruciating because, as Moses constantly reminds him (you livin' in the stone age, *Snowman*, even Barney Rubble got a cellphone), he knows nothing about texting, messaging or email, he gets put on terminal hold when he tries to call on his landline, he stands *in* line for hours to schedule appointments, most ending in—dead-ends. Six months later he signs a contract and rents a pocket space in the mini-strip mall on Maynard, previously a frozen vegan tofu shop featuring a kale, collard and mustard greens combo, didn't last a month but the set-up's perfect, tiled and stainless-steel surfaces, commercial sinks, two eighty-quart floor mounted mixers, a walk-in industrial freezer, a pair of chilled holding vats. He signs another contract with a local produce distributor for his ingredients, hires six full and three part-time employees, offers Moses a significant pay raise and puts him in charge of production. And ... we're off to the races, right? Sorta. There are some speedbumps along the way.

Still new on the job, Roland or Rhonda or Raymond confuses *mix* with *agitate* (employing an inverse Bond mnemonic, the Snowman has reminded them numerous times it's *stirred*, not *shaken*) and the whole batch explodes, knocking over mixers, vats, blowing out doors and windows, mountains of this foaming rainbow sludge spilling into the street, and everybody and his grandmother (people are beginning to wonder about these two), all the free-ranging (it's a thing again) neighborhood kids and all the sitting on their butts all day work-at-home techies, are there in a heartbeat stuffing their faces. Not too many minutes later the whole hood's glowing like a giant leprechaunic pot of gold at the end of the rainbow and everybody's got that goofball grin on their faces like a great acid trip's just starting to kick in. In the end this fiasco proves to be an enormous PR boost, forever after remembered as one of those iconic Osberg events (cf. the first Eeyore's Birthday Party) and everybody (and his ...) will claim to have attended.

There are other obstacles. One evening, everybody else gone home, the Snowman and Moses discussing ways to increase production, Moses' cellphone rings. And, yeah, he knows how much the Snowman hates these damn things, it's written across his face like a backslash circle, until Moses informs him that he's just received an anonymous tip. The Health Inspector's gonna show up first thing in the morning. Uh-oh. The sound system blasting the soundtracks from *Shaft*, *Super Fly* and *Foxy Brown* (the Snowman's choice), and The Mamas and the Papas and Joni Mitchell (Moses'—apparently they both have this misbegotten and outdated notion of each other's musical tastes), they spend the entire night sweeping and mopping the floors, emptying trash cans and flushing them with hot soapy water and a light solution of bleach, scrubbing and rescrubbing all tiled and stainless steel working surfaces, endless applications of sanitizers, disinfectants, deodorizers, can't quite get that damn pee smell out of the restroom even with gallons of bleach and Pine-Sol. They're just giving the mixers a final swipe with Progel sanitary lubricant when the doorbell rings at two minutes to eight and Carlitos Límpez limps in (gout—hazard of the job) in his circuit preacher/vaquero outfit. He wouldn't admit it to his best friend (Geronimo, they play dominos on weekends) but you can tell he's still got a bone to pick with this Snowman dude for eluding him at SXSW, so isn't he surprised to find all the papers and permits in order, everything spic, span and orthodontically shiny, and both Moses and the Snowman (at the last second) properly hair-netted. Just opening up, the Snowman says, trying his luck. Puttin' on a pot of Chopahuac's finest coffee right now, care for a cup? Hey, have you tried our product? This'll wake you up! It's on the house! *Pop! Fzzzzt!* Not sure Mr. Límpez will remember what he came in here for when he strides out the door in a super-caffeinated rainbow haze. (The Snowman will learn later, thanks to a slip of the lip from Moses, that the anonymous tip came from Carlitos' twelve-year-old son, Baldo, a huge fan of *PoPoPops!*™.)

More road-blocks, potholes and detours pop up along the Snowman's entrepreneurial highway. He's constantly down at City Hall applying for permits, waivers. His little office in the back of the shop next to the employees' restroom is buried in paperwork. Invoices, tax forms, rent, insurance, employee records, new orders, canceled orders. He's trying to keep track of everything with a second-hand pocket calculator. He lies awake at night tossing and turning, his mind like the squeaking, squealing data stream of an old reel to reel tape recorder, it sounds like it's saying *help me* over and over again at a very high speed *helpmehelpmehelpme.* Yes, that's it. He needs help, someone to schedule, organize, coordinate— in other words, take care of the business part of business—but who? A familiar little button face with Brillo pad hair and bright blue bird's eyes behind wire-rimmed glasses appears on the screen in his head.

Evelyn?

Yes ... who is this?

The voice on the other end of the line is wavery, watery, afraid, nothing like the snippy, bitchy Evelyn he remembers. Forced into early retirement, borderline destitution is more like it, her ICIN stock worthless, her liquidity evaporated, unemployment benefits run out, a tad too young for Social Security or Medicare, husband Fred's beset with health issues, VA benefits and social security checks are insufficient and never arrive on time, their re-refinanced mortgage is in arrears, Evelyn's practically in tears when the Snowman asks her to come on board.

Her first day on the job is a perfect restorative. Everything, the random, stochastic and chaotic, is transformed into simplicity and order, the entire shop and everyone in it enters the binary realm of yes or no according to formulas on Evelyn's computer where she taptaptaps away while—the door of the small but brightly lit office in the corner she has commandeered from the Snowman ever ajar—she keeps a stern eye on daily operations over her wire-rimmed glasses. Every time he enters the shop he hears a shrill, familiar, *Snowman,* stop tracking fruit pulp all over the floor! You're gonna kill somebody! And stop leaving the refrigerator door open every time you sample the starter! You're wasting energy! He freezes on the spot and he and Evelyn stare squinty-eyed at each other across some kind of wormhole between two not entirely compatible memories of the same event before they both break out laughing, sure, a little bit nervously, not entirely certain of each other's intent. Because, yes, there is a lot of history between these two. There's also that nagging suspicion. Wasn't she part of a plot to kill you, Snowman?

Moses, meanwhile, seems to be summoning up years of untapped energy. Free of the entropic pull of Ice, he's like a rogue planet spinning in its own orbit, a mad jinn laughing and singing to himself as he tears apart a mixer-housing, yanks out and replaces a worn drive belt and a second later jumps on the production line to fill in for an absent employee and pretty soon the whole line's butt boogeying and chicken wing flapping, if you took a poll right this minute, what's the best job you ever had? they'd

all say *This one!* (Boone has been accused of
misappropriating this scene from a seventies' Black
sitcom but until somebody can identify which one he's
off the hook.)

Once Evelyn and Moses have the show under way,
the Snowman comes to the best part of the day, pushing
his cart, and this one's a doozy. Aching to put his low-
rider chops to use, Angel has constructed a photovoltaic
and lithium battery-charged motorized cart that conveys
a sense of old-time ice cream socials while projecting the
attitude of a chrome-grilled muscle car, with a lime-green
and Mandarin-orange telescoping umbrella for shade and
a step pad in back for the operator's riding convenience.
The cart is the heart and soul of the Snowman's business,
the public profile, the personal contact, the *ring ding ding*
bells and chimes of tradition, the familiar shouts, *Yo,
Snowman! Over here!* It's that inborn business acumen
again. He's got a plan he doesn't understand, a program
someone else wrote, it's in his blood, in his genes, in his
pavement pounding feet. He's gotta get out there at least
a coupla hours every day, get himself seen, promote his
brand. He's become a popular figure about town. He's
got that Michael Katz cachet (Remember him? Naw, you
ain't from here. Ha, neither was he!), that Norman
Vincent appeal, that Eagle Scout Optimist's Club
American-do attitude. People from out of town in town
for South by Southwurst, for the music and film festivals,
the 10 Ks, marathons, tech conventions and rodeos (it *is*
Texas) wanta take selfies with this *Snowman dude*
they've heard about.

And just like that he's beaming into homes in Yreka,
California, in Mars, PA and Polecat Junction, Missouri,
in faraway places like Marrakech, Timbuktu and

Zanzibar. He's a guest on Sister Sunne Rae's show, and for a dude who's normally an introvert, he acts like he's made for the stage, he's wearing brand new waxed and polished huaraches, lime green cargo shorts and probably the most eye-catching Hawaiian shirt in his closet (pink orchids and killer whales devouring dolphins). It certainly catches the Sister's eye, she gets the whole story out of the Snowman, how his father bought this classic piece of haberdashery while honeymooning with his blushing new bride on the now submarine Polynesian island nation of Tuvalu. Sounds like there was plenty of fun afoot in the capital that night, the Sister mugs for the camera and the Snowman grins good-naturedly as the audience bursts into laughter. He joins the Sister in a duet of *Singing in the Rain* (she compliments his Kermit the Frog imitation), he pulls wheelies with his cart on stage. At the end of the show the whole audience is on its feet (with the assistance of canes, walkers, caregivers, mostly they just need to get home and change their Depends).

He can feel this force, this energy, this vibe welling up inside himself. He's on the ~~floormat~~ doorstep of something BIG and he knows it. He's been receiving inquiries from distributors, marketing reps, off-beat, new-age, neo-hippie entrepreneurs in other states. Evelyn's blowing up his cellphone all day—yes, he has one now, had to cave to reality, Moses helped him pick it out, and, he's gotta admit, it's pretty fucking amazing, except when it isn't. *Brinnnggg!!* Snowman? We have to talk when you get in! Evelyn's got skyscraper stacks of paper correspondence teetering on her desk from *every damn state in the union,* ten thousand emails in her inbox from *freaking Borneo alone.* Before he can sneak past her

office, she shoves her screen in his face, at least take a
look, would ya, *Snowman?* We have to *do something!*

And here he takes a fateful step—well, according to
causal analysis they've all been fateful steps, but on a
scale of one to ten this is a fifteen. The next day he's
pushing his cart down the Drag, the above concerns
gnawing at his brain like hungry beavers, when he hears
this drums-booming-in-the-forest voice say, What planet
you on today, Snowman? and only then realizes he has
stopped in front of M'Shaka's display table, not entirely
by accident according to Freud and astrology. M'Shaka
glances at his cart. Can't stay away from making snow,
can you, *Snowman?* He smiles a crooked bullish/bearish
line graph smile, extracts a *PoPoPop!*[tm] from his cart,
gives it a quick canned whipped cream shake, pops the
top *fzzzzt* and hands the frosty rainbow-colored
confection to M'Shaka, who cocks a skeptical eye at it for
about one second, but it's a hundred and two in the shade,
he's got a river of sweat streaming down his face, and, *ha
ha*, he notices now, holding the *PoPoPop!*[tm] close to his
rainbow robe , *they're the same color!* just before he takes
a bite and *man oh man oh man* has he seen the light, he's
got that rainbow glow in his eyes, he's got that rainbow
aura about his head, he minces neither meat nor words
when he says, How these things even legal, Snowman?
(There's that specter of drugs again.) M'Shaka takes
another bite, his brow furrows, pondering an unfamiliar
but pleasant taste, and he says, I see you on the Sister's
show the other night. Seem like you doin' all right for
yourself. So what's troublin' you, bruh? Da biz givin you
da biz? It's supposed to be a joke, right? but M'Shaka has
hit the proverbial nail on the toe. Skipping a detailed
account, the Snowman admits that, yes, he could use

some business advice, it's kind of *complicated*. M'Shaka takes another bite, ponders further the phantom taste while observing him for a disquieting minute, then says in his booming timpani *Arthur*. Arthur? Yeah, Snowman, my son, Arthur. Hmm.

Shattered stained-glass fragments of memory, he and M'Shaka in the neon blue and maroon interior of the Blue Heartbeat Nightclub, bluesy music, cigarette smoke drifting, glasses clinking, the rising, falling surf sound of conversations, occasional laughter. A brief a.m. interlude with a young woman named Tropique that did not lead to wild or even tame sex but left him with residual suggestions of some kind of international intrigue he still can't wrap his head around. Later that morning, more or less coming to his senses again sitting in the pews of a Baptist church clapping his hands and croaking *rocka my soul in the bosom of Abraham* and *swing low sweet chariot* and *amazing grace* next to M'Shaka, apparently none the worse for wear, rocking and singing along in a beautiful baritone. Sometime around noon seated at a large family gathering over a huge soul food feast, the authenticity of which M'Shaka and Boone's writers seemed in disagreement about, somewhere in this stew (no, that wasn't part of the menu) a round-faced little boy with a high forehead and thick glasses looking up at him as if he, the Snowman, were an extraterrestrial. Isn't he a kid?

Baby-faced, bespectacled, slight of build, Arthur looks like the nerdy guy in your twelfth-grade physics class who not only knows all the answers to the test but asks questions that stump the teacher because he is or rather *was* that kid—when he was eight. Not even old enough to order a drink, indeed, just barely old enough to drive to an establishment that serves alcohol, he has already completed an MBA at Harvard and is finishing up his LLD in business law at that ~~venal~~ *venerable* institution. So exactly why would this kid who's going to be pulling down millions in another year or two stoop to help the Snowman with his little local yokel enterprise? Makes even less sense when M'Shaka announces Arthur will be doing this pro bono, which, hmm, the Snowman and Arthur look at each other like *say what?* The camera draws in on Arthur's eyes gleaming like hot black coffee behind the round window panes of his glasses and in those delicate organs of sight we see a glimmer of resentment or contempt or *something* that is decidedly not happy with this arrangement. Does Pops owe this Snowman dude some unspecified debt hearkening back to a darker time in the old man's life that he, Arthur, has scrupulously made a point of not tracking down *despite the rumors?*

While he's away at school up (or down—depends on your perspective, *ayuh*) east, Arthur conducts business meetings with the Snowman, Moses and Evelyn via the social media giant *InYourFace*, with occasional on-site visits during holidays and long weekends (no reason to stay in Cambridge, he's way too young to participate in any reindeer games with his fellow Vardians) when he flies into Osberg, first class, the Snowman's dime. He strolls about the premises like a baby-faced regent, intimidating the employees with his lettuce-wilting superior attitude, condescending to the Snowman for the nice *little* operation he has here, even Evelyn holds her breath until he pronounces *alles in ordnung* when he dares examine her accounts. Moses alone seems unimpressed. Yo, *Sir* Arthur, y'all still pimpin' the law books? Get you a legit job, bruh, I take you on. Arthur smiles at this witticism, maybe even digs the legitimacy it gives him, but there's also something ugly, accusatory here, a negative electrical undercurrent surging back and forth between Moses and Arthur that *could* be read as *you shuckin', jivin' sell-out nigger!* versus *listen to who's calling the pot black!* not just because their more or less equal levels of melanin make them both indisputably Black, but also because they are both deeply involved in a capitalist culture that has never smiled kindly on *their kind.*

Any reservations about Arthur's youth are quickly dispelled when, while clerking over the summer for Republican Senator Warren Bucks, he expedites the *PoPoPops!*® registered trademark, in the process dispatching a couple of upstarts who claimed to be start-ups marketing a disingenuously similar but clearly inferior product (*pip! peep!*) called, respectively (but not respectably, the courts decided) *PopPop'sPops* and *PoppyPops*. He also easily secures trade secret status for the *PoPoPops!*® "special ingredient" from the FDA, although this does require that the Snowman largely clue him in on the nature of Maria's magic potion, not, once again, without some awkward hemming, hawing and minor dissimulation. It's, um, an *ancient* formula? Extremely *rare* ingredients? Almost *impossible* to find? There's this old *curandero* over on the Far East Side? And, hmm, Arthur's giving him the old skeptical, must've picked it up from his dad, not just because it's obvious this Snowman dude is lying through his teeth, but because Arthur's extremely rational mind doesn't allow for things like *curanderos* and *fórmulas antiguas,* much less *magic,* which the Snowman did not mention, but, sure, it was implied. Nevertheless, thanks to Arthur's undeniable brilliance and an odd but infectious optimistic streak (hubris?), everybody in the shop is abuzz and aglow. Well, okay, the *PoPoPops!*® they nibble on all day doesn't hurt, but there is this general sense of something big happening here, get in on the ground floor and who knows—bonuses? stock options? the millionaire's club?

What the Snowman has in mind is something like the funky, earthy, hippie-dippie WistVille Co-op of olden days, but with an updated WholeFloods business model, in-house products gradually replacing corporate brands, supportive of local businesses, everything holistic, healthy, free range, organic, *natural*. What Arthur has in mind is—oops, apparently Arthur's intentions haven't been made public yet but this might give us a clue. At a catered party with top-shelf booze flowing like Niagara, Arthur (he's having a vanilla milkshake, thanks for your concern) now introduces the Snowman to a group of deep-pocketed private investors he's met through his Harvard ties, who, after gallons of pricey liquor and complimentary *PoPoPops!*®, are all rainbow aglow and chortling ho ho ho, sign me up! And, boy, do the Snowman's eyes go wide when he sees those rows of zeros.

With this hefty chunk of cash, and the assistance of Ms. Guppy, who has become increasingly less snarky *and* invisible (that *is* love light in her eyes, isn't it?) as the Snowman's trajectory of success has become more hyperbolic, as well as the help of Cristina DesVals from the commercial realtor, *Tías' Tierras*, a venerable, woman-run family firm (the name says it all), the Snowman moves his operations into a much larger piece of real estate on the Near East Side whose architecture has attracted him for years, a four-story yellow-brick building with white sandstone cornices and lintels and tall arched windows with mullioned panes that takes up the better part of a city block (of note for historical buffs, the original brewery of *Ol' Rattler Beer* c. 1883 when the German braumeister Helmut Hübsch, recently arrived from Bavaria, made his mark with a hopsy lager that did not fare so well when it was introduced as *Alt Klapperschlange* but quickly gained local fame thanks to the Americanized name his savvy youngest daughter, Renate, seven years of age, *but I'm almost eight*, gave it).

The upper floors are completely renovated into modern office space, administrative, marketing, accounting. The first floor and cavernous basement are assigned to production and storage. Industrial foods consultant Gabrielle Gyurmande designs the layout and supervises installation. Five-hundred-gallon commercial mixers, two-hundred square-foot walk-in freezers, thousand-gallon stainless-steel holding vats, conveyor belts, injectors, packaging line. Machine operators and mechanical engineers in hardhats, neckties and white lab coats mill about. Scores of future employees in training. To the Snowman it's all as incomprehensible as Willy Wonka's chocolate factory. For Moses, whom the Snowman has promoted to line manager and who is now in charge of one hundred full-time employees running two eight-hour shifts, seven days a week, this is the backyard swimming pool everybody dreams about and he dives in headfirst, devoting all his hours off the job to studying technical manuals, taking on-line engineering and management courses. All very good because Arthur has expressed his doubts about Moses with a poisonous black coffee gleam in his eyes and a casually dropped piece of wormwood that will fester in the Snowman's ear. I'm not sure he's up to the task, *Snowman*, but if *you* think so ...

Evelyn is promoted to general manager, and, yes, the Snowman's old suspicions still hold true. There is very convincing circumstantial evidence (You were saying, Inspector Clouseau ...?) that she was part of a conspiracy to kill him, but she's also nonpareil at what she does, which is everything. And besides, Arthur is there at his ear, *Keep your enemies close, Snowman*, which, hmm, sounds ominous. Shouldn't it have been something innocuous like let bygones be bygones or whatever (sic) under the bridge? Of course, Evelyn's absolutely thrilled, she's positively beaming, she has her own fully appointed private office, she has a three-person staff, above all she has *finally* been recognized as more than a *frigging* secretary. Let's see how that works out.

Lastly, the Snowman signs on Roger Wilco. It's mostly an act of charity. Unemployed, unwashed and, frankly, unloved, Roger has been moping around the office in the same nerdy loafers, skinny jeans and plaid shirt with a pocket protector day after day trying to interest the Snowman in all kinds of patently wacky ideas. What if I built a machine that made *fruuuit*-flavored fish sticks? Or how about a *gunnn* that shoots *frannnk*furters into people's mouths—great for hot dog eating *connn*tests? But when Roger sketches out a design for a greatly improved high-speed, high-volume assembly line that moves the product from start to finish three times faster than the current model, the Snowman's interest *is* piqued. Unfortunately, this also means hasta la vista to two-thirds of his recently hired work force and a de facto demotion for Moses (salary remains the same, but his responsibilities drop about fifty percent). Of course, the Snowman feels terrible but before he can do anything rash like offer these former employees some kind of separation package, the cherub-faced Arthur, barely past the age of majority but still not old enough to legally order an alcoholic beverage anywhere in the USA, is there at his ear reassuring or, to be perfectly honest, instilling in him this poison, *Snowman, Snowman, Snowman*, that's the nature of business. People have to learn. Life isn't fair. You don't get handouts forever. By their bootstraps, *Snowman!* They have to *pull themselves up!*

To increase their identity as an Osberg icon, they open a large public reception area that sells *PoPoPop!*® themed novelties, T-shirts, mugs, Frosty the Snowman hats and Hawaiian shirts. They offer free tasting on *Ice Cream Social Sundays* during which the public is allowed to tour the facilities and sample new flavors. Moses achieves modest success (the Snowman shoots Arthur a snarky *I told you so* look) with his creation *The Black Cat.* (*ME-yowwr!* Well, okay, some credit goes to Me'th for the name. *Mrrt.*) Coffee and dark chocolate from the mountains of Chopahuac, Mexico, a hint of cinnamon and ... Moses sticking his finger in the pot, tasting, his Moms' voice in his head, I don't know, Mo, maybe a little nutmeg, your great grandmother Althea always said ... Moses originally called it the *Coalman*—I ain't no *snowman*, bruh, mugging thuggishly for the camera before adding in a surprisingly spot on Sidney Poitier voice, They call me the *Coalman*, the *cool* Coalman—but everybody and *their* grandmother (them again? can't we get these people another line of work?) already knows the

Department of Good Taste is going to say Ix-nay to all
the negative connotations.

Meanwhile, Roger suggests a tweak in his assembly
line that will double production but requires a snow cone
wrapper that is both sturdier and lighter than what is
commercially available. The Snowman barely mentions
the subject to Evelyn and by day's end she has several
bids on his desk, the most promising of which will require
some entrepreneurial wooing and salesmanship. I've
arranged for a business meeting over lunch tomorrow.
And don't dress like a slob, okay, Snowman?

For once he takes Evelyn's advice and, man, he is
barely recognizable to the viewing audience when he
enters the restaurant, hair perfectly coiffed and wearing a
tailored charcoal gray suit (Armoani) and cobalt blue tie
(Versakes), and exuding a casual confidence that suggests
he's not unfamiliar with haute couture. And still he's
unprepared when the maître d' shows him to his table and
for an instant, maybe two, he stands stunned, unable to
reconcile the aggressive young alpha male or female sales
rep he had pictured in his mind with the person seated
across from him. It's Judith, of course, in a casual gray
blazer over a lighter gray V-necked cashmere sweater
with a simple silver chain necklace that combines
simplicity and elegance. Her hair is sculpted around her
face like the veil of a nun's habit or the aura of darkness
around a candle flame. Her posture is erect, fit, suggesting
her usual rigid military discipline in diet and exercise. As
always, he's startled by the alien gleam of intelligence in
her eyes, by that odd cobalt blue that seems outside the
normal range of human eye color (if you're thinking Liz
Taylor, it's more than that), not, coincidentally, unlike the
color of his necktie. Judith, too, seems to be appraising or

maybe better said reappraising him, not exactly an Aretha Franklin ALL CAPS shout-out, more like a grudging lowercase *r-e-s-p-e-c-t*. Under Judith's stewardship, PPP has resurrected itself as a corporate powerhouse recognized by the EPA for its commitment to a wide range of environmental concerns including recycling, reforestation, wetlands reclamation, revitalization of barrier reefs, restoration of prairies, re-introduction of endangered wildlife species—all the "*res*" an indication of how far south the environment has sunk. Sure glad to know *somebody's* working on it. The Snowman, to his credit, has recently been recognized by the Osberg Chamber of Concrete for his successful track record in hiring (and firing) locally, as well as raising (by fractions of an inch) Osberg's profile for niche industries.

Their conversation begins monotonically, camouflage for old battle wounds. Hi Judith. Hi Snowman. Thanks for coming, Judith. It's business, Snowman. She informs him that normally this sort of transaction would be beneath her purview but when she saw his name, Well, naturally, I took a personal *een*terest. He tries to comment on the irony of their company names, both contain, you know, three Ps? *P-P-P?* B-b-but for some reason this little bon mot comes out in a P-p-porky P-p-pig stutter that, to a trained medical professional's ear, might suggest the onset of a stroke. Judith asks if he's okay. He says he just swallowed his wine the wrong way (she ordered, it's a pricey red, he couldn't begin to guess its provenance or its cost, Evelyn will remind him later). This minor display of vulnerability on his part and compassion on hers kindles a small campfire of warmth. They order a second bottle of wine and now they're both having some linguistic issues. Kinetic energy rolls back and forth between them like a warm ocean current. Tapping into some old lovers' code, it appears to the audience they're arranging a tryst, most likely at the Driskoll, when *brrrinnng*, the Snowman's EyePhone® rings and on the other end he hears that familiar nasal whine.

Snowmannn.

Yesssss, Evelyn?

And, yes, he knows he sounds like a British prig because, *shit*, just when … but his tone quickly changes when Evelyn mentions problems with the fruit distributor in Honduras. No, he didn't explain, Snowman. She heard gunfire and the line went dead. Oh brother. And just like that Judith's all business again and he's straightening his tie and buttoning and rebuttoning his suit jacket like a preening talk show host, and whatever coulda shoulda woulda won't. Have your people talk to my people, okay, Snowman? and it's all the fault of this damn EyePhone®. Before they part, Judith's eyes meet his as if searching for whatever might be defined as his soul. Finally she says, Goodbye, Snowman … and good luck. In her voice he hears not just finality but a certainty of that finality that hollows him out like a mined-to-death mountain in Montana.

Voice: *I know it's hard to understand, but you still can't tell him. Not now. Not ever. Besides, your work isn't finished.*

17
BIG Business

JUDITH'S WISH FOR GOOD LUCK is appropriate because the Snowman's about to enter uncharted waters. Recognizing the need for a wiser guiding hand, Arthur has set up a meeting with Wolf Bärenhaut, Chief Investment Officer for International Brokers Investment Group. Attired in a black wool morning suit with vest and tails, a black bowler derby, and a monocle in his right eye, Wolf enters the Snowman's office with brisk military precision, sits down beside his desk, unlatches a brown leather briefcase of a kind not seen since the nineteenth century, lays out a sheath of manually typed (Remington c. 1873) pages of onion skin and, over tumblers of hundred-year-old single malt scotch and thousand-dollar Gurkha Golden Dragon cigars (the baby-faced Arthur abstaining on both fronts), begins to describe a marketing campaign that will soon put the Snowman's product in the face of every citizen in the nation. We'll employ all means available, telegraph, railroad, stagecoach, pony express fliers. The Snowman's first thought is, where the fuck did Arthur find this guy? He also has the (p)funny suspicion that Arthur has let a wolf into the sheepfold.

Shortly afterward they contract with a major nationwide distributor and begin shipping *gourmet*

PoPoPops!® to all fifty states. To ramp up their PR campaign, they sign on with *GrowNuts*®, a hotshot startup consortium of brilliant young women and men so full of drive, ambition and energy that people passing in cars on 6th St. in the middle of downtown Osberg can hear a beehive *hummm* emanating from their building. There are rumors of disembodied ideas swarming up and down the halls, brainstorming sessions that set off fire alarms. Despite these slightly *preternatural* events and the "Keep Osberg Wacky" bumper sticker someone posted on the community bulletin board, these people mean business. Everything is quantified, codified and extrapolated through an algorithmic distillation of bell curves, Venn diagrams, pie charts, bar graphs, line graphs, statistics, probabilities, game, chaos and other Mad Hatter theories. The young team at *GrowNuts*® is aiming for hip, cool, cutting edge but with a timeless underlying theme and they totally kill it with a narrative that plays on the American mystique of the lonesome cowboy as the Snowman appears in a ten gallon hat, wraparound shades and his Hawaiian slacker dude outfit munching on a *PoPoPop!*® while he sits astride an enormous longhorn steer with horns as wide as the Trinity River (during a drought), not entirely unlike Saul Bunyan's giant blue ox Bubalah, as they invite all of America to trot along (or trample under, depends on your politics, aesthetics, etc.) with them across a virtual map of the United States from California to the New York island as the sun rises in the east and sets in the west while Wiley Nilson and Freddie Jupiter join in a twanging coloraturistic duet of *We are the Champions of the Planet*.

The reception is beyond expectation. Demand far exceeds production, stores are sold-out in hours, shelves bare, and dissatisfied customers are making their voices heard. *Give us our PoPoPops!® We don't want no stinking gum drops, sugar dollops or lollipops! If you don't give us our PoPoPops!® immediately, we'll bust your balls like you wouldn't believe!* It doesn't help, or maybe it does, that a common belief persists that *PoPoPops!®* contain a mind-altering secret ingredient. Well, it does contain a secret ingredient, Maria's magic potion, but mind-altering, narcotic, a *drug?* The controversy will continue. Neither the FDA nor the DEA can identify any active agent that fits the bill as a controlled substance. Researchers speculate that an unknown enzyme in the *PoPoPop!®* formula activates the drug only upon ingestion. Regardless, everyone agrees that eating a *PoPoPop!®* creates an extraordinary sense of well-being that lasts the entire day (or night for you artsy, hip, music and lit types, also janitors, municipal maintenance and utility workers, EMS, police and medical staff—congrats on the pay raise, y'all, *ha ha*, just kidding). As an added plus, *PoPoPops!®* contain half the calories of rival products and preliminary studies show that eating one a day may actually lower cholesterol as well as the risk of diabetes, heart disease and early-onset Alzheimer's. And everyone everywhere wants one. Just about everybody you meet has that rainbow glow in their eyes. What next? Pots of gold and unicorns all over the place? The whole nation turning gay? Maybe. Maybe not.

Okay, so this Bärenhaut guy's clearly brilliant, a genius of capital gains and profit making, except for this little eccentricity (apparently some form of Asperger's) that causes him to dress, act and speak as if this were the nineteenth century. Building upon his success, Wolf announces the next step is to go public, first nationally and then internationally. *The wagons shall roll westward, the steam ships sail east, lighter than air ships circle the globe.* This Churchillian pronouncement presages top to bottom reorganization of the Snowman's burgeoning enterprise, albeit with the Snowman mostly sitting on the sidelines wrinkling his brow over incomprehensible financial formulas and mission statements, among which, he notices, the original *PoPoPops!®* brand will be subsumed in a corporate entity now titled One Pyramid Enterprises North.

Wait a minute! he emerges from a brief back-in-elementary school, drooly, head-on-the-desk visit to slumberland. Whataya mean *subsumed?* Everybody *and his grannie!* (peanut gallery) knows *PoPoPops!®* We've got a *following.* People in fucking *Fairbanks, Alaska* are raving over 'em. Fucking *Eskimos* are going wild for them. Exactly, *Snowman.* (Why, he wonders, does everybody pronounce his name with these condescending Italics?) Which is why it's wise to create some distance between our top-selling product and the corporate brand as we begin to diversify into other fields. Hmm, he's not sure if he understands the reasoning here. He also balks at the "corporate brand." And whataya mean "diversify? And what the fuck's this One Pyramid Enterprises *North* supposed to mean? Texas isn't in the fucking north! Wolf snaps shut his briefcase, removes his monocle and stares at the Snowman as if he's trying to make out a faded road sign in the middle of *nirgendwo.* Northern hemisphere, *sir. Ohhh,* he says as if now he gets it, even though he doesn't, not really, but just to be sure, there's Arthur at his ear.

Arthur, who knows the Snowman is a sucker for clever word play, has little trouble convincing him that the acronymous OPEN represents both the transparency of their business affairs as well as inclusivity of diverse cultural views. Listen to it, Snowman. The welcoming open *O* at the beginning? The warm soft *N* that doesn't quite close at the end? Hear how it invites you in and asks you to sit for a spell over a cup of coffee and a piece of pie? In sharp contrast to his laser sharp intellect, Arthur, like any lawyer or politician worth ~~shit~~ his salt, has retained these homely homilies for precisely these occasions when it's infinitely easier to convince the country bumpkin with wit than wisdom. And all the Snowman can do is nod his head yes or venture a hesitant, oh, I guess. (Why if things are going so swimmingly does he have this monkey of suspicion hanging on his back so tightly it's like the damn thing's trying to buttfuck him?)

Wolf now announces it's time to pull together a C-Suite. Whataya mean, we're gonna open a hotel or somethin'? No, *Snowman*, Wolf, barely able to conceal his impatience (are those fangs?). We're putting together a board of *directors. Chief* Executive Officer, *Chief* Operating Officer—*C-Suite? Ohhhh.* Following several high-powered meetings with several high-dollar attorneys and accountants, all the bylaws drafted, the requisite fees paid and incorporation documents filed with the SEC, Wolf and Arthur call to order an initial shareholders meeting to approve policies and elect officers. And these two have cast their nets over a wide Sargasso Sea of business and ivy league connections, deep pocket investors and Wall Street rainmakers, all high-stakes players used to swimming naked in shark tanks. And, sure, things get heated, sometimes they use language their mothers wouldn't approve of, there's the occasional wet-sounding *smack* of a fist striking flesh, weapons are sometimes flashed. Afterwards they'll be all buddy-buddy. It's like joining a street gang, you gotta take your beatdown. The Snowman feels like a little kid in a room full of scary adults. He tries to act like he knows what the fuck's going on but, let's face it, he's basically twiddling his thumbs and whistlin' Dixie past the graveyard on a dark and stormy night.

Finally the show arrives at the top floor, the aforementioned penthouse of the corporate world, the C-Suite. Despite innumerable and very sound reasons why he should not be, the Snowman is named CEO (it's his ball), which almost makes him giddy even as that homuncular little voice in his head is screaming *what the fuck are you doing, Snowman?!*

Arthur naturally morphs into Chief Financial and Legal Officer (*naturally*—no one has the balls to challenge him).

At COO—of course, *Evelyn!* the Snowman exclaims. Arthur seems mildly enthusiastic. Good idea, *Snowman*. The optics are perfect. A woman, mature, *experienced*. But while Arthur supports Evelyn in private, when the vote is opened on the floor, he goes along with the ~~gang~~ majority, "out of touch, a woman (the gender thing can go in either the plus or minus column), *old*," and she's subsumed (*that* word again) into an *upper lower management position* with about six months projected longevity. Once again Arthur is right there at the Snowman's ear. Let's be honest, Snowman, she wasn't up to snuff for this level of play and, quite frankly, there's something about her I don't trust. And *bingo*, Evelyn disappears forever into anonymity (subliminal shot of Evelyn, arms and legs flailing, as she swirls down an enormous drain).

The Snowman is, however, nonplussed by Arthur's alternate choice, both his and Evelyn's former boss, *Mister* Gastreaux (no Christian name has ever been mentioned), but Arthur dismisses his objections. Sure, the guy may (circumstantial) have tried to kill you, *Snowman*, and, yes, he is a cold-hearted son-of-a-bitch (factual). But that's exactly why we need him. In a nutshell, or an iron mask, Gastreaux will act as enforcer among the contentious members of this elite club.

Of which Wolf Bärenhaut signs on as, naturally, Chief Investment Officer (he doesn't need a telescope to see the sails of a treasure ship on OPEN's horizon).

The legendary Eunace Guppy (sometimes referred to as the *Guppy* but *never* the *Gupster* much less *Gupstress*) is appointed Chief Negotiating Officer, an odd choice, anyone (and in a sense that's everyone) who has never seen Ms. Guppy in action might think. Strict vegetarian, abstains from tobacco, alcohol and, by all accounts, sex, drinks English Breakfast tea from Nymphenburg china, with milk, on rare occasions is seen, when she *is* seen, dipping a ginger cookie in her cup, her almost preternatural blandness (she goes unnoticed in a party of two, the wallpaper stands out against *her*—you get the idea) disguises one of the most ruthless negotiators in the corporate world. Her opponents leave the boardroom shredded, shell-shocked, gasping for oxygen and clutching at crumbling fragments of terra firma. Which has the Snowman shaking his head in disbelief. I mean, wasn't she that *mousey* little loan officer at that *chintzy* little bank? Musta' got an MBA at night school, fought her way up the corporate ladder? No, wait, wasn't that *Eunice* Guppy with an "i"? Hmm, is Boone playing with a doubling thing he doesn't have a handle on yet? Or just doubling up on the roles his actors play to cut his payroll?

Filling the position of Chief Accounting Officer, Natasha Bolsavitch, a bitter-looking, Soviet bureaucrat type whose face is drawn taut around the obscene pucker of her mouth like the strings of a money bag. For everything that goes wrong, she will be blamed, for everything that goes right, she will remain unnamed. For which reason she can be quite candid in her assessments of a company's financial health, *blunt* is the word, but, well, c _ _ _ is more often heard, probably coulda copped a job as an oracle back in the day (hey Aeschylus, check this out, there's a voice coming out of this hole in the ground, female, I think, sounds *angry*), and is generally recognized by all as a *bitch*. Perfect, Wolf opines. We shall have no worries of anyone dipping in the till. There shall be no thumbs on the scale, no sticky fingers, three-dollar bills, wooden nickels or repurchases of the Brooklyn Bridge.

Cash Dullard is brought in as Chief Marketing Officer. Ivy league, Cape Cod accent, patrician features, terminally sangfroidal. Enthusiasm? Exuberance? Ebullience? Jubilance? About as much as your average oligocheaetologist describing the mating habits of earthworms (*wow, look at 'em go*, right?). How does someone so pathologically aloof or removed or maybe just sociopathic become a master of marketing? It's all in the heart, he says, placing his hand on his chest in the general proximity of that most vital organ although not quite on target.

Assuming the newly created title of Chief Data Officer, the twenty-six-year-old hipster genius of data metrics, Pernell Humpworthy, also known as the

Dromedary, in part due to his name but also his unfortunate and, according to medical literature, extremely rare physical attribute, that is to say, a hump on his back that visibly swells from mere foothill status, barely noticeable at all, to Matterhorn proportions (oddly, a turn-on for the ladies, visualizing, one surmises, an equally prodigious swelling elsewhere) as he bends over his screen for hours on end drinking up vast quantities of Red Bull and raw data.

Finally, Roger Wilco comes on board as Director of R&D. *I ammm the DOC-torrr*. Oops, wrong cue.

At this point blurry-eyed and brain numb, the Snowman can only nod in acknowledgement as the general secretary reads a list of the army of investment advisers, sub-advisers and legal counsel, including the renowned Houston firm Habeas, Corpus & Moot, no relation to Boone's gaffer—oh, wait; an independent registered public accounting firm, Y. Yu Ohus; a transfer and shareholder service agent, Watts N. Anehm; and, finally, a banking custodian, Newmus Mattock, Esq. Is that it? Oh, wait, let's not forget. At the back of the bus, er, um, room, Moses. Despite Arthur's continuing efforts to shove Moses out of the picture, the Snowman manages to keep him on in what many see as the largely ceremonial role of Chief Taste Tester. (I'm sorry, Moses. That's awright, Snowman.)

Finally, business over, champagne corks are popping like Fourth of July skyrockets (well, okay, there's a mistake right there—*PoPoPops!*® should be the obvious metaphor). Arthur has his usual vanilla milkshake. Eunace Guppy, for the occasion, gunpowder tea (high velocity). And the Snowman? Yeah, sure, a drink'd be great, several of them, but what he really needs is a boost

from the ol' *PoPoPop!*® starter batch, a five-gallon glass
jug of which he has begun to keep in his office closet,
'scuse me, I'll be right back (not that anybody notices his
absence). But *zingg!* They sure do notice his return. Just
like that he's on his feet again, he's back in the ring, he's
throwing punches left and right, he's clever and
charming, his timing's perfect, his wit brilliant, the other
board members are turning in astonishment, THIS is
exactly the *Snowman* they want to see out on the
frontlines.

And that's exactly what they're going to get as the
young *GrowNuts*® team once again nails it. To a retro
Beach Boys soundtrack of pounding drums, shredding
guitars and a downright eerie theremin with liminal
images of Bela Lugosi in the background, we see the
Snowman in what has become his trademark Hawaiian
shirt, a pair of fire engine red cargo shorts and tire tread
and Bossie the Cow leather huaraches *hecho en México*,
holding up a frosty, rainbow-colored *PoPoPop!*® like
Lady Liberty's torch while catching a wave on the back
of a killer whale on the Banzai pipeline surrounded by
dozens of buff young surfer dudes and dudettes cutting in
and out on their boards while also holding up
PoPoPops!® like flaming torches. The same image
playing now on the enormous screen behind the
Snowman, fashionably casual in his Hawaiian slacker
outfit, as he strides out on stage in the main hall of the
Osberg Convention center a year later to announce to
raucous cheers OPEN's launch of its IPO. The entire
financial world from Wall Street to Shanghai and Dubai
is on tenterhooks. The buzz is so loud people claim
sightings of enormous flying insects as big as small
airplanes. Word is this is a sure thing but you know how

that goes. People wanta see this Snowman dude in action and they sure as hell don't wanta listen to him drone on about *positive indicators* and *future prospects*. They want a fucking *performance*, they want *pyrotechnics*, they wanta hear something that'll *c'mon baby* set the markets on *fire!*

But what *does* this Snowman dude have to say? No nerdy business major in high school or college, he. Never inspired by Rockefeller, Mellon or Carnegie. Never aspired to be the next Perot, Jobs, Gates or Dell. No Zuckerberg, Musk or ~~Bevos~~ Bezos did he want to be. He looks out over the *thousands* of expectant faces packed into this giant hall and asks himself that perennial *question existentielle, what the fuck are you doing here, Snowman?* His knees are knocking, his teeth clenched, his expression more a rictal grimace than that confident Tim Apple grin shareholders want to see. The first words out of his mouth sound like *Squeak! Squawk!* His first sentence and his second are rambling, disconnected, punctuated (or not) by awkward starts and stops. He seems to be grasping for a coherent thought. And then it comes, it's like he's been struck by pentecostal lightning, like he just visited Moses' burning bush and now the holy ghost is speaking through him in the voice of a Gilded Age robber baron. Really, where's this stuff coming from? In his head he sees walls of computer screens, international stock indexes, container ships in the Atlantic, Pacific, Aegean, huge lumbering transport planes, convoys of tractor trailers, miles of rail cars, he sees a minefield, no, wait, wrong connotation, a *meadow* blossoming in North Korea with rainbow-colored *PoPoPops!*®, and somehow he's weaving all these disparate pieces together into a little choo choo train-that-could narrative of OPEN that in his telling traces its origins all the way back to the Dutch East India Company interlaced with crowd-pleasing new-agey tropes and pithy wisdom he attributes to a sixteenth-century Puritan forebear *Listen and heed, for ye shall invest wisely and gather unto thineself great benefit which thou shalt accumulate through good and profitable acts and deeds*, which he translates into the even pithier, more contemporary and fashionably off-color, *Go forth and multiply your assets, motherfuckers!* All in all, the sort of soaring rhetoric you'd expect to ignite a lynch mob—er, roomful of hungry venture capitalists. Everybody and his granny (officer, can you do something about those two?) is staring at the Snowman with this *holy cowabonga!* expression because there is no doubt in anyone's mind that they have just witnessed genius, at least it sure as heck *sounds* like genius (the religious stuff was a tad creepy, but the evangelical contingent is feeling pretty damn *included*). The shareholders are on their feet again and again, they're roaring like Romans at the slaughter of Christians in the Coliseum (okay, *that* didn't go over so well with the evangel crowd). Of course they're happy, they're nearly fucking delirious. They're toting swag bags packed with two or three thousand dollars of cool cutting-edge *stuff*, they're about to stake a claim in the Lost Dutchman's gold mine, and they've all got a wonderful feeling everything's going their way. Shares soar four hundred per cent above the opening price. It's a total feeding frenzy on Wall Street. It's like tossing a pig in a pond full of piranhas, like a night of fire fishing in Taiwan, the *mattanza* in Sicily. Brokers are yelling *buy! buy! no, wait, sell! no, buy!*

OPEN's stock continues to climb to dizzying heights with aggressive marketing policies, mergers, buyouts, new product offerings. Perhaps sensing his survival at stake, Moses' latest inspiration, the Halloween-themed, orange and black-spotted *JaguarPop®*, will prove to be an enormous success among the growing Mayan-American demographic. And what's not to like? A lush, succulent, totally indulgent blend of pumpkin spice, peanut butter, dark chocolate, orange extract (all certified organic products of Mexico's Mayan community) and Moses' own secret ingredient derived from the juice of a rare herb found only in Mali, so *he* says, which does indeedy give it that extra boost, you just feel so good, like we knew you would now, *so good! so good!* They're flying off the shelves in every outlet across America as well as those newly opened in Canada and Mexico, sales are exponential, impossible to keep up with demand. And the Snowman darts another snarky *I told you so* in Arthur's direction.

18
Downtown

IT'S NOW ABOUT THREE P.M., the hottest time of day, the
city of Osberg's sweltering in a sauna of heat and
humidity that will last well into evening. And where has
the Snowman gotten to? Still crashed in the shade? On his
feet again plying his trade? The errant grasshopper is
searching for him all over the place. Most afternoons he
circles back downtown on the S. 1st St. Bridge, there's
always a fair or farmer's market or musical event he can
check out, or a protest at the Capitol or the new City
Hall—it's that architectonic collision (his opinion) of
limestone slabs, Corten Steel and jutting copper spars
buried in native landscaping, looks like one of those
dystopic, sci-fi films where civilization has collapsed and
the world is ruled by troglodytes and humanoid primates.
(Like now, *Daddy?*)

Inside, the city council is stretching its limbs for what
promises to be yet another marathon session, a vote by
four a.m. would be welcome, at which point most council
members are simply holding on for the free Oma's
Country-Style Kolaches and Warbucks coffee. Outside, a
group demanding voting rights for domestic animals
(One Thump for Yes!) has set up camp, they've got a
volunteer medical team, food and hydration stations,

porta-potties, and a sympathetic reporter from the *Osberg Chronicler*. A handful of counter-demonstrators across the street is completely bedraggled from a day in the wilting, hyperthermic, one hundred-and-fifty-degree pavement temperature, but just enough of a breeze to stir the leaves of the sycamore tree they're standing under for shade has revived them sufficiently to chant, *Just Say No to Votin' Bovines!*

Playing the bipartisan card, the Snowman distributes several dozen *PoPoPops!*® gratis to representatives of both camps, leaving in his wake a consensual *pop! pop! pop! pop!* as he pushes onward along his desultory route. Which leads him next past the old municipal power plant (*appealing* Art Deco façade, *clean*-looking white metal smokestacks, *scary* Dr. Frankenstein electrical stuff) and onward to Osberg's new public library, another architectural clash (his opinion again) of native limestone, Corten Steel and walls of tinted glass (from one angle it oddly resembles the head of Picasso's deluded Don Quixote wearing the barber's basin for a helmet). Joined at the hip on its north side to the city's hip, happening urban center. To the south, library patrons can look up from their reading, snoozing, googling and gaze out over Municipal Lake and the hike and bike trails. And why does any of this matter to the Snowman (or Boone's audience for *that* matter)? Because he's been meaning forever to stop in and see if they have an obscure novel called *Unburbling*. A friend loaned him a copy when he was a freshman at UT, he didn't get it at all but a line at the end about a magic carpet ride on a giant slice of pizza stuck in his head and recently he saw the title listed at the very bottom of literary critic Clarissa Hopplightly's top one hundred dystopian novels of the last century. (Boone, who is not only a great fan of literature himself but has reimagined (some would say destroyed) a number of classic works of fiction in his films, has been trying to get his hands on a copy for years.)

But what's all the commotion? People are rushing out of stores, restaurants, offices, cafés, they're lining up on the sidewalks of Congressional Avenue. Has the circus come to town? Is it time for the ACL music festival? No, it's the annual Juneteenth parade celebrating the arrival of emancipation in Texas (two years late, but what the heck, it's a big state, word travels slow). And, true, it's not even June, or the nineteenth, they had to squeeze it in on the city's calendar of events. But where is everybody? There's maybe half a dozen participants. A ninety-five-year-old lady in pink cat-eye glasses and a salmon-colored Sunday going to church outfit with ruffled hem and sleeves, banging a tambourine and shaking her bony old booty with a mile-wide smile on her face because, sure, she's kinda stiff, a little clickety-clackety arthritic, but she's *alive* and she's moving! A very round middle-aged lady in a high school marching band outfit tootle-ootling on a clarinet. A high school break dancer who blasts out rapid fire volleys on his snare drum while spinning on his head. A nine-year-old girl in a shiny pink and blue sequined majorette costume playing a glockenspiel and intermittently tossing her mallets overhead (and catching them). A well-meaning eighteen-year-old co-ed from Minne*soh*ta, white as the freshly fallen snow she left behind, a slightly bewildered look on her face as to why she's here, nevertheless she's keeping up a pretty good bassline on her tuba *Oomp-boomp, Oomp-boomp-boomp.* Oh yeah, and *Ha!Ha!Ha!* there he is, the Snowman, pushing his cart behind like the guy who cleans up after the elephants and tossing out preshaken *PoPoPops!*® to grasping hands in the crowd, those radioactive atomic neon rainbow clouds exploding everywhere, adding a spot of color to the proceedings, you might say (but you might also get taken to the woodshed). And that's it. All the Black bodies they could find, minus Ingrid, the, um ... (she's kinda shy) white girl and, well, of course, the Snowman. The African American population has been gentrified out of central Osberg, it's at least an hour bus ride (provisional route) from the Far East Side, police and border checks at every intersection, and you know what they say about driving while Black.

A shop door opens and an ice-cold blast of molecularly combined air fresheners, disinfectants, cologne and perfume sends a barrage of shivers cascading from the Snowman's occiput down to his calcaneus and back up again along a river of sweat. But it could just as well be the unease one feels in the tenebrous depths of the urban canyon, especially understandable as one approaches the halls of power. And there it is, the Capitol. Modeled after the Capitol Building in D.C., it's a Texas tad taller but just as buttfuck ugly (the Snowman's opinion again), its pink granite Renaissance Revival dome an architectural eyesore that makes him think of deposed kings, fallen empires *Look upon my works ye mighty* ... Osberg's exponential vertical growth and continually refined interpretations of an antiquated municipal ordinance that restricts obstruction of the Capitol view from various sight corridors have so diminished this illustrious edifice that, seen from a vulture's eye perspective, it looks like a fireplug at the bottom of a ventilation shaft in an NYC housing project. The State Troopers who guard the Capitol grounds hate to see the Snowman pushing his cart up the mall, which, thanks to cost-cutting, budget constraints and the loser-end of some ill-advised Snopesian real estate deals (thanks, Guv), at this point resembles the front lawn of a modest, middle-class residence. Well, okay, free *PoPoPops!*® all around keep the Snowman on pretty good terms with these peace officers. It's just that for the next half hour they're not going to know if the sporadic *pop! pop! pop! pop!* they hear comes from ice cream cones or gunfire. The halls of government these days are aswarm with survivalists, paramilitaries, historical re-enactors, guys in Davy Crockett coonskin caps, gals in Annie Oakley fringed leather jackets, they're toting blunderbusses, muzzleloaders, AK-47s, tugging behind them 3 pounder French and Indian era cannons, 105 mm howitzers. And in case all these guns make you nervous, rest assured, it's part of the plan.

Plan?

Scene: the Governor's office in the Capitol Building, purple draperies, polished cherry, oak and pine shutters, molding, credenzas, ormolus, mirrors, cabinets, arm chairs, tête-à-tête, creaking leather, carpeted floor. The Governator, Abe Bismol, is seated at his desk surrounded by Lieutenant Governor Dern Halfprick, Attorney General Akin Apoxton, Congressman Lemur Smeetch, Senators John Crony and Teddy "Toad" Crooze, with the venerable Reverend K. James Fallible in attendance for spiritual guidance, aged, like the rest of us, his upswept golden pompadour gone Grecian silver, his orthodontically enhanced smile bottle-cap crimped. The center of their attention, one might even say admiration, an odd object on the Governator's desk. Constructed out of leather and iron, it looks like a cross between a bear trap and a child's swing seat, although many women, especially from the Middle Ages, would recognize it immediately. It's a chastity belt, of course, but, counter to hi-tech trends toward smaller, lighter, more efficient, it's noticeably larger, more cumbersome and intimidating than its predecessors. And thanks to—no, it's not a fly on the wall, it's a grasshopper, a big 'un, and it blends right in with the mesquite flower pattern of the wallpaper—we get to listen in on these holders of the highest offices of state and national government as they plot—er, conspire ... um, collude? connive? scheme?

Hell, boys (there are no *girls*), there just ain't no other way to say it. We're gonna make it whereas all *women* aged nine years or above are required to wear these dadgum *prophylactic* devices. The Guv just can't bring himself to say *chastity*. He also doesn't bother to mention the fine print: the keys to said devices shall be held in safe keeping by the husband, father, brother or other responsible male family member (that word again). In unusual circumstances male offspring of the female in question may fill this role. (Which is why, when this new ordinance is passed, you might see a twelve or even six-year-old boy looking like a totally smug little shithead, his mother or older sister or even a maiden aunt unhappily in tow. Rumors will also abound of hurried assignations, bribes, occasionally you'll see a woman with a Madonna smile, her young keeper with chocolate smudges around his mouth.) Hell, I've got half a mind (you said it, not me) to try on one of them dadblamed thangs myself, just to see what it's like. What about you fellers? Shoot, Abe, you ought'n to be talkin' lak that. Yeah, Abe, that just don't sound right. Oh, c'mon fellers, you know I was just joshin'. (Grumbling.) Now, about this religious freedom issue. You mean where we give every kid a Bobble on the first day of school, Abe? Goldarn it, Dern, I'm talkin' about the way schools are dealing with this dadgum dinosaur business. Everyone agrees the goldang planet was created five thousand years ago, am I kee-rect? *Dang tootin!* Whooeee, Toad, I do appreciate your enthusiasm but that was a stinker! Which means the first human beings the Good Lord put on this here planet had to kill off them dadgum monsters. Am I also kee-rect on that score, Rev'rend Fallible? Yes indeedy, Guvnuh. I can point to the exact spot in the redacted, revised, rewritten or otherwise bowdlerized Good Book that describes the final battle between mankind and those ungodly minions of Satan.

Which, of course, leads to talk of another kind of battle, the perennial 2ⁿᵈ Amendment fight over gun ownership. And that's where *the plan* comes in, and this is right up the alley of the proponents of TEXIT, so-named as Texas drifts farther away from the state of reality. Look, fellers, let's just lay it out in the open. Who buys guns? The fellers look at each other nonplussed like *duh!* Um … paranoid schizophrenics? Rightwing extremists? Lunatics? Domestic and foreign terrorists? Insecure white males? That's right, fellers—our guys! Them dadgum Satan-loving *liberal*—excuse my language—pussies won't stand a chance when the day of reckoning comes, ain't that right, Reverend? *Reverend?*

Completely lost in this modern Knossos—the governor's mansion. The Snowman can see it ghost-like glowing back there in the shadows of the Capitol Complex. It's that white antebellum structure with tall white plantation columns stuck on a little grassy plot like a cenotaph or tomb to a past that is gone but not forgotten (nor remembered very accurately). And this is where white-sheeted ghosts start whooshing about and we hear scary music in the background (clarinet *whoo-hoo-hooing* up and down the scales—is it the lady from the parade?). Visitors report liminal sightings in glass doorknobs, beveled glass cabinet doors and cheval mirrors of Black men and women in livery and work clothes from the mid-nineteenth century. Slaves? Servants? They certainly weren't invited in the front door, even if they did build the damn place. The Snowman also remembers (even if you don't) that a number of years ago a shadowy figure was caught on security cameras trying to burn down the Guv's residence with a Molotov cocktail. The culprit was never apprehended and no one knows if this attack was meant as political or architectural criticism. Taxpayers were disinclined to waste more money on reconstructing this abomination but you know how that goes. Anyway, don't bother knocking because the Governator's never in.

Warte! Hörst du mich nicht?! Das ist aber sehr schlecht! A disturbance has broken out on the set. An unidentified male voice with a heavy German accent the Snowman recognizes from *somewhere* attempts to interject a historical factoid regarding the Second and Fourteenth Amendments that muddies the waters in liberal and conservative camps alike, and which Boone, shaking his head vehemently and muttering *are you out of your fucking mind?* will immediately edit out: *Cut! Cut! Cut!*

Well, thanks to this confusion, the drone seems to have lost track of the Snowman again. Oh, there he is. Instead of heading straight downtown this afternoon, the Snowman, whose route seems even more desultory than usual (Procrastinating? Maybe. He has a history of putting off or trying to avoid undesirable tasks or

situations dating back to his childhood: see subject's
Educational Records—Glenda), has made a brief detour
to the SoCo district where Boone's hyper-caffeinated, old
school cameraman has inserted a bunch of sunny, bright
overexposed black and white stills from the thirties and
forties when this part of Congressional Avenue was a
typical southwestern cow town main street, hitching posts
outside feed and hardware stores, gas stations, used car
lots, diners, a couple of spanking new stucco and tiled
motor lodges frequented by traveling salesmen (What the
hell is this silk stocking doing in your suitcase, *Fred?!*),
Westward Ho! vacationing families (*See the U.S.A. in
your* ... Ford?) and newlyweds (so they said), oh yeah,
and the Osberg School for the Deaf, the oldest continually
operated school in Texas, bet you didn't know that. (Say
what? You heard correctly.)

Back in the day when the Snowman first pushed his
cart out this way he kept seeing these kinda glamorous,
kinda trashy, severely under (or over) dressed women
hanging around the once-upon-a-time ballroom classy
turned adult cinema shabby Osberg Theater. Slow on the
uptake, it took him a while to realize they were
prostitutes—well   before,   of   course,   this   street's
miraculous (dollar signs, *not* a radioactive spider bite)
transformation from a scattering of shops, cowboy boots
(tried on a pair, didn't work with the cargo shorts) and
western wear (same for the Stetson hat and pearl snap
shirt), costumes for all occasions (can't get those sweat
stains out of his mind), tacos for güeros (and margaritas
for Margaritos), a store full of *tesoros*—terrible at
choosing presents, he usually ended up here in desperate
last minute attempts to buy Judith something for
Christmas or Valentine's Day or her birthday, a burnished

silver heart (kinda large in retrospect) necklace from Mexico that she wore once (*twice?*), antique glass earrings from Victorian England (three or four times?), glossy painted carved wooden earrings from Branson, Missouri (I think these will look nice on the *Chreestmas* tree, *Snowman*)—and finally, The "Grandaddy of Osberg Music Venues"! The number one live music club in Osberg and the world!! Rockin' around the clock since 1955*iiiiivve!!!* Ladies and Gentlemen!!!! The *Continental Club!!!!!* (Side note: the Snowman has never been inside, probably the only native Osberger who hasn't, don't ask why, maybe because of his nocturnal work life, maybe because of his tendency to avoid crowded noisy places where he might, oh, I don't know, meet someone and have fun?)

And from that bit of history into trendy, expensive, New Osberg chic, posh, tony and ultra-hip shops, bars, clubs, restaurants, boutique hotels and upscale condos and apartment buildings. And smack dab in the middle of this postmodernismo Osberg snapshot comes the grungy, grumpy, grumbling Snowman, *look at all this shit!* sounds like Popeye after a night of port call @!#%! muttering to himself and cursing everyone in his path, *get outa my way asshole! and get that goddamn mutt offa me!* Somehow this makes him even more Osberg wacky attractive to the street traffic (is this dude really *the* Snowman?). He sells a couple dozen *PoPoPops!*® in a blur of app and hard currency transactions to in-the-know locals, tourists, future (maybe ... not sure yet) transplants from snowy Michigan and sunny California, they're swarming over the borders in hordes, *The Progeny of the Prophylaxors of the Texas Republic* (apparently named by the same guy who came up with Ku Klux Klan) are stringing hundreds of miles of Occam's razor wire along the frontier with Oklahoma and New Mexico. Overwhelmed by this twenty-first century land rush, land grab, grabbing hands, *Snowman! Snowman! Snowman!* the Snowman gets his ass out of SoCo as fast as he can *slap!slap!slap!slap!* pursued by a stampeding herd of snorting, bellowing, red-eyed longhorns and ghost riding cowboys (CGI).

19
Growth (pre-cancerous)

OPEN'S GROWTH CONTINUES UNABATED as they now cut the ribbon on a huge new industrial plant in an equally new industrial park in the burgeoning southeast sector radiating outward from the Osberg International (and soon to be Interplanetary) Airport. Asphalt, concrete and huge boxy buildings cover several thousand acres of formerly prime farmland. Marketing, Cash Dullard at the helm, sells this move as a tribute to Osberg's "Grow Local" campaign. Th-th-that's not exactly what we had in mind, liberal-leaning Council member Angeline Trout sputters. Is *too*, conservative Standish Miles snaps back. Is not. Is too. Is not. *Lalalalala*. And there you have it, folks, your city council at work.

As part of its commitment to the Grow Local campaign (detractors call it *Go Loco* but, sour grapes, right?), OPEN announces a number of new plant openings across Texas. Rumors of political aspirations spring up when a regional news station shows the Snowman in a Stetson, western cut jacket, string tie and pearl-snap shirt (he's wearing his cargo shorts but you can't see 'em), behind the wheel of a 1924 Cadillac V63 Touring ragtop convertible, top down, rumbling through dusty, barren, sepia-faded cow towns and dried-up oil patches. He's smiling and waving howdy to all the plain folk in their shabby dresses and baggy, threadbare trousers out on the sagging front porches of weathered gray pine-board houses in the hundred-twenty-degree heat holding up little American flags (made in China, penny apiece—Marketing distributed them in advance) and ~~jeering~~ cheering him on, and why not? He's doing a great service to these near ghost towns where cotton, cattle and oil have long ceased to be king. The people love him, right? He's bringing back jobs! He's making America great again! The soundtrack is blasting what many believe to be a patriotic song by Bruce Springstring (it's not, and attorneys for Mr. Stringbean—er, Springsprung—um, Spring*stine*? It's Spring*string*, you idiot!—have just issued a cease-and-desist order to Boone Weller, no, wait, wrong guy, this is for Mister, um, *Snowman?*).

Meanwhile, buried in the read-between-the-lines microprint of jargon and legalese, certain important details escape the Snowman's attention. These desperately poor towns are granting OPEN a one hundred percent tax waiver for the next thirty years as long as OPEN promises (*hee hee*) to hire a certain quota of locals, minimum wage is top wage, there are no sick days, paid vacations, bonuses, health insurance, overtime pay, pensions, retirement funds or anything else exuding the insalubrious odor (*who cut the camembert?*) of a benefit. And, yep, there's that word again. *Camembert?* No, you cheesehead, *benefit* (n. late 14c., "good or noble deed," also "advantage, profit," from Anglo-French *benfet* "well-done," from Latin *benefactum* "good deed"—Ed.). In other words, one man's good deed, or even, one might say, act of desperation, that is, the commodification of his labor, is another man's advantage or profit in that perennial game of winners and—let's just call a spade a shovel—*losers*. And yeah, sure, there are the naysayers, sticklers for facts, community and environmental impact statements, etc., but their protests go as unheeded as Cassandra's warnings to her father, King Priam. (Say what?)

Thanks to the Guppy's understated brilliance at the negotiating table (she does this wheedling, inveigling, nasal thing with an underlying psychopathic razor's edge that makes your nervous system search for the nearest exit, plus you never know where the heck she's coming from, she could be standing right behind—look out! *eee! eee! eee!*), the OPEN juggernaut buys out, acquires, consumes and/or unabashedly crushes small businesses across the nation. Co-ops (co-opted), mom and pop operations, specialty and boutique shops, aggressive little start-ups swelling into fragile chains whose team members are all immediately cashiered and replaced with a new *team* consisting of half as many employees rehired at half the salary and made to understand immediately that they will be expected to ruthlessly compete with each other if they wish to keep their jobs. And just to be sure the message is clear, while the Gupster—*What?!*—that is, *Ms*. Guppy does her stuff, the highly respected (feared is more accurate) Chief Officer of Spanky-Spank, i.e., Chief Human Resources Officer Carlton McCowum (a belated appointment to the board, something about a sexual harassment lawsuit (under appeal), nothing that concerns us) personally takes charge of managerial issues.

Bulldog face, built like a brick shithouse (it's a real thing), McCowum's reputation precedes him as not just a brutal bastard but—all right, let's say it, a real *prick*, a

genius of labor busting, lower wages, cuts in benefits(!!),
longer hours, shorter vacations, known for swooping into
district and regional headquarters for lightning strike
inspirational visits. That poor wretch, Bob Crutchett—
quality control manager over in the Southeast Sector?
Wanted *time with his family*. Can you *fucking* believe it?!
McCowum shouts into the terrified faces of the Southeast
management team. Crutchett wants *time!* We can't have
an *absentee* manager, Crutchett! We need a *company*
man! Someone who's *always* here! But of course *you* can
take a coupla days off, *Crutchett*. That'll give you time to
find another job! Then the collapse, the cave-in, the
cascade of nervous tics, twitches, the look of utter
incredulity, voice quavering, breaking, you mean
terminated? Crutchett is actually on his knees, he's
groveling at McCowum's feet, he may even be licking his
shoes, tears stream down his face, please, sir, I have a
wife, kids, my little Timmy is deathly ill, I'll do anything,
wash dishes, scrub toilets. Get him outta here! McCowum
snarls and a squad of burly security guards in Sam Brown
belts and black leather jackboots frog march the sobbing
Crutchett out the door while pummeling him with their
nightsticks.

    And, sure, the Snowman does think some of this
seems like a bad thing, but it's also a good thing, as
Iago—*Who?*—er, I meant to say *Ar-Ar-* ... the Snowman
struggles to say *Arthur* but he can't get the name out. His
lips, tongue, mouth, throat constrict like they've been
soaked in gasoline. What the fuck's going on here? Is he
having a stroke? Has he been drugged, poisoned? (Vlad?)
He finally manages to extrude Arthur's name in a kind of
ga-ga goo-goo baby talk *Ee-arhh-go*, which, oddly,
Arthur responds to, albeit with a slight how-did-you-

know? tilt of his head. Iago né Arthur now leads the Snowman on a virtual tour of their newest factories where the employees are working at an admirably robotic pace with equally robotic perfection and, sure, they do show signs of stress, faces gaunt, hollow eyes, obvious hair and weight loss, but, heck, studies(??) suggest *some* stress can contribute to productivity. Lean and mean, *Snowman*. Survival of the fittest. Darwin, Rousseau, the Social Contract through a jaundiced lens. Eat or be eaten, *Snowman*. Sharks, all around you, circling. *Piranhas* (Iago pronounces it *pee-rahn-yas* like the Brazilian Portuguese, although, yes, Hector, it is Tupi in origin). Tough, you gotta be. *Ruthless.* You crush them, *stomp* them, before they stomp you. But why does it have to be like this? the Snowman asks in his *guileless* voice. Iago rolls his eyes. That's how you grow, *Snowman*, and growth is the name of the game. You gotta grow, grow, grow. But *why?* he persists like a child who isn't receiving the answer he wants. Finally Iago loses it. Christ, *Snowman*, are you really so fucking *stupid?!* So you can dominate the fucking industry! You consume them or they consume you! It's the soul of capitalism! It's our national legacy, our *heritage*, for God's sake! Iago makes it sound like it's not only within the legal boundaries of the law (and no, that's not redundant) but a moral imperative. Although, sure, one does wonder again at a descendant of slaves taking ownership of that part of the national heritage. And the thing is, the poor Snowman (that *stupid* really did sting) has been so deeply sucked in by the corporate mentality surrounding him that he can kind of see the logic behind Iago's words. I mean, you gotta look at the *BIG* picture, right, *Snowman?* You gotta understand the *benefits* to society, right, *Snowman?*

What's good for OPEN is good for the nation, right, *Snowman?* And, oh brother, the audience sighs, not sure if he's really convinced himself of this crap, or he's simply parroting Ar—*Iago.*

What's good for OPEN is certainly good for, well, OPEN, which now, *ahem,* opens its Corporate Headquarters in the newly launched postmodern-classical Osbergdorf office tower in downtown Osberg, at two hundred thirty-two stories and almost half a mile high not quite the tallest building in the world but close. The Snowman, of course, merits the penthouse office. Cutting edge furnishings, ergonomic work station, curated art, Banksy, Basquiat, Botero, Warhol. Three-hundred-sixty degree view of the city. Directly below him, barely discernable, the winter blue and silver, cloven glass spire of the Jack Frost Building, a cross-over between art deco and sixties modern, briefly the tallest building in Osberg but reduced long ago to a mere dwarf among giants, practically street-front by today's standards. Gazing up yonder to the north, he can just make out the Dopie Mall, that rectangular, flash drive-like little edifice on the southwest corner of the university's forty acres where, just between you and me, he spent many stoned nights watching often bizarre and sometimes incomprehensible foreign and indie films. Newcomers'll never believe this little novelty once laid claim to Osberg's tallest. If he looks across Municipal Lake and just south of Congressional Avenue Bridge where the Osberg Statusman offices once stood (the clattering presses long fallen silent, the old guard of print newsmen and women, well, not exactly retired, but made … *obsolete?* by tidal changes in the print media and the Supremacist Court's reinterpretation of the 1st Amendment—anything *we*

don't like), he sees, or rather *winces* at, the gleaming
burnt orange Texas Two Step Towers condominium, an
architectural atrocity (yes, *his* opinion) shaped exactly
like the Jackalope ears hand gesture, ubiquitous after
every victorious varsity glazed donut eating contest, that
burnt orange pride burning even brighter knowing these
deep-fried heart-stoppers are baked fresh right here in
Central Texas. The whole thing's a big plus. Health
experts report a steep decline in brain injuries since
interest waned in college football (cholesterol's skyhigh
but that's another story). The stadium has been renovated
to look like a giant burnt orange-iced donut, fans
participate by trying to keep up with their favorite players
C'mon, Joe, eat! mph, mph. Sales are through the roof.
Jackalope souvenirs, apparel and paraphernalia available
at the front gate. Snack vendors in the stands sell donuts
by the dozen, white pastry boxes of glazed and jelly filled,
frosting, sprinkles, M&Ms, *Get 'em while they're hot!*
Employment's all good, tax coffers bulging.

 Boone! Hey *Boone!* Where the bloody 'ell you goin'
with this shite? Bloody fokkin old fool's got another
wanderbug up his bloody fokkin' arse. We'll be half way
to bloody fokkin Timbuktu before he gets back on track.
I dunno, Moot, one'a these days you'll really piss the old
boy off and then we'll be in a bloody fix.

 Ignoring this background chatter (Moot and Jeef's
badinage is notorious on the set), and turning his gaze
westward toward the hills beyond, the Snowman can see
raw white patches of caliche bulldozed out of the dark
green cedar and live oak, the endless creep of civilization,
new gated communities, clubs, private villas encroaching
upon, exiling, depleting, destroying wildlife, aquifers,
ancient ecological systems, natural habitats. Things he

and, let's face it, most Osbergians don't think about very
often. (Who let that guy in here, anyway?) He also has a
much more up close and personal view of the Eye
levitating in its gleaming emerald pyramid than he would
like. Every time he looks, it's staring right back at him,
pretty much at eye level but not exactly eye to eye, more
of a skeptical glance, like, what are *you* doing there,
Snowman? A question he does not fail to ask himself on
a quotidian basis.

Despite the Snowman's celestial occupancy of the
loftiest office in Osberg, this isn't one of those
hierarchical corporate structures, the big guys on top and
everybody else hidden away in a warren of matte gray
dens, nests and cubbyholes way down below. Team
members enjoy a wide array of amenities. Open work
spaces, lounges, gyms, lap pool, indoor track, yoga and
meditation centers, natural lighting, tropical plants,
ergonomic furniture. A lavish buffet lunch is provided
free and attendance is encouraged, well, *expected,* indeed,
monitored (discreetly), not only by the usual biometrics,
facial, retinal, digital, but also chemical identifiers (BO,
halitosis, f-f-flatulence, you get the drift). And even
though this makes the Snowman feel just a little bit
icky—i-i-isn't that an invasion of privacy and maybe
even i-i-illegal?—Iago's there at his ear. Look, *Snowman,*
it's just good business practice. Left to their own devices,
team members scatter across the city like hungry mice
looking for diners, restaurants, coffee shops, losing their
focus on the job, engaging in *intrigues,* returning to work
late, sometimes *intoxicated.* This way we keep them close
at hand, the mission ever present in their minds. It's the
perfect construct, *Snowman.* On the one hand everything
seems out in the open, *transparent.* On the other, we've

got that all-embracing big brotherly awareness *and* control.

And, sure, the Snowman makes an effort to do his part. He announces an *OPEN* door policy between the hours of two and four (although, let's face it, most of his visitors come for the view, which does result in some awkward hemming, hawing and flimsy excuses). Under his stewardship, team meetings are lively, everyone is encouraged to participate, marketing, management, R&D, team leaders, first day on the job newbies. Let him have his fun, McCowum smiles at Iago, or at least one assumes that's what it is on his face. Talk costs us nothing, employees let off steam, makes 'em feel included, boosts morale, we're in the money (by the way—take names!).

Completely ignorant of these machinations, the Snowman circulates among the work stations, the break rooms, making an effort to appear informed of team projects' progress, to participate in the repartee and polite gossip, the backslapping, joking, schmoozing, eating— above all *eating*. Because it never stops, really, lunch-time more or less folded into an all-day feast. You can always find breakfast ready if you arrive on the job early, pancakes and waffles, omelets and French toast, home fries, grits, eggs boiled and over easy, biscuits and gravy, yoghurt, oatmeal, an endless variety of pastries. Throughout the day pit masters hand out steaming platters of barbecued brisket, sausage, ribs. Slabs of pizza as big as table tops. Sashimi, sushi, kimchi. Everybody encouraging you to eat! eat! have another! Plates of glazed and jelly-filled donuts, kolaches and Danishes everywhere on display. Baristas dispensing double cappuccinos and triple strawberry mocha lattes. In the gym, team members munch on corn dogs, burritos and wasabi-flavored taco chips while they dutifully push, pull and pedal.

And the Snowman's right there with them, stuffing his face like a politician on the campaign trail. All day long somebody's glad-handing him, inveigling him, high fiving, fist bumping and generally *selling* themselves. Hi, *Snowman* (along with the open-door policy, he has encouraged team members to act on a first-name basis—mistake), it's me, Blake, again! Or Taylor or Madeleine. Did you get a chance to look at my … ? Have you seen my suggestion for …? Do you have a moment to discuss that idea I … ? Or else it's some stupid office party. Come on, *Snowman!* It'll be fun! Roger's making the punch! He's coerced into wearing a jester's cap and uttering inane jingles on OPEN's blog. We're hopin' OPEN helps you with copin'. He adopts the modified Trekkie outfit that has become standard apparel at OPEN, the Starship vector on the chest replaced by a swooshy *OPEN!* Comfy, yes, casual, sure, not, however, particularly flattering given the average team member's, um … *d'ya eat yet?* But if the Snowman raises the slightest complaint, if he suggests that some of this is excessive, that perhaps his time could be better spent actually looking at the books and trying to understand their mission, there's Iago at his ear again. *You* are the heartbeat of OPEN, *Snowman!* Company morale depends on you. You've got to make your presence felt. You can't hide away like a hermit.

Even when he excuses himself and escapes to the little boy's room there is no escape. Standing at the urinal in a post-pee moment of bliss before the final shake, tuck away and zip, he hears a pair of black brogue wingtips smack the tiled floor behind him and in strides that prick

McCowum who naturally (alpha male thing) chooses the urinal right next to his, although he stands a good two feet back, ostentatiously opens his fly and takes out his tool, which, for all the Snowman knows (he makes a point of not looking) really could be a two-footer, at the same time angling for a glimpse of *his* equipage, figuring that in order for this *Snowman* dude to make it this big he's gotta have (be?) a huge prick. The Snowman, however, isn't having any of it. He tucks, zips up, flushes and heads to the sink.

Exiting the men's room, he is accosted by Eunace Guppy, or rather a gnat-like swarm of pixels in the middle of which he can make out a faint outline of Ms. Guppy's face. Why do you keep avoiding me, *Snowman?* she says in a creepy Joan Crawford come-on voice that could easily be misconstrued as some sort of declaration of love or lust but more likely has to do with her lobbying for higher numbers on her performance evaluation. I'm not *avoiding* you, he says to an art deco floor lamp. I can't even *see* you. Oh, how dare you! I'm standing right here, *Snowman!* Sorry, he apologizes to a coat rack and, dashing to the elevator, he flees back up to his office muttering, *Snowman, Snowman, Snowman,* what are you doing *here* with these *people?*

20
Pushin' the Cart

ONE DAY IN THE MIDDLE OF THIS MADNESS the Snowman locks himself in his office, changes back into his Hawaiian slacker dude outfit to the medley or maybe better said cacophony of Superman, Batman and Hawaii Five-0 theme songs, takes his private elevator down to the basement, pulls the tarp off a row of ice cream carts, loads up the first one in line with *PoPoPops!*® from a convenient freezer (for team members' convenience they're everywhere), and pushes it out the door into the street. And so he begins to push the cart again. It wasn't a planned thing, impulsive, sure, that desperate need for escape, freedom, but maybe also nostalgia for simpler times. Doesn't take long to discover they never were. It's been years since he pushed a cart. His hands are soft, the metal push-bar hard, the cart heavy, awkward, unwieldy, one of the wheels wobbles and squeaks and, *man*, he's not in shape for this shit. I mean, sure, he hits the gym, he lifts weights, he swims laps, but none of that's real work like, say, swinging a pick and a sledge and busting rocks all day in the hot sun. He's not used to the heat, he sweats like a *frog*. But at least he's outside in the fresh air and sunshine, he's back among *the people*.

Well, sorta. His old clientele has faded away, no one calls out to him in a fond, familiar voice, Yo, *Snowman!* No one even recognizes him as *The* Snowman, zany CEO of OPEN. He's just a lowercase *snowman*, humble ice cream vendor. Sometimes somebody will say, Hey, you look just like … and he'll finish, *the Snowman?* and they'll go—What? No, that other guy, not Gates, um … *you know*. It's just like starting over, relearning old routes, establishing new ones, entirely random. One day he realizes he has been inadvertently following an intermittent trail of cans and bottles fastened to tree limbs, No Parking signs, telephone poles, interspersed here and there, he begins to notice, with makeshift crosses and crude crucifixes made with strips of cloth or pieces of cardboard or wood and laid on the sidewalk or on top of a manhole cover or sometimes a dead animal, road kill flattened by the passage of traffic or just happened blood and guts. Ahead of him he spots a strange, wiry, bearded little figure with a tattered brown fedora on his head and dressed almost entirely in black or else in clothes that have gone so unchanged and so unwashed for so long that they have turned black. Curiously enough, he's pushing his own cart, albeit the shopping kind, purloined from the local HUB grocery store. He's also more or less maintaining his distance so that he and the Snowman almost seem to be working in tandem or else running some kind of odd relay except that, unlike the Snowman, he's also gesturing wildly and muttering to himself and at times he makes half-hearted attempts at running up a tree or the side of a building. It's Bum, of course, the bummest bum of all, grown older, raggedier, his disintegrating combat uniform gradually replaced by Salvation army duds, dumpster dive finds, the booby traps and IEDs he plants on his mutable perimeter gradually giving way to crosses, memorials, as his memories of the killing machine fade or maybe more accurately disintegrate into oblivion, replaced by a vague neanderthal brain awareness of loss and maybe mourning for buddies killed in combat, perhaps even for those he has killed, possibly, as well, for his broken connection to humanity with which he has minimally learned to reconnect, if only transactionally, like a feral cat.

The next time the Snowman encounters Bum he will find him with his shopping cart left untethered nearby like a trustworthy old horse while he busies himself industriously sweeping the parking lot of Kamel's convenience store with a largely straw-less broom, which doesn't matter in itself because he's not really making any attempt to sweep up cigarette butts and broken glass. He's just sweeping, sweeping, sweeping in widening and intersecting arcs, like a vodka-drunken Russian Cossack dancer at the Bolshoi, like a demented chimney sweep sweeping across the stage in an off-Broadway production of Mary Poppins or a tale of lost men (*Waiting for Goddamned?*). And, yes, he is indeed putting on a performance, for an audience of one, the proprietor of this convenience store, Kamel himself, you can see him through the front window waiting on a customer at the cash register. Kamel's also showing signs of time passing, his hair and neatly trimmed beard gone gray, lines around his eyes, weight around his middle, a slump in his shoulders, his American dream become a little more dream than reality. While Bum sweeps he repeatedly glances over his shoulder in Kamel's direction, his gleaming black little ferret eyes watching, his mossy yellow teeth clenched in a grotesque grimace that is meant to be an ingratiating smile accompanied by little canine growling sounds *grr grr*, which is about as much politesse as he can muster. He's seeking Kamel's approval, *urging* him to see how hard he's working in exchange for the five-pack of Swisher Sweets Kamel sometimes bestows upon him and which Bum smokes down to soggy stubs while relaxing in his parlor or den.

Bum has found a permanent residence. It's the concrete foundation of an old building set back about twenty feet from the DR-35 frontage road, just a short hike up the hill from the conglomerate *Las Lomas Bajas* taqueria, *Cracked* windshield repair shop, *Le Rouge et Le Noir* erotic clothing boutique, *The Oneiricist's* adult video store and the *Chiquitas Bananas* strip joint, all of which sit on the fringe of a tony, gentrified neighborhood of breeders and karens separated from this urban blight by an invisible osmotic membrane that keeps the white in and the dirt out. Bum has a caravan of shopping carts purloined from Fiesta and HUB parked in front of his castle, each loaded with treasures that only a connoisseur of the streets could appreciate, probably why nobody steals from him. *Gaaaahh! Dead squirrel!* He dances around his carts, rubbing his hands together, cackling and muttering to himself *good good good* as he inventories his possessions.

Bum is a man for all seasons. In winter, the fire he has kept burning for the last week with lumber scavenged from construction sites reduced now to a smoldering pile of embers and gray ash, the temperature hovering around zero, a light dusting of snow on the ground, he lies unmoving under a low grave-mound of carpets and blankets on a wooden pallet in a near-hibernational state, maybe gnawing on a stale loaf of artisanal bread picked out of the dumpster behind Texas French Toast Bakery, quite likely answering all of nature's calls without bothering to hit the loo, hot chocolate sludge oozing out into already caked layers of jockey, boxers and possibly even ladies underwear, hot streams of pee saturating the already foul cotton, wool and polyester of two, three, four pairs of sweat pants and trousers and offering some degree of warmth before the inevitable heat exchange, not working in his favor, leaves him lying wretched in a cold, soggy mass. One morning in the spring, which comes the very next day, that's how it works in this capricious central Texas clime, chili today, hot tamale, the sun shining, the pungent green of newly sprouted grass and weeds exploding out of alleys and empty lots, there's Bum stretched out on his pallet, shoes and socks off, toes wiggling with hobo contentment as he puffs away on a Swisher Sweet cheroot, courtesy of the charitable Kamel.

Kamel's is the nexus, one might even say the mecca, for the homeless population who work the corners of 38th and the DR-35 frontage roads. Between shifts they take breaks on the deteriorating railroad tie planter situated out front right against the sidewalk and just a few feet in from the street. Makes it convenient to haul in handouts from cars stopped for the red light or pulling in for gas. Also makes pedestrian traffic uncomfortably close, not that you see a lot of people on foot, it's a fucking wasteland, trash and broken glass everywhere, sun blasting off the pavement, temperature above one hundred, the air stinks of gasoline, car exhaust, human excrement.

There's a crowd gathered here now. It's Big Earl and the gang. The Snowman's gotten to know most of these folks by name, he's familiar with all their shticks, tics and idiosyncrasies. There's Hopalong. Guy's got a *bum* leg.

He's holding a plaster cast in his lap that he was wearing on the corner just a minute ago. Yeah, yeah, I know, bad optics. His leg *is* fucked-up, old break never healed, but he's lost so much weight out here on the street the damn cast keeps slipping off. His story changes all the time, drunken brawl, motorcycle wreck, stepped in a gopher hole, on a land mine. Sometimes he's got a crutch or a cane but mostly he hops along like Ratso Rizzo (don't call me that!).

Hopalong's sitting next to Peg Legge. That's her real name and it's almost enough to make you believe in coincidence, destiny, *something*, because she only has one leg, the other amputated at the knee, some story about hopping a freight train outside Bakersfield. There's always a story. Sometimes she wears a wooden pirate peg she fashioned on a lathe at the job-training center (no job offers though). She says *arrr* a lot, probably due less to piratical propensities and more to a chronic respiratory issue, that street life thing again. And, sure, she's got a few crow's feet and missing teeth, but she's still country girl pretty with a blond shag, clear blue eyes and a great body (minus a leg). She and Hopalong seem to have a thing going on. They make a great team. Arms flung over each other's shoulders, they hop along at a good pace.

Sitting next to Peg, Penurio Centavo, this Mexican guy who speaks zero English except *thank you* and *goodbye*, which he also uses to mean hello, kind of like *shalom* or *aloha*. Penurio's been giving the Snowman the evil eye as he approaches, seems they share some unpleasant history—maybe you remembered.

Next to Penurio, Handsome John. You'd never guess this guy actually used to be handsome, Texas photo ID in his wallet proves it. One day he appeared on the corner, his kisser black and blue as a Concord grape, eyes puffy as marshmallows, brain knocked loose in his skull, fragmented memories of some dude whaling away on his face like a punching bag *flibbita-flibbita-flibbita*. And there he was, waving at cars, throwing peace signs, making a grotesque attempt at a smile. Putting on a brave face, you might say, even though he also looked like he had tears streaming down his cheeks. His face healed into a not exactly recognizable facsimile of its former self. Homies called him Leatherface for a while but it didn't last, just too damn cruel. Now he stands on the corner, thoughtfully (pretty sure you mean *thoughtlessly*) tugging at his long, scraggly beard and throwing shaky peace signs.

Next to Handsome John, One-eyed Jack. Jack is a skinny, bashful, boyish-acting forty-year-old with thin flaxen hair, thin nose, one good eye, the other a concavity of red scar tissue over which he wears a black patch when he stands on the corner to make himself less frightening to potential donors. He's an easy-going guy, friendly, *mischievous*. One day the Snowman witnessed him sticking his fingers down Peg's exposed butt crack (okay, maybe that's another *M-word*). Peg jumped like she'd been stung by a bee, shrieked *Acckk!* And then swore *what the fuck, Jack?!* And then smacked him in the face, not once but two-three-four-five times, *hard*. Jack looked pretty damned taken aback, face red, eyes watering. He blinked several times, then slapped his knee and bent over laughing but he also just might have been crying.

And last but by no means least, Big Earl. Big Earl always has a smile and a wave for everyone. Most of the time he's wearing hospital scrubs, blue, green, magenta, depends which hospital he was discharged from.

Sometimes he's limping or his arm's in a sling or he's walking with a crutch, or, more recently, he's sitting in a wheelchair, usually with a stream of pee running out from under him into the street. Big dude, maybe a former lineman gone to ruin, big grizzly face, bushy brows, looks a little like a former Soviet premier (starts with a B). Greets drivers with the palm-downward fascist salute popular among politicians and talk show hosts *heyyyy!* (they don't know) or else, index and little fingers extended, the famous UT Jackalope ears victory sign. Big Earl acts like a celebrity, he *is* a celebrity, in his own mind, in the collective consciousness of all the hundreds and in fact thousands of motorists who see him on this corner every fucking day. So when they *don't* see him (well, maybe it takes them a day or two to notice), they think, hey, what happened to that big smiley guy. Did they lock him up? Did he die? And then he appears again two or three days or a week or even two weeks later with a new sling or cast or his leg bandaged or gauze surgically taped over his forehead. And damn, those must be good meds, he's smiling and waving and throwing his signs jubilantly, triumphantly, Benjy idiotically to all the passing cars. And while some might envy what they perceive to be an Edenic state of innocence, Big Earl's essentially a fifty-year-old, six-foot, three-inch, two hundred-fifty-pound baby, and *somebody's* gotta take care of him. (Oh, sure, I know. There are plenty of you bleeding heart types who'd say just shoot the bastard and save the rest of us some grief and tax money.)

These folks are part of a clique, a crowd, a circle, if you will (early resonances of that cycle thing?). They hang together, more or less as a family unit. It's best if you team up, somebody's got your back when you're crashed under the bridge and some punk kid or homicidal maniac wants to douse you with gasoline and light you up or he's just dying to try out the heft of this lead pipe or the edge of a machete or maybe it's the homeless psychopath bully who's imposed himself on your unit. You wake up to this strange sound and a woman whimpering and this fuck's humping your old lady, he's got a knife to her throat and you're pretty sure he'll cut her whatever you do or don't.

Maybe that's why the bums congregate here. Kamel tolerates them, watches out for them, calls the police or EMS when he sees one of them in trouble, doesn't mind if they loiter a bit inside for the air conditioning when they're buying beer and smokes. Works out for everybody. Kamel makes a little profit off the bums' business when their tips are big, when their social security and VA checks finally come in. He cuts them a break when they're short. *Allah be praised, charity is virtuous in the eyes of God.* And you know, Kamel's got something there. Because panhandling isn't just a job, it's a penance. The bums are like an esoteric holy order without the monastery walls. In return for the alms they receive, they take the burden of society's sins on their bent, broken and humbled shoulders. They're a living object lesson, a cautionary tale of where we ourselves might end up if … oh, if any of a million things. The luck of the draw, a bad business decision, drug or alcohol addiction, PTSDs, voices in their heads. All born innocent babes. Born into poverty, sickness and abuse. Born into wealth, privilege and power. Doesn't make a damn bit of difference now they're fallen into ruin. Ain't nobody prayin' for me, *ain't nobody prayin' for me.*

And man, are these folks glad to see the Snowman pushing his cart up the bunny trail, to receive his largesse, his suckerness, cuz he's always good for free *PoPoPops!*® And why not? He's got a million of 'em *ahhh, yeahhhh!* Sometimes he goes back to their camp with them, sits for a while on an upside down five-gallon paint can, the throne reserved for the guest of honor, maybe he has a cold beer with them, maybe takes a hit off a joint, old habits, etc., until everyone else dozes off in a dope and alcohol slumber and he realizes, oh shit, what are you doing, *Snowman?*

He comes back to the office sweaty, disheveled, a light buzz on. He's lost some weight pushing the cart, his clothes are a little saggy. Rumors will spread that he's in training for the upcoming Osberg 10K, that his eccentricities include extended bikram sessions, that he has a life-threatening illness. Mostly the other team members don't even notice his absence. His contributions to the board meetings have never amounted to more than ponderous, painfully extruded um …uh … yesses, noes and maybes, depending on cues he receives from Iago. True, there are those rare, in fact, legendary, *inspired* moments when he appears to be speaking from Mt. Sinai and everybody in the vicinity whips out their EyePhones® to capture a few drops of this lexical manna. He never knows himself when it's gonna strike. It's like somebody's remotely driving him, not exactly mind control, just using him as an imperfect vessel to get across a message from another dimension (granted, sometimes slightly garbled). *For we shall not be what we are now, soft no longer, all the circuits open, everything that has ever been shall be known and all that is known shall be shared by all. But first ask yourself this, what does it matter to a machine what a rose smells like?*

Otherwise, he's pretty much invisible, even when he forgets to make a pit stop in the phone booth and transition from the *Snowman* (humble street vendor, eccentric personality, Hawaiian slacker dude outfit), to, well, *the* Snowman (mild-mannered CEO, eccentric personality, trekkie outfit). The only person who notices his disappearing acts is Jimmy, the mailroom guy. Hi, *Mister* Snowman, did you just step out for a moment? And glancing at his Hawaiian shirt (orange plumeria and hummingbirds), faded green cargo shorts and huaraches, Gee whiz, Mister Snowman, are you doing a photo shoot for a new commercial?

21
Back to Business

TO FURTHER ENSURE OPEN'S unobstructed expansion, an army of lobbyists has set up a permanent encampment in Washington, which is somehow more acceptable than a homeless camp. It's like an infestation of cockroaches. They're in the elevators, the stairways, the hall closets. They're sneaking over the transoms of senators, congressmen, cabinet members. They're sitting at the bar waiting to pounce on anyone with a whiff of political clout. They contribute huge sums to political campaigns on the left, right and down the middle. In another victory for (capitalist) freedom, the Supremacist Court declares all banks, financial institutions, businesses and corporate entities to be private citizens with all the attendant rights and privileges of any (white) citizen. No one's going to tell Mrs. Bard's Bread or Ms. Victoria's Top Secrets they can't vote or that they have to sit at the back of the bus. When Mister Dour Chemical is accused of poisoning thousands of people in a developing nation that's so far off the average American's radar it might as well be on Pluto, Mister DC breaks down in court, *boo hoo hoo*, why is everyone so mean to me? *Case dismissed.* And when Ms. Victoria's Top Secrets appears before the judge (known to cop a squeeze here and there, swills beer like strawberry soda, boys will be boys, etc., gonna be up for Supremacist Court himself someday) in a foxy red satin outfit with white lace and flashes of black fishnet, the verdict is ~~onani~~ *unani*-mously decided.

Which presents the Snowman with a ~~condom~~ conundrum. (Someone is having trouble maintaining focus again.) What gender is your corporation, sir? Um, I never considered that aspect. Well, you must if you want your corporation to become a fully certified citizen with all the civil rights afforded any other (white male) citizen, including the right to own property, have sex w/o protection and pee standing up. Um, I guess male then. So that would be *Mister* OPEN? I suppose. And what is Mr. OPEN's racial preference, keeping in mind that in addition to the aforementioned entitlements, this includes the right to vote, the right to sit down at an all-white lunch counter, play golf in an all-white country club, drive, eat and breathe in public without police harassment and, most importantly, the right to a fair trial by a jury of your, need I say it, white peers. The Snowman scratches his head. According to the above criteria? I'd have to say white. Wise decision, sir.

Wise indeed. The blindingly white (Iago has been voted white by the other board members and actually seems to be turning lighter-skinned by the day) *Mister* Open, MO (*Moe*) to his close associates, is now virtually untouchable by either the long arm of the law or a myopic reading of constitutional articles and amendments. When MO receives word that the workforce at the El Paso plant has walked off the job en masse, he takes it as a personal insult. You've hurt Mister OPEN's feelings. I'll handle it, McCowum growls with an Edgar J. Hoover bulldog scowl (subliminal flash of the Director). Despite nationwide union protests, lawsuits in Federal Court (rotsa ruck) and a sympathetic letter writing campaign from a dozen mixed-age students in a one-room schoolhouse somewhere in Appalachia where coal and tobacco once were king, the plant is closed for *renovation*. It opens again six months later, staffed by an entirely new work force, largely illegal immigrants (Don't worry, President DeBoche assures his constituents, they're essentially slaves, we'll boot 'em out of the country as soon as the job's done). And by the way, these people are working for peanuts, literally. Each month they're issued a thousand pounds of raw, unshelled goobers imported directly from Nigeria in huge cargo ships that disgorge leguminous mountains onto the wharfs in Ports Galveston and Houston. They have to drive across the state, a long day's journey even *without* police harassment, after which they're given (well, they have to lease them) wheelbarrows and shovels to load up their cars, pickups and donkey carts and it's left to them to turn a profit.

To facilitate tranquil labor relations, McCowum enlists the aid of Roger Wilco, who, in short order, comes up with another nifty invention in his ~~little shop of horrors~~ R&D department, the Static Employee Aptitude Tester, a cranial-rectal monitoring device to screen job applicants' tolerance for sitting on their butts for hours on end and occasionally taking it up the ass when called upon to do so. The prospective employee wears something that looks like a spaghetti colander with a bunch of wires sticking out on his head and sits on a specially designed cushion (pretty much toilet seat-shaped) packed with chips and sensors that detect tics, twitches, changes in blood pressure and neural activity, as well as the various vapors and effusions escaping from the imperfect O-ring of the

applicant's sphincter. (It shouldn't surprise anyone that
Boone, who has never outgrown his proclivity for
adolescent pranks, insists on modified whoopee cushions
so that when an applicant sits down there's this loud
flatulent *blommmpph!* that attenuates into a gaseous
wheeeeee.) When the Snowman pops into the laboratory
for a look-see, he finds Roger wearing one of these seat
cushions around his neck like a horse collar and
mumbling abstruse and in fact *alchemical* equations that,
even to the lay ear, have very little relation to the tenets
of established science. Years of cutting-edge research are
clearly taking their toll on Roger, not to mention an ever-
evolving regimen of personally patented psychotropic
drugs, none of which has ever achieved over-the-counter
or prescription status. Nervous tics flash across his face
like sheet lightning, his eyes, nose, cheeks, chin and even
those silly little *way-hay up she rises* anchor-shaped
dimples at the corners of his mouth are tucking and
puckering, winking, blinking and knotting, he grinds his
molars, hunches his shoulders, when he speaks he's just
a tad too ebullient, sounds like he's leading into a 50s'
rock n' roll tune, yep yep yep, uh-huh, uh-huh, sha-na-na-
na, we can do that, yes sir, you betcha we can can can.

Riding the tide of profit and power, the until now
monolithic Mister OPEN quickly moves beyond the
prepared foods industry into cosmetics, followed by
investments in IT, AI, robotics, genetic engineering, the
always profitable pharmaceutical industry, and energy,
meaning, of course, the traditional coal, gas and oil. But I
thought we were trying to get away from all that, you
know—*Greta?* the *climate?* Iago, patience tried beyond
saintly, once again has to explain. It's an intermediary
step, *Snowman, before* we transition into renewables.

You can't just abandon an entire industry—think of the jobs lost! The dent in the economy! Well, gosh, when you put it like that.

The Snowman now learns that Mister OPEN has ventured into space development and exploration, and it doesn't take much for Iago to convince him that it was his inspiration. Remember when you said *Space is the place?* Um ... pretty sure I was just talking about a long-ago Sun Ra concert at Liberty Lunch but, um ... space, did you say? Like most kids when he was growing up, the Snowman was thrilled by space stuff, and now, *wow,* here he is, building his own rockets, planning colonies on Mars, *holy cow!* MO's constructing a huge spaceport down on the coast, he's bought up thousands of acres of fragile eco-systems, sand dunes, rare plant and wildlife, bird sanctuaries, saw grass, wild morning glories, sea turtles, rattlesnakes, fox, coyotes, pelicans, herons, the occasional roseate spoonbill, clandestine nudist colonies. Of course there are protests, locals all sour grapesy about the "in my backyard" thing, terrorist threats from rogue Audubon Society members.

Iago dispatches the Snowman to take care of the situation with some of his oratorical magic. At a huge OPEN-sponsored barbecue and beer festival, he gets up on stage just before Wiley Nilson plays and addresses the crowd, among whom the skeptical locals are enormously outnumbered by a bunch of mostly drunk and raucous outsiders Iago has bused in. Of course, the Snowman doesn't know that. He figures these folks are just as excited about the new spaceport as he is when he assures them they ain't got a dadburn thang to worry about. As the CEO of OPEN he ain't gonna let them dadblame bankers take away their land. That ain't the way it works in this great state. And another thang, I can promise y'all this talk about pollution ain't nothing but a red snapper (*yesss*, Larry, it *should* be *herring*, the Snowman is appealing to folks down here on the gulf—Glenda). They ain't no chance in hell one of them dadblame rockets is gonna blow up and scatter toxic doo doo and unsightly body parts everywhere. Talking to these folks in the vernacular, ain't ain't ain't, like a country boy who grew up on swimming holes and fishing poles, bob-wire fence and cattle pens, while *Grapes of Wrath* stealing the land out from under their feet. Wait, what? But before the Snowman's doubts, second thoughts and pangs of conscience can catch up with him, Iago's already grabbed him by the arm and diverted his attention to Mister OPEN's latest project as they team up with Hollywood to launch a new TV weekly *Billionaires in Space* (in the earlier versions they don't come back, each week another one takes the skybus and just sorta disappears, kinky, yes, but viewers love it).

By now Mister OPEN has become the bellwether, the benchmark, the gold standard of the nation's economy. Secretary of Finance, Donald Dukkets, is more or less relegated to the role of liaison between Mister OPEN's board of directors and the Federal Reserve. Quinienta Megawatti Dharma-Smythe, head of equity research at Phyvendeimer & CO in the Big Apple, constantly issues glowing over the top (cheerleading costume, pompoms *yeeeee*) forecasts for the future, not what you'd expect from a plumpish, bespectacled, middle-aged lady more used to appearing in a lehenga choli and dupatta. Upper management, in a constant state of euphoria as stock options continue to soar, spontaneously breaks into chorus lines, legs kicking, heads rotating in synch, million-dollar smiles as they sing, to their credit mostly in tune, *We're in the money*. Black and white security footage that looks suspiciously like a clip from *Modern Times* shows a huge metal tube running directly from the Federal mint in D.C. to underground garages on Wall Street where it gushes forth packs of brand new hundred-dollar bills that entry level employees outfitted with GPS ankle bracelets shovel into the trunks of their bosses' private vehicles.

And the biggest joke is that the biggest boss, the man sitting on top of this whole heap, is *him*, the Snowman. Thanks to that Peter Principle thing and the non-scruples of Iago, Wolf and the rest of the gang, he has become a man of wealth and means, rich beyond the wildest dreams of the richest men on the planet. He rules an international conglomerate. He has factories, franchises and outlets all over the world, most of which he knows nothing about. He has more personal wealth than all the former kings of England, France and Spain and all the emperors of Germany, Austria and Russia combined in today's currency. To give you an idea of just how much money he's got, he has a pyramid-shaped *objet d'amusement* on his desk made out of about twenty-five kilos of solid gold encrusted with rare green diamonds, its pinnacle fashioned out of the world's largest emerald, Sotheby's values it at over a billion, and the fucking thing serves no purpose at all, it's just a thing (welllll ... okay, Glenda has informed us that it was actually a gift from the Caliph of the long forgotten empire of Hudustan to the 17th century Raja of Eyesore, purportedly stolen by British adventurists and later sold to a notoriously shady dealer of antiquities, but who's keeping score?).

How little could the Snowman have imagined when he experimented with that first frozen concoction at his kitchen sink that one day billions of consumers around the globe would live for their daily *PoPoPops!*® (stock photos of people enjoying *PoPoPops!*® in front of the Eiffel Tower, ~~the Kremlin~~, the Leaning Tower of Pisa, a grass shack in Uganda, a cave in Afghanistan). President DeBoche declares *PoPoPops!*® the best ambassador America has ever had. The Snowman has been nominated for the Nobel Peace Prize. He flies to Saudi Arabia and Abu Dhabi, Istanbul and Athens, to Frankfurt, London, ~~Moscow~~, Rome, Seoul, Singapore, Shanghai, Hong Kong, Tokyo, Rio, Buenos Aires, Cape Town and Beeville, Texas. He flies everywhere but sees almost nothing of where he flies. He lives in a rarefied existence of ease of movement, of every detail arranged for him, of chauffeurs, private planes, personal secretaries, managers, chefs, dietitians, personal trainers, golf courses, ski slopes, gaming tables, fox hunts. He arrives, passes through city and country scape, wines and dines in a glass castle in the middle of the Arabian desert, onboard a billion-dollar mega-yacht on a turquoise blue sea that may be privately owned (yes, the sea). On occasion, for the top dollar audience, he gives forth with one of his pentecostal orations that echoes both New Christian and old Monarchial understandings of wealth accrued according to merit (and, well, inheritance, theft and embezzlement). And the big, dirty, not-so-secret secret in the boardroom, in the secret chambers of Wall Street and the White House, in the legendary dungeon beneath the CIA headquarters in Langley, is that most of the time this *Snowman dude*, who wields so much wealth, power and influence, doesn't have a fucking clue what's going on.

Oh sure, now and then he makes some off-hand quip that roils Wall Street. The market bounces up and down like a tennis ball when a video surfaces in which the Snowman, seen passing a joint with legendary outlaw country singer Wiley Nilson at his ranch, says through a cloud of ganja smoke, *I've been thinking of channeling all my capital into improved cat litter*, and then, ha ha, joke's on them, it turns out this stuff, when saturated with cat pee, forms a super strong building material with none of the environmental drawbacks of concrete, and once again a few smart investors make a killing. (Insider trading anyone? Me'th? *Mrrt*.) But, yeah, most of the time the Snowman stands at the helm of the good ship Mister Open in his Hawaiian Islander outfit, daiquiri, martini or the occasional strawberry ~~blunt~~ smoothie in hand, ordering *Full steam ahead!* while Iago and Wolf steer his course for him (and it's not even clear they know where this juggernaut is going). And to the public at large, to the paparazzi and the celebrity trackers, he is that golden boy everyone *thinks* they want to be.

22
There's a Party Going On

WE HEAR POUNDING TECHNO-MUSIC, ice clinking in glasses, the thalassic rise and fall of conversations, bursts of laughter, as we now soar more than half a mile above the bustling, neon bright streets of Osberg to the glass-palaced penthouse of the futuristic Burj Osberg Condominium, winner of multiple awards for innovative architectural design and green building and, as you might have guessed, home to, domicile of, that same golden boy, the **Snowman**. Tonight this is also the galactic hub of Osberg high society. **Armoani, Gauchi, Frauda, Versakes** and **St. Luxuriant, Christian D'Odor, Dianne von Secontberg, St. Trezpassé, Channel 6, Cassassini** and **LaCost** mingle and greet. Valets circulate with trays of beverages, caterers replenish buffets. **The SexPak**, the hottest non-gender band in the world, is playing live. Strobe and laser lights. Fog machines. Synthesizers make a constant *Rant Rant Rant* sound. Twenty to seventy-somethings dance frenetically. Film stars, celebrities, hi-tech movers and shakers. Beautiful young men and women on loan from spa resorts, modeling agencies, sports arenas. The great tennis star **Raquette Williams** and the great downhill skier **Lindsey Von Schneeflieger** and the great swimming champion

Sirena Seesturm prowl with leonine grace and power. Also present, members of the NNFL (New National Football League, which much more closely resembles the gladiatorial sport it was always meant to be—spiked gloves, short swords and bucklers, razor-studded helmets and foot gear) and the NNBA (ditto—only mortal combatants need apply). **Travis Blocker** (performance enhancing substances, DUIs, date rape), **Bubba Hubba Jr**. (assault, assault and battery, aggravated assault, sexual assault of domesticated farm animals), **LaShawn LaGrande** (aggravated assault, grand theft, drug dealing), **Vlad Molesçu** (murder, sexual assault, drug dealing, conspiracy to undermine foreign democracies). Columnists from **Elle, GQ** and **Vogue**, from the **New York Times, Los Angeles Times** and the **Washington Post**, from **Fuchs News, SNN** and the blogosphere, circulate in a flurry of mikes, cellphones, sound and camera techs. Super celeb-chaser **Reahlly Rollie Rollert**, himself mobbed by a horde of cannibalizing paparazzi, twitches, twitters, tweets and selfies his encounters with the gods nonstop. *And here he is now*, the star of the show, a distinguished-looking, middle-aged gentlemen with hints of gray in his dirty blond hair, a tan that suggests tennis courts and swimming pools (but not pushing an ice cream cart), a cream-colored jacket open over a Hawaiian shirt (pink plumeria and ocean sunrises). It's the Snowman, of course. Rollie is on him like a cat on a pigeon with a broken wing but the Snowman deftly extracts himself like a killdeer who's only been faking. Without fanfare, he glides through the party, surprising guests with a pat on the shoulder, a touch at the elbow, a few flattering words. Everybody wants to know who he's with, is he seeing anyone, is he really the ascetic and

possibly even celibate bachelor he's rumored to be?
Everybody wants a touch of his garment, his magic, his
virtue. **Baxter Bruiser**, quarterback of the Punxatawney
Phils, three Super Bowl rings on each hand, recently
retired from the NNFL and looking for a cushy PR gig,
fist bumps *ow!* high fives, Yo, Snowman, about that ...
but before Baxter can launch his sales pitch, the
Snowman spins away with a move that surprises even the
great captain of the gridiron, exchanges air kisses with the
Brazilian bombshell **Pitanga Sanduiche**, stunning in a
scarlet thong and black leather bustier, stops to chat with
Osberg celebrity **Sister Sunne Rae** (they seem to be
sharing a private joke, have they stayed in touch since his
long ago appearance on her show?), gives a knowing nod
to **Me'th** who's also wearing a Hawaiian shirt (catnip
plants and mice in hula skirts) and a pair of dark glasses,
he's been keeping a low profile since the move into the
new digs but tonight he's a super cool cat with all the
kitties—with and without tails. The Snowman pauses to
greet the nonogenarian dowager **Bella LaBoeuf**, herself
a caricature of social column caricatures, excesses of
lipstick, mascara and rouge, prodigious nose buttressed
on the right naris with a wart the size of a Portobello
mushroom, bouffanted (**Sally Harshrinz**) in the
iridescent red, green and blue plumage of a bantam
rooster, torso puffed up pullet-like in a feathery **Chateau
le Coq** construction, gold lamé capri pants (**Frauda**) that,
far from flattering, further flatten her flat old ass,
toothpick gams that end in fire engine red **Christian
Lowbootin** stilettos of clodhopperish dimensions. The
grandiloquent **Ms. LaBoeuf**, caught pontificating (when
is she not?) to a circle of sycophants who dare not
contradict or interrupt, is herself surprised, upstaged,

disregarded when, attended by a bee hive hum and buzz of admirers, the staggeringly beautiful Italian import **Narcisa Guardami**, queen ascendant of the big screen's new *siécle d'or,* positively blossoms in a dandelion yellow outfit in the open doorway of the Snowman's private screening room where, in the flickering mothlight, we can see the ghostly faces of guests sitting on the floor, standing against the walls, all one hundred seats packed, on the screen a scene from the **Boone Weller** classic *The Abominable Snowman of the North* and—ha, there *he* is, the *Snowman!* No, wait, it's **Boone Weller**'s favorite leading man **Billy "Plum" Bob Bengay**, rugged, weathered, leaning against the wind on an equally rugged-looking mountainside as a vulture swoops down out of the blue sky and, in a symbolic gesture that will leave cineastes guessing for years, brushes **Billy**'s cheek with its funereal black wingtip.

But is this really the misanthropic **Snowman** acting so suave and debonair in the rarefied atmosphere of the hoiest of polloi, schmoozing and oozing with the glitterati and illiterati? Would it surprise anyone who's been paying attention that despite the golden glow and the million-dollar smile, the king cool cat of the coolest show in town is asking himself that very same question, as he has for most of his life, i.e., *what the fuck are you doing here, Snowman?* The absurdity of the situation grows. Maybe it's just **Boone** again—of course it's **Boone**, who can never resist another round of juvenile hijinks. Cannonades of champagne corks fly back and forth. Partygoers toss handfuls of pink Peruvian flake in each other's faces like Holi powder. Clouds of two-thousand-dollar-an-ounce ganja smoke drift overhead like **Michelin Man** dirigibles. A panoply of colored pills appears. Here and there people seem to be hovering several inches off the floor. Others stagger around with eyes fixed and arms outstretched like zombies. Still others zoom through the crowd, blinking and chattering like manic ventriloquists' dummies. The party continues outside. Someone jumps fully clothed into the boomerang-shaped infinity pool, seemingly disappearing into the abyss, and, like lemmings (reputedly), others plunge in after them. Women surface from the chlorinated depths with hundred-thousand-dollar cocktail dresses clinging to their bodies like seaweed. Clothes begin to come off, an orgy seems to be in the making. All captured on camera, of course, to appear later in social media, in underground cinema, porn films and finally the Federal courthouse, blackmail, libel, extortion. Curiously, although all present will testify to (or deny) their own personal and intimate conversations, *bon mots*, air kisses that promised more than a kiss, *guaranteed* job offerings and even full-blown (*ouch*) sexual encounters, not to mention the prevalence of EyePhones® and discreet bodycams, he, the **Snowman**, will appear in none of these mediums or venues, neither Ethernet nor web, celluloid, tabloid nor the marbled halls of jurisprudence. Indeed, there is zero photographic or electronic evidence of his presence at his own party. However, much later technology will reveal a shimmering hologrammatic image slipping through the crowd and occasionally the startled faces of those it has come in physical contact with. Some cineastes have suggested that the liminal character **Oscar** may have inadvertently wandered onto the set. Others that the **Snowman** has picked up a few tips on the art of invisibility, perhaps while browsing an obscure text at Half-Pence Books.

* * *

So, Annabellum, I see you've decided to include Ralph Ellison's *The Invisible Man* in your bibliography. Interesting choice. The title alone would seem to lend itself to the task at hand. Would you care to comment on that, Annabellum? For example, what methodology do you envision employing to explore this topic?

So, I thought maybe I could, like, do *illustrations?* (*Huh?*)

Like, you know, with *crayons?*

I see, crayons (*are you fucking serious?*). You do understand that might raise some questions with the committee regarding appropriateness?

So, like, I totally *agree?* Like black and white might be, like, you know, an *issue?*

Well, yes, in simple terms (*moron*).

I mean, like, you can't even see the white crayon on *paper?* And then the black gets, like, all *smudgy?*

Well, Annabellum (*Dumb*bellum), I see we have a lot of work to do.

Like, I know, *right?* My mom said she could, like, you know, schedule something with you, like, *next week?*

Your *mother?* Schedule something with *me?* (*What the fuck?*)

Yeah, you know, so you and Mom can, like, share what I'm going to *do?* You know, like, before I take *ownership?*

(*Are you out of your fucking mind?*)

But maybe it'll have to be, like, the week after *that?* Like, I think my grandpa might die or *something?*

Didn't you tell me your grandpa died at the beginning of the semester, Annabellum? (*Lying little bitch.*)

OMG! Like, I totally *forgot?* It was, like, a *miracle?* Like, he made a full *recovery?* But then he, like, had a *relapse?* So now he might, like, die *again?*

Jesus fucking Christ, and you said she's a graduate student?

What else would you expect from this fucking *Jugend Warenlager?*

* * *

23
What Goes Around Comes Around

WEALTH AND POWER SEEK EACH OTHER'S COMPANY. As much as these transactional relationships rub the Snowman the wrong way, at Iago's insistence he rubs elbows with people possessed of blimpish egos and Scrooge McDuck bank vaults of disposable cash. They don't wake up in the morning and ask, how am I going to pay the rent, buy food for my children and find another job before I get evicted? They wake up and ask themselves, how can I spend more money? Senator Warren Bucks, with whom Iago has maintained non-haberdashery old-school ties, inquires if the Snowman's *people* can come up with some kind of *tropical thing* for his daughter Ashleigh's twelfth birthday party. Nothing too fancy, maybe five mil? For you, sir? Not a problem. And that's how things work.

The Snowman, savoring a rare sense of empowerment, immediately puts R&D on it and once again Roger Wilco, more or less even-keeled at the moment (Roger has successfully completed a stint in rehab—"leave of absence to attend to personal matters" in the professional jargon, in the blue collar it's "You're fired!"), and his crew come through and this thing's fucking amazing. Young Ashleigh and her little friends, who, thanks to GMOs, hormones, heavy metals and industrial pollutants in the food chain, as well as taking ownership of their bodies via the current social media template, dress, look and act pretty much like what you'd expect from thirty-year-old pole dancers, grab hold of a pull-ring the size of a tractor tire while Senator Bucks counts off, oddly in the voice of Lawrence Welk, A-one, anna-two, anna-*three* and—*POP!* To preteen screams of delight, a tropical paradise blossoms around the back yard pool. Pink flamingos, parrots, palm trees, orchids and plumeria in iridescent pinks, yellows, reds and greens. Even better, this stuff's all edible, indeed, absolutely delish, brain-numbingly cold, tangy and above all *sweet*, and in the time it takes to say *Gee whiz, Mister Wizard* the whole party's bright-eyed and buzzing. Suddenly those old mainstays, pin the tail on the donkey, spin the bottle and blind man's bluff (buff?) are a heckuva lot *funner* than anyone remembers, including all the adults present who are helicopterally hovering considerably higher than usual.

And yes, there is that suggestion again of something not quite licit about this variation on the *PoPoPop!*®, but not to worry, the new drug czar's already on it. Oksi Constantine, Marvin Morfein's successor. He appears on TV in the latest iteration of the drug czar uniform, in this case a tribute to his Russian and Greek heritage, voluminous ermine robes open over a mirror and jewel-studded, embroidered brocade vest, on his head a Kremlin-domed gold crown encrusted with rubies and emeralds, for added gravitas, an ivory and gold scepter upon which Mr. Constantine is often seen leaning the full weight of his office (after, one suspects, substantial libations). His face glowing like a happy rainbow, the

Czar reassures the public that this new OPEN Industries product is perfectly clean fun. Next thing you know, the whole world (or at least that part of the planet that can afford it) has gotta have a Tropical Surprise. For the next six months that's all you hear. *Tropical Surprise! Tropical Surprise!* And man, doesn't that sweet, tangy, ice-cold treat beat the heat. Wait, what? There, now you've said it. No, not *meat*, Junior! *Beat the heat.* I mean, yeah, sure, who didn't enjoy those lazy, hazy summer days when the fish were jumpin' and the cotton high, but frankly, my dear, it's too damn hot. And just like that people (well, people of wealth and means) start to muse to themselves and then aloud. Wouldn't it be wonderful to go skiing in Aspen? Snowboarding in Vail? Trekking in the Alps? Remember when we used to have a *real* winter? And, who knows, maybe that's how you go from wholesome, family ice cream social to the big freeze?

It starts out innocently enough (as it always does). Somebody wants a winterscape for Christmas. *You* know, *Snowman*, like in the *good old days*. And once again Roger Wilco's can-do attitude (amazing what the right meds *can* do, is it not, Oksi?) proves true. He and his R&D crew produce the prototypical *Yuletide Special*. You pull the tab and *popopopopoPop!* It's like a string of Chinese firecrackers. It's like opening all the tabs at once on an IED advent calendar. It's like a Hallmark Christmas card in stunning 3D with ambient meteorological effects. Through the gauzy lens of nostalgia (thanks to Cash Dullard and his crew in Marketing, in tandem with the folks at *GrowNuts®*) we see snowmen, bobsleds, fireplaces, Christmas trees, candy canes, chestnuts roasting over an open fire, Jack Frost nipping at your nose, steaming mugs of eggnog, fluffy white snowflakes, and, yes, it's all edible and absolutely delish. Everybody and his grandma (Good God, can't we do something about the old bitch. Oh, all right. It *is* Christmas.) agrees it's like *eating* Christmas. The *Yuletide Special* quickly proves to be a great success, even among non-Christian faiths. Everywhere you go you hear friendly greetings from all religious persuasions. *Merry Christmas! Happy Hannuka! Ramadan Mubarak!* (One of the rare occasions Ramadan occurs in winter, indeed, begins on Christmas day.) Pretty soon everybody's gotta have a damn Yuletide Special. But this is no passing fad, no boxing day, take down the tree and the lights and thank goodness, that's over for another year. It's like a collective nostalgia for something distant and mythical (and also non-existent), a time of innocence and wonder, miracles and magic. (Skeptics in the crowd liken it to a heroin addict who starts using again, a taste is never enough.)

Meanwhile, the wheels have been humming like crazy over in R&D. With a great deal of fanfare, Mister OPEN begins to produce a cheaper *Christmas Tinsel Pop* for the common man (oops, shouldn't have said that ... um, blue collar? working class? sorta middle class? anybody out there?) Sure, it's not Rockefeller Center. It's a modest, relatively affordable little living room display, but it's still beautiful and yummy ... *so let it snow, let it snow, let it snow, and enjoy the winter wonderland in the cozy comfort of your own home.*

Of simultaneous note, in some kind of demographic equation economists can probably explain (or sociologists or psychologists or *somebody* who's good at 'splainin' these kinds of things), *Christmas Tinsel Pops* are *popping* up even among the impoverished classes.

Families living on a shoestring (and it's already been knotted together a bunch of times) spend their last pennies to buy a *Tinsel Pop*. The hell with groceries, diapers for the baby, electricity, for God's sake, they've *gotta* have this damn *Christmas Tinsel Pop*. (Climatologists blame the rapid spread of these winterscapes—but *we* didn't say it was poor peoples' fault—for changes in the atmosphere. NOAA reports the mean air temperature across the United States has dropped two degrees in the last month.)

By now the whole country's clamoring for the snow show. Put Christmas back in Christ! We want trees, ornaments, lights! We want frosty wassailing and Christmas caroling nights! Give us sugar plum fairies and cranberries (but, oof, hold the goose!), candy canes, holly wreaths and stockings hung over the fireplace with care! And presents under the tree, lots and lots of presents we wanta see, in Christmas wrap and FedEx packages, in crimson bows and mistletoe! And most of all, we wanta buy. We wanta buy buy buy. *Things*. So turn down the thermostat and *let it snow, let it snow, let it snow*. Everywhere the Snowman goes he hears Christmas carols. *Gangs* of carolers in Victorian garments have begun going door to door and singing or chanting or more accurately demanding, *Put Christmas Back in Christ!* And it is the wise homeowner, indeed, who assumes these folks are armed.

For once the Snowman finds himself in agreement with Reverend Fallible and Senator Snoops, both, as always, behind the times. I have fervently prayed on this matter and I don't see God's will at work here. Like any preacher worth his pillar of salt, the good reverend will change his tune when a midnight epiphany visited upon him by a host of angels—Michael, Gabriel, Raphael, Uriel, basically the whole gang, oh, yeah, and Moishe, his financial advisor—reveals to him the new truth, Christmas *is* Christ, the Eucharist, the wafer and wine updated for modern times. Senator Snoops, still reeling from the Operation Whiteout debacle of nearly two decades ago (in his home state he's thought of as a hero of the people—figures), adds his two cents. We must resist this here reackshunary temptation because reactin' to sumthin' we don't unnerstan' is lak tryin' to make a pillow out of a polecat or some such thang (there's actually some truth to that, and by the way, Senator Snoops, too, will see the error of his ways in time for the next election). But who the heck's going to listen to these naysayers? Bunch of lunatics, that's what they are. Besides, they've all been forgetting something very important. The Illegal Immigrant Issue!

The grand old man of the airwaves Uncle Bob reminds us in his gruff, somber, concerned fellow citizen voice, speaking, as it always seems, from the pulpit, the mount, ex cathedra, ex nihilo, the ineffable, unnamable (get outa here, Sam). A huge new wave of illegals has swept across the border. But these aren't the hardened criminals, the rapists, murderers and drug dealers President DeBoche has warned us against. They're kids, thousands of them, kindergartners, pre-teens, adolescents. Babies in soiled diapers crawl across the drought-desiccated Rio Bravo on their chubby wubby widdle hands and kneesies, or, where water still remains, they clump together like chains of fire ants and work their way across in rotation. In some cases parents launch their children across the river to awaiting "catchers" with makeshift catapults, which, unfortunately, does lead to some hard landings with fairly graphic visual and sound effects not entirely unlike that of fully loaded diapers dropped from a ten-story building. Eight, nine, ten-year-old girls and boys hang off the sides of rumbling freight trains, pack themselves layer upon layer into suffocating secret compartments of semi-trailers, clutching in their fists scraps of paper on which is scribbled a phone number or an address in a strange-sounding city in a strange-sounding state in another dimension on the far side of a black hole somewhere in that vast galactic place called *El Norte* which these *children* somehow must reach on their own. Young pilgrims, pioneers, cast into the wilderness by desperate weeping madres and steely-eyed padres for whom every waking minute and even every minute of sleep means grinding, unrelenting poverty, hunger, exhaustion and fear. Heartsick mommies and daddies no different than your own (well ... sorta) who have deprived themselves of everything but the barest of bare necessities, begged and borrowed from relatives, complete strangers, *starved* themselves, even sold their *fucking* bodies (no fucking pun intended), to scrape together the three or four thousand dollars—a fortune! more than they can ever hope to earn in their lifetime!—to send their kids out of this seething hellhole of poverty and violence where they face murder, torture, sex abuse and extortion on a daily basis, where they are forced into gangs, prostitution, drug dealing, where the drug cartels, paramilitaries and insurgents are no better and no worse than the corrupt police, military, government. Their country, their land, their social order devastated by decades of brutal, ugly wars fomented by *you know who* (lalala). And then when they finally do manage to arrive here in the land of the free they find—

salvation? Freedom from hunger, want, fear? Ixnay, Ose-
Jey. Men in uniforms tear them from the arms of their
parents, from their siblings and traveling companions and
Lock Them Up! in vast tent and razor wire encampments
in the searing hot desert like plucky little foreign
legionnaires on their road to a lifetime of foreign postings
in inhospitable climes. For added measure they all have
chips implanted in their brains, micro on/off switches,
any time they even remotely consider a criminal act or
even a complaint about the living(?) conditions, they hear
a stinging rebuke, *Bad dog!* accompanied by a sudden
blinding jolt to the old cerebellum, *Yeoowwwwooooo!*
Oh, but please, haven't we had enough of this bleeding
heart crap? (Really, who let that guy in here?)

This is when Iago (who has become so white he's
almost translucent) introduces the Snowman to a couple
of men in dark blue suits. Suit one, who has what appears
to be a dueling scar running from just below his left ear
to the corner of his mouth, gets right down to business.
The government is undertaking a top-secret defense
initiative. You are in a unique position to help us, Mister
… um … *Snowman?*

So basically you want to weaponize ice cream?

And dang if that crafty rascal Roger Wilco hasn't
come up with a new *PoPoPop!*® formula that recognizes
pigmentation and racial characteristics. Anyone who isn't
your basic Anglo Saxon white guy or gal (with a genetic
profile to prove it) takes a bite out of the new and
improved *AmeriPop!*® and, man, talk about brain freeze.
Everything, arms, legs, head, torso, the whole man, so to
speak (or woman) (or child), frozen solid on the spot. All
Customs has to do is drive around town and load 'em up
like cordwood on flatbed semis and haul 'em down to the

coast where they're deported in refrigerated cargo containers. And, yeah, there are some disgruntled African Americans, and Native Americans, and Kānaka Maoli Hawaiians (yes, they are also *Americans*), as well as Puertorriqueños (so are they, even if you call them Boricuas), and Guamanians (or *Chamorros* if you will), as well as your run-of-the-mill U.S. citizens of Hispanic descent, especially when they thaw out in an Inuit village in the Arctic circle (Rick gives them a helping hand navigating the place while on a nostalgic return visit, only thing is, he talks their ear off, Did I tell you how many pounds of pressure per square inch the individual knob in a three-inch knobby tire on a mountain bike is designed to withstand ... ?) or on a mountaintop in Peru (Rick again—detour on a return trip to Patagonia ... And the pressure is even greater at altitudes above the prescribed level for safe ...) or even a former Soviet Bloc country that looks like it's being sucked back into Mother Russia's buxom bosom ... but who's going listen to these losers? Besides, there's absolutely no reason to believe these blatantly racist and, who knows, possibly (probably?) unconstitutional acts are going to have any repercussions, is there? No, of course not. None at all.

There's a period of weeks, maybe a month, when a hazy pall hangs over the city, everything smells of smoke, the sky looks like it's swarming with gnats, black soot accumulates on window sills, rooftops, cars. It's like living in a roaring 24/7 mill town in the industrial northeast up until about midway through the last century. The official explanation is slash and burn agriculture in Mexico. The *indígenas* have practiced this method of clearing their fields and revitalizing the soil since ancient times. Effective, but not environmentally sound.

Especially bad for asthmatics and others with respiratory ailments. Clouds of smoke, dust and ash, as well as fungal spores and bacteria from Mexico and Central America travel as far north as Texas and other Gulf Coast states, sometimes blotting out hundreds of square miles of sky. And like it or not everybody down on the ground is breathing this shit. Yeah, but there's something different about this smoke, isn't there? Everyone senses it, a dark underbelly to the usual spate of climate disasters. Once again, the perennial, super-millennial Uncle Bob is the first to fill us in on the situation.

Good evening, folks. Well, there's been another flare-up south of the border down ol' Mexico way. In his somber but avuncular Uncle Bob voice, Uncle Bob informs us that militants have blown up a waste treatment plant in the colonial city of Guanopotto, a popular tourist and expat destination. Lisbeta Limón-Irituribe is live on the scene. Well, Bob, details aren't clear but something certainly hit the fan. There's *stuff* everywhere. General Buffy Wellington, commander of the Tri-Delta Force (Ninja Sorority Girls?), has briefed the president, who is having one of his less than adult moments. (Ga ga goo goo? *Goo.*) In a nutshell, the fires are raging and it's getting hot! Uncle Bob signs off with a time-honored reminder we haven't heard in quite a while. *An informed populace is a warm populace. Stay informed, stay warm.*

It doesn't take long before the hot winds of revolt are felt in *El Norte*. Unrest on the border, attacks on tourists, disruptions in supply chain orders. The public wants somebody to *do something*. The Party of Unabashed Fascist Fornicators is demanding increased military spending (of course they are). The calls for snow grow louder. Protestors gather outside the Federal Building.

Ho! Ho! Ho! Let it snow! Old-timers in the audience will catch the double-entendred reference to Santa Claus and the equally venerable former leader of North Viet Nam. Any perceived resemblance between Ho Chi Minh and Mr. Claus, however, is myopic at best. Is it any wonder, then, that the Snowman buries his face in his hands and moans a mournful Mister Bill *oh nooo*, because, yes, Virginia, he has seen this movie before. And this is what he sees:

He sees towering walls of orange flame roaring over towns, villages and vast stretches of agricultural land. He sees mountains of black smoke rising into the sky like the ashes of a thousand years of funeral pyres along the Ganges. He sees human bodies hanging from bridges like marionettes. He sees half-buried corpses sticking out of the ground like zombies rising from the grave. He sees a chamber of horrors where human beings are slaughtered like cattle with axes, sledgehammers, chainsaws. He sees severed heads stacked like coconuts, arms and legs piled like cordwood, sloshing wine vats of blood. This is Guernica and Goya, Bosch and Brueghel. But these are not photographs from *Smithsonion* or *Time*, not from *Life*, *Look* or some other venerable magazine extant or faded into the past. They are not fragments of dreams or nightmares—*cauchemar!* They are memories, his, that he has tried very hard not to remember but now the dam has broken and he's being swept away in a flood of horrors in a sea of blood in which he flails about grasping for a life preserver, a handhold, *something*.

Over the years he has seen the rare magazine article or five-second news clip about Subcomandante María on SNN or FUCHS News, bracketed by tourist brochures, images of turquoise blue waters lapping at white sandy beaches, buff, bikinied and Speedoed models snorkeling among schools of colored fish. Foreign journalists bring back apocryphal tales of jungle meetings with the near mythical Subcomandante María and her fellow guerilla leader Xuan Carlode Astraya that cause him momentary cardio-pulomonary contractions. The narrative has changed several times. Maria has been killed, tortured to death in a secret prison hellhole. She has died from disease, old war wounds. She's hiding in the mountains with her diminishing band of guerillas, disappeared into irrelevance, at best an asterisk. The Mexican government has done everything it can to discredit her, interviewed people who claimed to be aunts, uncles, ex-neighbors, former teachers, students. They say they have her entire biography, upper class background, ex-college professor, international law, economic theory. Which, if true, means what? That the purported truths she told him were lies? That he was even more deluded than he thought?

24
One Small Issue

ONE SMALL ISSUE. Everybody wants a return to the snow show (well, that's what they say now but keep in mind Brexit), only thing is, where's all this snow gonna come from? It's one thing to create fantastic bestiaries and Dr. Zhivago ice palaces and even bring in previously owned snowmaking machines from Sochi that cover entire mountainsides with piles of this soft slop that quickly melts away into milky runoff. It's another thing altogether to turn an entire city into a winter wonderland. And another thing still to bury a whole nation in snow. For that you'd need something like—and the bells of St. Peter's clang and bang in the Snowman's head—*Icine!* But Icine's gone and good riddance, right? I mean, that's not something we really want to get into again, right? The whole snow and ice thing, I mean, *right?*

He's been more or less been thinking aloud at the latest board meeting when he begins to notice the frowns, the doubtful and even baleful glances. Natasha Bolsavitch is shooting *hatchets* at him. Eunace Guppy's calumny is audible to more than just the dyspeptic-looking Dromedary into whose ear she has been whispering while his big mopey head with its unruly Alfalfa feathers sticking up in back nods in accordance. McCowum's glowering bulldog countenance suggests ruminations of CEOcide. Gastreaux's eyes are emitting the frozen halibut death-ray that the Snowman well remembers from their ten-year Gastromance. Iago's and Wolf Bärenhaut's heads are practically conjoined in collusion.

But wait, Roger Wilco has taken the ball and he's running with it, he's on the fifty, the forty, the thirty. Ohhh, too bad, the refs call him for illegal use of performance enhancing substances, fifteen-yard penalty. But hold the presses! The initial ruling is overturned. The DEA hasn't made a determination in the case. Another boost of rocket fuel and Roger's back on his feet, he's at the twenty, the ten, he's—touchdown! It has occurred to me that the secret in-*greeed*-ient in *PoPoPops!*® is very close to the mo-*lekk*-yu-ler compo-*zisssh*-un of Icine and with a few modifications—*whoooo knooows?*

Suddenly the room's abuzz. Eunace Guppy, the Dromedary and Natasha Bolsavitch are immediately on board (there's a brief and disturbing image of the three of them lined up on a surfboard in ill-fitting swimwear that just as quickly disappears—some greenhorn in marketing's gonna get a spankie for that). The brainstorming's so hot and heavy lightning flashes and thunder explodes over their heads and a miniaturized cumulonimbus cloud spontaneously drenches the room in a warm tropical deluge but everyone continues laughing and yakking like a bunch of kids at a pool party. And they're not just talking about starting up those clanking, banging, stinky old ice factories again. This time the snow show's going high tech, low profile. Cash Dullard's already pulling up some preliminary graphics on the screen and this new concept looks great! It's like a futuristic space station on Mars, a brilliant white ellipsoidal shape, like a giant hard-boiled egg lying on its side, with bright rainbow splashes of color on its discharge vents, which, children in mind, are designed to look like stylized rocket fins. There's even a child-friendly playscape feature. No more NIMBYs. The newly dubbed YIMBYs will be positively clamoring for ice plants.

To increase the concept's palatability to the public, Dullard proposes that this new snowmaking ingredient be called *Nicine,* short for *New Icine,* but, hey, you just know everybody's thinking *nice,* right? And not only *that!* Natasha Bolsavitch snarls. With this new *High Intensity Dispersive Element* that Roger has proposed—approving nods all around, minus the Snowman's, which you can be sure doesn't go unnoticed—we'll no longer need to send out crews of overpaid(?!) *troglodytes* in fleets of high maintenance SnowBiles (all eyes on the Snowman again, brows wrinkling, noses twitching with a mix of pity and disgust). We'll save *billions!* Ms. Bolsavitch bites the word out of the air as if it were a piece of raw meat. Hungry lupine eyes of the steppes narrow into cunning slits. And you know where those *savings* go, right? Iago certainly does. An open-ended contract with the government is a *fucking* gold mine! he chimes in with unusual exuberance. Practically *zero* accountability! This technology has the potential to carry civilization forward into a *modern* age. Wolf, as always, understated.

A phantasmal exhalation of ether, barely measurable on the paranormal activity gauge, enters the Snowman's nostrils and travels to his brain *Snowmannnn.* But this is going backward! he squawks. No, *Snowman,* Iago corrects him. It's future-thinking retrotech. *Huh?* We're taking time-honored traditions and carrying them forward into the next iteration. B-b-but we'll destroy everything! Undo all the good we've done! the Snowman sputters. Oh pish, think of the profit. Iago, dismissive. And from there it's a total pile-on, everybody's clamoring to be heard, each new volley of suggestions like a pile driver banging the Snowman's more or less ovoid head into a square hole as he sinks deeper into his chair.

The matter's decided. The board overrides all his objections. Is this outright mutiny? A coup? After the meeting he confronts Iago. But why? Iago squints at him as if he's talking to a microbe on Mars. Because it's what the *people* want, Snowman. It's what we *all* want. It's true. Talk show hosts, news commentators, politicians—that's all they talk about now, snow, snow, snow. And the voices of a new movement grow louder. Put Christmas Back In Christ! Let It Snow!

And, sure, you might ask why the Snowman doesn't just quit if this is such a challenge to his integrity. Resign his position as CEO, sell off his stocks, give all his fortune to charity, go live in a cave in the desert and survive on a diet of rattlesnakes and scorpions? But it's not so easy as that, is it? It's like a runaway train he can't get off, like he's Casey Jones at the throttle of the old 97 and he's so high on cocaine he just can't stop himself, he's gonna make this goddamn boiler blow or he's going over the side of the goddamn mountain trying and he's taking the whole goddamn trainload of passengers with him and for some goddamn and utterly unfathomable reason everybody (and his fucking grannie) thinks that's a good thing. Over and over he hears the same refrain. Your fortune is our fortune, Snowman. You're doing it for the rest of us, Snowman. OPEN's success is a success for everyone, Snowman. It shouldn't surprise anyone that the principal recipients of this corporate largesse (but let's not talk about welfare) are top level management and majority shareholders. Oh, but it's not just about *us*, Snowman. Think of the *beneficial* work we do. Ah, that word again. Iago is referring, of course, to Mister OPEN's recently launched Schneeland Foundation (Americans pronounce it like an involuntary nasal exhalation *Snee!*), a nonprofit philanthropic organization that supports ~~white~~ like-minded institutions around the globe with grants, trusts and endowments dedicated to fighting poverty and disease, improving maternal and infant healthcare, providing clean water and assisting in agrarian reform, all noble and worthwhile causes, nobody would argue with that, right?

In the spirit of giving (and forgiveness), Mister OPEN even makes a generous donation to the scripture-quoting Reverend K. James Fallible's Church of Jesus Christ Warrior-Redeemer. And yes, the Reverend has heard the message, he's changed his tune, he's all for the snow show now. *Put Christmas back in Christ!* Which is why we next see the Snowman storming through the offices of Mister OPEN, knocking over filing cabinets, water coolers, clutching in his white-knuckled fist a crumpled printout corroborating this "gift" and shouting, You're giving our money to the fucking church?! This is a fucking travesty! There will be blood! Terrified team members shelter in their work spaces, calculating their chances of making it to the safe room. Security is called in but they hesitate to take action because after all he *is* the CEO. Iago finally corrals the Snowman in a break area, where he has just smashed a coconut cream pie against a TV screen with Reverend Fallible's image on it, and guides him back to his office with a firm grip on his elbow and a lesson in realpolitik. Look, *Snowman*, we don't donate exclusively to Fallible's *racket* (and, yes, he said that). We donate to all major religious institutions including cults and covens. The religious base can make or break you, Snowman. Whether you're rocking in the bosom of Abraham—*my* people—or trampling out the grapes of wrath—*you* guys. At which the Snowman again buries his face in his hands and moans, Oh God, I don't wanta know about any of this.

He can't wait to get out of the office, out of the OPEN Building and push his cart, push away all these negative thoughts and the reality of what he's involved in by burning up hundreds and possibly thousands of calories a day in this futile pantomime of being a *working man*, futile because of course there is no escape from the screeching reel to reel monologue looping through his brain. *What the fuck are you doing, Snowman? You promised, you said you were never going to let yourself get stuck again and then you did, and you're not even a little shit, you're the big kahuna, the man in charge, your name's on the check even if you don't know what the fuck you're paying for. You've got to find a way off this merry-go-round, Snowman.* Which, roundaboutly, does bring us back to *that* word, *cycle*. Vico, of course (or rather of *corso*). Everything is cyclical, war and peace, birth and death, love and hate, slave and master. The same shit happens over and over throughout history. Just change the names, fashions, celebrity faces. It's like it's programmed this way, *destined*. Doesn't matter who plays the lead in this production, it'll still be played, indeed, must be played, acted out, a vacuum that has to be filled. Which, in *theory* at least, absolves the Snowman of culpability, reassures him that he isn't personally responsible, that he's not a prime mover, just an actor in the role he's been miscast in. Entrepreneur, Magnate, Mogul, Tycoon, Captain of Industry, *Capitalist Pig.* Excuse me, sir, did you just call me a *pig?* No, I didn't but you are a bit of a prig, aren't you, *arsewipe?* Which he didn't say, not out loud anyway, he *thinks*, because he is kind of muttering to himself and *accidentally* banging his cart into people and, yeah, grimacing like he's got fire ants in his britches. And then, just as he really is about to go off the deep end, men in white coats, strait jackets, *sedated*, for god's sake, somebody hits the pause button and the noise in his head, the cacophony, the screeching gears and jammed cogs—it all stops.

25
Oscar

STOPS AND STARTS AGAIN in a different realm, sphere, dimension when he hears—yes, it is, the sound of music, a flute of some sort. He doesn't recognize the piece and yet it sounds achingly familiar or rather pieces of the piece sound familiar because even if he wouldn't be able to name the individual composers it is indeed Mozart, but also Bach, Brahms, Beethoven, oh yeah, and Coltrane, Cherry, Rahsaan Roland Kirk, as well as ancient wind and string instruments from Africa, South America, from the Middle East and Asia, not to mention Laplanders, Incas, Orcas, it's the New Cetacean Orcastra, all woven together into a plait of sound but rolled up, cylindrical, a tubular green sheath, a shoot of bamboo becoming, a column of air blown through a hollow reed, in this case a shakuhachi, he knows it's a shakuhachi because (subliminal flash of a Japanese ideograph printed in black ink on a square of hand-beaten papyrus) Judith had in her possession a flute of this very kind, played it sometimes, mostly when he wasn't around, he surmised, because he often found it in different locations, sitting on the kitchen table, the couch, the windowsill, the mouthpiece sometimes still damp from her breath, the fingerholes gleaming from her touch, from the secretion of natural oils in her skin (so, alien-like but still human?), but, yes, heard it enough that he knows what it's supposed to sound like and this is it exactly. It's not a recognizable melody, he's not even sure you'd call it a melody. It's plaintive, melancholy, sometimes it shrieks and moans or laughs manically, mockingly, like a sea gull *ha! ha! ha!* For those who understand this tonal language it tells the story of a very strange enchanted boy who has wandered the world since the beginning of time, who is himself as old as time, and yet he remains perpetually a youth on the cusp of manhood. It is a melody of longing and loneliness, of suffering, hunger, of unbearable heat in summer, cold in winter, wrenching, debilitating illnesses that left him writhing in his bed of weeds, alternately soaked with sweat or shivering with body-wracking chills, and no doctors or medicine or even a mother's loving arms to heal and hold him. His face, his features are made of shadow, of cloud, of lunar light and darkness. His arms, legs, torso are like the bamboo reed, long and thin, but there is a translucence to them like that strange plant called ghost or Indian pipe that gives away to the whole world his utter vulnerability, his helplessness in the face of adversity, of anyone and that means many ones who would harm, would hurt, would *wound* him grievously for the pleasure and the sport, like shooting a fawn or a dove or even more perversely, a rare and exotic bird on the verge of extinction. Even to those who see him, who actually *see* see him, because that is no mean feat, to see him, this transubstantial being, he's hardly there at all, a wisp, a whim, a liminal thing, until his thin reed betrays him, announces his presence, calls eyettention to him. Where's that music coming from, Helen? Hear it? I don't see anything, George. It must be a trick. And the greater irony is he doesn't really know how to play, can't read music, he simply pulls this stuff out of the airwaves, the *matrix*, incorporates pieces of whatever he hears, has heard in childhood, infancy, in the—sure, why not, Sam?—womb. When he places those long spidery digits on the fingerholes of his shakuhachi he looks like he should be a concert pianist, indeed he might have been if he'd had lessons as a child, if he'd stayed in any school long enough for a teacher to discover his talent. One time someone almost did, in elementary school.

He was alone in the cafeteria-gymnasium-auditorium waiting for his father to pick him up. There was an upright piano on the small wooden stage. Someone had left the lid open. Curious, he put his fingers on the shiny black and white keys and pressed lightly, not so much tentatively but as if his fingertips were sensitizing themselves to the potentiality latent in these keys, the statue within the block of stone and the angle and degree to which the hammer must strike and the organization of those strikes into patterns that caused magical sounds to come out and they *were* magical. *Miss* Grimerge, fifth grade, tough lady with a tough reputation but a heart of gold, at her desk grading spelling quizzes, heard, didn't quite hear at first, maybe *felt* the vibrations in the air that carried the rain-soft tinkle of notes, her thoughts as always on the ever-receding imminence of her retirement and the simultaneous accrual of health issues, her hip and her heart and now this kidney thing, until the sound of this distant music finally penetrated her preoccupied brain resulting in the consequent but unconscious softening of the rigid geometry of her face into the betrayal of a smile. That's beautiful, she said to herself, is it Mozart? But *that* sounds like Tchaikovsky, and that—maybe something *oriental?* And is that *Coltrane?* I wonder who could be playing? And decided to investigate. But by the time she got up from her chair and unlocked and unbolted the bulletproof door, and checked the .380 semi-automatic on her good hip—clip in? safety off? okay, let's move out— the music had stopped and rather than limp all the way down the hall to the cafeteria, she locked and bolted the door again, with some difficulty sat back down at her desk, who's next? Oh Lord, *Raymond* ... and so she didn't see the boy's father—wait, is that Hanktheredneckasshole? Hard to tell. It *looked* like Hank. What were his kids' names?—storm into the auditorium-gymnasium-cafeteria snarling, *Oscar, what the fuck you doin' with that nonsense?* and grab his son, begotten of his own loins, *flesh of my flesh*, precious in the eyes of God, by his thin little arm and yank him up from the piano stool so hard the bruises would remain for two weeks. Even the story of how he obtained this flute is nebulous, apocryphal at best. He woke up one morning in his bedroll in the patch of woods he shared with a couple of other bums (you say *unhoused*, I say *potahto*), in the public park near the university, and he found it lying on the ground next to him.

But who?

T'was the *Magician*, one of the bums says, an old-timer, old, sure, but he's still got a fire in his eyes, goes by *Doc*.

Abrupt scene change. A dark form appears out of a snow squall. He looks like Toshiro Mifune, black hair tied up in a topknot, thick brows, fierce eyes, ragged beard. He's wearing black samurai robes embroidered in front and back with fiery red dragons. He's apparently some kind of wandering warrior shaman, technically homeless but, really, you don't picture a guy like this ever having a home—a cave maybe, or a rugged stone hut on the side of a snow-blown mountain. He kind of magically appears and disappears. The camera has caught him in a very private, very alone moment sitting in front of a fire, turning a piece of bamboo over the flames, slowly burnishing the wood into a mottled, caramelized brown and orange with a golden sheen. He extracts a long narrow iron rod from the fire, red-hot at the tip, inserts it in the hollow end of the bamboo. Wisps of blue smoke rise as he cleans out the papery membranes that separate each section. More wisps of smoke rise ghost-like as he burns the thumbhole on the underside of the reed and the four fingerholes on top. He finishes by searing into the flute a Japanese ideograph that Oscar couldn't possibly know means *darkness becoming light*, at first glance a fairly transparent message, at second not so much. Oscar picked up the flute, turned it once in his hands, his fingers found the right spacing on their own, just as his lips fitted themselves to the mouthpiece. He blew, ever so gently, his lips forming a perfect embouchure, soft as clouds. And the gods wept.

The music has stopped, disappeared with an odd Irish penny whistle trill and a will o' the wisp glimpse of a face so quick you may have missed that wistful, hurt look in his eyes. Orphan eyes, Oliver Twist eyes. It's like he's hiding some terrible secret behind those fragile window panes that he will never be able to share with anyone his entire life. Although, watching the Snowman push his cart away, there is something about that guy.

The camera now flies up and over west campus like a large bird of prey, a hawk or an owl, peering down into the concrete canyons where students are packed and stacked like factory-farmed chickens in windowless rooms in twenty and thirty-story residential towers. An owl out of its element. A day owl that might be searching for pigeons, rats, squirrels and other urban vermin in permanently penumbral streets bearing names reminiscent of a *mostly* Hispanic heritage where the Snowman once crashed for a year of his tenure at UT for $25 a month with ten other guys and sometimes gals in an old semi-Tudor-style house just off Nueces. But this owl is on a mission. It flaps its great wings once, twice, and circles back over campus, and so we arrive outside the window or, more practically, the door of room 221 in David Hall in time for Dr. Lilith Levant's nine a.m. class on, appropriately, *shh*, silence.

26
Silence

ALTERNATE YEARS, DR. LEVANT TEACHES another upper division Honors course called The Science of Silence. She knows a lot about silence. She carries in her genes knowledge of vast barren deserts, rugged mountains, endless sand dunes, absolute stillness except for the wind, shifting sands, rocks cracking in the scorching sun, the soft sibilance of serpents, the barely discernible skitter of tiny reptilian and invertebrate feet, the quick, darting movement of eyes watching from crevices, of women's eyes watching from behind black veils. She knows the silence of self-survival when you huddle in a tiny space in a closet or behind a filthy toilet and try to be as small and quiet as a dead mouse or a used tampon to escape the beatings and sexual assaults, to escape the shouting and screaming, the gunshots and violence exploding around you day and night. She has done case studies of sensory deprivation in controlled laboratory environments such as anechoic chambers, isolation units in mental wards, solitary confinement in prison, long tours under the sea in submarines, in the undersea world of Jacques Cousteau bathyspheres and other small submersibles that become a little bit scarier the longer you're down there, as well as more extreme settings like miners trapped in chthonic darkness and silence after mine collapses, people lost in the desert, the tundra, at the north and south pole, astronauts out in space—she'd love to talk to that guy stuck on Mars if he ever makes it back *please, please, I'm fucking begging you, get me the fuck off this fucking rock, I'm losing my fucking mind.*

All of which she has distilled and condensed into another richly prose-driven book titled *Shh ... Silence as a Subversive Dialectical Tool*, a treatise on the effectiveness of applied tactical and strategic silence in degrading, defusing and defeating the dynamics of political discourse run amok. Nonsensical or heated debates, tirades, perorations, rants, clownishness, buffoonery, outright lies and distortion of the facts, bullying, intimidation and actual physical attacks are all neutralized by the actions of randomly placed *silencists* whose unifying principle is: stand silent. They do not respond to the antagonists' theatrics with their own. No yelling or shouting, no jeers, catcalls, boos, hisses, chants, no tape across the mouth, no banners, signs, T-shirt slogans. They simply stand, or sit, faces expressionless as if they have been struck dumb, catatonic, caught in the soul-wringing grasp of some awful God who is calling them to account, and like miniature black holes they suck the energy out of the room, creating dead zones that communicate or Venn diagram overlap with other silencists (social scientists argue for some kind of quantum entanglement on a human scale, *real* scientists say ixnay).

The phenomenon spreads through small town community centers, big city convention centers, stadiums, auditoriums, arenas. Whether it's the half-dozen or so attendees at Sam's General Store in rural southwestern PA or the audience of twenty-thousand, seven hundred thirty-nine in Madison Square Garden, they sit as rigid as Rodin's thinker on the toilet or stand as stiff as Lot's wife turned to a pillar of salt and stare at the speaker in mute testimony. Huge metropolitan venues sink into the quietude of Trappist monasteries, Zen Buddhist retreats. Even TV audiences at home fall silent. The entire nation has sunk into a funk, a vacuum of near-complete noiselessness that reflects what—moral disapprobation? Shock? Horror? Even yammering political hacks are struck dumb by the deafening roar of silence, as if they have been caught in the middle of some heinous act, and indeed they have, and now everybody is waiting for the next thing they say and it better be mighty goddamn good. (Interestingly, this phenomenon had never been noted prior to the publication of Dr. Levant's book. A rare example of academia effecting change in society? If so, no one has given Dr. Levant credit for it. Nor has anyone questioned the Harvard professor who, having *observed* this phenomenon, in another bit of quantum legerdemain (the dead and alive zombie cat thing) claimed, in effect, to have created it.)

Dr. Levant premises the beginning of every semester by asking her students to define the nature of silence, which she explores with a Socratic line of questioning. What is silence? Are there degrees of silence? Can silence only be described in terms of absence of sound? What is sound? Throwing a bone to the science nerds, she writes on the blackboard in her impeccable cursive the word *Acoustics,* and then brings up on the wall screen the textbook definition: *the interdisciplinary science that deals with the study of all mechanical waves in gases, liquids, and solids, including topics such as vibration, sound, ultrasound and infrasound.* (And, yes, she *could*, and maybe once upon a time *would*, have made a joke about flatulence, passing gas, even sexual titillation, you know, just to break the ice, loosen up the ~~goose~~ *group*, but she doesn't. There's already too much silliness in Boone's oeuvre, and besides, it's not very likely any of her students will get the humor—teacher is obscure, vague, random, arbstact (sic), uses dirty language, talks about forbidden subjects, strip her naked, chain her to a tree, whip her, beat her, oh, please, let me). In other words, *ahem*, a perturbance in a medium such as air or water or even a mountain of solid rock that may be detected by auditory or acoustic devices, including the human ear, although comparatively speaking not the most precise. What if your dog starts howling at nothing in the middle of the night? Ghosts? A distant train whistle? A psychopath lifting the window sash you left unlocked in the dining room? What about an oscilloscope gone wild in a desolate arctic outpost manned by a couple of stir-crazy scientists who've watched the old black and white sci fi film *The Thing* wayyy too many times? Which raises another question. How, exactly, does one *observe* silence?

During one seminar, Dr. Levant requires her students to sit the entire three hours of class in Warholian stasis, no caffeine and sugar fixes, no trips to the bathroom (Lilith suspects Tybalt is doing the Burt Reynolds pee-in-the-bottle trick), no sound, no movement. The carrot here is that they're being filmed and it's already going viral which means they're all going to be—trumpet fanfare—*famous!* (For about one minute, maybe less, depends on the attention span of the … zzzzz.) Nevertheless, you can see itchy, twitchy digits yearning to grasp, to fire up, to tap tap tap the EyePhones® Lilith has ordered them to place a taunting, tantalizing two inches away from their fingertips, you can see the torture in their faces, the first lead pencil etchings of a permanent wrinkle, a frown, every sound is magnified, the creak of a chair, a sigh, someone's slow steady breathing—is he *asleep?*—a low guttural frog *burrrp*, an (*OMG, seriously?*) whistly whooshy poo fart that does sound a lot like a whoopee cushion and fills the room with the noxious vapors of steamed broccoli and refried pinto beans. (*Vegan?* Vegan.) When the second hand on the wall clock hits four there's a unanimous sigh of relief and the sudden loud ruckus of screeching chairs, backpacks, EyePhones®— Man, like I don't fucking *know?* Like, I've been totally fucking *incommunicado?* Like, for three fucking *hours?* (Oh man, *you* ain't going to Mars, bro.)

In the spirit of innovative pedagogy, Dr. Lil, as her students (one, anyway) affectionately call her, tasks her class with documenting silence *in situ* in and around the urban center. Before they're allowed to go out on this mission they're required to sign personal safety waivers absolving the university of any responsibility in case of physical or psychological harm (I was a witness to raw unfettered poverty *OMG*). Also, to arm themselves. Accordingly, university police will provide, at no extra cost, training (one hour) and loaner weapons (short barrel, six shot semi-automatic, .22 caliber, not very exciting *booo* but definitely gives you leverage over an unarmed opponent *yayyy!*).

Samantha (*Sam*, please) (you precious fucking *brat*) brings to class a video of herself in a flannel shirt, faded and torn blue jeans and "fringed moccasins, bought just for the occasi[o]n, on a rock a'sittin'" (*Sam* also has this extremely annoying habit of writing and even speaking in rhyme even if it requires absurd grammatical constructions that try Yoda's patience they would), in a dry creek bed in a bright, sunny stretch of canyon that has been completely truncated from the original meandering Parton Creek greenbelt by the encroachment of thousands of McMansions, condos, gated communities, IT industrial parks, retail businesses and millions of tons of concrete kerplopped right down on top of the long ago dried-up and forgotten New Bedford Aquifer.

Theobald (Lilith feels an instinctive distrust (repugnance?) for this Teutonic appellation with its suggestion of the master race, but to his credit Theobald prefers to be called Tybalt—now *that* does appeal to this irrepressible thing she has for bad boys) presents a video in which we see a silhouette of his lanky, black-clad body slumped in a penumbral crescent of light in the curvature of a large concrete storm drain underneath an exit ramp of MoPark Expressway.

Malfeasa (there's another good name, her parents obviously borrowed it from the evil fairy godmother in the eponymous Sid Ney film), looking like a boozy, smoke gets in your eyes Lauren Bacall floozy in a beige trench coat and short-brimmed fedora, sits on a wooden chair in a dim, dusty room in an abandoned house with a *Condemned* sign outside over on the East Side, broken glass on the floor, feathery skeletal carcasses, a baking soda pile of plaster fallen from the ceiling—this one gives Lilith vestigial prickly vibes up and down her spine, the frisson of fear, it has been called, but in her case a way too familiar familiarity.

Up next, LaShondra, subverting stereotypes (she's been interested in spelunking ever since her first subterranean expeditions in the municipal storm sewer system on the Far East Side as an adventurous nine-year-old girl), shows herself in a hard hat, goggles, gloves and thermal coveralls in the eerie glow of a 1200 lumen waterproof rechargeable caving headlamp wedged in a narrow, muddy crawlspace deep inside the famous Lost Aeronaut's Cave (about two miles upstream from Sam's location), the entrance to which is now accessed by a flight of stairs leading down from the basement of the former Dilley's Department Store in the long ago abandoned Parton Creek Mall, now the permanent squat for hundreds of homeless people (affordability-challenged?).

In every case, these students are convinced they have documented actual moments of silence and in every case Dr. Levant shoots them down. The faint sound of a jet airplane or a train whistle or an EMS siren in the distance. The traffic on MoPark that does, yes, disappear into a barely discernible white noise *but it's still there*. The trickling water, the scuttling cockroach, the cricket's chirr, the bird flapping its wings—yellow cheeked warbler, I'd say, Lilith, minor interest in ornithology, tilts her head. Possibly the last one extant. Might want to contact the Audubon Society. The screams of someone, man? woman? hard to tell, being assaulted in a homeless camp in the undergrowth not too far away. The sound of the wind soughing in the trees. Question: does a sylvan glade where the only sound one hears is the water trickling in a stream and the breeze rustling the leaves connote silence? If a tree falls in Brooklyn and no one hears, did anyone die? This last, an updated Buddhist koan, is lost on all of them.

Then there's a chromatic (*auditory?*) shift in the class. They become silence warriors, they're like hunger artists, novitiates in an ascetic monastic order (have mertoncy on their souls). It becomes an obsession, they out classmates who don't abide. I saw Sam *talking* to, you know, like, this *guy?* LaShondra gets caught passing a handwritten note to Tybalt whose lips whisper over the crush-weighted words like mosquito wings—still enough decibels to register on the snitch-o-meter. They're like a platoon of stone-faced North Korean soldiers on border patrol at the DMZ, like a youth brigade in the Chinese Cultural Revolution, like Rooski droogis, Hitler Jugend, like a bunch of bully *boy scouts*, for chrisesakes. Is this anything at all like Dr. Levant intended? Perhaps so. Familiar with military training, she knows that in order to build up your troops, first you gotta break 'em down, reduce them to obedient protoplasm and then you can begin to mold them into—no, not *men*, you fucking maggots! Killing machines! Now it's time to rein them in, draw tight the purse strings, make the whole damn show mean something.

So it is that the class finds themselves sitting in a circle at the bottom of an abandoned missile silo just west of Osberg listening for the sounds of silence or more accurately the absence of sounds. More or less like the difference between nothing and absolute nothing, Dr. Levant says, which leaves them all equally non-plussed. You know, *nothing* is something you can conceive of, it's a *thing*. Look, what's inside this empty box? *Nothing*. Whereas absolute nothing is, well ... do you know anything about the *Tao?* Okay, look, never mind. Now, I want you to allow yourselves to become receivers, you know, like Van Morrison says—*Who?* Are you kidding me? Anyway—turn it up, your radio, listen for signals, *messages*, telint, humint, alienint—*Gort, Klattu barada nikto*. Remember? No, they don't. Okayyy.

To encourage them in this endeavor she leads them in a group *Ommmm*, and while this isn't exactly like a bunch of tonally correct Benedictine monks doing a Gregorian chant of Somewhere Over the Rainbow inside the Cathedral of Notre Dame (restored, didn't come out quite the way they planned—*the Cathedral of Notre Damnée?*) it's pretty darn close, the whole silo's vibrating like a huge electric dildo (pretty sure there's at least one orgasm underway). Dr. Levant instructs them to focus on the blue center light in the middle of their foreheads, which, who knows, maybe it's mass hypnosis, the power of suggestion, but the second she mentions it, the blue light actually appears, they're like a circle of Aladdin's lamps with little blue flames at the tip of the spout. Tybalt reports hearing a screaming come across the sky. Sam's pretty sure she overheard Cleopatra talking baby talk to Mark Antony. Is that a *neutrino?* someone (not sure who) asks?

Now dial back the chatter in your heads, Lil says. Hear without listening, hear *without hearing*. The sound and the source of the sound and the receptacle for the sound are all one. Minutes, perhaps hours, later, she informs them that their heartbeats have hit the exact same rhythm (they're all wearing fitbits), they're also breathing at exactly the same rate, they're all feeling a megadose of warm tinglies all over. Individually, it's like a mind and body cheese melt. As a unit, it's like a Vulcan group fuck. They even share the same internal urges, um, Professor Levant? Is class gonna be over soon cause I really gotta pee? *Me too! Me too!* Because it can't last forever, this universal love-cohesion thing. It's like an acid trip, at some point you gotta come down, and truth is, you didn't really want it to last forever because, man, it's just too fucking intense.

There is some concern Ms. Levant has gone overboard with this silence thing when she's seen about campus wearing a U.S. Navy Flight Deck Crewman Sound Attenuating Helmet Assembly, commonly called "the cranial." But, no, she isn't trying to deflect Russian microwave bombs or subliminal US government propaganda, nor prevent some *other* malevolent entity from hacking her brain. She has been experimenting with the selective suppression of ambient sounds that may disguise existential threats, kind of a lizard survival mode, sometimes necessary in the teaching profession.

Which is probably why she doesn't notice the door of her classroom open one morning, just a narrow wedge, and close again with complete stealth and silence, although maybe it isn't stealth at all but the normal stride and carriage of the one who has opened and closed the door behind himself, the way a cat can enter a room unnoticed and suddenly *appear* on a chair or couch or multi-colored throw rug. But it is exactly this silence and this invisible presence that she senses. She can almost but not quite hear the breathing, as if one could hear a butterfly breathe. *Oscar?* She doesn't actually say his name out loud but he responds as if she did. Hi, Miss Lil. Jesus, Oscar, has anyone ever suggested that you consider a career with the CIA? No, Miss Lil. Should I? Fuck no, Oscar. You should work for the good guys. Who are they, Miss Lil? Is this kid fucking with her or what? He almost sounds like a simpleton and yet he's so damn smart. Wise is a better word, the wisdom of an old soul in the body of a young man barely out of adolescence. What kind of hell has this kid been through, what kind of cocoon has he been nurtured in, that he can know so much and still remain so humble and earnest and fucking *vulnerable*. And here she is, putting all this weight and all these expectations on this kid she can barely even see. It's like he's beaming down from the Starship Enterprise in a shimmering golden halo but he's only partially arrived, he kind of fades in and out, because even she has trouble believing he's really there.

The other students by now assume she's gone all the way over the edge, or maybe this is supposed to be some kind of innovative *performance?* Well, just wait until the fucking evaluations, *bitch*, I'll innovate your ass (Professor is mean, unfair, radical, *commonist* (sic), can't communicate, doesn't *empthasize* (sic semper), Professor is *crazy*.) The students are *supposed* to have begun rough drafts of their term papers by now. Of course none of them have even chosen a topic much less written a word and now they're all just sitting there staring at her (teacher doesn't teach). Except for Oscar, who has already submitted a proposal and a first draft titled *Becoming Invisible*. The only problem is that, naturally, he writes in vanishing ink. Thoroughly versed in detective fiction, Lil discovers that by breathing on each page she is able to read the text but it only lasts minutes, disappearing as the moist vapor of her breath evaporates. What she sees is enticing. Sections titled *Being and Nothingness, The Threshold*. Plus a personal narrative style that immediately pulls her in. *When I first discovered the portal I was afraid. I started to leave but something made me turn back, not exactly a voice but a presence that encouraged me to enter.* Dr. Levant's attention is distracted by a frantic thumping sound and she turns to the window where the great owl is beating its wings against the glass as if desperately trying to communicate with her.

27
Sistuh!

NOW WE SEE DR. LEVANT getting out of a modest, older model car (Studebaker?) and entering a modest two-story yellow brick apartment complex. We see the lights go on in a second-floor apartment. After a discreet pause, long enough for the professor to do whatever most people do when they get home from a long day, the camera enters the apartment and we see that—well, she's apparently already finished dinner, leftover roasted vegetables and grilled tofu, about half an inch of red wine remains in her glass, which she takes with her as she gets up from the table, goes into the living room and turns on the TV. We hear raucous laughter and a *loud sassy female Black voice*. It's the beginning of Sister Sunne Rae's monologue. She opens every show by telling an *off-color* joke and tonight she's really having fun with the pun as she relates an anecdote from her days as a waitress in a soul food joint in Louisiana (this is news to the audience, definitely strikes a chord among the working class).

One day this white dude comes in. After looking over the menu without a clue, he says, I'll have the soul food plate. Y'all want collard greens with that? I ask. White dude looks perplexed. Hey, I don't discriminate! he says. Just give me the regular greens! The Sister allows her audience a minute for this to sink in and even then the reaction is a spattering of uncomfortable laughter except among the few Black attendees who roll their eyes at each other *knowingly*. And, hmm, this is interesting, Dr. Levant—okay, she's at home, let's drop the formalities— *Lilith* is commenting on SSR. Still lookin' good, *Sistuh!* Got that mojo workin'! Which, hmm, does sound uncharacteristically Ebonic of her and, even more interesting, she's speaking SSR's lines *before* the Sister does. It's like this odd reverse echo thing. Tonight's guest ... *Tonight's guest* ... is Texas state Attorney General Akin Apoxton ... *Akin Apoxton.*

And, hmm, how does that work? The show's taped before a live audience but of course it isn't actually live on TV. Reruns? Maybe. It's also possible Lilith obtained the script in advance, thanks to a connection in the theater department, or, who knows, she even wrote it herself. Employing her ample gifts as a wordsmith, she's taken up scriptwriting to earn some extra bread, fortunately for her, her propensity for strong language immediately clicked with the Sister.

But this is serious shit. SSR's really digging into Apoxton, and when it comes to truth telling, brother, this sister tells it like it is. Now, isn't it true, Mr. Apoxton ...? and she ticks off his offenses and they are many. His as of yet unresolved criminal indictment for felony fraud, racketeering, bribery, poor taste in his clothing choices— it's been *eight years*, Mister Apoxton! His incitement to insurrection—*no recollection at all*, Mister Apoxton?! His anti-affirmative action policies, his attempts to ban books, police women's bodies, revoke civil and voting rights. With each charge Sister Sunne Rae's voice becomes less rhetorical, easygoing, and angrier, more accusatory. The audience is squirming in their seats, especially the white folks who, one can imagine, can't help but imagine themselves in Apoxton's shoes (well, *pee-yew!* not that far!). Akin's got mud on his face, big disgrace, and he doesn't even seem to realize much less care, what a fucking bigot he is. I stand on my record of ensuring the voting rights of those who deserve the right to vote (um, let me guess).

After lambasting this mofo's sorry white ass for another five minutes or so, or rather, letting him do the job for her, SSR invites him in on the joke, sorta. Well, Mr. Apoxton, you seem to be a man of your *convictions* … and I certainly hope you are! And Ha!Ha!Ha! a loud burst of laughter greets this apparent softball, everybody's happy again, or at least mildly relieved, 'cause, let's face it, when SSR's acting out like a n-n-n— come on, just say it—*Negro*, when she's loud and brash and making those *sassy Black female* comments, white folks be fearsome discomfited. But when she's singing and dancing, when she laughs, loudly and frequently, the mostly white audience loves her (on stage, anyway, in the supermarket not so much). This is the happy, dancey, *funny* Black lady they want to see.

And now, in one of those meta things Boone is so fond of, we see the Snowman in front of the wide screen in his penthouse retreat after a full day of pushing the cart, didn't even bother to go back to the office in the afternoon and he's pretty sure no one missed him except maybe Jimmy making his afternoon mail deliveries. He too is watching SSR. Oddly, he also seems to be speaking her lines at the same time she does and possibly just a heartbeat before. Does the Sister convey some kind of telepathic mind-ray to her audience? Is the answer something simpler, less sinister, her staff puts the script out on a blog immediately before the show for fans who want to participate (cf. *Rocky Horror*)? Apparently the Sister's show at night has become the highlight of the Snowman's day. Judging by his embarrassed groans during the collard greens monologue, one might suspect that he himself has been guilty of exactly this kind of cultural indiscretion at some time in his life, which may be why he also seems relieved and even happy to see that scoundrel Apoxton in the hot seat.

Incidentally, or coincidentally, or, probably more accurate to say, criminally, the following week, belatedly realizing just how badly the Sister sliced and diced him, Apoxton gets his payback with the announcement of a new campaign against violent crime. Not surprisingly, the word *gangs* enters the conversation more than once, tied, of course, to *minorities* and, unfailingly, *Black youths* (alert cineastes will later remember a minor reference to a group that calls itself *United Colors*).

The scene changes to a neighborhood in Far East Osberg and, wouldn't you know it, here comes a bunch of Black youths, and they are youths, boys and girls, thirteen, fourteen, fifteen. They're all wearing brightly colored hoodies, flamingo pink, raspberry red, lime green, grape purple, lemon yellow, orange orange, some with sleeves rolled up, some with hoods thrown back, in tight jeans with fashionable slashes at the knees, in plaid hip hop shorts, they're all wiry, lean, probably been hitting the courts since they were five, six. Yeah, I know, some of you hear *court* you're thinking Juvy, right? *C'monnn*, admit it. And, yeah, they're wearing some bling and a couple of them have nasty scars and missing teeth, but they're all smiling big happy smiles and they're singing, loudly, joyfully, *We are the world.* Is it meant as a parody? Sticking it to the man (i.e., whitey)? Because, look—they're pulling little red wagons piled high with cardboard boxes and shopping bags. What's this? Stolen goods? UPS and Fed Ex porch piracy swag?

And, uh-oh, that seed of doubt planted, the Snowman remembers now that while on a recent trip back to the hood to check on his old hovel, make sure it hasn't collapsed into the ground or been demolished by the city (he keeps meaning to have it fixed up, maybe rent it out cheap to some nice young folks, but you know how that goes), he did notice some kids in colored hoodies hanging around Moses' place, and, hmm, he hasn't seen much of Moses lately. He vaguely remembers him saying something about his Moms needing help at home and, okay, let's face it, his position as Chief Taste Tester doesn't require that he actually be on the job very often. But what if all this time Moses has been playing him like a chump-ass fool … ? And just like that those creaky old wheels of paranoia start turning in the dark recesses of his brain. Is Moses involved in something dirty? Are these kids dealing drugs? Fencing stolen goods? Are they part of the violent crime wave Attorney General Apoxton has warned us of?

That seems to be the question Sister Sunne Rae is asking herself and her audience as we now see her and her camera crew in a non-descript white van with tinted windows driving down increasingly shabby streets on the Far East Side, trash everywhere, overturned garbage cans, broken glass, piles of dog shit, human excrement, electric wires drooping from telephone poles, broken windows, shot-out streetlights, ramshackle houses and apartment buildings—the Sister's carrying on a running commentary of everything they pass. Here's another example of *invisibility* in our city. Talk about a beam in your eye! This ain't no plank of pine or even a damn yule log! This a thousand-year-old giant sequoia!

News outlets refer to these pockets of poverty, when they refer to them at all, as colonias, bantustans, territories, homelands (the words ghetto and slum occasionally pop up but, well, too many negative connotations). They're effectively shut off from the emerald city by "buffers," twenty-foot tall concrete walls studded with broken glass and topped with razor wire, impassable transportation corridors where multiple tracks of high-speed commuter rail and twenty-six lanes respectively of north and south bound vehicular traffic run 24/7 (occasionally some drunk, jonesing junkie or desperate mother trying to get her baby to a doctor will attempt to run across this DM(V)Z and *splat!* the Pietà reconceived as road kill), as well as man-made edificial canyons that plunge thousands of feet straight down into head-smashing bedrock limestone and turbid, vile-smelling moats filled with raw sewage and swarming with alligators, piranhas and giant snapping turtles as big as jeeps—all that remains of the once vast network of urban waterways, including the more familiar Onion, Boggy, Waller and Shoal creeks, largely known now for the eponymously named country clubs, malls and entertainment centers that have buried them in concrete. These urban islands of decay are connected to the "mainland" by single lane, rattling, creosote-soaked timber trestles, as well as several makeshift swaying rope and vine bridges, very iffy helicopter service (flimsy hang gliders and frail DIY lighter-than-air craft operated by clearly deranged enthusiasts periodically stand in, hang on tight!), leaky ferries that do sink on occasion, and, in even more desperate situations, catapults (*passengers* are issued inflatable sumo wrestler costumes and reminded to tuck and roll when they land—oh, and watch for the odd bounce, oh, and that pile of dog shit over—*oops*).

Unfortunately, this isolation from the rest of Osberg also results in medical and food deserts. The only source of emergency health care is—well, okay, this is embarrassing, there isn't any. The only source of groceries is the increasingly rare and heavily fortified convenience store, mini mart, mom ~~and pop~~ (our sincere regrets, Pop died in an armed robbery a year ago, good Samaritan accidentally shot him, ironically, a cop fatally shot the good Samaritan, the actual perp is now a tour guide in Barbados), or bottle shop where soda, malt liquor, chips, dips and prepackaged fried chicken *parts* are the primary source of nutrition, all goods marked at inflationary prices, no credit accepted.

There is one shining star in the middle of this steaming pile of shit.

The camera now follows Sister Sunne Rae as she and her crew drive through the gates of the *Organic Compound*, a militarized urban food and farming co-op. Looks like a combination Israeli kibbutz and hippie commune with a few disconcerting elements of the maximum-security prison, guard towers, searchlights, concertina wire. Gaean earth mothers in Rooski proletariat head scarves, ankle-length gingham dresses and heavy leather work boots, some with babies in slings on their backs or at their chests, and shaggy-haired, bearded pioneer farmer types in flannel shirts, denim coveralls and the same clompy leather work boots, out hoeing rows of butter crunch and oak leaf lettuce, tomato bushes heavy with fruit, bell and hot peppers, okra, sweet corn, huge purple mammary-swelling eggplants, as well as zucchini, cucumbers and several other members of the cucurbitaceae family, including the usual watermelon, cantaloupe and mush melon, plus various gourds, pumpkins, acorn, spaghetti and kombucha squash. Also pole and bush beans and a dozen different greens besides those already mentioned. They've got about thirty active beehives painted sky-blue out in a field of clover abuzz and ahumm with tiny apian wings. The men and women alike carry Uzi automatic pistols in belt or shoulder holsters, AK-47s slung across their backs. *Varmints*, they uniformly respond when asked why the need for weapons, without specifying what *kind* of varmints (note: Dr. Susan Bourbonne at the University of Texas at Osberg confirms the increase in previously unseen urban fauna imported intentionally or by accident from locations as distant as Australia, India and Thailand, for example, poisonous snakes, toads—they're *huge*, as big as groundhogs, and they have *teeth*—lizards, the kind you used to see only in sci-fi films, as well as unconfirmed sightings of saber-tooth tigers). And you don't have any issues with your neighbors? They all shake their heads, Nope, we're good with the hood.

With good reason. The Organic Compound donates to the local food banks. They hire young locals and teach them agricultural science (as well as proper fire arms safety and maintenance). They employ homeless, migrants, ex-convicts and otherwise unemployable people in a transitional program that works with local churches, mosques, synagogues, ashrams and covens (following Iago's advice, it seems). So it's really no surprise to see M'Shaka hoisting a crate of strawberries

into the back of a DIY conversion kit Cadillac Imperial
pick-up (Boone insists on this culturally insensitive
stereotype, which he thinks is iconic, and which is made
only slightly less offensive by M'Shaka's modifications
(not *entirely* unlike Harold's Jaguar hearse)). He's
already loaded up several crates and cartons of fresh
produce that volunteers in his church will prepare for free
community meals. The Snowman himself still stops by
the Organic Compound gift shop now and then to pick up
a quart mason jar of honey. It's golden and glowing,
almost incandescent, and so sweet it burns, it's like the
taste of solar energy. Indeed, OC honey was a prime
ingredient in his original *PoPoPops!*® recipe. In a
misstep that still makes him cringe, he urged OPEN's
board to approach the Organic Compound with a contract
that would have changed their status from niche industry
to corporate entity overnight. OC's response: fuck you
very much.

28
Ghost of a Ghost

ONE DAY, WHILE PONDERING THIS BLUNDER, among a lifetime of others, in the more or less non-stop tornadic activity in his brain, the Snowman notices a one-and-a-half-ton stake-bed truck go by in the street, loaded down with picks, shovels, rakes, push brooms, water hoses, plants in black plastic buckets, squares of sod, sacks of mulch and soil conditioner. Landscapers. City's crawling with 'em. Everybody's into the green revolution. So why does the Snowman fix on this one truck in particular? The men in the cab are all Mexican. Nothing unusual about that. It's the driver who catches his eye, in fact, causes him to do an over the top theatrical double take he (or rather Boone, directing him) most likely stole from a young Cary Grant (cf. *Arsenic and Old Lace*) (or Dick Van Dyke copying Cary Grant) as he follows the truck down the street to the next light *desperately* trying to catch a final glimpse of the driver's face, features, the dark flashing eyes, the bristly black mustache and mocking smile, not just because he recognizes them with bell ringing clarity but because the owner of this face and these features looks almost exactly the same as he did twenty-five-years ago, which he knows is impossible, not only because of the laws of nature, the inevitable aging process, etc., but because the person he remembers never existed.

A montage of familiar images runs through his mind, familiar because he has reviewed them multiple times over the years. He sees a movie-star handsome face with a bristling black mustache, laughing black eyes and a bemused, even mocking smile saying to him in heavily accented but otherwise perfect English *Here ees a crescent wrrench, what deed you want the espider for?* He sees himself in a midnight blue parka and puffy insulated coveralls sitting on his butt in a cushion-less couch in front of a roaring bonfire of construction debris, paralyzed by the cold, by the *mota* and tequila in his brain, the night black, the ground frozen white, snow blowing around him, staring at what, from a distance of almost twenty-five yards and as many years, he can unabashedly admit to himself now is the very attractive ass, even in puffy insulated coveralls, of the owner of this handsome face, at the moment bent under the raised engine cowling of a rocket-like vehicle. He sees this figure turn toward him holding in his bare hands the dripping black organs of internal combustion, his face, features morphing into a tortured mask of molten bronze, copper and terra cotta before it bursts into flames and then curls into black ash and disintegrates.

And just like that night turns to day, the snow melts away, the sun comes out, on the soundtrack we again hear *Mariaaa, I just met a girl named Maria* and we see a girl in a plain red dress, long black hair shining like a raven's wing in flight, eyes flashing like obsidian, lips like the red silken petals of the rose behind her ear, standing next to a tall, spiky cactus. At least that's the way she looked in Boone's original *bucolic* version before the new young screenwriter, Alma, yes, a woman, a first on Boone's crew, ran it through the shredder. We again see the black hair, but chopped short and streaked with crimson and henna, the flashing black eyes are angry, obdurate, hard, glistening like shards of obsidian, silver studs gleam like tiny stars in her eyebrows, nose, lower lip, the red peasant dress has been replaced with flannel shirt, charcoal gray jeans torn at the knees, a pair of black Doc Martens. The Snowman sees himself and this woman, Maria, in a *desperate* embrace, mouths pressed together *hungrily*. He sees a group of masked, armed men and women in ersatz military uniforms walking along a jungle trail. He sees one of them turn and look back at the camera. The film stops here as he re-examines for perhaps the thousandth time this moment. It's Maria again, almost unrecognizable in an olive drab military uniform, bullet-packed bandoliers across her chest, her face hidden except for her eyes and mouth by a green cloth military cap and black wool balaclava. He remembers no goodbye, no final words, only her bemused smile as she turned back that last time. And then she was gone, disappeared into the jungle.

29
L. Condor

WE NOW HEAR A BREATHY, full-throated pan pipe playing the melancholy refrain of a Peruvian folk song made famous by a pair of American pop singers back in the rocky, whole world's watching sixties and the scene changes to a gated estate carved out of the dark green cedar and blinding white limestone and caliche in the hill country just west of Osberg. Palm trees surround a white stucco Mediterranean-style villa with red terra cotta roof, splashing fountains, a sparkling turquoise blue swimming pool, a tennis court. A man in a smoke gray silk shirt with monogrammed gold cufflinks and a diamond pin in his avocado green silk tie stands at a leaded-glass window behind partially opened plush indigo drapes. He's tall, trim, tan, tennis and lap swimming are clearly part of his daily routine. His silver hair is immaculately groomed. He's probably about eighty but even after a lifetime of living not just on the razor's edge but in the bleeding edge he fits anybody's definition of handsome. Everything about him suggests the rare combination of expensive and excellent taste. He's watching the green and yellow-uniformed landscape crew mowing in the yard below.

One of them, a young man with a bristly black mustache, straw Stetson, wraparound sun glasses and orange ear plugs on lanyards (or are they ear buds? is he listening to music? *communicating with someone?*) mans a 2-cycle, gasoline-powered weed eater, his eyes, thoughts, mind like a zazen geometrician's, totally focused on cutting perfect lines and edges in rectilinear, triangular, circular and paramecium-shaped lawns and flower beds in the endless permutations of a job that must seem endlessly repetitive to an outside observer who could never imagine the chaos of fractals and stochastic elements assembling themselves in this young man's head into a composite whole that meets anyone's definition of perfection.

And yet, while he works, he sees, peripherally, occasional glimpses, stopping to wipe the sweat from his brow, to adjust his sun glasses, retie his boot laces, uniformed kitchen and maid staff moving like ghostly automatons behind the windows of this villa. He sees a plush purple drape shift slightly in an upstairs window. He sees the electric gate at the entrance open and a black SUV enter and the gate close again. He sees cameras, motion detection and tracking systems. What he doesn't see are any signs of security personnel. No armed guards, no Odd Job valet capable of crushing your skull with his bare hands or lopping off your head with a toss of his metal-reinforced bowler derby. But he senses a lethal presence everywhere, imagines the oily gleam of machine guns, RPGs, Hellfire and Stinger missiles, laser cannons, weapons, it would seem from his imagining, that he knows something about. When this young landscaper and his crew enter or exit this estate, he sees the red and green iris and bioscans at the gate searching his eyes, his facial profile, and knows he is being observed, quantified, assigned a certain value in an ever-expanding matrix of algorithms. That at this very second his head may be in the crosshairs of a Burris XTR II Riflescope with F-Class MOA Illuminated Reticle affixed to a Barrett M82 sniper rifle, but he never sees any human presence other than the aforementioned household staff, one of whom now announces a visitor to the older gentleman in the silk shirt and tie gazing down upon the landscape crew working below.

He likes to watch them work, to see his property groomed and maintained, to feel the sense of order. He has always liked order, even in the maelstrom of an extraordinarily chaotic career choice, which may explain why he is here now in the luxury of this gated estate, instead of dead, his mutilated body dissolved into nothingness in a vat of hydrochloric acid, or else rotting into imbecility in a six by ten-foot concrete cell in a maximum-security prison stuck out in some desert wasteland. Which probably also explains why this man, L. Condor, lives in anonymity. His neighbors (relatively speaking, the closest in any direction lives a mile away and that's old Jim, long time ago cattle rancher, sits in a rocking chair on the front porch and whittles gewgaws and gimcracks and occasionally takes potshots at turkey vultures and coyotes with his Winchester thirty-aught-six) know nothing about him, never see him. They might observe a vehicle turn off the narrow Ranch Road 13 onto a private gravel and caliche lane, a black GM, Mercedes or Cadillac SUV, essentially fungible in that they are all black, large, built like tanks with tinted windows (bullet, missile and blast-proof, but his neighbors don't know that).

Despite this order he has created among the vegetative anarchy of mesquite, cedar (ash juniper, to be accurate), agave and prickly pear cactus surrounding his estate, he senses something amiss, a perturbation in the cosmos, that butterfly flutter of stained-glass wings in Mauritius or the Seychelles setting in motion a tiny breeze that will grow into a great wind and possibly even a huge swelling storm that will pound the foundations of his world. At times he feels he's being *watched*, even though his security technician has assured him, after repeated sweeps of the house and grounds, that there is zero evidence of unauthorized surveillance devices. Nor have any drones penetrated his airspace (except for the one two years ago that disintegrated the instant it crossed his property line).

Nevertheless, a troubling little worm of doubt has wriggled into his head, triggered by the seemingly innocuous discovery he has made regarding the various hygienic paper products placed throughout his estate, beginning with a random glance at a surprisingly soft tissue paper napkin with which he had just wiped a spot of chocolate *mole* from the corner of his mouth and on which he noticed the logo PPP embossed in a corner in an elegant and shiny font as if it had been embroidered in silk (he couldn't possibly know it was modeled after an earlier embossed paper product common in the second century BCE China). And then sitting on the toilet one morning in his private suite's bathroom, trousers down around his ankles (yes, we all do, even the rich and infamous), he pulled a silky swatch of paper from the roll and again noticed the elegant PPP in the corner of each sheet. It doesn't take long before he's searching through the house and eventually the entire grounds in something approaching a frenzy, cold sweat actually breaking out on his brow as he discovers the same PPP monogram on all the rolls of toilet paper in the other bathrooms, on the paper towels in the kitchens, in the various laundry and utility rooms, on the boxes of facial tissues and complimentary notepads placed on the nightstands in all the guest rooms, even the paper hand towels in the chauffeur's maintenance cabinet.

Of course, regaining his composure, collecting his thoughts, that's the nature of business, as he well knows. You corner the market, capture the consumer base, make your brand the default, de facto, *only* choice, so that all other brands are *invisible* to the shopper. Which is fine if you think in rational terms, but not so fine if you grew up in a filthy, dirt poor third-world country where superstition and magic are rampant and even more potent than logic, so that even though you yourself are a rational man, Harvard-educated, with a pedigree you can trace all the way back to the House of Valladoides in the ancient city of Valladoides in old Spain and you live in a villa on a huge, gated estate with the most advanced, cutting edge, discreet and lethal residential security systems on the planet, you are still subject to the strange electrical vibrations you feel trembling in the air around you, to the liminal glimpses of things, one might even say *creatures*, that slip in out of dimensions still uncharted by science.

Do you believe in magic?

On the soundtrack we hear a brief excerpt from a top-ten sixties pop tune that living fossils from that bygone era will recognize at the very first drop of a D minor chord and nod their heads, see, I told you so, when the C major lands on the word *magic* and we return to the Snowman behind his cart, who apparently has also caught a snatch of this tune, possibly on a passerby's headset, just enough of a memory jostle that he hears again a soft, throaty female voice, *hers*, Maria's, say, *There are other ways to fight than with guns or a knife, Snowman. There is magic.* Yes, I know. In your greenghost world of logic, of cause and effect, there is no room for magic. But it's all around you, like the air you breathe, like those tiny creatures you can't see—you know, Snowman, *germs, microbes, bacteria?*

A blinding green slash of jungle fills the screen and the camera returns to the ragtag guerilla band, who look even more ragtag than before, their faces gaunter, bodies thinner, uniforms patched and worn. Subcomandante María is seen talking to a young man in a straw Stetson, blue plaid, pearl-snap western shirt, brown leather belt, straight-leg Levis over western boots. His back is to the camera so we can't see his face or his reaction to what Maria is saying to him, but we can hazard a guess from the mix of affection and concern in her voice when she says, mostly in English for the American audience but with a few words of Spanish for authenticity, This is a very important mission, *mijo*, the most important in your life. He's already done enough damage. Billions have been poisoned by this insidious illusion of well-being. We must put an end to it. *Vete con Diós!*

Of course the Snowman never expected to see this young Mexican landscaper again, so it really must be magic or at least another unlikely coincidence when not too long after this first sighting he again notices a landscape truck drive by in the street and behind the wheel he sees—*Look*, Snowman! *Look! Look! Look! Is it?* Yes, it is, that young Mexican guy, and he's laughing like a carefree gypsy but the camera zooms in on his face and his eyes are bright with anger and beneath his bristling black mustache his lips draw back from his teeth

as he snarls something in Spanish that sounds like ...
mierda?... mata? Well, there seems to be some confusion
among the translators. Stan? Eduardo? One of you wanta
take that?

30
Change of Heart (w/o surgery)

IT IS AROUND THIS SAME TIME that the Snowman is drawn back into the messy business of business when he begins to receive anonymous reports of inhumane working conditions in one of his overseas factories. In a nutshell, the workers are slaves. Men, women and children work fourteen-hour days, seven days a week. They never leave the premises. The doors are locked. The air is polluted with dust and fumes. There are no bathroom breaks. It's suffocatingly hot. There are horrible calamities. An entire line of workers loses their hands when a packaging device goes haywire. Several workers die in a fire in the company "cafeteria," which has no exits, and hard to say if that's worse than the rampant food poisoning. The Snowman decides to make an unannounced visit and orders his jet to be ready.

Yes, his jet, and this isn't one of those little eight-seater toys. This is a Boeing 777-9 private luxury jetliner, half-a-billion-dollar price tag, two VIP lounges, separate guest cabins, full baths. It's also armed with missiles, machine guns and laser cannons that can intercept anything from satellite-launched weapons to surface-to-air missiles as well as melt fighter jet cockpits (and their occupants) at a distance of a hundred miles. And, sure, it's extravagant. Back in the day the Snowman insisted on flying economy on business trips. And quickly realized his mistake. First class was an improvement, except for the resentful stares and occasional elbow in his face from the cattle class passengers fighting their way back to their stocks and pillories. Finally he let Wolf Bärenhaut, of all people, talk him into the private jet. I assure you, sir, these lighter-than-air ships today are much improved upon the Montgolfiers.

When it came to selecting a pilot he left the vetting to the experts, hours of flight time, combat experience, that kind of thing. What he was looking for was personality, a human connection, above all someone he could trust. In walks this blond, ruddy-faced, close-cropped, square-jawed, square-shouldered, rugged-looking outdoors type. Joe Palooka? Steve Canyon? He's trying to remember who this guy reminds him of when— *slap!* he smacks himself on the forehead—*Moll?* Because it's not a guy at all. It's Moll Flowers, first female employee on a snow crew, former combat helicopter pilot, oil rig roughneck, white water guide, snowboarded down Mt. Everest, sailed across the Grand Canyon in a wing suit, always on the lookout for an extreme challenge. She's more of a guy than most guys. And, sure, her blue-collar mill-hunk roots keep calling her back to more terrestrial pursuits, but sooner or later both she and little Dieter need to fly. Her most recent gig involved jockeying mothballed cargo planes, their destination unclear, the nature of their cargo also unclear, the planes barely airworthy, might explain why she jumped at this chance. Didn't hurt that I knew the guy I was gonna fly.

Laconic as always. Moll wears a standard commercial pilot's uniform, she salutes the Snowman,

Yessir, Nossir. She seems to prefer it this way, the professionalism. It's her military background, generations of family in uniform, her own life and death experiences in combat. (Boone's attempt to convey the seriousness of these experiences is less than successful when, in one of those near subliminal flashes, he brings up on the screen a clip of Moll leading a squadron of flimsy little DIY lighter-than-air craft piloted by— *teenage Mennonites?* Yes, they are, in sunbonnets and ankle-length gingham dresses, in straw hats, checkered shirts and denim overalls, flying these badge-winning, Junior Woodchuck assemblages of baling wire, canvas and pine slats powered by whining 2-cycle weedeater engines and they seem to be engaged in a dogfight with the Mexican air force and—*fire-breathing dragons?* Nawwww ... nobody's gonna believe that.)

On the flight over the Snowman sits in the cockpit next to Moll while she brings him up to speed on their destination (which will remain unnamed for diplomatic reasons). Today we're BFF, Most-Favored-Nation trading status, tourism's off the chart. In exchange we get government-sanctioned sweatshops, garment factories, electronics, toys for boys and girls, boy and girl toys for rich tourists. Moll's cynicism is refreshing. She's also being unusually expansive. Briefly. The joke is, twenty years ago we were bombing the fuck out of this shithole country (boyish chuckle). Shit, that time M'Shaka and I ... and, bang, just like that the door slams shut, the narrative stops, in an eyeblink Moll's expression transforms from what might be described as fond reminiscence to—oh, I don't know, tortured memory?

She doesn't finish but Boone does and, apparently to make up for the Mennonite farce above, he gives it to us raw and *in medias res*, more or less the way M'Shaka must have experienced it when he abruptly woke up one day *here and now boys* in a sun-blasted patch of desert in a maze of mud-brick compounds in a ferocious firefight, automatic weapons, incoming mortar rounds, RPGs, dirt, timber, sandbags and shrapnel flying everywhere, an enemy who viscerally hates his guts for reasons he doesn't understand screaming at him in a language he also doesn't understand but the screams of agony next to him he does. One of his men is writhing on the ground with his legs blown off. It's the tough little Irish guy, Cairns, Patrick. Sgt. Washington is tying tourniquets around the stumps and firing off shots. His face is wrenched with anguish and terror and absolute determination. No fucking way he's gonna give up and die. He's like John Wayne, Rambo, he's like Vince the Younger in the 2005 National College Football Championship, two minutes to play, down eleven points, but there's just no fucking way he's gonna lose this game. He's like a force of nature, charging through the defense, leaping over tackles, only now it's not Vince anymore, it's M'Shaka, aka Sergeant Washington, Frederick, and this isn't a game and he's not winning. Three of his men are dead, three severely wounded, three still functioning but low on ammo, and two hundred enraged jihadis are converging on their position. Out of nowhere we hear a choir of Valkyries screaming operatic scales in the upper register and then carbon steel blades chopping through the airwaves as a squad of helicopter gunships firing machine guns and rockets sets down and this big blond guy jumps out of the lead chopper, shakes hands with M'Shaka like they're meeting up for coffee and barks, Load 'em up! Except it's not a guy, it's a gal, Chief Warrant Officer 4 Moll

Flowers, and a shared history she and M'Shaka have never even discussed between themselves. It's the combat vet's motto, you man up, you woman up and you shut up. Although, true story, Moll has good-naturedly dropped her pants to half-mast in front of her gal friends to show them the scars where a bullet passed clean through her right cheek. Hunting accident, she says, laconic.

The Snowman, who has nodded off during this unspoken narrative, wakes several hours later as they're beginning their descent through the clouds with several doubts clouding his thoughts. The secret source who informed him of the purported atrocities has left it up to him to pull off this dodge. Of course he can't simply sidle up to the manager of this slave labor mill and say, Howdy-doo, y'all, I'm the Snowman and I own this place, because if they know he's the big kahuna they're sure as shooting not going to let him see the real thing.

A number of comic scenes ensues ("comic" is in dispute, see The Board of Questionable Humor vs. Boone Weller—Glenda) in which he first attempts to disguise himself as a local native looking for work with a shiny black wig and adhesives to give his eyes an Asian appearance, about as convincing as Brando in *Teahouse of the August Moon*. His Charlie Chan pidgin English doesn't help. The guards at the gate look at each other and then back at him like, I don't think so. One even bows his head and says, *So solly, Charlie*. Next he tries a middle-eastern look with a complexion-darkener, fake nose and beard. It's not exactly Omar Sharif but it isn't Peter O'Toole either. He barely manages to say *Assalamu Alaikum* before the guards, who also seem to have changed ethnicities (once again Boone's young scriptwriters seem confused about historicity), shake their heads no fucking way (in Arabic). Finally, he settles on the cover of a German arms dealer looking to diversify. He even manages a fairly passable accent (four years of German in high school and one in college). I am zehry interested in low vage skilled verkers. Well, in that case. The manager is only too happy to show him around the plant. Right this way, Herr Viertelreich, is it?

But the working conditions are nothing at all like the Dickensian nightmare he expected. Vases of flowers everywhere, fans blowing, the workers are all smiling (although, yes, most of them do look as if they could use some restorative dental work, and, true, they do appear, well, malnourished, and, yeah, some seem to have difficulty standing). A whistle blows and lunch is announced. There are buffet tables loaded with indigenous foods, fish and rice baked in banana leaves, fried plantains, jackfruit, pomegranates, melons, cucumbers and yoghurt, flatbread, roasted goat (again, some confusion over the cultural identifiers). The workers are encouraged to partake of this feast. This is great—I mean, *ausgezeichnet!* the Snowman says, snacking on fried rat and, well, yeah, let's call it *dirty rice*, while wondering at the workers' reticence to take even a bite of wilted lettuce, which he attributes to some traditional notion of decorum with guests. When he attempts to ask the employees about their working conditions, the language barrier is, well, a barrier. He does notice, however, a disproportionate, even desperate, one might say, effort to impress upon him their gratitude for the opportunity to work in this factory (according to the interpreter anyway).

The next scene shows the Snowman riding off in a taxi, he's in a great mood, chatting with the driver.

Dumbass Snowman got punked, right? But wait, what's this? We now return to the factory where the vases of flowers are being thrown in the trash, the food torn from desperate hands and mouths, the buffet tables hauled away and the workers driven back to work with whiplashes on their backs and the promise of an extra two hours on the line tonight, film footage, by the way, that comes via a tiny drone the Snowman has cleverly left buzzing behind, and darned if it doesn't look exactly like—yes, it's the grasshopper. (Reveal: the Snowman and the entomological drone have made a pact: the drone works on his behalf and he promises to pay for its children's (if the surgery works out) college education with the possibility of future employment).

Before we can dwell too long on this corporate *indiscretion*, Moll is flying us off again to a near neighbor where the Snowman wants to check in on the good works of his pet project, the Schneeland Foundation. This'll cheer him up, right? To encourage more efficient farming in developing countries, the Schneeland-sponsored MondoInsano Industries has begun a seed distribution program using highly specialized MGO seeds and fertilizers (nota bene: both a mandatory component of financial aid to the participating nations). The Snowman can't wait to get out there in the Land Rover and have a look at these endless hectares of emerald green and golden grains. He suspects something is amiss, however, when the driver, who is also serving as interpreter, insists he wear a hazmat suit and respirator. Nor is he prepared for the scenes of devastation they encounter. Fields of blackened crops, bloated bodies of people and animals, pools of fetid, orange and green mosquito-ridden water.

The driver now introduces the Snowman to the Khlam Chowdry family, some of the few survivors of this *event*, as it has been referred to by reporters (*when* reported). They're lying in rags on the dirt floor, coughing, wheezing, their bodies wracked with convulsions, seizures, they all have chemical burns on their arms, legs and faces. Stupid me, Chlam, the patriarch, says in a sing-songy voice that belies the circumstances. I must have misread the directions on the packaging. In an act of callousness that will haunt the Snowman long afterward, he reaches inside his hazmat suit, extracts a large wad of cash in U.S. dollars, dumps it on the dirt floor, mutters something that, muffled by his respirator, sounds like, *I hope this helps*, and, turning to leave, urges the driver to return to the airstrip as quickly as possible.

Back in the States, he confronts Iago, which has become sort of a stand-up comedy routine between the two of them, but the angry speech, the indignation and outrage he had rehearsed on the polished wooden stage of his imagination (which bears a close resemblance to his high school auditorium's) degenerates into a whiny protest. But why does it have to be this way? Why can't we pay these people decent wages with decent working conditions? Honestly, *Snowman*, Iago says as if he's talking to a recalcitrant child, I don't know how you've survived this long (which almost sounds like a threat). What for us may seem like harsh conditions and low pay are, for *those* people, a rare opportunity to enhance their lifestyle.

The final straw, the one that busts the camel's balls, comes when the Snowman belatedly discovers that he owns the largest for-profit prison in America and it's right here in the great state of Texas.

31
Young Dave

METAL CLANGS AND BANGS, male voices echo off tile and concrete. We see flashes of iron bars, cellblocks, floodlights, armed, uniformed guards on catwalks. The camera stops outside a solid metal door, then passes through the small rectangular glass window into a narrow cell, maybe seven feet wide by ten feet long. In the far corner there's a stainless-steel combination toilet, sink and drinking fountain. A small metal writing table is suspended from one wall, on the other a metal bunk on which a man sits. In his hands he holds volume three of The Loeb Classical Library edition of Thucydides' *History of the Peloponnesian War*, in which he seems to be thoroughly engrossed. His hair, once blond surfer floppy, has receded into a monastic, horseshoe-shaped gray halo. Inside these walls this man is known as Young Dave even though he is probably in his mid-sixties. Before Young Dave entered this unit thirty-some years ago, he was known to his work buds on the outside as Old Dave because, just turned thirty, he was the oldest among them. Ironically, when he began his sentence in this desert retreat, another prisoner, already on the far side of middle-age himself, went by the handle Old Dave. To avoid confusion, and possibly some rough play, the other prisoners called the new Old Dave Young Dave. In answer to the obvious question, Young Dave is serving a life sentence. His crime? Possession of less than an ounce of marijuana (this *is* Texas), which actually belonged to his girlfriend, but to avoid causing problems at her high-dollar white-collar job, he nobly, and stupidly, took the hit. And then, because he'd already had two previous convictions, the first also for possession of less than an ounce while he was a freshman in college, the second for ... *wellll*, he admits sheepishly ... *jaywalking*, the DA said he was clearly an incorrigible scofflaw, one, two, three strikes and you're out, or rather in, for life. And, while this is all mildly interesting, one might reasonably ask why Boone should give a rat's ass about this over-the-hill loser. Ah, well, as some of you in the audience might recall, Young Dave was once the Snowman's foreman on a snow crew.

The camera draws back through the window, out into the cellblock. Illuminated by glaring, twenty-four hour a day fluorescence, we see tier upon tier of cells stacked on top of each other in yet another Caligarian nightmare of shadows and angles in a man-made canyon of caged humans not terribly unlike an enormous wet market in Wuhan, China. The camera climbs higher, out of this cellblock, out of this wing, out of these prison walls, and hovers over a sprawling concrete fortress bristling with guard towers, chain link fence, razor wire. This is the privately managed, for-profit mega-penitentiary aptly named Wuthering Heights due to its wind and sun-beaten high desert location. In the summer the concrete structure bakes like a clay oven, the temperature inside climbs above one hundred-twenty degrees Fahrenheit, there's no air conditioning, the prisoners swelter and suffocate in the hot air. In winter, it's bitterly cold, often well below freezing, battered by howling winds. Heating is minimal. The prison staff suffers as much as the inmates. It's lahk we're doing tahm, too, Junior Boveen, a dayshift guard, says, mopping sweat from his frighteningly florid and incongruously Kewpie doll face.

This past winter ~~Kewpie~~ Junior had to take sick leave (unpaid) for two weeks to recover from pneumonia and severe frostbite. The mortality rate among prisoners at Wuthering Heights is ten times the national average but you wouldn't know that from the perorations of high-minded church fathers such as Reverend Fallible, who has felt the need to reassert his conservative credentials, and snake-in-the-grass politicians like Senator Theodore "Toad" Crooze, who decry the "country club atmosphere" and "gourmet catering service." (Clearly a desperate attempt to salvage what the pundits have proclaimed a floundering career on the part of the senator, known now in his nadir as *Grow a Pair* after that horrible interview on FUCHS News. Mr. Crooze, your opponent called your wife ugly. She is a little plain. He accused your father of assassinating a president. I've had my suspicions. He called you spineless. The X-rays are inconclusive.)

Half a dozen semi-tractor trailers pull up to the loading docks of this country club every day to deliver tons of bulk food, fifty-pound sacks of weevil-infested white flour, huge tubs of rancid margarine and lard, pallets of moldy white bread, barrels of stale cheese *food*, largely unidentifiable frozen meat *products*, neon-colored canned fruit saturated with corn syrup, crates of *fresh* produce, mostly potatoes, beans, onions, carrots and large bunches of bananas, much of it showing signs of putrefaction, spoilage and infestation, all far exceeding the government's maximum allowed quotient of insect parts, indeed, in some cases the insects are more identifiable than the food product (there's even the suggestion they were intended for the Mexican market—on the horizon for America's consumers).

Escorted by a phalanx of heavily armed guards, the warden, Joe Don Blocker (no relation to Travis), PhD in criminology (*The Criminal Mind Under Lock and Key*, Harpies, 2033), has been conducting a walking tour of this penopolis with the owner, Mister, um, *Snowman?* who, given his not exactly felonious but, by his own admission (among friends), scofflaw history, does note the irony of being on this side of the bars. Feeling the full weight of his position, he pronounces what he assumes to be a common sentiment. Our goal, of course, is to get these men rehabilitated and back out in the street in productive jobs. Apparently not, however, as common a sentiment as he thought. Warden Blocker explodes in red-faced outrage.

Are you out of your mind, *sir?!* That's exactly what we don't want! We want to fill these units with bodies, we want the prison population to soar! That's how we make our money, *Mister* Snowman. Sensing he's on the verge of insubordination, the warden, *call me Joe*, takes a step back, shrugs his shoulders in a rolling left to right motion like a street fighter preparing for a brawl and proceeds to enlighten this uninformed *corporate* type (yes, *him*, the *Snowman*—he *is* wearing a suit and tie).

Do you know (*Joe's* highland gorilla chest expands proudly) that the United States incarcerates more of its own people than any other country in the world? And even better, this whole operation costs taxpayers almost a hundred billion dollars a year? And do you know why that's better, *Mister* Snowman?

Um ...?

Because a big chunk of that hundred billion goes directly to *us*. Apparently Joe doesn't think it worth mentioning to *Mister* Snowman that at least a third of the prison population is probably innocent and that many of the inmates are here by mistake. Court fuck-ups, incompetent lawyers, corrupt judges, half the time it's simply because they can't afford bail. Fucking losers sit in jail for years for a minor offense like, oh, you know, public urination. Sometimes the prisoners don't even remember what they're in for.

I'm also proud to say (Joe *does* say) that we've had tremendous success with our new juvenile outreach program. Well, at least that sounds positive. For about two seconds. What Joe really means is that criminality has been taken to a new low—er, rather, it has been redefined to include a lower age demographic, which now covers the whole range, K-12. Joe has an entire block dedicated to kids who misbehaved in class. What are you in for? one eight-year-old asks another. Squirting milk out of my nose. You? Throwing a spitball at Joni Hensen's head. Every month a new delivery of *pre-young adults* arrives. For *hygienic* purposes, Joe has these little lambs stripped naked, fitted with diaphanous cupid wings and halos, and then paraded on their way to the showers past tiers of hardened criminals in the notorious Z cellblock who'd make that highland gorilla shit his pants. Which also happens to be where Joe is escorting the Snowman now. Joe pops a large powder blue umbrella open over their heads as golden showers, gobs of cum and handfuls of excrement rain down from above, along with a cacophony of catcalls, lewd and probably physically impossible sexual suggestions and the sloppy barbecue sauce sound of smacking lips. Joe grins. I'm sure you can imagine how much these fellows would love to get the little ones in their cells and give 'em some daddy bear love. Which is how Boone, leaving his audience to digest that morsel, transitions back to Young Dave.

Young Dave's small social circle includes Clancy McCluhan, a soft-faced seventeen-year-old busted for possession of half a gram of meth in Cowtown, Wyoming and sentenced to twenty years in prison, to be served in Texas thanks to a kind of barter system (the state of Wyoming takes a cut of the profit). As the sheriff led young McCluhan from the courtroom, his mother collapsed on the floor sobbing, *Texas? Twenty years?* I won't never be able to see my boy again. I can't afford a trip all the way down there and with my heart like it is. Aw, dry up, lady, the sheriff sneered. You do the crime, you do the time. It's the only way these kids'll learn.

Clancy certainly had some learning to do. One day Young Dave came into the shower and found Clancy on his hands and knees, naked, a cock in his mouth, a cock up his ass, and a line of guys barely able to keep their hands off the erections sticking out of their pants. Young Dave yelled for the guard, which, although monosyllabic, still required a considerable passage of time to enunciate in his attenuated west Texas drawl, which also really pissed off the sodomites (that's not meant judgmentally, folks, just saying), who, based on their expressions, looked like they were about to give Young Dave the same treatment when *Boom! Boom! Boom!* the tiled walls and concrete floor shook beneath their feet as if King Kong was stomping through the jungle and, not too far off the mark, in trotted Pakalolo, this huge Hawaiian dude, native Kānaka Maoli, he's at least seven feet tall, easily weighs five hundred pounds, in the weight room he benches eight hundred for reps (lots of 'em), squats about two thousand, he has full facial warrior tattoos, shark tooth necklace made from the teeth he tore from a great white's jaw when it chose him to dine on by mistake. He's also part of the Snowman's little circle and he enjoys nothing more than some friendly roughhousing. He swings his massive arms and bodies fly everywhere, skulls crack against concrete, bones break, and Pakalolo's belly laughing like a kid with a new game station. From the expression on the guard's face when he finally shows up, he was expecting a different outcome, including some sloppy cleanup on his part. The injured are hauled off to the infirmary with exaggerated dissembling from Young Dave and Pakalolo about a hotly contested soccer match. Clancy disappears for weeks. Unfortunately, Young Dave has a pretty good idea what that's about.

Doctors, hospital and emergency services are provided to the Wuthering Heights facility under a blanket contract with the Texas State Medical Extension Program. It should come as no surprise that, in exchange, Texas state medical schools have access to large numbers of cadavers, as well as volunteers (guinea pigs) for experimental drugs and procedures (a rumor persists of a cellblock X where the products of some of these experiments are kept: humans with pig snouts, donkey ears and penises, extra legs, extraordinary psychological aberrations, e.g., gourmet cannibalism). Naturally the doctors are all quacks. During a visit to the prison infirmary for the treatment of an infected big toe, Young Dave found himself in the hands of a doctor Benway, who, after regarding Young Dave with a skeptical arch of the brow, said in an adenoidal drawl, It's clearly a case of *brainnn* disease (the attentive audience member might notice a disturbing resemblance to OPEN's R&D man, Roger Wilco—that rascal Boone again, cutting corners in the casting and payroll departments?). But ... I ... on ... ly ... have ... an ... in ... fect ... ed ... toooe, Young Dave said, his own drawl perhaps suggesting a competitive if not professional challenge to the good doctor's diagnosis. To which Doctor Benway replied even more archly, *I ammm the DOC-torrr!*

And, yes, he is, despite the Board of Medical Examiners' revocation of his license for unorthodox practices, i.e., inducing or coercing or, in some cases, physically forcing female patients and young boys to perform various sex acts as part of their therapy (I like my lunch *naaaked*, Doctor Benway snarls), leading to a number of suicide attempts, at least one successful(?), after which Doctor Benway himself was ordered to undergo psychiatric treatment, or, as he likes to joke with a Dick Cheney smirk, to be *rewired*—new logic board, hard drive, clean out the transistors, and we're good to go. In the spirit of new beginnings, when Doctor Benway was introduced to the head doctor at Wuthering Heights, he said, I feel I should inform you—Shush! the supervisor hushed him with a forefinger to the lips. Not another word! We are an equal opportunity employer. And *smik smak*, the rehabilitated Doctor was on board with a six-figure salary and unlimited specimens for his experiments. Hostile prisoners, the severely depressed, suicidal, schizophrenic, *innocent*—Doctor Benway drugs them into drooling stupefaction and then turns them into his unwitting sex toys (the good doctor prefers this kittenish language to the harsher *meat puppets*), dresses them in women's lingerie, clown costumes, little Lord Fauntleroy outfits. He's got a drawer full of flash drives, thousands of photos, enough evidence to have him medically castrated and sent to prison for life. What is it about these Mengele types who just have to keep records of their misdeeds? *Whoooo knowwwws*, maybe one day I'll write a *booook*. Young Dave remembers none of his treatment. Nor does he understand why an infected big toe required general anesthesia and two weeks of heavy sedation. Sometimes he has disturbing flashbacks, images of Doctor Benway in various states of undress, himself trussed with electrical cords, also undressed. He also suspects that Doctor Benway has installed some sort of internal *device*, a little reminder of who's in control here. At odd times his face crumples in pain or he gasps and his eyes roll back in his head.

Meanwhile, *Joe*, who has caught on to the Snowman's liberal bent, says, I wouldn't want you to get the idea that our prisoners are treated in anything less than a humane fashion. Let me remind you that our *residents* are allowed visitation privileges with family members and friends. Although, true, these visits are limited to once a year, the visitors have to drive several hundred miles out in the fucking desert (there is no public transportation), and, yes, they are more or less treated like prisoners themselves, patted down, scanned electronically, body cavity checks at the guards' discretion, *hi, cutie*. They're assigned a small booth with a two-inch-thick glass partition separating them from the prisoner, the prisoner and the visitor are provided with tin cans connected by waxed string for communication. Even shouting, it's almost impossible for them to hear each other and even worse with two dozen other prisoners and guests shouting in the background. The system's perfect, Joe says. There's no way for the prisoner and visitor to exchange contraband. Or hugs. Or love. Or reassurance that little Tommy and Lisa at home still love them, and yes, Frank, I do too, although it's hard, it's really hard, you're not there and—sob—I get offers from other men, you know, they say, why're you waiting for that loser? But it's you I love, Frank, know what I mean? *What'd you say?!*

As you may have observed, Joe says, we have a quota system in this facility. Quota system? Yeah, you know, so many Blacks, Hispanics, Asians, Whites, etc. Strictly in accordance with Federal guidelines, deferring to states' rights of course. Minorities currently represent sixty percent of our prison population but our goal is seventy per cent. You have a goal, Warden? Isn't that putting the cart before the horse? Really, Mister Snowman. Your liberalism is unbecoming. Statistics show that the majority of prison inmates are minorities. It stands to reason, therefore, that the more minorities we incarcerate, the less chance they have of committing crimes.

At this moment Joe and the Snowman are passing a dark, steep stairway blocked by a rusted iron gate secured with a large brass lock. What's down there? the Snowman asks. Solitary confinement, Joe replies with a shrug that can only be described as dismissive. So that's where you lock up the really bad guys? the Snowman persists. Joe sniffs, nods stiffly. So they're down there for what, like, days? the Snowman, not letting up. Joe pushes out his lower lip. Weeks? Joe remains stolid, stoic, lips zipped. Months? Joe's as mum as his dead mum. Now the Snowman's curious. So, just to clarify, *Warden.* Are you saying you've got guys locked down in some kind of dungeon, *alone*, for *years?* Joe swings his head from side to side, all aw shucks sheepish. Um … *maybe?* I mean, I don't *know?* I haven't *personally* been down there in *ages?* To which the Snowman says with an inexplicable French accent, Well, *eef* you don't know, who does? Look, Joe says, regaining his composure. It's not our business to pamper these thugs. Not to put too fine a point on it, *Mister* Snowman, but what we're talking about here isn't just punishment. We're giving the people what they want. Retribution.

And when it comes to retribution, Texas does it big. Executions on a weekly basis, public participation encouraged. Licensed gun owners can sign up for Civilian Execution Brigades (CEBs), known informally as the Civilian Public Whacks program. A couple hours of instruction, mostly tall tales and BSing about the good old days (lynchin' nigras—oh, sorry, Fred), a trip to the firing range, human silhouette targets are cheap and effective, head shot's best, ladies and gentlemen, right between the eyes, however for the novice we recommend large body mass just to make sure you hit your target, strike the general area of the heart, liver, lungs and you're in like flint. Before each execution, the warden explains to the condemned inmate the purpose of his punishment. Normally, these hardened criminals wouldn't give a flying fuck what Joe has to say, but, after all, he does have an, *ahem*, captive audience. As I am sure you are well aware, Mister Bruno, there are many theories regarding the application of the ultimate penalty. *Huh?* In this institution, we are solely concerned with facts. The fact is, you have committed a despicable desecration of the Lord God's Holy Gift of Life. *What the fuck?* For this, society deems that you must be punished with the loss of your own life. For if you suffer no punishment, neither your victims residing in the arms of God in the high holy heavens, nor your victim's loved ones struggling with inconsolable grief, nor society at large outraged by your despicable act, will feel justice has been served. We do not delude ourselves that this punishment will act as a deterrent to others. And please, let's not split hairs over the nature of retribution. In short, you have hurt people very badly, Mister Bruno. Now we are going to hurt you very badly in return. *Dude, seriously?*

To the witnesses on the other side of the glass partition, it looks as if the warden, who has a solemn, thoughtful, brow-furrowing expression, is offering words of comfort. So they can't begin to understand the condemned's anger and frustration when the warden briefly turns the mike on, Do you have any last words, Mister Bruno? *Fuck you, dickhead! Motherfucking cock—!* Public participation in executions goes over so well that courts are encouraged to pick up the pace of capital punishment cases. To make the kill more exciting for the CEBs, the condemned are locked in modified exoskeletons, basically body-contoured cages, that can be arranged in various attack positions, knife raised overhead, pointing firearms, etc., and sent scooting forward on metal tracks directly at the shooters. You can imagine the adrenaline rush when you squeeze the trigger and lead hits flesh, and then that second rush, sucking down an ice-cold brewskie afterwards and reliving the thrill of the kill with your fellow CEBers.

Following the execution of Leroy Philateles Brown, a prisoner from Mississippi who pretty much everyone knows was innocent, the Black wing rebels, twenty thousand Black men in five thousand eight-by-ten cages, they're all banging on the bars and stomping their feet in the exact same rhythm to the exact same beat *BOOM-ba-Boomba! BOOM-ba-ba-Boomba!* The vibrations overwhelm Wuthering Height's electrical system. Every gate, door and lock in the prison springs open at exactly the same moment. Prisoners are climbing out of windows and down drain pipes. They're pouring out of doors and storm sewers. They're piling into delivery trucks, laundry vans, prison guards' private vehicles, prairie schooners, pedicabs and wheelbarrows. Teams of escapees run in relays, others take turns going out for long passes. SNN and FUCHS News drones are first on the scene. Overhead camera shots show a mass of humanity swarming away from the prison in what *Osberg Statusman* political cartoonist Ben Corporal likens to an enormous ink spill with the caption **Your Tax Dollars At Work**. Apparently those tax dollars have already been spent (or placed in private accounts, guess whose?). There aren't enough resources to round up all the escaped prisoners. The authorities realize it's simpler to carry on as if nothing's happened, just make sure the paperwork looks good.

It would be heartwarming to report that, just as a formality, doing the dewiest of due diligence, the Snowman asks to have a look at prison records and, while scrolling down the list of inmates, he happens upon a familiar name, or, even better yet, as he nears the end of his tour he spots Young Dave in a chow line and, thanks to his vast wealth and connections, finagles his release on the spot. Doesn't happen. As things stand now, Young Dave will spend the rest of his life in prison.

32
One of Us

AND MAYBE THAT'S HOW you go from a cheesy, candle-lit Hallmark Christmas Card, benign, reassuring, frosty snowmen and sleigh bells jingling, sugar plums dancing and stockings hung by the chimney with care, to an arctic barrenness of ice and snow, of Klondike cold, frozen Frankensteinian ice floes, of soul on ice. And from there? The deliciously wicked possibilities of absolute zero, complete stasis, of an infinite night of frozen blackness, all movement and life stopped, even the process of thinking arrested, the last unfinished thought of the last sentient being suspended for eternity, the hand of God flipping the switch, goodnight, Irene?

And what of our Snowman? Did he know what was happening all along? Was he the perfect *Mister Freeze* after all? Cold and calculating at heart, Boris Spasskily planning out every move five, six hundred moves in advance? All his protestations of innocence (I knew nothing, I was simply obeying orders, etc.) a façade—okay, say it, a *lie?* You just kept making excuses, you looked away, averted your gaze, convinced yourself you weren't responsible, that it wasn't what it was, that you didn't understand when Iago explained to you. Come on, *Snowman*, fess up and it'll be a lot easier for everybody.

Okay, look, I never knew what the fuck was going on. I mean, I thought I knew. Sometimes. Like I basically understand internal combustion without the chemist's or the physicist's or the engineer's knowledge of molecular structures, thermodynamics, the optimal design and specifications of a crankcase. We've heard this before, Snowman. I didn't know, I wasn't informed, I was out of the loop, I vass not a Nazi, I ... I ... I ... I ... Yes, *you*, Snowman. Remember that big world-wreathing conspiracy you were always so paranoid about? Well, you were right. There is a conspiracy, and you're part of it. In fact, you're one of the top conspirators. But how? What? When? I never signed anything, never agreed to anything, never plotted against anyone. Yes, you did, Snowman, when you made your first penny of profit off your first *PoPoPop!*®. But what's wrong with that? Nobody works for free, everyone's out to make a buck. Sure, a buck, two bucks, five, ten, a hundred, a thousand, a million, a *billion* bucks. When does too much become never enough? That's when you climb on board the train, join the team— cabal, if you like, when you become a player of the great game, the unspoken conspiracy of mutual interests, everybody working together for each other's benefit (*that* word again), everybody working toward the same goal, the unabated accumulation of wealth. It's a global hive mind, a matrix in which everyone communicates, speaks the same language, thinks the same thoughts, entirely democratic, anyone can participate, everyone has a voice, a vote, sure, some bigger than others, some much bigger, that's how it works, how it has always worked, the law of the jungle, the Darwinningest, Rousseauian *anti*-social contract. If some crash and burn along the way, if they fuck up, miscalculate, get eaten, that's the nature of the game. This club is open to anyone, even the untermensch who, somehow, through genius, desperation, obsessive work ethic or pure criminal intent, manages to claw his or her way up out of the cesspool and into the stratosphere where, magically, in a single generation, okay, sometimes two (*three?* depends on the genes), they shed all their thuggish, bumpkin mannerisms, assume ownership of their exulted rank. It's an honor to welcome you on board, *Mister* Snowman. But I didn't ask … I don't want … Come now, Mister Snowman, there's really no choice. Everyone, let's give the Snowman a hearty reception. All together now. *We accept you, we accept you. One of us, one of us. Gooba-gobble, gooba-gobble.*

And, sure, there is some history here, some gold in them thar cerebral hills that a decent psychologist, not necessarily even a *good* one (*I ammm the DOC-torrr!*), might mine for all it's worth. Because, yes, giving it some thought, the Snowman does remember now that sometime in the ninth or tenth grade, as usual staring out the window at a hawk in a tree top or up at the acoustic panels on the ceiling or anywhere but the completely unintelligible algebraic equation or diagrammed sentence scrawled on the blackboard like a message from Mars, he frequently fantasized about becoming enormously wealthy. Exactly how he would accomplish this was unclear but that's beside the point. He'd live in a fortress mansion on a mountainside in some exotic tropical or Alpine location and he'd have private jets and helicopters and a huge yacht, heavily armed, of course, more like a cutting-edge Chinese destroyer. He'd basically own the entire country, in fact, he'd essentially be king of the world, and if people didn't do what he told them they'd be sorry, real sorry, but if they were good and obeyed his orders he would reward them. In a ~~nutshell~~ (repetitive; suggestion, why not alternate with *clamshell?*—Ed.) (Dude, *seriously?!*—Edwige.), i.e., something between enlightened despotism and *progressive* feudalism. A philosophy that, in his young adulthood, evolved, due in part to world events, the influence of more informed friends, but also the very real possibility of his being drafted and sent to fight in a war that made absolutely no sense to anyone, into the desire to do something good that benefited (*sure* about that word?) all of humankind. So how, he asks himself again, has he come to this? A player in the planetary endgame of capitalism? Maybe it was there all along, a wrinkle in his genes or an errant forbearer (Rocketmania?). That urge for oblivion, capitulation to the fear of death, to entropy, and, shucks, why not take the whole world with you? Ragnarök, Götterdämmerung, for the romantic young evangels we have the Apocalypse.

To say the least, he's stunned, blindsided by events. How could something that started out so well and made so many peoples' lives happier turn into this—dare I say it?—corporate monstrosity? How could he allow Maria's magic potion to be used for such *evil?!* No surprise that by now some in the viewing audience have divined a kind of Tolkien ring (*ouch*) to the whole sordid affair. Nor does Boone fail to confirm that suspicion as he gives us a glimpse of the corrupted Sauron bent over his Palantir in his tower, searching for that very piece of elvish jewelry, the source of all power, *my precioussss.*

33
Addiction

WE NOW HEAR DEEP MALE VOICES chanting, *O-Ee-Yah!*
E-oh-Ah! and we see a brief, disturbing image of—flying
monkeys? Wrong film. We see the Snowman in his
Hawaiian slacker dude outfit being escorted by four
heavily armed guards. Has he been arrested? Committed
some crime more monstrous than the white-collar kind?
He and his escort approach a giant vault with a huge iron
door, perfectly round, on either side of which two more
guards are posted. He glances at the bioscan, waves his
hand over the palmscan, taps in a six-digit code and,
lastly, withdraws from his right front pocket a large brass
key with what do appear to be (the camera zooming in)
elvish inscriptions, inserts it in the keyhole, turns it with
a loud *CLANK* and the door swings open revealing—
Scrooge McDuck piles of gold coins? Nope.

In the center of the vault stands a large stainless-steel
tank, maybe a thousand gallons at a quick guestimate,
with a metal stairway on the side. The Snowman's
huaraches make faint clinging sounds on the rungs as he
climbs to the top. He takes a small glass vial out of his
shirt pocket, unscrews the cap, inserts a syringe through
the self-sealing aperture, extracts a single drop of liquid
and squirts it into the tank, which is filled with nothing

more than municipal tap water. He then presses a button, initiating a very gentle stirring process that will transform this simple, inexpensive drinking water into extremely valuable "heavy water," which will then be distributed in single liter units via secure couriers to production plants all over the world, where it will serve again as a starter batch.

Once a month the Snowman performs this ritual and every time he does so he thinks of just how ridiculously precious this single drop is. An entire industry, a corporate empire, the hundreds of thousands of employees, the millions of people in ancillary industries, transport, distribution, the grocery chains, convenience stores, Mom and Pop corner shops, managers, cashiers, shelf stockers, delivery drivers, the billions of consumers around the world who live for their daily *PoPoPop!*® (stock photos of people enjoying *PoPoPops!*® in front of the Eiffel Tower, ~~the Kremlin~~, the Leaning Tower of Pisa, a grass shack in Uganda, a cave in Afghanistan), and it's all contingent upon this tiny drop of liquid. Even crazier, everyone (and his grandmother) assumes the Snowman's supply is endless, that he has some kind of secret formula, that he produces this stuff himself. They'd never guess that not only is his source finite but he's been running on borrowed time. He has discovered that at some point the effectiveness of the starter batch fades and he has to rejuvenate the whole process with a full drop of Maria's potion. He tries to extrapolate into the future how long the remaining potion will last, given that he originally had— how much, boys and girls? that's right—ten milliliters, which he figured equaled about two hundred drops or a thousand micro-drops, divided by twelve, minus spillage and evaporation, equals, um … I don't know, maybe sixty-six point-six years? Well, shit, that's enough to last his lifetime and keep the show going long afterward, right?

Welllll ... yes, except for another small issue that theory and algorithms don't account for, which he has confided to no one and, as far as he knows, no one else knows about, not even Iago, although he suspects Moses suspects and by now *you* might have guessed even though it's still hard as hell for him to admit even to himself. He can't even remember how it happened, gradually of course, as it always does, an occasional sip of the starter batch now and then, call it taste testing or quality checking, and, sure, getting a pretty good buzz on. It perked him up, put some lead in his pencil, in his tank, in his backbone, made him ready to face adversity with a smile and a song, well, okay, let's not go that far (ask anybody who's ever heard him mangle a tune). And from there to swilling the stuff like communion wine, scooping up dippers of happy juice from the vat he kept in his office every time he faced another crisis, Iago, evolved from precocious brat into fully matured Svengali, dragged him deeper into the abyss. And, well, *you* know how that goes. Experimentation leads to habituation leads to *bingo* addiction.

One time, purely by accident (he tells himself), *whoopsie*, he spilled an entire drop of Maria's magic potion in his hand and, purely out of reflex (so he also tells himself), licked it off and, *Bonnnggg!* That sure did ring some bells. (He has a blinding photo flash of another ten-milliliter glass phial containing a clear liquid that *looks* like water or maybe rubbing alcohol or even vodka but is neither aqua vitae nor uisquebaugh but liquid acid, not sulfuric or hydrochloric, LSD, that he obtained from a college friend who happened to be a chemistry major and …) It was like the fountain of youth, the Lazarus effect. The shadow of gloom lifted, the negativity and naysaying evaporated, he was a *new man*, extroverted, outgoing, a good word and a glad hand for everyone. OPEN team members figured his disease was in remission or he was in therapy or he finally ran that big marathon. Months later he was still experiencing the afterglow, all is good with the world, not a cloud— *rrruuhhnnn* (sound of machine running down).

And then it happened, true, belatedly, maybe for that reason all the more severe, the crash, the acid blues collapse. His spirits sank to a new low, he felt seriously suicidal, nothing but black clouds on the horizon. And so, no accident this time, he took another pure drop of Maria's potion … *and we're off* … off to the races again, off on another spin cycle (that word again, what is it about that word … cycle? … cycle? … cycle? …) wired, wild-eyed, full of light and energy, channeling god knows what deity, Carnegie? Mellon? Jesus Christ? (Um … the money lenders' tables? Not likely.) We can make this business greater than ever! We can dominate the global market! (We already do, sir.) We can launch our product to worlds beyond with our new space program! We cannnnnn … *crash* (sound of breaking dinner plates, cars slamming into each other head-on).

The rest is a story as old as the ink in the Dead Sea Scrolls. He started to sneak drops of the pure stuff on a regular basis, *sneak* because even though nobody else knew what he was up to, his guilt and paranoia convinced him they did, and as much as he didn't want *them* to know, he really didn't want to admit to himself what he was doing, and you know how *that* goes. The lies, excuses, I need it to keep going, I deserve it, *my preciousss*. And why not, right? He's *the guy*, the number one, big honcho, all the weight's on him, all the pressure. Besides, it's only a drop now and then, right? He's got enough left to last—what was it, sixty years—something like that? Okay, now maybe it's fifty? forty? Recalculating the entire timeline every time he steals another drop—thirty, *twenty* years? Pretty soon he's down to single digits—nine, eight, *seven*—the realization of what he's doing every time that much more poignant. No matter how he spins it he's approaching zero and there ain't no *less than* in this game. Which, he also understands, means something unimaginable, not just life without that special pizazz, that ol' black magic, but, on a much grander scale, the *imminent* loss of *PoPoPops!*® and the inevitable collapse of OPEN and with it the one shining light in this whole damned enterprise that he has relied on to maintain any shred of self-respect, the unspoken social contract with humanity that has mostly kept the world economy running and the snarling dogs of war at bay (true, slightly delusional, but that *is* the nature of addiction).

At night he lies awake tossing and turning, imagining continents devastated by drought, famine, nuclear holocaust. During the day he suffers panic attacks, paralyzing fits of paranoia, self-doubt, he's unable to face team members or deal with the simplest tasks, he nearly breaks down in tears for no apparent reason, which—and you twelve-steppers know how that goes—causes him to indulge even more. He tells himself again and again that he has to stop, that he's addicted to this shit, that he's sick, which—only makes it worse. Adding to his troubles, Iago has been tighter than his own shadow, alternately obsequious and wheedling, inveigling, cajoling and outright bullying in an attempt to extract from him the secret ingredient. As a precaution, Snowman. In case you're … *debilitated.* Which once again sounds like a threat and doubly so after an encounter the Snowman has with M'Shaka on the Drag (another of Boone's *coincidences?*).

M'Shaka has aged, like everybody else, his shiny black dreads gone to ashen gray snakes, the furrows in his brow deep as cracks in blackland prairie during a drought. He inquires how Arthur is doing in *the business,* which, to the Snowman's already paranoid ears, sounds like a criminal enterprise (if not an indictment). Struggling to pronounce Arthur's name, he says *Arrrrooo* is fine, but his voice doesn't sound fine, he sounds like a hound dog baying at the moon, and M'shaka doesn't sound fine either when he shakes his head from side to side like a weary bison and says, I don't know where I went wrong with that boy. I can't see him no more. This is news to the Snowman. What, you mean like you're disowning him? He's disowning *you?* No, man, I mean I can't *see* him. He gone beyond white, he ain't there no more.

And then there's this, courtesy of the grasshopper: video that, due to a minor mishap (low battery on his cellphone), the Snowman will not have a chance to view until much later of an OPEN board meeting to which, apparently, he was not invited (Iago, who has caught wind of the Snowman's alternate life pushing the cart, tells the other board members the Snowman is indisposed at the moment—*not* the first time this has happened, I'm sure you have noticed). Laying his cards on the table (but keeping them close to his vest), Iago presents the current state of the Nicine Project as a two-pronged problem with a single solution. One, in order to obtain government funding, they must first prove the efficacy of Nicine, and for that to happen they need the secret ingredient in *PoPoPops!*® so Roger Wilco's crowd can do the necessary testing and development. And two, they need to substantially increase revenue to finance this operation.

And here Iago introduces the concept of "enhanced popular appeal," by which he means increasing the ~~addictive~~ *quality* of *PoPoPops!*®, and then, of course, we'll have to raise the price to keep up with demand (*of course! of course!*—concurs the board). Marketing, a nod to Cash Dullard, will target minority demographics, i.e., the poverty level crowd. Let's face it, these people are miserable, they're desperate, it's like playing the lottery and buying booze, they'll spend their last dollar on a fantasy and some feel good instead of food on the table and baby formula. We'll get Big Pharma in on it, talk to Oksi (the fact that Iago is on a first name basis with the drug czar should set off alarms *somewhere*). Of course we might meet resistance from diehard constitutionalists, the moral values crowd, we'll have to pay off—I mean, consult—with Reverend Fallible on that issue. Everybody else will be so blissed out they won't give a damn what we do. Keeping in mind what Marx's brother Groucho said, Opium is the religion of the people. Wolf ... if you please? Inserting his monocle, Wolf reads aloud from a Victorian Era pharmacological manual in a deadpan voice that sounds disconcertingly like Madame Psychosis': belladonna ... cocaine ... ergot ... ether ... laudanum ... morphine ... nitrous oxide ... opium ... shall I continue? Thank you, Wolf, I think that's sufficient. People have always loved their drugs. You've just got to make the concept palatable. The only hitch is, in order for all of this to work—and here Iago makes a dramatic Perry Mason pause (he is a lawyer)—we've gotta get that *dumbass Snowman* (Iago's exact words) on board.

No fucking way! The dumbass Snowman is outraged when Iago presents his case. *One,* we're not in the business of making profit off of poverty! And *two,* I sure as hell am not giving *you* the goddamn secret ingredient!

Despite the Snowman's adamant opposition (since when has this *bozo* gotten so recalcitrant?), Iago has little trouble convincing the other board members to greenlight the project. It's only a matter of time before we have the secret ingredient in our hands (he doesn't explain how but we can assume they assume he knows). As for financing, I'll feed the Snowman some line about inflation, rising costs. That dumbass *(again?)* will buy whatever I tell him.

Which *Brrriiinnnggg!!!* is why we next see that *dumbass* (again) taking Iago's call on his EyePhone® when he's pushing his *damn* cart down the *fucking* sidewalk trying to earn an honest *goddamn* living and, let's be honest, put business as far out of his mind as one of Jupiter's moons. Look, *Snowman,* I've talked with the distributor, fuel costs are up, union's busting his balls, he says he's gotta get fifty-thousand per shipment. To which the Snowman, beginning to get just a tad sick of Iago's schtick, not to mention this new distributor's endless price-gouging, replies in a feral growl that sounds like it might have come from one of Me'th's larger feline brethren, Tell that scumbag twenty thousand tops!

Now what? Iago lets things settle for a while and then *Brrriiinnnggg!!!* not too much later we see the Snowman receiving another phone call. *What the fuck now?!* He won't go for it, *Snowman*. He wants a cut himself, he has his own people he's gotta pay off. Yeah, well then fuck him! He's a dead man! he shouts loud enough to be heard within an entire city block (heads turning). We'll never do business with that lowlife piece of shit again! Uh-uh, Snowman, We need him. Oh, fuck me.

34
Anomie

YEAH, FUCK YOU, SNOWMAN. And once again all he can do about it is go back out on the street and push his cart like a damn donkey. It's pretty much a full-time job now. He starts in the a.m., finishes in the p.m., and day after day his mood descends farther into the abyss, that Joe Btfsplk's dark cloud of gloom hovering over him like a permanent insecurity blanket. Sure, in the beginning he had this totally misguided idea that he was getting back to his roots among the *people*. Wrong. There's been a change in society, a tectonic shift. He sees it in the anomie, the anger, in the koyaanisqatsian breakdown of ancient bonds and the trending toward chaos. Everybody at odds with everybody else, social and mainstream media full of lies and hate, people getting shot over a box of wings, a pair of shoes, a wedding cake. Fuck comity, right, *Snowman?* Nobody gives a fuck about anybody else, everybody's in it for themselves, everything is a fad, fraud, fake. Look at this fucking place. *Yoga Yogurt?* Yoga with yoghurt in thirty-three ~~flavors~~ poses. Fucking yoga with tea, coffee, beer. Yoga with goats, glazed donuts. Yoga with tomahawks, throwing knives, with fucking *guns* (it *is* Texas). Wasn't the whole fucking idea of yoga to clear your fucking mind and get rid of all the

fucking clutter?! What's this shit? **We the Living!** He
bends down, squints at the flyer in the window. CLASSES
COMBINE CROSS-TRAINING, URBAN SURVIVAL AND
A PALEO DIET! WE'LL TEACH YOU HOW TO RUN
DOWN AND KILL WILDLIFE WITH YOUR BARE
HANDS! COOK IT OVER RUSTIC FIRES IGNITED BY
IRON, FLINT AND PRIMITIVE BOW DRILLS! DEER,
BOAR, TURKEYS, RABBITS, DOGS, CATS, PEOPLE!
(Cannibalism is somewhat in again, still testing the
waters, trying to get some buzz going, get past the *yuck*
factor with aggressive marketing, experts from Bora
Bora, Papua New Guinea and New Zealand are on hand
for personalized instruction, a dab of wasabi or dollop of
Stubbs Barbecue Sauce helps you get that first bite
down.) Makes perfect sense, right? People eating people?
(... muttering continued ...) Won't be nothing else to eat.
Climate change killing everything, all this AI shit taking
over everything. None of which you had anything to do
with, *Snowman*. Nobody could blame you for any of that.
You were just a small fucking fish fry, little guy, cog in
that big fucking wheel, the zeitgeist. It's happening in
spite of you, not because of you, this transformation of
society into whatever the fuck it's becoming or rather
unbecoming.

At the next corner a shimmering, feathery, ninety-
foot tall hologrammatic *Angel of Mercy* leans down from
a Schneeland Foundation's *Peace Through PoPoPops!*®
VRBL and, briefly morphing into a voluptuous red
demon lady with horns, says to him, *Snowman, Snowman,
Snowman,* don't be such a schmuck all the time. This
thing's way bigger than you.

His clientele has changed too. They're rude,
impatient. Snot-nosed kids screaming at him *Snowman!
Snowman! Snowman!* Snotty poseurs who take tiny bites

of his *PoPoPops!®* while rhapsodizing over this *nice little ice* they had in Ven-*ice* (C'mon, Sam, you know that doesn't work). So why don'tcha go back to fucking Ven-*ice* and eat their goddamn *nice* ice, *stronzo?!* What did you say to me?! Carabiniere, would you please beat up this horrible man? They all think they fucking own me! Not a single goddamn one of 'em realizes I am the *original* fucking *Snowman* and head fucking honcho of OPEN! They all think I'm some random old loser *posing* as the Snowman, right? Like the guy who plays Santa at the mall? Those two or three weeks a year the only gig he can get. All right, sure, the holiday season's gotten longer, he's in Santa's chair August through January (Epiphany, divisions between the Julian and Gregorian calendars)— that's beside the point. *I'm* the loser?! I could have any one of you assholes hauled off and shot! I could do the fucking job myself and get off in a court of law! I could … he stops in mid-rant, stares wildly at the startled faces staring back at him like a garden full of fucking posies and he's got a pair of hedge-clippers in his hands. What the fuck are you doing, *Snowman?* You're out in fucking *public*, remember? You can't do this shit. They'll lock you up in an institution. You'll end up in the street like one of these … *bums.*

And, wouldn't you know it, maybe this really is a coincidence, maybe it's Boone doing another doubling thing, projecting the Snowman into a different role or potentiality, because now another ghost appears before him. It's Bum himself, the one and only, the original brand. Years of living rough have taken their ~~troll~~ *toll.* The Bumster has shrunk into a hunched-up little gnome, his head permanently planted at a crooked angle on his chest, his beard an ashen gray nest to several species of vermin and at least one very shy house wren. It's still above a hundred degrees and he's wearing a once quite elegant black men's wool winter topcoat by Sears, Roebucks & Co. (c. 1950), as well as a tattered but still rather natty black fedora on his head, although he has also been seen modeling a Mexican sombrero with pink and green stitching, a white, broad-brimmed lady's sunhat with a green visor, a bicycle helmet, a hardhat, and, more recently, a pointy, fire engine-red knit cap in which he does closely resemble a garden gnome, albeit ambulatory, his long-time private residence on the side of the DR-35 frontage road, along with his caravan of shopping carts, recently displaced by a new highway construction project, that incoming he feared for so long finally landing with the soft thud of a demolition order to all landholders in the vicinity to vacate their premises within ninety days before the bulldozers present their case. He shuffles from one locale to another in his multiple layers of clothing like a turtle in its shell or a drydocked hermit crab in someone else's shell, his peripatetic course determined by voices in his head, by messages from God. In his golden years (sure, *dotage* is appropriate), Bum has deigned—condescended, one might even say—to accept an occasional *PoPoPop!*®, there's even a detectable rainbow glow around his dark and furtive little eyes after he takes a bite, maybe even, briefly, a glimmer in his brain, a memory of happier times when he was a boy with a mama who loved him and hugged him close and a pappy who patted him on the head and said, I'm proud of you, son. Bum doesn't have long to go on this earthly plane, his tormented wanderings soon to end, but the toll takers, tally keepers, statisticians need not worry, there will be more to take his place. There are plenty of winners in the "Taking It To The Streets" lottery, and more all the time.

A car rolls past like it's on a movie set, an older model, banged-up, trailing smoke, probably needs new valves, ring job, a pathetic-looking family scene inside, white trash dad and mom in the front seat, both showing signs of extensive meth use, missing teeth, ruined faces, broken nose that never healed properly (hers), three kids in back, two boys and a girl in worn, ragged clothes, they all look glum, unwashed faces tear-stained. The Snowman turns to watch the car pass and—wait, is that *Hanktheredneckasshole* behind the wheel? He calls out, Hank! Hank! But they're gone. Then he remembers they were gone a long time ago. Hank couldn't find work after the snow industry collapsed, he relapsed into terminal alcoholism. About the same time the oldest, a boy, disappeared into the streets. Marfy-Ann took the other kids and went to live with her morbidly obese and permanently disabled mother in a trailer somewhere out near, um ... what was that address again? And that's how you drop off the radar.

A new stencil graffiti has begun to appear around Osberg, the Snowman sees it everywhere he goes, on walls, windows, doors, a pastel green pyramid (more or less U.S. dollar colored) with a fierce, probing, condemnatory eye in the center and human arms, legs and heads sticking out from under the base where an inscription reminds the public *all wealth flows upward ... losers!* He remembers a college seminar in which the eccentric and radical Economics Professor Johannesphär Knebel explained the economic pyramid in a nearly unintelligible accent nevertheless infused with sarcasm. Evrysink ees deesiignt to diirrrekt vealth upvard from labor unt prodookshun to zee koffers of zee plutocrrraatik vun perrrcentile who, in zee vords of our prezeedent in perpetueety, "best know how to manage zee Kountry's uf-fairs." Of course *they* fucking know best. It can't get much fucking better than this, can it? Everything works in *their* fucking favor. C'mon, man, stop it with the "they." It's you, bro. It's fucking you. *Snowmannn*, you're doing it again.

35
Eventide

IT'S NOW ABOUT SEVEN PM, still hot as hell, the temperature above one hundred, the sun a fiery orange disk in the west where the sky is infused with strange pastel pink and green hues that seem to be coming from outer space. Leaving the SoCo district in his rainbow phosphorescent wake, the Snowman's approaching the Congressional Avenue Bridge, at this hour a bumper-to-bumper assembly line of car horns, brake lights, hot exhaust, AC not working, windows down, heart-pounding, teeth bared, baboon-screaming road rage with live ammo. *BANG! BANG! Ow, ya got me!* Murder! Meyhem! *To the bat cave, Robin!*

And off the Snowman's mind goes, over the railing and underneath the bridge where one-and-a-half million Mexican free-tailed bats are suspended in the dank, dark, lime-stinking, guano-reeking crevices like wisps of charred newsprint awaiting some mysterious signal more or less concurrent with the arrival of dusk to send them swarming out into the twilit sky and down the Colorado River like a mile-long cloud of flickering black tacks that gradually disintegrates into smaller hunting parties—John, Steve, Harriet and Martha, break left, Earl, Sam, Betty and Lois, you're up next—to dine on the billions (and billions) of tiny insect droids and drones flitting, fluttering and buzzing in the balmy night skies over Osberg, among whom, or which, is a familiar face doing his or its best to fit in.

The Grasshopper's Lament

Oh, to be wanted, desired, wooed even,
but for love
and not appetite;
to be invited to dinner to dine
and not to be dined upon.
And should you survive this feast,
oh, sublime procreation.
True, awkward, hasty,
not a lot of time for champagne and foreplay.
Some species have but minutes to live,
others hours, months—a year.
The lucky ones, that is.
Oh, mortality.

The Snowman makes another dozen or so sales to the rabid fans of *Chiroptera* already stationed on the bridge *Snowman! Snowman! Snowman!* and, fleeing a flurry of grasping hands, *Take your cone and get outa my way! I don't have all goddamn day to stand around making change! PoPoPops!®* popping behind him like champagne corks (like *PoPoPops!®*, you dork!), he crosses busy Cesar Chavez at the light and begins a slow slog up Congressional Avenue, depth-of-field telescoped into a dusky, simmering 3D matrix of shadowy green oak trees, traffic lights and brake lights glowing red, neon signs coming on over restaurants, bars, coffee shops, boutiques. He stops again beneath the phantom blue luminescence of a sign that says simply in spectral white AVENUE CAFE over a gaping hole that has just appeared in the urban scape, a tear in the canvas through which the ghost of a long deceased popular eatery, sleeves rolled above his elbows, apron an artist's palette of coffee, orange juice, egg yolk, bacon grease and salsas rojas y verdes, has just stepped outside for a quick cig. The ectoplasmic eating establishment bows deeply, After you, my dear *Snowman*, and disappears back into the black hole which, time-lapsed, cartoon-like, is immediately *Cask of Amontillado* bricked up behind him.

The Snowman's mind snaps forward in time again, another memory dissolved into cannabinoid vapor as he takes another quick, surreptitious toke before starting across dirty old Sixth Street. Glancing sideways *ouch*, his super X-ray vision telescopes down the one and two-story brick and mortar canyon of bars and clubs, windows and doors thrown wide open, the bass-thumping heart-beat of Osberg's entertainment district where the neon lights are already bright, the street-life coming to life, Osbergers off work, out-of-towners in town for a good time, police foot and bicycle patrols gathered at strategic intersections for another night of wild west shootouts, cowboys, gangbangers, thugs, kids—fucking *kids*, where do they get all these guns? (Ha ha, it's a rhetorical question, everybody and his grannie knows Santy Claus brings 'em.) (Is that guy *still* here?) Which is one of the reasons the Snowman never goes down that street anymore, too much trouble, too many ghosts (Antone's and the Black Cat and Joe's Generic and ...).

His brain is like a city map of all the great places that disappeared before all the great places that replaced *them* disappeared, clubs, restaurants, diners, cafes, concert venues, head shops, bicycle shops (si? psi?), running emporiums, gyms, boutiques, gone out of business, shut down, torn down, forced into subterranean labyrinths carved out of limestone by millions of years of hydrology or driven out into the hinterlands where cactus and cattle still roam. Every street, every block, every building in this dirty old town another memory. The Trailways Bus Station where he went to pick up Judith at three a.m. after a trip into Mexico soured (some kind of research project, he never understood and Judith didn't explain—I'm sorry, Snowman, it's too com*plee*cated). The Greyhound Bus Station where he caught a slow coach up to Branson, Missouri for an unhappy attempt at a family reunion, basically a bunch of Martians banging into each other like awkward pieces of furniture—oh, right, *that's* when he bought Judith the parrot earrings that ended up on the Christmas tree). But no use dwelling in the past, *Oh, murderer of the spirit, no-stäl-gí-a, leave me be.*

Beneath the Paramount Theater's bright green blade the Snowman notices they're showing the perennial cult classic *The Abominable Snowman of the North* and cinephiles in the audience go wild when his reflection in the glass poster case is momentarily superimposed over B-movie star Billy "Plum" Bob Bengay's. But his image little resembles that of a movie star in the next shop window he passes. He looks like a slavering orc pushing a tumbril of dead bodies back to his cave for dinner. He's grubby, grimy, hot and sweaty, his neck's stiff, his back aches, his knees are sore, his spirits are depleted, he can barely move his feet … *slap … slap … slap …* His breath rasps in his chest as he starts up Ninth Street. This short steep climb gets harder every day. He turns down a service alley ripe with the urban gastric smells of rotting garbage, rancid cooking grease, vomit, urine, diarrhea, both ends of the alimentary process represented.

He stops in front of a rusty steel shutter, glances at an iris scan on the brick wall, the shutter begins to crank open. He pushes his cart inside and parks it at the end of a row of similar carts, all in some state of disrepair, peeling paint, damaged frames, broken wheels, torn and faded green and yellow umbrellas, one, partially covered by a black plastic tarp, appears to have been charred. A gallery of ghosts. He knows every one, remembers its history, shot up by a drunken cowboy on horseback, collision with a pedicab, set on fire by exploding Fourth of July fireworks. Each time he was going to give it an overhaul, new axle, wheels, umbrella, paint job, straighten the frame, update the ice box. Until it made more sense just to buy a new cart. And now this. He has been summoned. *Summoned!* Like a fucking lackey, house servant. How *dare* they summon *me?* I give my life to this shit and this is what I get? I'm the fucking *soul* of this business. Whoa, whoa, you're doing it again, Snowman. *Huh?* C'mon, you know what I'm talking about. Oh yeah, talking to … um … myself. Well, yeah, that too. I'm talking about your fucking self-esteem, Snow*bum.* You're acting like a fucking chump. Remember who the fuck you are, *Mister* Snowman. Don't get so damn ~~apoplectic~~—*apologectic*—alla' time. Yeah, yeah, you're right. *I'll* show 'em.

He waves his hand over a palmscan, a stainless steel elevator door slides open and he enters. The camera zooms in as he touches the button for the 233rd floor to let us know we're in for a long ride as Boone welcomes us back aboard the memory train, and, yes, Louise, it is fair to compare it to Einstein's glass elevator traveling through space.

36
Death Comes

INEVITABLY, FOR ALL OF US. Boone has been at a loss how to fit this scene in. Timing is everything, placement just as important. The following event has obviously occurred sometime in the past, how long ago isn't clear. Once again we see the Snowman pushing his cart up the Drag as the student tides part around him. The film switches to grainy, technicolor Super 8 and we watch as the president's car—wait, wrong film—as two OPD motorcycle cops cruise down the Drag in slow motion, the camera catching various details, the sunlight glaring off chrome, white helmets, wraparound sun glasses, creaking black leather. The motorcycles pull up to the curb where M'Shaka is standing behind his display table in his colored robes, incense smoke swirling around him, a set of windchimes ringing faintly *is that a breeze?* From his here-we-go-again expression it's obvious the cops have hassled him before. Nevertheless he greets them with a jovial, deep as thunder, How you doin' today, my brothers in blue? See anything here that interests you? The cops don't say anything, don't even bother to dismount. Straddling their bikes, boots planted flat-foot on the pavement, they draw their weapons, shoot M'Shaka multiple times, reholster, push back from the curb, rev their engines and exit stage left at almost the exact moment the Snowman enters stage right behind his cart and ejaculates the first words that come to his mind, obscene, yes, maybe, but less so each time he repeats them with a new degree of disbelief, *what the fuck? What ... the ... Fuck? WHAT THE FUUUCK?!* as through the steamy summer haze he sees and sees and sees and still doesn't see, can't accept what his eyes, brain, tell him he sees. A large, bear-like body in rainbow-colored robes lying on the dirty pavement in a storefront alcove with a dark red puddle of blood spreading outward like spilled paint that unaware passersby slog through and only belatedly become aware of, *what IS this sticky stuff?*

Utterly untrained, unprepared, un-*anything* for this kind of contingency, the Snowman drops to his knees, jams his hands in M'Shaka's thick beard and coarse bundle of dreads and cradles his head in his arms, repeating futilely, ineffectually, C'mon, man! C'mon, man! Brief candle of hope, M'Shaka's eyes open, his lips move, *Arthur*, he whispers. He wants me to tell Iago. Of course I'll tell him! M'Shaka's face contorts with pain, his head slowly rocks from side to side, his features relax, the heavily furrowed brow smooths out, probably for the first time in his life, and his eyes close. C'mon, man! the Snowman says as futilely as before. Somebody! *Help!*

Then, sirens, flashing lights, EMS, cop cars, voices shouting, What happened? Did you see anything? Nope, nobody knows anything, nobody saw anything, heads down, minds, eyes, thumbs absorbed in an alternate electroidal reality. The one or two bystanders who *maybe?* saw something are totally nonplussed. I mean, like, they're *cops?* I mean, like, they have a right to, like, *shoot him?* I mean, like, he must have done something *bad?* And the Snowman? Dragged off to jail, grilled in a dark dank cell in the basement, *C'mon, fuckwad, we know you're buddies with this guy.* No, that didn't happen, he drifted away, slipped back into the crowd, an itinerant ice cream vendor in a faded Hawaiian shirt, palm trees and—what is that red blotch, an *orchid?*

Later everybody will agree it looks like a coordinated hit, but who? The Osberg Chief of Police denies her people had anything to do with it, denies the existence of rogue elements, paramilitaries, "sporting clubs." Someone suggests a connection to old drug ties. There are reports that M'Shaka's ministry has been infiltrated by the FIB, rumors that he was advocating for violent overthrow of the government, attacks on police stations, military bases, free school lunches (choose the correct answer for a free *PoPoPop!*® offer valid while supply lasts).

Once again the headlines are splashed with accusations of police brutality, racial profiling. Riots break out. Sorta non-lethal rubber bullets and beanbags fly, batons flail, people are bloodied, beaten, on their knees, here and there bodies crumple to the ground. A big chunk of the Far East Side cracks loose from the rest of Osberg. You can see this Grand Canyon-like crevasse open up on the city map and what had (mostly) been a figurative separation of the races becomes a physical reality. While attending M'Shaka's funeral, a black silk, satin, veils, tails and crepe affair on one side of the family, a floral and fashion shop collaboration of color and texture on the other, the Snowman finds himself seated next to an older Black man with snow white hair and beard whose face brightens with recognition. You the *Snowman,* ain't you, M'Shaka's burden? *Burden?* he says, thinking maybe the old gent means, I don't know, *brethren?* The village elder, because that's what he would have been where his ancestors came from, tilts his head sideways, gives him a bemused smile. C'mon, man. M'Shaka never tole you 'bout that? Um … *noooo …*

Which is how the Snowman now learns that at some time in their life, every Black person in America is assigned a *white* person to redeem (also known as the *Black man's burden* but the gender-neutral *person* is preferable). Black men, women and even children have been serving in this role for centuries, first as slaves, then as servants, butlers, maids, childcare and healthcare providers, co-workers (grudgingly) and finally even *friends*, often times without any appreciable success. Dem ol' white folk be ornery troublesome rascals, the quartoseptcentennial-something Mammy says, and she's been taking care of white folk since she nursed a wounded Confederate soldier back to health when she was a nine-year-old girl—Glenda, the fact-check person.)

*   *   *

Ding!
Going down? Oh, sorry, I must have pushed the wrong button.
Damned straight you pushed the wrong button, motherfucker! Trouble with people today, don't pay no fucking attention!

*   *   *

37
Sister Claps Back

STILL IN THIS FILMIC TIME CAPSULE, the camera now flies across Guadaloupe onto the UT campus, circles the Tower, upthrusting, phallic, stone spear, missile, where we learned how easily a single individual, a disturbed individual with a gun (okay, a couple of guns, *rifles*, bought 'em at Chuck's Gun Shop just up the highway), could launch tiny lead projectiles with deadly force at the soft bodies, insufficiently hardened coffers of the skull, kill, murder, destroy the lives of innocent people and with them all their loved ones, family, friends, co-workers, unsettle and terrorize everybody who read, heard about, saw it on TV, the screen, just like that, any time, any place, out of nowhere, this fatal bee sting, murderous hornets. *Thump! Thump! Thump!* But it isn't the sound of gunfire, muffled, somewhere in the distance, that we hear now, but the great owl beating its wings against the window of room 221 David Hall where Dr. Levant is staring down at the chaos of wailing sirens and flashing lights of EMS and cop cars on the Drag. She turns to the blackboard, takes up a piece of white chalk, and in her immaculate hand writes in block letters as if she were carving them in the pediment of the temple of Saturn in the Roman Forum, CLASS CANCELLED, puts out the light and closes the door.

Now we're outside Lilith's apartment building. The camera focuses on a lit window on the second floor, hers, and, stealthy as a cat burglar, slips inside her bedroom just as she opens a walk-in closet and—*oops*, are we about to intrude on a private moment? No, Boone hasn't stooped to that. About five seconds of film that we understand to represent five or ten minutes of trying on and taking off elapse and Lilith emerges from the closet and *wtf?* because it isn't Lilith—well, it is, but it's also ... *Sister Sunne Rae?* Nothing has changed. It's just that once she puts on that orange wig, rhinestone tiara, sequined butterfly glasses, colorful robes, oh yeah, and that big prosthetic butt (she's grown quite attached to it, they're like BFF, it has its own wardrobe, chauffeur), suddenly she looks about three or four hundred pounds heavier, her face chubbier, her cheeks cheekier. She's like a superhero, reserved, demure (most of the time) academic by day, warrior-goddess by night. And, amazingly, no one makes the connection. It's like Clark Kent and Superman. You'd think everybody'd figure it out, but, nope, they don't, not even Lois Lane, Jimmy Olsen or the janitor, *'Night Mister Kent.*

Now we see *Sistuh* on stage. As with the beginning of every show, the orchestra is playing the sixties classic *Let the Sun Shine in,* not this time, however, as the pop-soul-psychedelic anthem to peace, love and brotherhood but as a dirge, slow, funereal, accompanying the mule-drawn buckboard bearing the coffin to the graveyard, which should clue the audience that something's up but, nope, totally tone deaf, they're applauding raucously, they can't wait for whatever outrageous thing the *Sistuh*'s going to say tonight and she's sure as shootin' not going to disappoint them. Eyes blazing with the flames of several centuries of caged fury she announces that this show is dedicated to Brother M'Shaka M'Baka aka Freddy Washington aka *Sergeant* Frederick Washington, and she then bows her head for a minute of silence that outright unnerves her audience.

When she raises her head again, the ridiculous costume, the tiara and orange wig, the oversized rhinestone glasses, the orange and saffron robes, the big prosthetic butt, have become something else altogether. She is a goddess of fire and her heat radiates outward, consuming onlookers in the theater and at home, immolating them in its wrath. Which is uglier, people? The word *nigger?* Or the act of *murder?!* The word *fuck* or the act of *rape?!* Why is it still legal to kill Black people? Why are women still not allowed to own their own vaginas? Why are men allowed to insert their penises in any convenient pound of flesh they desire? Why is it always the woman's fault? The woman's responsibility? The woman's crime? Why are you sitting on your asses waiting for a good laugh instead of *doing* something?

Sister's voice breaks and she chokes back a sob. Tears stream down her face. It's hard, people, she finally says. It's hard. The audience is stunned. Some, more or less following her drift, are also in tears, a few sobs escape. Others struggle to squelch uncertain guffaws that suddenly seem as out of place as at, well, a funeral. Never has anyone seen the Sister so angry. Nor so vulnerable. Is this a new shtick, a trick to catch her audience off guard and then send them careening into even more uncharted waters? Or just a hitch, a glitch in the facade of a public persona otherwise honed to perfect pitch (*that number again is* ...)?

Well, how about this? Here's the Sister, Lilith, back at home, sitting on the couch watching her performance on TV with tears streaming down her face. When I started this gig I was just trying to supplement my income. But it quickly became a way to vent about every damn thing that bothered me and that's a lot of things. You might say Sister Sunne Rae is my acting out persona. I should add that my therapist wholeheartedly encouraged me to explore this role, although I'm not sure she'd still agree with that decision. The truth is, I've been doing this damn show for almost twenty years and ain't nothing getting any better that I can tell.

Until this last sentence Lilith has been staring straight ahead into the blackness outside the window beyond the TV, but she now turns and looks at the person seated next to her. Is she being interviewed? Is this part of a documentary, *Black Comedy in Osberg?* The camera draws back and—*WTF?* It's the Snowman, who, we can also see now, has placed a comforting hand on Lilith's shoulder and is looking at her with what one might call sympathetic or even *referred* pain. Their physical proximity, their familiarity, suggests an intimacy that exceeds mere friendship. But when did this happen? *How* did this happen? Does Boone expect us to buy some impossibly impossible romantic plot twist? One day Lilith's strolling down the Drag, feeling good about herself because she's had a better than usual class, when she spots the Snowman pushing his cart and, despite her health-conscious diet, on a whim she buys a *PoPoPop!®*? But when she reaches for her purse to pay, the Snowman, gallant, perhaps already smitten, waves her money away, growling Tom Waits-like, It's on the house, lady? And in that moment there's something, an improbable spark, an exchange of energy, an endocrinological entanglement, a hormonal cloud meld, i.e., chemistry? Maybe it happened when she laughed and unlady-like said *No fucking way*. Maybe when he laughed back and said *Fucking A*. Maybe when they somehow ended up sitting on a bench at the outdoor market on 24th street while she ate her *PoPoPop!*® Maybe when she said to him, mocking, taunting, in her sassy Black Ebonic voice, before he knew she was a fucking university professor, much less Sister Sunne Rae, Ain't you 'fraid when you blush you gonna melt yourself, *Mister* Snowman? Because he was, wasn't he? Blushing? Like a fucking adolescent boy? And even more so when she smiled at him, a wide-open smile with that rainbow glow already showing in her remarkably green eyes. And are we further supposed to believe that from this unlikely encounter however many years ago that was (don't bother counting, it's Boone's math) she, Sister Sunne Rae to many, Lilith to a few, became the one later love in the Snowman's life? And, even more unlikely, he hers? (You knew, didn't you?) And to further complicate this intrigue, they thought it best to keep their relationship quiet, discreet, hide it from the public, she, a truth teller, challenging the status quo, the privileged quo, he, what—a capitalist pig, corporate hog? (*Excuse me, sir.*) But she saw through that, knew he wasn't that, right? Maybe because he was a white man who wasn't afraid to wear colors—is that a *pink* shirt in your closet, *Snowman?* Lilith, the rare black lily of the Nile, the luminous black light of the night, of the ball, of the dance, the lively, lovely Lil who in her youth danced all day and all night (according to one report, later suppressed) before she went off to tend to her flock, not of sheep but—ephebes?

But things don't look so loverly now, do they? There is chemistry, yes, but it's the volatile kind that sets the retort bubbling doubly, threatens to explode the alembic, causes thunder to burst from the sky. And what's this? A symbol? A metaphor? The great owl is perched on the back of the armchair across from them, glowering at the Snowman with its wide orange eyes. Lilith, his *mistress*, she whom he is assigned to watch over, protect, is angry, distraught, and this *man*, whom his deep raptor instincts have never trusted, is the presumed cause. Fuck this shit, *Snowman!* Stop lying to me! Stop lying to *yourself!* You're never going to change anything from the inside. They're fucking eating you up. You're dying before my eyes. I don't want this, Snowman. I don't want you like this.

38
He Said, No, man!

THE ELEVATOR STOPS, the door opens and the Snowman trudges across the lunar-lit foyer as if he's carrying a sack of moon rocks on his back (they're a lot heavier here on earth). He looks grizzled, grimy, he hasn't shaved in days, his sweat-stained Hawaiian shirt is hanging off him like damp laundry, his wallet's about to fall out of a hole in his rear cargo pocket, one of his huaraches is falling apart. In the receptionist Ms. Nexus' crisp, Good evening, *sir*, he detects a note of something less than respect that immediately puts him on the alert. He hesitates in front of the polished oak door of the boardroom as if he's preparing to enter an arena of mortal combat, then grasps the cudgel-like handle and heaves the door open with a loud vacuumous *whomp* that draws a collective gasp and momentary look of shock from the faces seated around the conference table. And there they all are, after all these years, still together, aged, sure, but, improbably (one might even say impossibly if this weren't Boone's show), essentially the same. Iago, Eunace Guppy, Carl McCowum, Natasha Bolsavitch, Wolf Bärenhaut, Gastreaux, Cash Dullard, Roger Wilco, the Dromedary, who, sure, doesn't say much, but in his computer brain he keeps a running tally of every single tit and tittle, jot and iota down to the Ticonderoga pencil stub in the box of miscellanea in Ms. Nexus's desk, which, according to both game and chaos theory, figures in here somehow.

The conference table, the Snowman notices now, is spread with assorted delicacies, platters of Wagyu and Kobe beef, Almas beluga albino caviar, Piedmont white truffles, flutes of champagne, artisanal drinks upon request, a banquet in appearance, his last supper, he senses. The round wall clock says nine p.m. Through the green-tinted plate glass window he can see the final orange flare of the sun setting like an enormous Georgia peach over the hill country in the west. He turns to take his seat and only now notices that his modest but dignified executive chair has been replaced with an old vinyl recliner with cracked upholstering and stuffing bulging out everywhere. Snickers and sniggers skitter around him like cockroaches on the wing. *Fuck you*, he mutters, audibly to some, and defiantly sits down. And down it is, he's barely sitting at eye level with the table. More smirks and chuckles ensue. Oh, so that's how they want to play.

Scrunching his butt around so that it makes loud farting sounds, he grins at the other board members with shining, psychopathic Jack Nicholson eyes and clenched teeth, carefully places some food items on his plate, a spoonful of caviar, a slice of truffle, pours some champagne. The others load their plates like it's meatloaf, mashed potatoes and gravy and begin to chow down like barnyard animals. Cash Dullard appears to have traces of coke under his nose (but it *could* be confectioners' sugar). The Dromedary is unabashedly picking his. The Guppy eats like a fish catching flies on the surface of the water, after each bite releasing gaseous little urpy burps that she politely attempts to disguise behind a tightly clenched fist. McCowum, clutching a Texas-size slab of seared Kobe beef in his hands, tears at it with his bare teeth. Wolf, wielding ornate Gorham Victorian Buttercup flatware, methodically cuts his meat, truffles *and* caviar into incrementally smaller pieces, which he inserts into his mouth with machine-like precision and chews exactly forty-seven and a half times.

This decorum last about two minutes. Someone— Cash Dullard?—launches a truffle across the table that lands in the Snowman's plate, splashing caviar on his shirt. A crouton sails past his face. Soon truffles, caviar and other comestible projectiles are flying from fork and spoon catapults and trebuchets. McCowum, of all people, is holding up rabbit ear fingers behind his neighbors' heads and making gooney *who, me?* faces when they turn around. Roger Wilco is setting off stink bombs and laughing like a hysterical James Cagney. The Dromedary is doing this weird, highly suggestive erectile thing with his hump that's causing a stir among the female faction. Gastreaux is making farting sounds with his hand in his armpit. The time has come (*oh, oysters*).

The Snowman takes a sip of his champagne, pats his lips with his napkin, places his hands on the table, sits up as erect as he is able, and like an undeluded Lear or resurrected Theoden, the scales fallen from his eyes, his ancient strength revived, he says in a stentorian voice, Enough! This must stop! Shut down the *Nicine* project now! I order you!

There's a moment of shocked silence, startled faces. Fear and uncertainty flicker in the ocular assemblage. Boone, playing a Hitchcock trick, manifests their unease in the physical surroundings, the gilt-framed portrait of a stern-faced Andrew Carnegie, slightly askew, the white faces of the electrical outlets in the walls, their eyes and mouths frozen in shrieks of horror, the tremor in the wine and water glasses—oh, wait, that's Tarkovsky. For a moment it seems the Snowman might have taken command of the situation, but, ohhh nooo! It's like that scene in *Zhivago* when the Russian officer climbs up on the water barrel to address the crowd of deserters. At first he seems to have arrested the mob's momentum, but then the lid collapses under his feet and *splash* he falls into the cold water like a clown in a dunking booth and everybody bursts out laughing *Ha!Ha!Ha!* One of the deserters then dispassionately shoots him and everybody drifts away still laughing.

Pretty much what happens to the Snowman right now. The damn chair collapses beneath him and he sprawls backward on the floor and *ow! ouch! ow!* bangs his elbows and jams his neck again. But instead of sympathy or a helping hand, just as in *Zhivago* everybody's laughing and pointing at him *Ha!Ha!Ha!* He struggles to his feet, rubbing his elbows, rolling his head on his shoulders, trying to regain his composure. But here comes Wolf with the coup de grace. I'm afraid the course of the Nicine Project isn't your prerogative anymore, *Mister* Snowman. The train has left the station, the steamship has sailed from port, the air ship has cast off its moorings. The Nicine project shall continue on its forward trajectory.

The Snowman is now informed that he's no longer majority shareholder and therefore his opinion counts for diddlysquat. His neck's too stiff to fully turn his head but his eyes roll in Iago's direction. Iago gives him a nothing-I-could-do-about-it shrug and tosses out this breadcrumb.

Because of your public image we wish for you to remain as CEO *for now* but your role will be exclusively as a figurehead. Yeah? Oh yeah? he sputters, his face flushing betanin red. We'll see about that! From the other board members' smug expressions, it's pretty obvious they don't think so. (More than one long-time fan of the boob tube will see here a reprise of beloved TV comedian and First Amendment champion Tommy Smothers' "flustered chump," and as every Tommy Smothers fan also knows, in the end Tommy is often vindicated.)

What the Snowman can't understand is, without the secret ingredient they've got nothing, right? Does Iago have something else up his sleeve? Maybe. He's had little trouble convincing the other board members that the *Snowman* is too unstable to retain sole possession of this vital resource—his behavior of late certainly does nothing to dissuade them otherwise. The point is—Iago's eyes, bright, gleaming with black coffee ferocity, fix on the eyes seated around the table—*something* must be done about it. Agreed? Well, yes, *maybe*, heads nod, kind of wishy washy, yessy noey, not sure what Iago has in mind and not so sure they wanta find out (*Watergate?*). What he does not tell them but, thanks to additional footage provided by the grasshopper, we see is this: Iago and Bärenhaut in what appears to be a conspiratorial huddle with rogue elements among the R&D gang. (Roger has had another *episode* and is required to wear a self-protective garment, okay, let's just say it, a *strait* jacket. He has also been placed on some mighty powerful meds that supersede even his home remedies and was last heard muttering something about a Doctor Benway.)

Later the Snowman will learn of the many other changes that followed upon this kangaroo court martial.

He will hear Iago, apparently reclaiming not only his name but his throne, referred to as *King* Arthur. He will see his own image fade from the break rooms, the hallways, the PR packages of swag, and replaced by *Iagarthur's*. It is also at this time that the Board orders a reorganization. It seems that Mister OPEN, too, will enjoy a rechristening, appearing in public now as Mister *NOPE*. King Arthur is positively gloating as he says to the other board members in a smarmy Mister Rogers voice that is right on target. Do you hear that already negative *Nnnn* at the beginning telling you don't even bother? Joined by that big *O no!* tone of regret? Followed by that hard, aspirated P slamming the door behind you on your way out? And finally that silent E for Exit, a reminder there's no going back? Rumors will abound that the real reason for this name change is to escape pending lawsuits, the simple rearrangement of those four capital letters leaving the litigants hopelessly tangled up in the courts for years, if not centuries (cf. Dickens, *Bleak House*—Ed.). Which might also explain the very quick ubiquity of a new piece of graffiti. NOPE—*No One Profits Elsewhere*. But now we're getting ahead of ourselves, or rather, Boone is, it's his bloody show, innit, bloody old shite.

Peals of laughter echo behind the Snowman as he stomps out of the boardroom, head crooked on his shoulder, left huarache disintegrating into disconnected pieces of cowhide and tire tread. Adding insult to injury, the door does indeed bang him in the butt, nearly knocking him to the floor again. Furious, fuming, that dark Joe Btfsplk storm cloud rumbling ominously (but impotently) over his head, he limps past Ms. Nexus, who makes no effort this time to hide her contempt, enters the elevator and pushes the button for the basement. And down he goes. For about thirty seconds.

The elevator jerks to a stop at the hundred-tenth floor and the door opens but no one's there. The door shuts and the elevator lurches as if it's going to continue but the bell dings, the elevator shudders and the door opens again and again there's no one. The door closes and in its stainless-steel surface the Snowman sees an orange glow like firelight or the sunrise in the desert. He blinks and now he sees a monstrous serpent head with fiery bronze, copper and terra cotta scales, huge eyes and fangs and a tormented human face emerging from its mouth. The image fades from the door but he still sees it in his mind, knows it is an omen of something yet to come, a reminder of unfinished business even if he doesn't know what that business is.

The camera now focuses on the green digital floor indicator to let us know the elevator has continued its descent. Half a minute later it stops again, the door opens, the Snowman exits into a garage and climbs into a shiny black, custom-design sports car that easily cost enough to build a hospital and several schools in Uganda or Rwanda or some other godforsaken Petri dish of foreign meddling and homegrown ineptitude and corruption. He waves his hand over the palmscan, glances at the bioscan, the car purrs alive and he pulls out into the street. Traffic's still heavy but his car's Privileged User's Traffic Facilitator does indeed facilitate his passage, changing red lights to green, opening closed lanes and closing open lanes as he heads east under DR-35. Not true for other drivers who wonder (or more likely go ballistic) at sudden red lights, hastily set up detours and *whoop! whoop!* unexpected traffic stops.

39
The Rose Redux

THE SNOWMAN FEELS LIKE HE JUST LOST a high-noon showdown. His mind, his whole body, is vibrating like an incandescent lightbulb filament about to burn out. He drives through the long dark tunnel of his interiorverse unaware of cars, street signs, spaceships falling out of the sky. Past auto body shops, junkyards, mom and pop convenience stores fortified with metal shutters and burglar bars, shabby houses, apartment buildings, taquerias with garish hand-painted roosters, cactus and dancing señoritas. And doesn't wake out of this dreamscape until he spots a slightly anthropomorphic neon green cactus covered with pink flowers on the green-tiled rooftop of a Mexican restaurant called *La Rosa del Desierto* in the same pink and green neon. It looks pretty much the way it did twenty-five years ago, a little shabbier, a little more forlorn. The parking lot in front is nearly empty. His headlights flare up in the large plate-glass window, on which the name of the restaurant is also painted in pink and green, and then fade into platinum glowworms when he turns off the engine, revealing the silhouette of a hooded figure sitting in a booth inside.

Then he's inside, sitting in a booth, maybe the same one occupied by the hooded figure, the aftertaste of outrageously priced artisanal drinks and curated cuisine gradually receding as he begins to drink methodically from a bottle of El Residente brandy while increasingly bizarre images flash through his brain. Crowds of drunken, laughing people wearing motheaten donkey ears on their heads. Himself transformed into a donkey with special effects Boone has shamelessly lifted from Max Reinhardt's *Midsummer Night's Dream*, except, one guesses, for the embarrassingly erect equine equipage. Something that at first glance looks like the Joker's bloody leering mouth but resolves itself into a man with his throat slit. As the Snowman refills his glass, he stares myopically at the label on the bottle, which depicts a man climbing out of the Rio Bravo with a red sash across his chest that reads in Spanish (but for the viewer's convenience here in English—Eduardo) *I'd rather be a resident in the US than president of Mexico.* In his mind he sees the blurry image of a young man, a boy, maybe fourteen-fifteen, wading naked into a dark river, at the same time a soft throaty voice that could be male or female begins to narrate.

Warm black muck sucked at his feet. The stench of sewage and chemicals filled his nostrils. A large black snake undulated toward him through the reeds. He'd never learned how to swim, never been near enough water to learn how to swim. He pushed his plastic bag of belongings before him and began to kick his feet. Half way across, the water turned cold, colder than anything he'd ever felt in his life. The cold penetrated his arms and legs, turning them into heavy blocks of wood, he felt his cojones *shrink into a little package* (odd girlish giggle), *and then, nothing, numbness and an overpowering desire to sleep. All he had to do was give up, stop fighting, let the water take him. No! he shouted into the snow drifting down from the black night. He wanted to live! Struggling against the cold water, against his exhaustion, he broke through the snow-covered sheet of ice on the far shore and, naked, his hands and feet raw, bleeding, staggered up the riverbank through waist-deep snow. A cold wind blew. He was shivering violently. He tore open his bundle. Miraculously, his clothes were still dry and had even retained some warmth. Standing on the plastic bag, he dressed quickly, pulling on socks, underwear, shirt, sweater, coat, gloves, hat and boots. Fully clothed, he began jumping up and down until the warmth returned to his body. Suddenly he started to laugh. He was alive! He made it! His joy quickly faded. Before him loomed the wall, thirty feet high, iron and concrete, topped with razor wire, impenetrable. Except, that is, for a fairly roomy rabbit hole burrowed under a bad concrete pour that he had been instructed to look for. He dropped to his knees and crawled under the wall. On the other side, frozen whiteness stretched beyond sight.* El Norte.

By now the Snowman has done a pretty good job of getting himself fucked up. He's hunched over the table with his face in his hands, his melancholy made worse by the music coming from the jukebox glowing in the corner where male tenor voices are singing in Spanish of an *amor perdida* (interestingly, the Tennessee Williams spelling, in which case the feminine ending is probably more accurate—*Eduardito*, tee hee.) A noise rouses him. He lifts his head and stares blurry-eyed and incredulous at the person who has sat down opposite him, incredulous because damned if he doesn't recognize this guy, indeed, doubly recognize him. His first thought is *Margarito!* But, no, of course he knows it's not Margarito, can't be, even if the young man sitting across from him in a pearl-snap western shirt and straw Stetson, which he now takes off and places on the table, looks almost exactly *like* Margarito, the Margarito, that is, that he knew, thought he knew. It's gotta be Boone playing tricks on him, right? But wait, now he knows. It's that young Mexican landscaper he's seen around and right now the dude's staring at him like he's either IDing him for a police line-up or marking him for a Zeta hit squad.

You look like shomebody I didn't used to know, he shlurs, playing it cool or just too drunk to know better. The young guy looks at him like *huh?* He starts to say something else, then waves the thought away like a pesky mosquito. Sh'too hard 'shplain. S'bout an old friend. *Mar-ga-ri-to.* He enunciates the name drunkenly, syllabically. The young guy looks startled, confused. *My* name is Margarito, he says in perfect English.

Now it's the Snowman's turn to look confused. He squinches up his face like he's trying to solve a tough math problem, pushes the nearly empty bottle of El Residente across the table. Drink? (For those interested in movie miscellanea, it's worth mentioning that Boone had toyed with the title *Conversations in the Cantina* for an earlier film in which the Snowman and the presumptive Margarito are seen hunched over a diminishing bottle of tequila like drunken monks in their hooded parkas as they engage in an extensive and increasingly incoherent conversation. Is Boone taking another shot at this vision? The young man seated across from the Snowman quickly shoots down this idea when he says with enough disdain to sink the Titanic a second time, I don't drink. Besides, the film's running time is stretching beyond the Producer's tolerance so it looks like they're going to have to get all the conversing done in one sitting. With that in mind the Snowman takes another stab at 'splainin' (shouldn't there be a close parenthesis somewhere here?—Ed.).

What I mean izh, I thought you were you but then I remembered you were her. But that doesn't make any sense either. His face goes through an additional set of contortions before a dim bulb of comprehension glows over his head and he struggles to get the word out. You're Maria's *s-s-son?* Which elicits from *this* Margarito an even more confused and menacing glare, like, what the fuck do you know about my *mother?* But before *he* can say anything like that another dim bulb incandesces over the Snowman's head and he sees a man, himself, swimming naked in slow lazy circles in a deep turquoise blue pool illuminated by dusty yellow sunlight and crowded with tropical foliage. Now he sees a young woman, Maria, also naked, the tawny globes of her buttocks pushing out of the water as she swims in lazy circles in the same pool. This is followed by a rapid montage of images, the water sluicing between her wet gleaming breasts, over his bare butt crack, that *suggests* to the audience that they are not only swimming together but making love. The camera moves to the Snowman's face as he seems to be experiencing a powerful orgasm, and then Maria's as she too seems to be in the throes of ecstasy. Now we hear a voice, Maria's, repeating a covenant from an ancient Mayan text that sounds oddly biblical or at the very least legalistic *nor to know carnally nor to have sexual congress with nor by any means to violate this covenant.* Because she didn't violate the covenant. She circumvented it thanks to an unwritten clause those wise Mayan shysters understood as implied. It's a union that did and didn't take place, an intrigue of camera magic, cinematic congress, as we now see on a split screen the Snowman climbing out of the water and beginning to dress behind a giant philodendron at the same moment Maria appears and begins to undress, so that he is caught in an awkward position. Announce his presence and admit he has violated her sacred place, or, as he did in reality, watch like a skulking onanistic church elder as she finishes disrobing and slips into the pool.

The Snowman's head has started to sink to his chest but he snaps awake again with a painful cervical *crack* and stares bleary-eyed at the young Margarito sitting across from him. And yeah, now he notices differences, a lighter complexion, the features less Latino, more Caucasian, and are his eyes *blue?* Of course he could be wearing contacts. And the blond highlights in his hair? Dye, right? Fads, fashion trends, next it'll be topknots. Yeah, let's see how well those arguments hold up in a paternity suit. The question is, and, let's face it, the Snowman is not thinking this through quite so cogently at the moment, could his sperm have survived long enough in the warm water to enter Maria's vagina in a viable state? The Snowman and Margarito *Junior* (MJ for the sake of brevity) look at each other again and some kind of telepathic exchange seems to be taking place as MJ's lips move and he whispers *¿mi padre?* even as the Snowman mouths the words *my son?* in what to the viewer might appear to be an odd catechism or prelude to a confession despite the fact that the Snowman is decidedly not Catholic nor any other denomination. Several thoughts are now swirling around in his already discombobulated head. Why is this young man here? Did Maria intend for them to meet?

As if to confirm his supposition, MJ now (improbably, but, again, it's Boone's show) tells him the tale of a Zoltec queen and her sacred well and it's very much like a tale Maria once told him. The queen gives birth to a baby boy who grows up to become a powerful warrior, his triumphs thanks to the magical water his mother anoints him with before each battle. Poisoned by greed, he kills her so that he can have all the water he wants and become even more powerful. The next day the queen's pool dries up and a great king from the east defeats the errant son in battle. Except that in a reversal of *that* tale, it is the queen who has been mortally wounded in combat and the son is desperately trying to save her, but an evil sorcerer has caused her pool of magic water to dry up and only one drop remains in the entire world. MJ stares directly into the Snowman's eyes, pellucid equatorial blue meets blurry, bloodshot arctic blue. Even in his stupor, the Snowman grasps—well, about as well as you can grasp a cloud—two things from this parable. One, the prospect that Maria may be gravely ill. (Scholars will later argue that the dried-up pool and the queen's wound are metaphors for a sick and moribund Mexico. Boone's reply: I don't do metaphors. *What?* Since when?) And the second, that somehow MJ knows that he, the Snowman, possesses the last of Maria's magic water. Which also seems to be confirmed when MJ, in what Boone probably intended as comic relief but instead comes across as just plain creepy, says in an annoyingly fake Mexican accent, *JaJaJa*, Meester Snowman, you make water from water, no? *¿Sólo una gotita*, no? *Meester* Snowman, by now completely blotto, slurs, How you know 'bout that? His head slams onto the table and he passes out.

Then they're heading out to the car, MJ striding ahead, the Snowman stumbling behind. Give me the *pinche* keys, *güero!* MJ snarls, slipping into Spanish. You're in no shape to drive! He feels around in his pockets, then slurs again with a sloppy grin, No keyszh. He manages to pass his hand in front of the palmscan on the door and it unlocks, but then he's so plastered, he can't sit up straight in the seat or keep his eyes open, MJ has to assist him with the iris and bio scan. *¡Muévete, pinche viejo! ¡Siéntate derecho! ¡Mira! ¡Aquí!* MJ's anger seems way out of proportion. Through the narrow slits of his barely sentient eyelids, the Snowman sees a black obsidian gleam at MJ's belt. Knife? Gun? A wave of cold Arctic air floods his besotted brain. He's gonna kill me. Dark, scowling, MJ looks very much like he has murder on his mind. But maybe he's just trying to figure out how the hell to drive this *pinche carro*. It's nothing at all like his *troca*.

And, no, it's not. Even with the Snowman loudly sawing logs, this AI ride carries them safely back across town to the Snowman's residential tower where we next see MJ helping the Snowman inside his condo. C'mon, *puto*, look at the fucking scanner! Put your hand up there, *cabrón!* The Snowman immediately crashes on a couch but before he slips into oblivion he hears MJ rustling around and wonders stupidly, Whazh he looking for? Shomething to drink? Glassh of water? Ohhhhh, right, *the* water. Haha, ain't gonna fiiiind it.

40
The Soup Thickens

HE WAKES AGAIN out of an oneiric sludge in the middle of which MJ's face, oddly conflated with the Wicked Witch of the West's, appears in a pool of lurid green and pink neon when he hears someone bang into a table and utter *fuck!* In the dim light sees—*Iagarrrthurrr?* What're *youuu doooing* here? Iago stops whatever it is he's doing and says in an irritable if-you-must-know tone that he received a message from the security bot a short while ago. *Secooory bot?* We had it installed *last month?* In the event of a *medical alert? Remember?* Umm ... not *reary?* Well, anyway, *Snowman*, I just wanted to check up on you after, you know, *the meeting?* Oh, God, he groans and passes out again. Iago stares at him for a full minute before the camera draws in and we see his face transform into a shifty, sidelong, Snidely Whiplash sneer *Heh! Heh! Heh!* as his eyes focus on a small red thermos on the mantel. That's it! his expression says. Pretty obvious, right? It's like the Holy Grail, *Raiders of the Lost Ark* version, not a pricey, cutting-edge, hyperthermic-hypocryogenic brand, but a sturdy, inexpensive, reliable commodity made of simpler dross.

The screen now goes dark and, inexplicably, we hear crickets chirring, an owl hoots (It's gotta be Wilbur,

right? *Wilbur?* Lilith's friend? *Wilbur?!*), and then—can
it be? yes, it can—birdsong. Natural light gradually fills
the room. Morning arrives and passes. Sometime after
noon, the Snowman struggles awake like Count Dracula
with a missed appointment at the blood bank and a stake
through his heart to boot. Groggy, head pounding, he
stares bleary-eyed at his surroundings, sensing and indeed
expecting to see something out of order and there it is or
rather isn't, the empty spot on the mantel where the little
red thermos sat. Did he forget to put it back in its place?
Did he suck down the last precious drop in one of those
let's-just-keep-going plunges into excess and afterwards
toss out the thermos?

Frantic, he digs under cushions, behind furniture.
Where the fuck is it? Where has it gone? My *preciousss!*
A shard of memory with Iago's face imprinted on it
dislodges itself from the cluttered archaeological ruins of
his subconscious. He finds his EyePhone® in his back
pocket after looking everywhere *but*, listens for Iago's
voice on the other end and in as casual an I'm-not-
accusing-you tone as he can manage, says, Did you
happen to see a little red thermos at my place last night?

Prolonged silence. Iago finally says, I have no idea
what you're talking about and hangs up.

Hmm. A review of security footage after the
Snowman has had a couple industrial-sized mugs of
espresso and a prolonged hot shower and is more or less
alert (one on a scale of six), will indicate a gap of exactly
eighteen and a half minutes and, even more telling, the
complete absence of Iago's presence. And here it gets a
little tricky. Complicating matters, ghost images on a
discarded thumb drive that turns up in a garbage bin
months later reveal an awkward near encounter between

Iago and—*Moses?* And that's interesting because ... hold that thought.

Sick in body and spirit, the Snowman shows up at the office about mid-afternoon (it's only a five-minute walk from his condo). He's jittery, on edge, his hands are trembling, he can't sit still at his desk. An eight-ounce glass of his remaining starter batch tastes weak, watered down, and gives him about as much relief as 3.2 beer does an alcoholic. Finally he takes the elevator to the basement to pick up his cart, maybe a few hours of honest labor will help clear his head, but before he can get out the door he has another awkward encounter, the crystallization of a precognitive awareness of something else amiss in the universe that has been nagging at him and he's about to discover why as he now spots Moses in a U.S. Navy deck-gray janitorial uniform, pushing his way on stage with a wheeled bucket and wet mop, his face aged, his bundle of locs gone ashen, his once vast reservoirs of kinetic energy diminished to a brittle, slow as molasses shuffle. This leads to embarrassed smiles, fidgeting, what-can-you-do-about-it shrugs. The Snowman tries to explain, to apologize, I'm sorry, I didn't know. Moses cuts him off with his succinct, centuries of explanations and empty apologies behind him, that's awright, Snowman. At least I still gots a job. Bowing his head in what at first seems like a gesture of resignation, Moses takes off a thin leather necklace with a small black pendant carved in the shape of a male figure with distinctly African features and, slowly, solemnly, as if bestowing knighthood upon the Snowman, places it over his head. It's *magic*, he says as if they are mutually agreed on that possibility. At the touch of the pendant on his chest the Snowman flinches as if he's received an electric shock and he wonders with only slightly less ingenuousness than Dorothy, but is it good magic or bad?

Now what? Fallen from corporate grace, his nerves frayed by the abuse of joy juice and the terrifying prospect that there will be no more joy juice, still trying to process the revelation that he might be a father, the Snowman doesn't notice the landscape truck that has been tailing him on different occasions. It appears out of an alley or side street and follows behind him for a block or two before veering off. Apparently, for plot purposes, Boone's not going to take us inside the cab, but it's gotta be MJ, right? One could surmise that discovering the Snowman might be his father has caused MJ some personal conflict too, as well as ambivalence about his mission. And what exactly is that mission? We now hear voices speaking in Spanish. Presumably we're listening in on a conversation in the cab of the landscape truck, but the words are muffled, indistinct, *mierda? mata?* something like that? Then there's something in English that is neither indistinct nor ambivalent, *whack, off him, dispose of* ... oh, wait, those are subtitles at the bottom of the screen. Well, to this uninformed viewer it sure seems like they're plotting an assassination.

But what is Boone thinking? Does he have in mind a twisted Greek tragedy of vengeance in which Maria has sent MJ to kill the Snowman, his (putative) father? Why? What is her motivation? His corrupt use of her magic potion? *He's already done enough damage. Billions have been poisoned by this insidious illusion of well-being. We must put an end to it.* But why then did she arrange for them to meet, knowing they would discover their relationship, which might cause MJ to abandon his mission? Also, if he kills the Snowman how will he ever find the final drop of water that might save Maria's life? Boone seems to be struggling to tie together complicated plot elements. His harshest critics will say he failed miserably. His dwindling number of supporters will say, look to Yogi Borges who famously said, when you come to a fork in the garden path, take it.

And then there's the dream. The Snowman's had this dream so many times it has become an actualized event that has lodged itself in his subconscious where he mostly manages to keep it caged and under lock and key during his waking hours but in his sleep it roams freely. He's naked, bent backward over a stone altar. A figure in a grotesque mask, like a giant serpent's head with huge square teeth and a tortured human face emerging from its mouth, stands over him holding a gleaming black obsidian blade. He hears a familiar voice, hers, Maria's, say, we know you have suffered a great deal, *Snowman*, but now we must ask you to suffer some more. He sees the blade descend, he feels an odd tugging in his chest, before darkness descends he sees a bloody hand hold a still-beating heart up to the bright hot sunlight slicing across the green jungle canopy.

The scene changes. The sky is early morning shades of gray, lavender, pale blue. The sun's first light touches the post and live oaks on E. 31st, turning their dark green leaves golden. Squirrels scamper in the tree tops, birds sing, the milkman makes his deliveries through a narrow fracture in time. Despite this tranquil picture, the crescendo of ominous music (solemn woodwinds, frantic strings) in the background warns us this is the fateful day and, yep, we now see a familiar one-and-a-half-ton stake-bed pick-up loaded with landscape accoutrements following the Snowman as he pushes his cart down the street at the beginning of his route. He turns a corner and the truck goes on by but then there it is again, right behind him. But wait … is it the same truck?

Boone does a series of quick cuts, we see the back of the truck loaded with tools, the truck in profile, sunlight blasting off the cab, the windshield. Then we see MJ behind the wheel, his face grim, his jaw set. The camera moves down to his belt where we can see a black obsidian gleam, then back to the truck-bed where the suggestion of violence is heightened by the camera panning over various sharp-edged tools, axes, machetes, pitchforks.

The camera returns to the Snowman who seems totally unaware as the brake lights of the truck behind him flash red and it slows to a stop. The driver's door opens and—it's not MJ. It's another man, crewcut, soul patch, swarthy, heavily five o'clock-shadowed, he's holding a gun. And then MJ is behind him in his green and yellow landscaper uniform, the obsidian blade in his hand. Apparently the grasshopper has switched loyalties again, recognizing in MJ a compañero (*¡Pero, no me comas, güey!*), and warned him of the Snowman's peril. *Whooop! Whooop!* Sirens, flashing lights, screeching tires. Osberg police officers, state troopers and ICE agents descend on both of them. *El Agua!* MJ shouts to the Snowman, who has just lifted his head at the sound of this commotion.

41
Down Ol' Mexico Way

Goodbye to my Juan, farewell Roselita
Adiós mis amigos, Jesús y María
You won't have a name when you ride the big airplane
All they will call you will be deportees

WOODY GUTHRIE'S OKIE TWANG fades away in the background as the audience sees an American Airlines passenger plane descend into Mexico City, but the surprise is universal when not MJ in handcuffs escorted by U.S. marshals but the Snowman strolls down the ramp inside the terminal, although he's completely unrecognizable. Sunglasses, wide-brimmed fedora, overcoat, leather gloves. His face is wrapped entirely in bandages, except, oddly, for his nose, which is a strange bubblegum pink and clearly fake (Boone once again unabashedly splicing in footage from the original *The Invisible Man*). It's been almost twenty-five years since the Snowman last visited Mexico, but the circumstances of his departure (drug cartels, political intrigue, a bloody revolution) understandably require that he keep a low profile. Also understandable that the other passengers were a bit nervous about his appearance. Is this greenghost dude a mad bomber? Does he have something contagious? And, sure, the cabin crew had their doubts. And you can bet Customs would too. Concerns that were whisked away like pixie dust with a story about a severe skin condition he was traveling to Mexico City to have treated (medical certificate stamped and approved by the Mexican consulate in Osberg), as well, of course, as a generous disbursal of pesos all around.

Discarding his disguise in a stall in the men's room in exchange for a faux Indiana Jones outfit, wide-brimmed, high-crowned sable fedora, brown leather bomber jacket, poplin shirt open at the neck, pleated, khaki wool twill trousers and sturdy trekking boots, the Snowman next boards a little twenty-seater, twin-engine propeller plane that wobbles up into the sky like it's got a load in its pants and soon they're droning over a rugged mountain range whose jagged peaks appear mere meters from scraping the plane's belly, none of which seems to bother the other passengers, a mix of crisply dressed tourists, sweaty paisanos and a couple of unlikely business types (suits) packed in among a clutter of wheeled carry-ons, sacks of garlic and tethered chickens. Quarters are cramped, the ambient smells intense, flatulence rampant *beans*. The Snowman tries to breathe through his mouth but this only adds to his anxiety, causing an uncomfortable tightness in his chest that briefly disappears when they safely touch down outside the colonial city of Chopahuac an hour later, but returns when he spots heavily armed soldiers stationed everywhere on the bus ride into the *centro*.

Thanks to that old anchor around his neck, nostalgia, he has made reservations at the Hotel Caulifornia where he stayed during his last visit to Chopahuac. It's almost a reprise of twenty-five years before. The desk manager,

Peter Lorre, is still behind the receptionist's desk and he still looks exactly like *that* Peter Lorre, sure, older, aged, lines at the corners of his eyes and mouth, lips slightly pinched. He also shows signs of having gone through some pretty extreme duress (but let's not use the word *torture*). He has a limp, a twisted hand, a jagged scar over one eye, part of an ear's missing. Nevertheless, his face brightens with recognition at the sight of the Snowman, then quickly dims again when he says not very convincingly, Oh, *Mister Snowman*, it is so good to see you again, *hnn, hnn, hnn*. The aged, not *that* Peter Lorre then inquires officiously if the purpose of his visit is business or leisure. Good question. He's here to find Maria, of course. But he also knows he's not going to find her unless she wants to be found, which makes this whole trip quixotic at best and chaotic at worst.

After hauling his bag upstairs to his room and some minor ablutions, he spends the rest of the afternoon strolling about Chopahuac, noticing here and there pock marks that a regular tourist might not recognize as bullet holes in the pastel pink, yellow and blue stucco houses and white limestone walls, pediments and façades of Spanish colonial buildings. Phantom gunshots echo in his head. He sees flashes of men and women in a motley mix of military uniforms from several different centuries bearing an equally eclectic assortment of modern and antiquated firearms. He sees the bodies of people he knew and loved, *friends*, lying in spreading pools of blood on the cobblestone streets and his lips move as he silently speaks their names, *Nico, Bombástico, Grandpa Mexico*.

Lengthening shadows and the retreat of the warm yellow light remind him that it's getting late. Tired and hungry, he goes in search of a restaurant that he remembers serving a delicious *pollo asado con mole de chocolate* (roasted chicken in chocolate sauce—Stan) (everyone knows that—Eduardo) but not only does this tiny café seem to have disappeared, but also the alley, street and entire neighborhood where it was located. He finally settles for a plate of chicken enchiladas verdes and a cerveza at a brightly lit taqueria but the enchiladas are soggy from watery salsa and the loud American tourists at the nearby table annoy the hell out of him. Leaving his dinner unfinished, he heads back to the hotel for a night of restless sleep compounded by a case of indigestion riveted in the center of his chest that he blames on the lousy meal.

After a light breakfast (huevos a la mexicana, papas fritas, fresh corn tortillas, sliced papaya with yoghurt, coffee—well, okay, his appetite has returned) in an outdoor café near the zócalo, he continues his search, but a full day of pounding the pavement and what he hopes are discreet inquiries (Is it true, *amigo*, that this famous Subcomandante Maria is still hiding in the mountains? And is it also true that she sometimes disguises herself as a man?) turn up nothing.

Discouraged by what he has found (bad or at least uncertain memories) and not found (Maria), he enters the first bar he sees and orders a double tequila, which he's just polishing off when he notices an attractive woman with long chestnut hair sitting alone at a small table. Never great at guessing age, he'd nevertheless guess she's probably in her mid to late forties. She also looks familiar. Suddenly his heart beats faster, his breathing comes quicker, both of which, the tachycardia and the shortness of breath, should serve as warning signals of *some* sort.

When he looks again, however, she's gone, and just as well, right? No need to reopen more old wounds.

He's just about to leave and head back to the hotel when he hears his name pronounced in a female voice that is also familiar in its haughtiness if not outright disdain, *Snowman.* To which he replies, also as a statement not a question, *Amanita,* and, looking up, he sees that, yes, it is her. Battle-scarred, harder, sure. She's also just as striking as she was twenty-five years ago. What follows is more or less a replay of the first night they met. She says with sarcasm that is also familiar, Thanks for inviting me to sit down, *Snowman,* I think I will. Oh, don't look at me like that. What, you're still angry because I tried to kill you? She signals the waiter and they both order a drink, she a Manhattan, he, his second double tequila. You look well, he says, meaning, yes, I'd still fuck you but I hate your guts. She smiles, a dark smile that looks as if it's not only used to attending funerals but causing them. I live well. My father was farsighted. He set up a very generous trust fund, untouchable by the feds—U.S. or Mexican. Oh? And how is her father? She shakes her head, says she doesn't know anything about him, hasn't seen him in years—since, you know, the *event?* Mind if I reserve the right to some healthy skepticism? he says.

They both have another drink, her second Manhattan, his third double tequila. A multitude of doubts swirl in his by now swirling brain, the predominant one why and how, out of all the gin joints in the world, does she walk into his. Not exactly accurate, of course, it's not his joint and she was here first (another of Boone's unlikely coincidences?). When it's time to pay, she glances at his rumpled Indiana Jones outfit and signals to the waiter, I'll get this. And, sure, why not, she *did* try to kill him. But just as old wounds fester, old desires rekindle. While they're waiting for the check she suggests they go to her place nearby for another drink. Now what? Is he going to fall for this trick, moth to the flame, Charlie Brown to Lucy's perennial promise that *this time* she'll let him kick the football? Twenty-five years ago you can bet he'd say you bet. But, well, he is pushing sixty and, even if shaky, he does have some kind of commitment back home. Plus, what about that venomous spider gleam in Amanita's eyes? Does she have unfinished business in mind?

Before the check arrives, the Snowman excuses himself to go to the restroom and, taking the coward's route, out the door he goes and, in an alcohol haze, starts making tracks, sort of like a lucid dream in which his brain recognizes a fatal danger and extracts him from it. Sort of. In what initially seems to be an Alain Resnais rip-off, he enters the next bar he sees, sure, not quite the same, a dive cantina this time, and again notices a woman sitting alone at a table and, something about her posture, profile, for one second he thinks *Amanita?* Except this is nothing like the Amanita he just left behind. She's wearing an outlandish Mexican outfit, a black dress with bright red and green floral patterns and a large yellow rose behind one ear, which, well, doesn't really work with the copper scrub-pad hair (a wig?). Boone Weller fans will have recognized her immediately—well, okay, maybe it'll take a sec. *C'monnn*, it's Mona Moondrake, former porn star cum (couldn't resist) B-grade screen queen. Sure, a close-up of her mug is a bit of a shock, her features are coarse, lumpy, the layers of pancake and rouge can't cover the five o'clock shadow, she looks like she's taken more than a few beatings. A drag on her cigarette also attracts(?) the Snowman's attention to the miniature dumpster fires of her ill-chosen vermillion lipstick and matching nail polish. He hears himself say like a film noir dick (take your pick), Long time no see, Mona. She squints at him drunkenly and, her voice thick with booze and cigarette smoke, says in a masculine falsetto *Billy?* This too registers in his memory but before he can go too far down that lane she examines him more closely and says with a ditzy cross-eyed look, Oh, you're that *Snowman* guy.

Again his instinct is to get the fuck out of here, but, too late, suddenly she's all tears and heartache, down on her luck defenseless dame, and boy has she picked the right shoulder to cry on. Oh *boo hoo hoo*, Snowman, I'm so *boo hoo* glad to *boo hoo hoo* see you. Followed by a lengthy narration in a booth he has discreetly suggested they retire to, where, fueled by more booze (like either of them needs that) and bar snacks (and, yes, they are—roasted grasshoppers *¡mi familia!*), he learns that, following an abominable fiasco that was in all the entertainment pages, *that son-of-a-bitch* Boone dumped her after *that jerk* Billy skipped town with some floozy and she's been stuck in *this shithole* ever since *boo hoo hoo*. (Boone Weller fans who still insist the Snowman is actually B-grade film star Billy "Plum" Bob Bengay will be disappointed by this revelation. There are those contrarians, however, who'll argue that it's the Snowman who's playing Billy Bob, with a certain prosthetic prop. In yet another of Boone's quantum entanglements, for about one second the Snowman and Billy Bob will lock eyes on the set.)

Apparently Mona was initially quite the novelty in this *cuello de los bosques*. (That doesn't work in Spanish, Stan.) (What the fuck do you know, *Eduardo?*) (Mucho más que tú, obviamente, *Stanley*.) When, that is, she was still young and attractive to both male and female admirers and her laughable attempts at Spanish were considered endearing. In recent years, however, she's had to earn her keep dog-sitting for wealthy Mexicans and waiting tables in this crummy cantina. Mostly she just gets fucked up on cheap booze and *mota*, 'least it's legal here. So she sure as hell is surprised when the Snowman hands her a wad of cash in U.S. dollars that'd choke a *caballo* and tells her to fly back to the States at her earliest convenience, and to ensure that she does, he writes her a sizable check, good only upon presentation at the NOPE Bank of Osberg.

This scene is followed by some fuzzy plot devices. The Snowman gentlemanly escorts Mona to her boarding house and then heads back to the Hotel Caulifornia, but along the way he senses that he's being pursued by someone or even some *thing*. (Strange noises in an alley. A cat coughing up a furball? A psychopath stropping his razor blade?) In a cutaway we see Amanita talking on her EyePhone®. On the other end we hear Peter Lorre's unmistakable laugh *hnn hnn hnn*. Something diabolical is clearly afoot here. Should we try to warn the Snowman? Is it too late?

42
¡El Agua!

MAYBE NOT BECAUSE WE NOW SEE the Snowman the next
morning driving a rental car east of the Edenic green
Chopahuac valley into the barren, sun-blasted desert in a
scene that should ring a bell for fans of Boone Weller's
earlier oeuvre. He notices a cloud of dust and in its midst
he sees a man with a long white beard walking behind a
steel-share plow pulled by a huge black ox, also with a
long white beard. He spots a large bird-like creature
perched on the side of a strangely toxic-yellow mountain
that resolves itself into an unusual outcropping of stone.
He swerves to avoid the desiccated carcass of a fairly
large animal that seems to combine both reptilian and
mammalian features. At last he comes upon a weathered
wooden sign buried in an enormous prickly pear cactus
covered with fuzzy white cochineal webbing that points
to Las Riquezas thataway and thataway he goes but not to
the Las Riquezas he remembers as he passes crumbling
stucco, stone and adobe buildings with collapsed terra
cotta roofs and termite-eaten wooden beams. The palapa-
like cantina, *Mi Sedecita*, where he fondly recalls
enjoying a beer or two, has vanished into the dust.

A sense of hopelessness has begun to press down on
his shoulders. The discomfort in his chest has also

returned. Heartburn? Heartbreak? Heart *attack?* Maybe
he should head back to Chopahuac, look for a doctor.
You're almost sixty, *Snowman.* You gotta pay attention
to these things. He's also a guy. He continues to drive,
another destination in mind, one he both desires dearly
and deeply dreads to find. And, yes, it is that bad.

Maria's house has been destroyed, turned into a pile
of rubble, the barn burned down, the once verdant garden
disappeared into the sandy rocky soil. He gets out of the
car. Pieces of charred wood and broken pottery crunch
under his boots as he wanders among the ruins, searching
for something to call to mind even for a moment the
bucolic life he remembers enjoying here. He feels a sense
of futility and with it an odd sense of lassitude. His feet
drag as he approaches a rocky hillside beyond the
foundation of the house where a cleft in the stone, clotted
with a faded brown macramé of dead moss and ferns,
reminds him of the verdant spring and the fresh water that
once flowed here. The camera follows his gaze to a
horizontal band of red and yellow sandstone sundered
vertically by what, from this perspective, appears to be a
jagged crack but, as he approaches it in an unsteady
tacking motion that has as much to with this strange
fatigue that has come over him as it does his dread of what
lies ahead, we can now see that, hidden by a parallactic
trompe l'oeil, this crevice is actually a narrow cave
entrance.

The thought of entering this dark door into another
dimension, as he knows he must, causes him even greater
trepidation. He feels physically and mentally exhausted,
as if the entire stretch of the space-time continuum
between now and the last time he visited this place
twenty-five years ago has been compressed into a leaden

mass he's carrying on his back. Taking a deep breath that rasps in his lungs and causes a sharp pain in the center of his chest, he enters the cave. The weight on his shoulders immediately increases, causing his back to bend, his legs to buckle. He feels as if he has just landed on Jupiter without a spacesuit. He sinks to the ground and begins to crawl forward on his hands and knees. He feels like falling flat on his face and passing out and who cares if he never wakes up again. He hears a voice shout *El agua!* and just ahead he sees light. A dusty yellow sunbeam illuminates a fairly large grotto shaped like an upside-down wineglass. Dead brown tropical vegetation surrounds a deep hole. Dragging himself forward on his stomach, he peers over the edge at the sandy bottom where, in the dim light, he can see flashes of gold and what appear to be human skeletons.

The pressure in his chest has become unbearable. His hand instinctively goes inside his shirt to his heart and closes around the pendant Moses gave him. It weighs a ton. It's like a chunk of kryptonite weakening him, draining him of his will. His arms feel leaden, disconnected as he struggles to remove it over his head. He stares at the carved wooden figurine like a myopic drunk trying to read the label on a bottle of something that might be booze or toilet cleanser at the same time he hears Moses' voice say, *It's magic.* Willing his hands to act, he fumbles with the pendant until the head comes off with an aqueous *pop.* Inside is a glass ampule, about the size and shape of a decongestant capsule. He lets it fall into the palm of his hand where it gleams like a tiny star, at its heart a drop of clear liquid no bigger than a dormouse's tear.

Now begins another struggle. He knows what he should do, what he *must* do, but a desperate voice, his own, is shrieking *No, wait! Let's think this through, Snowman!* This is the last drop in the entire world! The last taste you'll ever have in your life! What difference can it possibly make? He peers down at the sandy bottom of the hole again. Water out of water, right? But there is no water, no well to prime, no starter batch to start. Go on, Snowman, don't be a chump, take it! You've already given more than enough, you're *entitled*. He wants it so badly. *It* wants him to have it. Just put it in your mouth and bite down and the hell with the glass, Snowman. His hand is shaking, his whole body trembling, *my preciousss*. He puts the phial to his lips, a kiss, a taste of the glass and what the glass contains, *bite! bite!* No! he cries, his voice barely a croak as his hand flops over the edge of the hole and the phial falls, falls … but what? He doesn't hear it hit bottom, there's no shattering of glass, not even the tiniest tinkle. He peers into the depths. The light has shifted. He can't see anything. The camera zooms down to show us what the Snowman can't see or know. The phial has landed intact in the gossamer membrane of a spider web a few feet from the bottom.

Exhausted, he sinks into a deep sleep. And dreams of a snake swimming toward him in lazy undulations in a pool of clear turquoise blue water. Of a screaming human face emerging from the jaws of a huge serpent. Of an obsidian blade cutting into his bare chest. Of an extremely intense orgasm that involves Maria even though it doesn't. And wakes five or ten minutes or even an hour later as if he has just returned from a year in outer space. He struggles to his feet, staggers back through the tunnel, his strength returning the farther behind he leaves the empty pool even as his spirits sink lower. Any hope he had of finding Maria dashed.

43

ESCAPE FROM ZOL!

THE SNOWMAN NOW RETURNS to the rental car and starts back to Chopahuac. He wants to get away from this place as quickly as possible, get back to the hotel, pack and leave. But he must have made a wrong turn. He's now driving on a lonesome desert highway, a two-lane strip of worn gray asphalt cutting through a landscape of scrub and cactus. The AC has stopped working. Hot air pours in the open windows, lulling him into a drowsy, dreamlike state. He passes a small black bundle on the side of the road that resolves itself into a squinting, hook-nosed (prosthesis), witch-like little old woman who turns to watch him go by with a toothless mouth open wide in what seems a mirthless cackle and he thinks *Doña Hermosa?* Has Boone revived this motheaten old prop as some kind of symbol or forewarning? We again hear Incan panpipes playing the mournful, melancholy refrain of *El condor pasa* as the Snowman drives beneath a mountain whose entire top seems to have been blown off. He knows this mountain, knows the secrets it harbored in its hidden recesses, remembers things that he does not want to remember, rotting corpses sticking out of the sand like zombies rising from the grave, a human slaughterhouse where people are butchered like livestock.

He remembers waves of blinding, white-hot pain searing his eyes, his brain. He remembers an ill-conceived, desperate, but ultimately successful attempt to retrieve the Coupe, out of loyalty, yes, maybe even love, but also and more practically as a vehicle of escape. For himself, anyway. For Boone, well, an opportunity for the venerable director, in an act some critics call meta-meta, others crass commercialism, to insert the trailer for the long-awaited sequel to his last critical disaster (but acclaimed cult classic), *Escape From Zol,* starring Boone's favorite leading man Billy "Plum" Bob Bengay. You can bet he's giving away ninety percent of the plot, everything else'll be schlock, but fans'll still flock to the movie, at least for the popcorn.

Accompanied by the soaring strings and brass of Maurice Jarre's theme to *Lawrence of Arabia,* we now see a small cloud of yellow dust rapidly crossing the desert. A micro-tornado? A Looneytoonish Tasmanian devil? No, it's the Snowman, twenty-five years younger, helmetless, wraparound sunglasses, wind whipping his hair around his face, roaring across the desert on a motorcycle even though, as far as we know, he's never driven a motorcycle before in his life, which may explain the slides, spins and unexpected leaps and wheelies he makes as he climbs higher and higher into the rugged mountains. The audience unfamiliar with Boone's notorious stinginess is probably thinking this has gotta be a stunt double, right? I mean, has that fucker Cruise really set the bar so high? But, nope, the camera pulls in and it's the Snowman all right. Where is he going with such steely-eyed determination?

He screeches to a halt at the edge of an incongruous and blindingly green patch of jungle that seems to have appeared out of nowhere. Ditching the motorcycle he begins to fight his way through the dense tropical foliage with a machete he discovers in a scabbard on his hip. Suddenly it occurs to him that this is exactly the kind of place where you'd expect to find **POISONOUS SNAKES!!** Thought become reality, he glances down at his feet one second before he tumbles into a pit seething with the oily reptilian gleam of hundreds of poisonous serpents in a scene at least one cineaste will claim Boone expropriated from the Snowman's childhood favorite *Bomba the Jungle Boy.* Avoiding this Freudian pitfall at the very last instant, he shifts his momentum and kind of hops, skips, jumps around the snake pit and takes off running again but *look out!* **HERE COME THE BEES!!** and a swarm of Africanized killer bees sporting natty dreads and hypodermic stingers descends upon him in a loud angry buzzing. Just before they can inject their fatal venom he splashes headfirst into a rushing river. For about two seconds he thinks, great, saved from the bees, when he starts to feel little stings all over his body. Minor annoyances at first, they really start to hurt and now he understands, they're **PIRANHAS!!** Luckily he's already across the river and dragging himself up on the other bank when he hears a splash behind him and an **ALLIGATOR!!** lunges out of the water and clamps his foot in its jaws. Just when he thinks he's a goner a **JAGUAR!!** bounds toward him, claws and fangs bared for the kill, but instead of joining in the feast, the giant feline leaps over the Snowman, twists in midair like a ninja assassin, sinks its fangs in the back of the alligator's skull (it is, in fact, a caiman lizard—Glenda) and, glaring at the Snowman like *you owe me buddy*, drags the lifeless reptile into the reeds and he's on his feet again and running through the jungle at full speed.

We again hear the familiar Incan panpipes and just ahead the Snowman spies a large Mediterranean villa crowded in with bright pink and red bougainvillea and the blazing green of palm trees. Grabbing onto a sturdy vine (it's a giant pothos, common name Devil's Ivy, but botanists disagree on the exact taxonomy—Glenda again, *new meds?*), he swings over a twelve-foot-tall chain-link fence topped with razor wire, pole vaults on a piece of bamboo over an eight-foot stucco wall studded with broken glass, forces open a heavy wooden door with his shoulder and enters a large car barn. And there she is, stabled among several other automotive classics, the Coupe in all her Plasticene beauty (the Coupe has never been assigned a sex before, perhaps *she* had some gender reassignment work done under the hood?), the shark fins in back stacked with brake, backup and turning lights, the shiny chrome grill in front Cheshire Cat grinning at him coyly—well, okay, let's be frank—more like, *What are you doing here? I thought we'd parted ways long ago.* He hears gravel crunching outside, voices. *¿El Condor? Ya se fue pa'l Norte, ¿verdad?* Then silence.

He waits five more minutes, climbs into the Coupe, turns the key and ... for the first time in their storied relationship the Coupe is uncooperative. Rather than fire right up she coughs and stalls. *Please*, he begs her. I'm the one who got you out of that junk yard, remember? I always treated you well—okay, maybe not so well but we had a thing! And, who knows, maybe he struck an old chord of allegiance. The Coupe clears *its* (reverse surgery?) throat with a final internal combustion cough, expelling the residue of the overly rich fuel mix it's been swilling lately, and its mighty eight-cylinder, four hundred and fifty-six cubic inch, four hundred and sixty-seven horsepower engine built back in the day when men were men and cars were Wehrmacht tanks roars to life and just like a Wehrmacht tank crashes through the garage door without a scratch, bangs through the ornate wrought iron gate ornamented with cut copper palm trees and flamingos at the entrance without damaging its paint, and barrels down the mountainside, apparently home free. But, nope, spoke too soon.

In the rear mirror the Snowman sees a column of black SUVs roaring up behind him with men firing automatic pistols and machine guns out the windows *Bang! Bang! Ratatat!* Bullets zing and ricochet all around him and—oh no! The camera leaps ahead to a heavily fortified guard post manned by a bunch of tough hombres armed with AK47s, RPGs, Uzis. The camera now flies overhead and from this bird's eye view we see the Coupe being squeezed into an increasingly smaller space between the SUVs behind him and the guardhouse in front. Zeno's paradox notwithstanding, things look bleak. Which is when the Snowman remembers that on the single occasion Amanita agreed to ride with him in the Coupe she pointed at a button on the dash and said if you ever find yourself in a jam turn that and push. How she obtained this piece of information he doesn't know but he turns the button and pushes and *holy thunder!* a sheet of oil sprays out the back of the Coupe and *wheeeeee* the SUVs slip and slide and swerve off the road and down into an arroyo as the Snowman tromps the gas pedal to the floor and the Coupe surges forward eighty, ninety, a hundred miles an hour and before the armed men at the guardhouse can fire their weapons crashes through the gate, again completely unscathed, and the Snowman and his trusty steed roar down the mountain into the valley below while behind them we see marble columns, pink stucco, terra cotta roof tiles, palm trees, TVs and appliances blowing up in slow motion as a lurid purple, orange and green mushroom cloud rises in the sky.

44
Masked Ball

BOONE NOW MAKES A CLASSIC (some would say hackneyed) match cut as we see another Mediterranean villa, also familiar, situated in the rugged hill country just west of Osberg. The camera takes us inside, no invitation or RSVP required, to show us the elegant older gentleman we've met earlier, a mister L. Condor, shifting between his manicured fingers a silken square of toilet paper, in the lower right corner of which is the embossed monogram PPP. He is picturing a striking, somewhat alien-looking woman with unnaturally blue eyes not entirely unlike the azulejos in the vestibule of the Cathedral of San Lucífero in Valledoides. He remembers the circus atmosphere of those dreadful congressional hearings after the snow industry collapsed, and how easily this woman manipulated all those clowns. He senses something recondite, even deadly, about her that he also finds alluring. He has long suspected she is complicit in the great tragedy that befell his empire in Mexico, for which he would dearly love to see her pay, although in his younger days, before he had her hacked to pieces before his eyes, he would first like to have made love to her, if that is what one wishes to call it. He also has a special place reserved in his heart (or, more accurately, his private torture chamber) for this *Snowman* buffoon who has not only managed to escape his clutches several times before, including this recent *fuck-up*, to use the crude American expression, by his *until now* most trusted lieutenant, Horacio Ignoménez, but, even more aggravating, this *muñeco de nieve* has become very rich and famous.

L. Condor crumples the square of toilet tissue into a tiny ball and pitches it into the toilet. How he would love to do the same to these two *putos*. Surely there is some way to have them in his grasp. His personal valet and confidant, Clive Hedgeworth Yñagez-Irrutia, himself aged, slightly bent, rather becoming in his profession, suggests a masked ball. We invite noted Osberg celebrities, promote it as a charity event, from there it will be easy to do as we wish with selected guests. This idea excites Condor. The opportunity for vengeance, yes, but also because he has become somewhat vain in his golden years and the irony of receiving public recognition, even from a bunch of ignorant *greenghosts*, appeals to him. He has Clive contact Beatrice Biscott, who did his villa's interior and is a renowned mover and shaker in Osberg's social order. She immediately draws up a guest list and invitations are sent to various socialites and bigwigs.

The night of the event, L. Condor, costumed appropriately as a dashing Diablo in a tuxedo accessorized with a red eye mask, horns and tail, is the perfect host, greeting and exchanging pleasantries with his guests, so nice to meet you, so glad you could come, complimenting them on their costumes, oh, of course, Joan of Arc! His guest of honor, herself unaware of that title, comes dressed as the biblical Judith. Not Gentileschi's realistic portrayal of a stout, workwomanlike Judith assisted by her equally robust peasant maid. Klimt's art nouveau version, an austere Judith, albeit in a multi-colored outfit with her left breast and midriff sensuously bared. His other intended victim, the Snowman, who arrived back in the States in time to receive his invitation, is très meta as a slimmed-down Frosty the Snowman, top hat, scarf, and a white flannel leisure suit with over-sized coal-black buttons. Seeing past or through Judith's disguise, which doesn't require X-ray eyes, he feels pangs of regret, which only add to the crushing weight of failure he has brought back with him from Mexico. His dilemma is complicated by the presence of Lilith aka Sister Sunne Rae (Condor has no idea, Clive is an ardent fan), who comes as Scarlett O'Hara (can't disguise that butt even beneath an antebellum bustle) in the black mourning gown Scarlett is wearing when Rhett gives her the kiss-off.

Now here's where things get interesting. L. Condor has begun to suspect that some of his guests are impostors. There's something nightmarish about their costumes, not because they are ghoulish or frightening but because they all signify something to him. For example, this woman in the olive drab military uniform with bandoliers of ammunition across her chest. The green cloth cap and black balaclava she's wearing hide all but her eyes, which still manage to convey a certain bemused look despite being gaunt and sunken. She's also smoking a tobacco pipe, a mottled briar with a large bowl, and one can't help noticing that her teeth don't look particularly healthy, indeed she has an overall consumptive appearance. It's Maria, of course, in a transcendent fashion statement, which may explain why L. Condor hasn't recognized her as a ghost from his past.

She has also been conspicuously avoiding the Snowman, who oddly doesn't seem to have caught on yet either, even though she's accompanied by Xuan Carlode, who comes as Cuauhtémoc in a plumed serpent mask and loincloth, an intimidating figure even older and warworn (Boone has been accused of stealing from *Machete*). L. Condor also searches warily behind the mask and cape of the dashing swordsman in black, Zorro, of course, whom the audience will recognize immediately as—*Antonio Banderas?*

No! No, no, no! I told you a thousand times no! You know we can't fucking afford him! And here Boone once again rushes onto the set, absolutely apoplectic, gnashing his teeth and waving his cane in a threatening manner. Uh-oh, looks like somebody has royally fucked up. For about one second the renowned Spanish actor appears on the screen, the question to be determined in court later, does his brief visit qualify merely as a cameo, or did he appear long enough to demand full pay scale?

And just like that, in Señor Banderas' stead, we see MJ, recently released from a U.S. immigrant detention center, not a *whole* lot worse for this little misunderstanding (turns out he has dual U.S. and Mexican citizenship, the legalities are a bit complicated but it does involve the issue of paternity and a legal document presented in Spanish and English).

And who is *this* fascinating creature, a Marvel superhero? She's wasp-like, spider-like, cat-like, *something*-like in a sleek black leather outfit, her face hidden behind a black mantilla veil, her chestnut-brown tresses flowing over her shoulders. *Amanita?* Why, yes, it is. Does Condor know his daughter is here? Does he know *why* she's here? Does she? Even weirder, Mona

Moondrake is also present, which can only be explained by a lung-bursting plunge into the oxygen-less depths of quantum mechanics. There is this odd sheen about them both, kind of *subatomic*, and if we haven't already gotten the message, there's a brief shot of Amanita's face superimposed over Mona's with theremin music in the background (warbly, quavering, *spooky*). For tonight's occasion Mona is wearing a powdery green Venetian carnival mask shaped like a Luna moth—quite striking, really, against her copper curls—a sleeveless, ankle-length white dress with a wide brown belt, and a necklace of large jade beads, a lovely ensemble, made just a bit slovenly by Mona's blowsy appearance.

Iago, or rather *King* Arthur, who must have got wind of this affair and copped his own invitation, comes dressed in Elizabethan costume as, who else, Othello. Moll Flowers comes as Joe Palooka in butt-hugging Navy whites (enlisted). M'Shaka appears in luminous rainbow robes and, well, nobody's sure about this one, I mean, the dude's dead, right? And true, he's not saying much, he nods his head in acknowledgement a few times, he does a couple of smooth dance moves when the party heats up, but that doesn't prove anything. Virtual? Maybe.

Everyone at this gathering is kind of luminous or liminal, there's this odd light, like a movie projector behind them. Oscar even makes an appearance, or rather, he doesn't, but he's there all right, the Snowman recognizes that feathery touch on his arm and at one point Sister Sunne Rae seems to be having an animated conversation with an empty doorway (an overheard snatch of their conversation includes an earnest encouragement for *you two to patch things up and get back together*). There are also a few guests from the original list of invitees who wonder why they haven't recognized *somebody* by now—Fred? Wilma? Is that you?

The camera returns to L. Condor. Surveying his party, his heart has begun to beat rapidly. He feels somehow out of control, something he has only felt a very few times in his life. But he is also a gambler and his doubts vanish as he feels that old thrill of the big stakes game. Let fate take its course, the blade fall as it may.

The night begins with a chamber orchestra, recorder, viola da gamba, viol and violin. Everybody finds themselves involved in intricate Renaissance dances, the gavotte, torneo, saltarello. Oddly they all seem masters at this balletic craft. There are genteel exchanges of partners, polite bon mots *vous êtes très chic!* and battute spiritose *ma va, bugiardo!* Ah, but as so often happens at adult parties, the alcohol begins to flow, the powders blow, the ganja glow. Somehow the chamber quartet has disappeared and in their place the cutting edge(!!) band ICIS is slashing and shredding and everybody's dancing frantically and, frankly, my dear, most folks here are a tad too old for this shit, they're huffing and puffing and gasping for breath.

And this is when things really get interesting. People begin to drift off into other rooms, they're bumping into each other in the dark (Mona and Amanita do this shtick where one gets bumped and the other one says *ouch!*). Matches flare, EyePhones® glare, there are moments of hilarity, laughter, silly giggles, *oh, it's you*, moments of repulsion, genuine fright and terror, *It's You!* It's like a comedy drama, like the board game Clue or an Agatha Christie movie, that scoundrel Boone's grabbing whatever he can, *The Masque of the Red Death,*

Traumnovelle, House of Wax. Everybody's suspicious of everybody else or out to get somebody else with, of course, de rigueur sexual inuendoes and complications.

The Snowman and Judith have a brief encounter in a dark corner of the party when they accidentally slam into each other, full body contact, and the Snowman feels that old muscle memory or at least some body part memory, but the refs are already calling foul and they spin away from each other like satellites in space and *whomp*, he crashes into—*Maria?* And again there's this full-body recognition, muscle memory thing and even at his age Johnny Doolittle downstairs is getting all sproinga-boinga acrobatic. And then splat, he slams into Lilith that is to say Sister Sunne Rae and, oh boy, there's some splainin' to do here, like, fool, haven't you made up your mind yet? And away he spins again for a very close flyby of Amanita and Mona and once again the air is charged, the sparks fly, magnetic forces are at work, energy fields collide like galaxies, and, implausibly, he, the Snowman, is the very event horizon at the center of this chaos. Even if they don't exactly *want* him, they lay claim, possession, ownership, they cast spells, utter curses. Barb-wire strands of electric blue light sizzle and crackle around them like Van de Graaff generators. Lights flicker on and off. There are gunshots, screams, we see horrific images, mutilations, beheadings.

Life imitating art, the lights go back on and *WTF!!* the entire party gasps. Judith is holding L. Condor's head on a silver platter. And now the whole theater goes up in a collective scream. Audience members are shouting, It's John the Baptist! No, it's Robespierre! Apparently Boone's young screenwriters have gotten history confused with myth and scripture. Is Judith indeed supposed to be Salome? Is she Perseus holding the head of the serpent-tressed gorgon? No, of course not. She's playing herself! It's the biblical Judith and Holofernes! We told you that above. Which, neither a scripturalist nor a student of apocrypha, the Snowman once again mishears as *Hollow Furnace* even as a bunch of longtime Boone Weller fans collectively slap their foreheads and go *Dooohhhh!*

But is Judith really a cold-blooded murderess? Is she still throbbing inside from the carnal act, yes, satisfying, wildly so, this barbarian chief, huge, an animal, that preceded the slaughter? Or simply relieved that a distasteful chore has been expedited? But wait, as even a beginning law student can tell you, the fact that Judith is holding the severed head doesn't necessarily mean she did the severing. Evidence will show that she found this grisly trophy in the dark, she thought it was a panettone. Well then, who is the culprit? And here Boone, in a quick cut away, shows us Inspector Clouseau, Sherlock Holmes and—*Philip Marlowe?* speculating aloud about possible motives. We quickly discover that none of our familiar cast of characters is guilty. It was the swarthy, five o'clock-shadowed Little Bo Peep nobody could figure out, some dude—Harold? *Horace?* But where has Miss Peep gone?

Suddenly we hear screeching tires, convoys of black SUVs crash through the gates, behind them flashing lights, sirens screaming, hundreds of state, county and municipal police cars, swat teams, National Guard APCs. Everybody looks at each other like, uh-oh, the jig's up. Secret exits, trapdoors and false panels spring open and slam shut as everyone scatters and once again there's no

long goodbye between the Snowman and Maria or
anybody else for that matter.

45
Adiós, Mis Amigos

THE SNOWMAN STANDS AT THE WINDOW of his Penthouse condo, staring directly at the Eye. They seem to be having a staring contest. The Eye looks angry. *You have betrayed me, Snowman. After I gave you so much*. The Snowman is defiant. *You who were supposed to watch over and protect us have betrayed us all*. Not sure who blinked first but the next shot puts us in a dimly lit alley in front of a soot-blackened red brick wall on which is painted a mural of a rattlesnake coiled around an ice-cold bottle of Ol' Rattler beer, a vestige of the days when this was the service entrance to the rough and tumble Rattlesnake Den (bikers, diesel dykes, trans cowboys, pretty authentic-looking extraterrestrials). The wall swings up and the Snowman's long-time automotive companion, the coal-black Coupe du Jour emerges with himself behind the wheel. He can feel the Eye's resentful gaze follow him as he drives across town and under the concrete bastion of the sixty-eight lane DR-35, where the camera loses him heading east on 7th street. We pick him up again cruising through a maze of narrow backstreets in a tiny pocket of miraculously ungentrified shotgun shacks, bungalows and outright hovels that looks like a setting from *In the Heat of the Night* and knowing Boone it probably *is* a setting from *In the Heat of the Night*. The Coupe pulls up outside a modest, slightly dilapidated, white wood-frame residence listed in the tax records as owned by a Manfred Snow, although when asked, neighbors will report having never seen this Mister Snow.

The wind has picked up. One of those capricious Central Texas cold fronts seems to be moving in. The Snowman retrieves a key from a slot in the doorframe, unlocks the door and hurries inside bent and shivering like a decrepit Bruce Wayne retreating into a damp, cold bat cave stinking of guano, or the aged and kryptonite-weakened Superman slinking into his hovel of despair. The place has remained largely as it was when he lived here, the kitchen table and two chairs, the couch and sofa in the living room, the rat's nest he slept in on the bedroom floor, the old, rusting freezer in the seldom used back room. In the bathroom he stares at himself in the cloudy, chipped mirror. Nothing he hasn't seen before, the same old face, or more accurately, the same face older. Older and tireder. He feels lost. He feels lonely and untethered. He misses Me'th. It's been years since he last saw him. The penthouse scene apparently turned him off and one day—*fffft*, gone. Maybe he went off to die somewhere or, more likely, he packed up and left, disgusted with what you've become, *Snowman*.

This is where Boone would really like to pile on the saccharine, a man and his cat, separated, torn asunder by forces of nature. But that's not going to happen because here comes Me'th in the door now, carrying a rat the size of an opossum between his teeth. The look of surprise or shock or even horror on the Snowman's face is understandable. Either he's having a flashback, a distinct possibility, or else Me'th has gotta be the oldest cat in the world. Somebody call Guinness, get him in the book. It also confirms some viewers' long-held suspicion that *Me'th* is short for Methusaleh. His fur is speckled with white and he appears to be growing a beard. In later scenes he will be seen using a walker. (*Mrrrwhat?!* No later scenes?!) From past experience the Snowman knows better than to attempt any overt display of affection, so, no hugs. He and Me'th sit at opposite ends of the couch, Me'th gazing sleepy-eyed past the prey he is clutching almost lovingly in his paws, sometimes blinking at him in that slow-motion optical gesture signifying whatever it signifies in cat, I come in peace, all is well with the world, I will watch you until the end although I may not be able to protect you.

The Snowman takes out a bottle of pills and sets them by the ashtray on the small end table next to him. The camera pulls in so we can read the label and these are exactly what drug czar Oksi Constantine had in mind when, dressed in his full emperor regalia, he warned the public of the dangers of prescription drug abuse (code words, with a wink and a nod, for big profits in the pharmaceutical industry). He opens a bottle of whiskey, a smoky, peaty, single malt, fills half a glass, lights a cigarette. His eyes fix, as they always do, on a luminous white square of hand-beaten parchment tacked to the wall on which is printed a Rorschach blot of black ink that in Japanese means something like *the path to harmony is scattered with thorns* (*tacks*, actually—Glenda). Was it never what he remembered, thought, believed it to be, even for a little while? *Love?* Was her androidally bright mind incapable of love? Is that what it takes to plan and execute a revolution?

He continues to drink methodically while lighting one cigarette after another. The camera occasionally returns to the bottle of pills. Are there fewer than before? Can't tell from this angle. What about now? The last cigarette has smoldered down to nothing in the ashtray. The Snowman looks as if he's fallen asleep. His crooked smile suggests he's having a pleasant dream. One might even surmise that in his mind he has been transported back into the warm sunshine down ol' Mexico way. Somewhere in the distance we hear a rooster crow. A brass trumpet blares and a high tenor voice sings *Méxicooo* with an attenuated final note that erupts into a lonesome coyote howl *ay! ay! ay-yyyyyy!*

A disconnected shot shows a vintage black Coupe du Jour heading south on DR-35 at night, a string of taillights stretching out in front of it like red-hot cinnamon drops, the city of Osberg a white mound of phosphorescence receding in the rear mirror. Long-time cinema buffs will recognize this as a reprise of the original shot from Boone's earlier release *The Abominable Snowman of the North*.

46
The Following Morning ...

... THINGS BEGIN TO CHANGE. Snow starts to fall. Soft, silent, disconcertingly rainbow-colored. People go outside and lift their faces to feel this cold wet stuff coming down from the sky. Is it real? Will it last? I mean, heck, it's the end of August, it's a hundred and ten degrees. It's also delicious. People are seen eating their way to their cars through sparkling rainbow snowdrifts. Children lag on the way to school, eating handfuls of neon red or green or blue snow, each with its own distinct taste, cherry, lime, blueberry, although it's the wise young lad or lass indeed who heeds Uncle Frank's admonishment, *Don't you eat that yellow snow!* And then—that crazy Central Texas weather—just as suddenly, the snow begins to melt. Temperatures quickly soar into unheard of territory. All across the nation paperboys in pancake caps, suspenders and knee breeches are out on street corners shouting in high shrill voices, *Extra! Extra! Read all about it!* The public is on tenterhooks for the latest word hot off the press. Shake up at Northern One Pyramid Enterprises! Mysterious disappearance of CEO! (On an unrelated score, it is also around this time, cineastes note, that Billy "Plum" Bob Bengay, aka William Bengay, also known as *William the Bulge* among a certain giddy crowd, fades from public view. There are rumors of a paternity suit, law suit, a terrible accident, disfigurement, early-onset dementia—*whooo knowwws?*)

But wait, that's not it. It's something worse, much worse. The great tragedy! The outcry is universal. It flies across the entire nation, circles the globe like a hypersonic missile. In every country, city, province and state people of every race, creed, religion, ethnicity and cookie dough preference wrinkle their noses in disgust. *Thees PoPoPop!®* tastes like *sheet!* And the thing is, that's exactly what it tastes like (or so says a noted coprophagologist with a shit-eating grin). Angry customers with what do look like brown smudges around their mouths mob shops and stores to complain. Warehouses and distributors are overwhelmed with cancelled orders. Chemists at NOPE announce with their usual understated irony that a slight change seems to have occurred in the molecular structure of the *PoPoPops!®* secret *enzyme.* No matter how they adjust the formula the result is the same, the product tastes and smells unmistakably like *doo doo.* Roger Wilco is brought in from the looney bin for his opinion but his response is so over the top crazy (nonstop lip flibbing *blbb!blbb!blbb!*) the video is destroyed and Roger is sent back to the psychiatric ward where Iago, er, *Arthur*, who just can't wrap his big rational brain around this turn of events, is caught on camera with his hands wrapped around Roger's neck, Roger's got that cartoonish strangled, cross-eyed look. But the truth will out as *somebody* said because, yes indeedy, Arthur owns this fuck-up as we now see him staring *perplexedly* at the little red thermos in his hand as if this inanimate object has betrayed him and not a chain of rational assumptions on his part that failed to account for the irrational.

Northern One Pyramid Enterprises stock is worthless within days. Board members are seen plummeting from upper story windows to the pavement half a mile below, sometimes assisted in their defenestration by an anonymous flurry of hands. Natasha Bolsavitch glides down on a broom. Eunace Gup—oh, what the hell—the *Gupster* descends at a slightly slower rate beneath a flouncy pink silk parasol that to the observer seems to be falling on its own. The whole nation quickly sinks into a depression that is as deep and black as the Mariana Trench and growing deeper by the hour. Here Boone inserts a black and white film clip that he almost certainly stole *somewhere*. It could be a scene from Dante's Inferno or *The Seventh Seal* or a newsreel from the Great Depression. An endless queue of gaunt, hollow-eyed people, men and women, senior citizens, children, all bent in the posture of penitents or condemned, all staring transfixedly at the glowing mini-palantirs in their hands, plod toward the edge of a yawning abyss where, due to one of the usual fuckups in this low-budget film, special effects puts on a brief, glorious CGI of a sunset over the Grand Canyon (unless it's intended to suggest the gates of paradise.) Psynancialogists are sent out in droves to council devastated members of the financial industry (and ensure their complicity in the face of the next inquisition *mum's the word*).

A cloud of gloom settles over Osberg as the city slouches toward a colder than usual fall and an earlier than usual winter and what promises to be a bleak holiday season. Throughout the city, in apartments, homes, condos, basement workshops, grocery stores, offices and coffee shops, disconsolate Osbergians nod along to the moody, melancholy, universally beloved if unabashedly sentimental (some would even say mawkish) Vladimir Lennon classic, *So This Isn't Christmas* (the young, ultra-hip crowd puts it right up there with the pirated video of the Sid Vicious and Tony Bennett duet *We Did It Frankie's Way*). Hopes for a brisk Christmas retail season plummet even further after multiple toy stores report a complete disaster with their most popular item, "Baby Blue Eyes," which comes in male, female and non-binary genders as well as algorithmically determined skin colors. When caressed by children's hands, Baby Blue Eyes' angelic face morphs into the sad, twisted face of a child-laborer in the country it was made and the doll blackens and chemically burns into a hideously deformed corpse. "Some phenomenon of plastics," a spokesperson for ToyZRD® suggests, phlegmatic as a horned toad.

How has it all gone so terribly wrong? How could this universally popular taste treat that once upon a time united the entire globe in the rainbow glow of peace, love and groovy all-inclusiveness (dates please—when did you say that was?), now cause that same world to fall apart? Was it possible, through some kind of causality that doesn't exist according to the laws of thermodynamics *as they are currently understood*, that the same someone who got the ball rolling with her magic potion not only foresaw this outcome but orchestrated, arranged, engineered the entire chain of events, earthquakes and car chases, revolutions, volcanic eruptions, bizarre meteorological aberrations? *Bru-ja-ja!*

The scene changes. The camera shows Lilith at the blackboard looking tired, aged, a kind of graphite gray in her hair and even the highlights of her face. Her voice quavers slightly as she explains the scientific underpinnings of magic to a bored-looking classroom (heads on desks, ear buds in, EyePhones® out, half asleep and still *tap tap tapping*). The entire universe is connected through a kind of quantum entanglement, Einstein's "spooky action at a distance." One might even define this phenomenon as a form of communication. The universe is talking to itself but not everyone can hear. Rarely, certain individuals not only learn how to hear but to "speak," that is, to cause things to *happen* even at impossible distances, things that, for lack of a better explanation, seem magical. Reputedly, it takes years of training, a perfect match between shaman and pupil, lots of suffering and deprivation are involved, and sorry, there are no chai or kombucha breaks. Can you imagine something like that, class? *Zzzzzzz*.

And, who knows, maybe Lilith is right because as if things weren't already weird enough, in a news flash Uncle Bob announces a crack has occurred in the space-time continuum. A blond, bearded man with strikingly blue eyes and, well, a suggestion of a Levantine complexion (it could be tanning beds, skin toners, something like that), but otherwise your typical Anglo-Saxon white guy dressed in a long white robe and crude leather sandals, albeit with spurs, has just ridden into town on the back of a *Tyrannosaurus rex* and both the man and the T-rex are wearing six-shooters in tooled leather holsters on their hips, although the T-rex is sporting absolutely the biggest, baddest pair of long-barreled Colt .45s you've ever seen in your life (they're more like mini ICBMs, and sorry you NRA folks, they ain't on the market—*yet*). It also doesn't escape anyone's attention that martyr boy (several bystanders swear they saw a golden halo floating over his head, could've been the light, maybe hidden wires—wait, is that Brad Pizzoccheri?) and the big lizard both look pretty darn pissed. They ride up to the huddle of reporters, who appear understandably concerned, martyr boy leans down and, speaking in Texian with a Middle Aramaic accent (*Tex-Aramaic?*), says, Howdy, folks, can y'all tell me which way to the Apocalypse?

Is it any wonder then that in his final appearance behind the pulpit a much diminished Reverend Fallible is seen addressing his equally diminished congregation in a much weakened voice that echoes like a creaky windmill in the huge and largely empty nave, his once proud mien humbled by age, the golden *surf's up* tonsorial wave sweeping back from the noble promontory of his brow thinner and gone from Grecian silver to dog-piss yellow, the once armor-piercing blue eyes fading behind an aqueous gray fog, the bulge in his pants that legendary torpedo with which he is rumored to have converted many a recalcitrant gal—or have his Depends bunched up? He also sounds a tad too much like one of those Old Testament prophets, not just inspired but *deranged*, when he proclaims Darkness is upon us! Go in search of the light—preferably one hundred watts or higher!

There seems to be no end to the scandals. Judith has been discovered (*alleged*, but let's not split cunt hairs) to have ties to the ultra-radical, global anti-corporate underground army CESS. Rather than stick around for the four a.m. kick down the doors and frog-march her outa here routine, Judith does indeed go underground. Her name and any trace of her presence are Sovietskily stricken from the annals of PPP and in her place the board installs this new guy Montag who has this brilliant idea if he can just sell it to the shareholders. It's very simple, ladies and gentlemen, *Fire*. Why continue to waste time and money recycling? Get rid of it all! Everything! Immolate the problem in its own clothes! *Paper*. We'll burn everything, all the books, newspapers. Libraries are full of this shit (*excuse my English*). In the name of patriotism we'll demand that people surrender subversive texts such as personal diaries, journals, old love letters. What we want here is total commitment to digital technology. Our new director of R&D, Roger Wilco (miraculously recovered—*newwww medddds?!*), has suggested a small chip implant at birth, some sort of cranial port or WIFI connection, direct transaction between brain and machine. All we gotta do is get it past Congress.

47
Cartography

By NOW BOONE'S ALL OVER THE MAP. He's desperately trying to tie this whole thing together, he's cramming in tons of material he'll never be able to justify, scenes of hope and hope not only deferred but destroyed.

The camera takes us through a dark tunnel into a large grotto shaped like an upside-down wine glass. A dusty ray of sunlight illuminates a deep hole at the bottom of which we can see human skeletons adorned with gold jewelry partially buried in the sand. The camera directs our attention to a spider web attached to an exposed root and the faint gleam of a tiny glass ampule trapped in its silky membrane. At that moment a rock dislodged from above by a scuttling scorpion falls and tears the web, causing the ampule to drop the remaining three or four feet to the bottom where it shatters against the gold bracelet on a skeletal wrist. Suddenly a stream of water gushes out of the sand. Thanks to time-lapse we see the hole fill completely and become a deep, turquoise blue pool as dense green tropical foliage flourishes around it. The camera now draws back through the tunnel, out into the bright sunlight and satellite-high into the sky so that we can see the vast barren desert below begin to turn green following a blueprint set in motion during the

Cambrian period. First moss, liverworts, lichens, then grasses, small branching plants, large leafy plants, cycads, giant ferns, vines, trees, the desert transformed into tropics, the deforested forest reforested. Is it a dream? Virtual? Cinemagic and after the film's over it all disappears again?

The camera returns to the States and the booming city of Osberg where we are now visiting one of this vibrant cosmopolis' many homeless camps (courtesy of the grasshopper—he, she or it is selling *their* services to any and all buyers). It's surprisingly tidy, the tents and lean-tos arranged in an orderly grid, sidewalks made of bricks, boards, flagstones. It's a crisp autumnal day. A small group of men and women dressed in slightly shabby but sensible clothes for this time of year is seated in a semi-circle on plastic milk crates, old chairs, sofas, they've all got this healthy glow about them like they just spent the last two weeks at a beach resort. They're sipping hot mochas and lattes, herbal teas. A CBD joint with negligible THC (.2 %) is making the rounds. Everyone's attention is focused on an individual whom they address as Mister Bill, possibly a reference to the venerable and vulnerable SNL character, but here in Texas more likely out of old school Southern respect, although they could just as well call him Howard Hughes. He's completely unidentifiable, probably in his early sixties, bearded, shaggy hair, a wide-brimmed hillbilly hat, clunky black horn-rimmed sunglasses duct-taped together at the bridge, faded denim coat, pants, blue chambray shirt, brown leather work boots. His arrival in their midst is a mystery. Whether he descended on Jacob's ladder or beamed down from a Martian spaceship or just walked here from the next town over is anybody's guess. In

addition to English, he speaks passable Spanish and
occasional phrases of a strange language the others think
really is Martian, although it's also pentecostally possible
that he's just babbling pure nonsense during one of his
infrequent Wernickean dysphasic attacks. They all agree,
however, that he sounds like one very smart chocolate
chip cookie.

Lately he has begun to talk about forming a
consortium, to be called Bums Alliance for Good. The
idea is to pool their earnings from panhandling and
compound them through a range of investments, stocks,
bonds, real estate, the latter also including single family
residences and small apartment complex fixer-uppers to
provide shelter for homeless *associates* while they
renovate the property. Mister Bill fills them in on the
details. We begin locally, here in Osberg. We'll cover all
the major panhandling sites, every street corner,
intersection. Each associate will be outfitted with an
EyePhone® and expected to keep in touch with home
base—and no, Rosco, it has nothing to do with trust. Yes,
I know the government shoved a transistor up your butt,
pretty sure everybody here's got one. We just want to
keep our bookkeeping straight, nickels and dimes add up.
We'll have to increase gross receipts. That means not just
more time on the corners and more corners covered. It
means a smarter approach to *cornering*. And that means
the three Ds, dress, deportment, dialoguing. The way you
look, the way you act and the way you speak to the client.
Ragged, shabby, down and out, but basically clean,
decent, friendly—all good. Blowsy, slurring, aggressive,
surly, vomit on your collar—no good. We want to
establish a degree of professionalism. In order to
accomplish that goal we'll need absolute integrity among

our sales associates. No dipping in the till, no drug and alcohol binges on company time. Every associate will be guaranteed a minimum daily allotment for food, drinks, personal necessities and a place to sleep, plus adequate funds for stimulants *after* hours (snickers.) We will also assist with legal expenses incurred during interactions with the police. In the event, however, that you are found guilty of a crime you will be expected to reimburse the general fund in a timely fashion. (Groans.) We will also have a bonus program for you hard-chargers and innovators who want to earn some extra income. Enos here ferments wine out of mustang grapes that he harvests from the urban forest. Word on the street? It's not a great wine, it's not even a good wine. It's sweet and oaky and way too heavy on the tannins, but at least it is wine, sorta. Plus, Enos makes a few extra bucks selling his product to a counterfeit kosher spirits dealer under the name Mazel Tuff.

Hey Enos, I wouldn't drink that cat piss with your mouth! All right, all right, let's quiet down. I've put together some spread sheets, worked up a couple of helpful algorithms. Hopalong, Peg, One-Eye, you'll be sector managers. Ha! Ya hear that, hon? *Managers.* You know it, babe. All right, you two lovebirds, save the PDA for your own time. Once we've got the show up and running here in Osberg we'll expand into all the major cities in Texas, then nationally. Eventually we'll go international, *Workers of the World Unite*, etc. The disenfranchised, diasporas, displaced persons, refugees, immigrants, exiles—the cities of the world are teeming with them. We'll have to draw up discrete constitutions for varying constituencies, we'll need a legal branch to ensure we adhere to international law … *Honnnk!*

Snorrre! Zzzzzz ... Well, it looks like Mister Bill's losing his audience. All right, enough palaver, let's break for a *PoPoPop!*® *Yayyyy!* And Mister Bill's not skimping. He's brought along a whole ice cream cart. He must have stolen the damn thing from the Smithsonian. These have to be the last *PoPoPops!*® in Osberg, maybe the world.

The camera now travels to the mean streets of Far East Osberg, where it catches up with a bunch of kids in multi-colored hoodies blowing clouds of steam on this chilly morning. It's the United Colors gang. Now what are these hooligans up to? Let's follow them and find out. Hmm, they're approaching a ramshackle bungalow, sagging front porch, worn siding. Probably a crack house, right? These kids are gonna be sucking on those pipes 'til their eyes pop out. Or maybe this is their fence, they're selling stolen goods, somebody's beloved heirloom, a porcelain woodchuck, for ten lousy bucks. One of them goes up the stairs with a cardboard box in his hands. He knocks on the door, three quick raps. A minute later there's the sound of someone approaching, tentative, unsure. The door creaks opens and an old man with a little brown walnut-wrinkled face peeks out. When he sees who it is he breaks into a wide smile, pats the boy on the shoulder and takes the box. Aged fingers clumsy, slow to obey, he opens the lid to inspect the contents as the camera zooms in on a home-cooked meal of baked chicken, steamed broccoli, black-eyed peas and cornbread, and a fresh fruit salad. We briefly follow this gang of miscreants as they now go from door to door, handing out home-cooked meals and food baskets to the homebound and handicapped, the old, lonely and forgotten, here and there stopping to chat a spell, do some chores around the house, sweep the floor, wash the dishes, take out the garbage. And for those of you who were still wondering what the hell Sister Sunne Rae was doing with all those donations she solicited on her program (*that number again is ...*), here's the answer as the camera cuts away to Lilith's apartment and inside where we find Dr. Levant seated at her dining room table, writing a substantial check to the "United Colors Distribution Fund."

Well, that's pretty hopeful too. Looks like we're on a roll. Nothing but blue skies ... oh, wait, are those storm clouds? The forecast didn't say anything about inclement weather. Geez, the temperature must have dropped twenty degrees. Is that snow?

Turns out this will be the last check Lilith writes. The *Sistuh's* show has been canceled. Made white folks uncomfortable, the attorney general complained (officially). Made him uncomfortable all right. The same charge that will end her (non-)tenure at the university— uncomfortable white kids (maybe they oughta change those undies now and then).

The capitalist axe will fall on many fragile necks. Here's Moses pushing his Moms up the sidewalk in a wheelchair, she's wrapped in a blanket, head's kind of lolling to one side. She's been doing poorly again, can't afford her meds on her reduced health care. Moses is trying to find work. Lucky for him, he wisely (so it wasn't luck) cashed in on his stock portfolio before the crash, but he spent it all supporting extended family and friends. Now the furnace has gone on the blink.

A faint gleam on the frosty ground catches the camera's eye, a mottled brown and yellow pattern that, in a warmer clime, could be reptilian, constrictor or tortoise shell, but which resolves itself into a very simple but ancient musical instrument made of a hollow reed at the very moment a heavy black boot, hob-nailed, *jack*, stomps on it, splintering it into mute shards useless for anything but setting poisoned boobytraps for unsuspecting GIs, at the same time we hear the sound of a body crumpling to the ground, if, that is, you can imagine the sound an angel or even a fairy, a composite of pixie dust and imagination, makes when it falls to earth, although there will be no mention of this body, heavenly or otherwise, in the police report.

The wind blows harder, snow drifts down.

We now see a homeless camp of a different stripe altogether, snow-covered tarps, tents, a fire pit filled with smoldering garbage in front of which a woman wrapped in blankets and a tattered flower print shawl is sitting on the ground, clutching in her lap a brown paper shopping bag out of which some old video cartridges have fallen. The camera moves to the woman's face, a grotesque, crudely painted clown mask of despair with a noticeable five o'clock-shadow. How can this even be her inside this slow-moving old body with this old drooling wound of a cunt that isn't even real, her flaccid tits sagging parabolically down to her navel, hair sprouting all over her body, her arms and legs and even her back *owoooo*. Tonight will be very cold. She has some booze, pills, she hopes it's enough. She couldn't afford anymore, all that money gone so fast. She meant to go by the post office to see if there was a reply from her estranged brother. She couldn't possibly know there's a letter informing her of a generous lifetime trust fund set up in her name.

48
The Cutting Room Floor

A SENTIMENTALIST AT HEART, Boone will hold onto these final two clips until the very end when his producer finally convinces him to dump them. *You're way over fucking budget, your film's a piece of crap, nobody gives a shit how the hell you end it, basta!*

Through the Looking Glass

An old woman sits at the window of a small adobe house with whitewashed walls as the first pale pink and yellow morning light spreads across the desert, perhaps watching an unfamiliar car coming up the lane or a flying saucer landing. Her expression shows neither surprise nor fear nor even curiosity.

The scene changes. Now we see the woman going through her daily routine, collecting eggs from under sleepy-eyed brooding hens in the chicken coop, milking the goat, drawing water from the well in a wooden bucket, scratching at the rocky soil with a crude wooden hoe where a few ragged green plants are struggling to survive, the accumulated aches and pains in her aged body remote and yet never far from her mind every time she bends over the hoe or reaches up to hang chiles from the rafter. To the romantic, a simple bucolic existence, to the realist, hardscrabble poverty. In one narrative, mythical, the aged Earth Mother Gaia, in another, more or less accurate, simply an old woman who sometimes wonders that she is still alive.

The scene changes again. Now we see her sitting on a wooden bench in the shade next to the open front door, watching the chickens scratch in the dirt as she herself did earlier, the raggedy, one-eyed kitten playing with a grasshopper *help me, Snowman!* the scrawny goat stretching its neck to chew on the dried leaves of the rattlepod tree. In the lines etched into the woman's face, in the obsidian glitter of her small black eyes, one senses that these things, these daily chores and these creatures, have woven themselves into her life and become her life until she has no other life apart from them. An old woman on a small plot of sandy, rocky soil in the middle of a desert strewn with cactus and scrub, the sun burning like an incandescent lamp in the vast blue sky, a vulture drifting overhead, symbol of death, eater of death, ancient death itself dressed in tattered, flea-ridden black mourning cloth, the ochre mountain behind her stolid, mute, brooding over hundreds of millions of years of memory in which these creatures who think themselves close to God and cast in the image of God should only figure as an insignificant part and yet who have laid claim to the title destroyers of the earth.

In the evening she eats a plain dinner, pinto beans and corn tortillas, water from the well, then prepares for bed and the dreams that will come on the wings of night and the name that will flutter like a moth between her lips until she wakes calling *Margarito!* in a quavering voice and her eyes wet with tears but no voice answers back full of masculine laughter and joy of life *my Maria!* Dear God, whatever god that is, to hold him in her arms one more time, to embrace his beautiful youth in her aged flesh. How can it be possible that after so many years she still wakes in tears or that an old woman like herself can still yearn for a young man not much more than a boy she loved so long ago?

Would it be any surprise then if she were not surprised by the apparition of an old woman's face floating in the silver lake of her mirror as she prepares for bed one night? Her own reflection, of course, seen through rheumy, cataract-dimmed eyes. But, no, it isn't her reflection, she realizes as she begins to detach individual features from the face in the mirror, the pale green eyes that are the color of cut limes or Atlantic sea ice, the strong nose that speaks of Iberian nobility, the lips tightly compressed to prevent the escape of a kind word, the serene and icy beauty, even at this age, that suggests a lifetime of privilege. The apparition returns the following night and the night after that.

Who are you? The old woman, Maria, finally asks. What do you want from me? The woman in the mirror looks alarmed. Her eyes dart around the room as if searching for a precious object and then she disappears. The following night, however, she returns, suspended in the pool of quicksilver, her face pale, imploring, her hands clenched at her chest. This time at the question, Who are you? the woman only looks annoyed, as if at the insistent ringing of a telephone in a neighboring apartment, and again she disappears. Maria is perplexed as much as disturbed. Why is this cold, unresponsive old woman intruding upon her dreams of Margarito? The next time the woman appears a name rises up from the dark well of memory.

Amanita?

Yes, Maria, of course it's me.

What are you doing in there? Don't you at least have the decency to come out and face me?

I don't have any control over this thing, Maria. I'm just a passenger on a train. I can look out the window, I can watch the scenery go by, but I can't get off. I should have known better. I promised the brewhag a fortune. Yes, witchcraft, superstition, all that primitive nonsense I despised. I was desperate. I didn't know I'd show up here. At first I was as startled as you. I thought it was like a one-way glass, that you couldn't see me. I watched you several nights before you noticed me.

Life's been good to you, Amanita. Maria's own words surprise her.

Amanita smiles, a *cruel* smile, one that in the prime of her beauty might have launched a thousand ships with no other purpose than to see them crash on the rocks. How you must have hated to hear my name spoken.

Maria says nothing but it's true. Amanita's name is like shrapnel from an ancient wound she has carried deep in her flesh all these years, or a vestigial poisonous sac whose original purpose, whether some sort of defense mechanism or a vehicle of self-destruction under extreme duress, has long been forgotten. But the pleasure of poison is not in swallowing it and keeping it forever a secret while it slowly destroys you, but in spitting it out and watching its acid burn in the eyes and the face—in the soul of the one who has caused you so much pain. And still the words taste bitter in her mouth.

Of course I knew about you and Margarito.

Amanita flinches as if Death, anthropomorphic, yearning for its own form of consummation, had caressed her throat with its icy fingers. You don't know what you're talking about. Clearly Amanita isn't interested in this meeting either, doesn't wish to see it to the end, wherever it's heading now, the struggle still to come, the things they will have to say, the stilted dialogue the scriptwriters will give them contributing to the pain they must endure, and to discover what? That death is real? That we are all going to die? So easy to say when you are young and life is yours forever, but to speak of death now when it has drawn so near, when the carriage stands outside the door, decorated in black crepe and plumed feathers?

Boone had originally conceived of this scene as a stage production with Margarito presented as a Prince Hal-like protagonist, a rascal, rogue, Lothario, a dreamer, poet, would-be revolutionary, ever young, ever dashing, his Dorian Gray portrait sustained by the love of two aging women, his deeds and exploits continuing well beyond his expiration date. But even Boone concedes such sentimentality is out of place in this day and age. Which might explain why the following scene has been furiously, childishly, one might even say, crossed out with what appears to be red crayon. (Or is this the handiwork of Boone's young granddaughter? Yes, he has one, he brings her on the set now and then, perhaps to demonstrate what—his humanity?)

Maria: Don't act so surprised, Amanita. How could I not know? Men are clumsy, they come to you trailing the threads of other women's desires, they litter your home, your sanctuary with the traces of their infidelity, a smudge of lipstick, a whiff of perfume, a strand of hair, the feel of her breasts in his hands when he touches you, the taste of her mouth in his mouth, rotting there like dead meat. Why is it so easy for men to lie down with any bitch who comes along, to sleep as easily with an adoring lover as a whore? (The anger that has risen in Maria's voice trails off in remorse.) But I always forgave him. I opened myself up to him entirely, I gave him everything, my laughter, my happiness, my (Maria's voice quavers again) … youth.

Amanita (turning one hand in the other, examining her nails, her skin, as if she has just discovered a startling change in their appearance): I didn't know him when he was a boy. Only as a man. But like all men, he was weak, he gave in to my desires. Poor me. I made the mistake of falling in love with him. But the more I needed him, the more he despised me. He threw away all I offered, power, money, *respect*, for a barefoot country girl. (Amanita's eyes turn a furious emerald green, the fury of betrayal betrayed). Fool! How could I not see that he was only using me, that I was the skeleton key to unlock my father's innermost sanctuary. That was my mistake—and his. (Amanita's eyes dull into a leaden green and her face falls, shatters, cracking porcelain, chipping paint. Suddenly she looks as if she has pulled a silicon mask of an old woman's face over her own. She lets out a moan, as if someone had inserted a large needle in her spine. When she speaks again it's as if from a distance.) After that I blocked out all thoughts of him, denied memory and recollection, created in my mind a stone wall with iron gates that refused entry to his name. And then the dreams started, he came to me in my sleep. It had been so long. I thought maybe he was forgiving me. Instead he brought me here. (Amanita begins to weep in barely aspirated sobs.) *Uh uh uh*. (Maria too begins to weep. Maybe it's tension or pain or an arc of sympathy between ancient adversaries. For some time the two women's tears flow, their faces riven and haggard with grief, their arms clutched over their breasts, the hands of one thick and rough from years of labor, the other's thin, milky white, with fine blue veins.)

In keeping with this theatrical version, Boone had also envisioned the following scene as something like a Greek chorus, strophe and anti-strophe, as Maria and Amanita now cross back and forth on a raised stage and directly address the audience.

> He wasn't like other men—
> He was a dreamer—
> A visionary—
> He could have been a great poet—
> Or famous actor—
> His name passed down through the ages for the pleasure of all women—
> And the envy of all men—
> Rather than a nobody—
> An asterisk—
> Failed revolutionary—
> *Dead*—
> (both women let out a loud sob)

It should also be mentioned that Boone originally intended to have Irene Papas play Amanita, and Maria Callas, Maria, until, that is, he was reminded of a minor inconvenience.

Sir?

What is it, Moot?

They're dead, sir.

What?

The actresses you mentioned. They're dead, sir.

Nonsense, Moot. This is film. No one in film ever dies.

As high-minded (and ambiguous) as that sounds, what Boone really has in mind is some pixelatin' hijinks—*snip, snip, snip*.

The silver lake spreads outward, flooding the house and the yard and the entire theater. Patrons are pulling on sweaters and jackets. Is the theater's AC on the blink? Is it that freak cold front the weather people warned us about? A freezing wind howls across the desert, sweeping away chickens, cat, goat, house (note to sound: include music from the tornado scene in *Wizard of Oz*). High overhead Grandfather Vulture soars through the thin blue ether, watching this small human drama take place on the earthly plane below, tallying the actors' little mistakes, keeping track of their mortal wounds. Sooner or later they all add up.

Or was this, too, a dream, a fabrication, filtered through the celluloid membrane of an eight-year-old boy's imagination, sitting in a row of creaky fold-up seats with dried snot and pink fetal wads of bubble gum stuck to the bottoms at the Saturday afternoon matinee, watching in wide-eyed fascination after the mushy stuff was over and the good stuff came on again, bandits in floppy hats and bushy mustaches splashing across the Frío Grande on horseback, soldiers in blue uniforms with yellow chevrons on the shoulders and yellow stripes down the legs right behind them, carbines blazing in the flickering white light of a movie projector?

Crossing the Rio Bravo

The old man only closed his eyes for a minute and only then because he'd been rowing for so long and the hot sun beating down on his head made him sleepy. *Snowwwmaaaaan!* A clear, ringing child's voice calling across the water woke him again, a little boy with shiny black hair, in a red t-shirt and dark pants, standing barefoot on the sunny southern bank of the river. *Margareeeeto!* the old man called back in a hoarse rasping voice, but the boy didn't answer and the old man's eyes closed again. When they opened, the boy was gone. Maybe he went home. Maybe he was never there. Whichever it was, he better not do that again. Fall asleep and wake up half way down to the sea with this school of fish swimming next to him. Or, squinting, peering closer, was it only a flock of seagulls reflected on the water's surface?

He started to row again, the *creak, thunk, splash, creak, thunk, splash* of the oars breaking the water's surface and the sounding board of the hull echoing across five or ten thousand years of the human diaspora. He stopped rowing. His winter-frosted eyes traveled again to the south bank of the river where the hot yellow sunlight gleamed on a weather-beaten board shack perched on stilts like a very large wading bird in a bright green patch of willow and giant cane. His gaze traveled back across the water to the frozen whiteness of the north bank where a nearly identical shack perched like a gloomy stork, a foot of snow on its roof and its weathered board face sagging beneath the lowering gray sky. But no smoke rose from the stovepipe to tell him he spent the night there. He glanced down at his faded pink tank top and tattered khaki trousers, and then at the checked flannel shirt and wool-lined canvas coat lying next to him on the seat. He could have taken them off five minutes ago. Or he could just as easily have been getting ready to put them on.

He pulled on the oars again, *creak, thunk, splash, creak, thunk, splash*. Then stopped. His chin sank on his chest. Through drooping eyelids he examined the white hairs springing from his faded pink top and his sagging old man's breasts and the sinewy arms sticking out of his toad-like body.

In the past he rowed other men across the river, always for free, knowing full well they'd pay soon enough on the other side, not just the old men with broken backs who expected nothing more than to be treated like donkeys and maybe earn a few dollars to send home to their wives and families whom they might not see for the next year or two years or never again, but the young men with dreams still intact of earning wealth and glory and returning home like conquerors to build big mansions and do great works and restore the honor of their cities, towns, villages.

One morning an old greenghost showed up on the north shore, his brows hoary, his eyes the pale blue of the Arctic sky. He said his name was Billy Bob but he didn't act like a Billy Bob. Unlike the other men, he demanded to be rowed in the opposite direction, south of the border. At first he sat in the prow of the boat and stared at the water as if he might throw himself in at any moment. It wasn't long, however, before he began to demand answers to unanswerable questions. How do you say, Time's up? On the ropes? End of the road? How do you say, Goodnight? Turn out the lights? Don't let the bedbugs bite?

It doesn't matter anymore, Snowman. You can stop asking questions now.

But I want to know the answer.

To what, Snowman?

Snowwwmaaaaan!

The camera returns to the little boy standing barefoot on the sunny southern bank of the river, his mouth open wide as he calls across the water to the old man slumped over in the rowboat drifting down stream.

Most of the audience, except for the eight-year-old kid, who does kind of identify with the boy on the riverbank, and a few die-hard Boone Weller fans, and they're fewer every year, have gotten up from their seats and departed the theater long before the credits begin to roll. Too bad for them because there's a final scene. It's time-lapsed so the passage of hours occurs in no more than a minute or two. In the flickering, grainy, almost excruciatingly lurid colors of vintage Super 8 we see a classic top-hatted snowman with lumps of coal for eyes and mouth and a carrot nose, wearing an incongruous Hawaiian shirt (palm trees and, yes, hula girls). The snowman seems to slump and sway drunkenly beneath the hot yellow sun. The camera moves in for a close-up of individual crystals of ice beginning to melt and trickle away in deepening fissures as the snowman morphs through horror show grotesqueries of decay and decomposition and a leering death grin until all that is left is a sodden top hat and Hawaiian shirt and a few lumps of coal. The camera slowly draws back to show a donkey dispassionately munching on a carrot.

Voice: The old man? No one knows. Nobody ever saw him go in or out.

Voice: Who knows? Whatever the cat dragged in, I guess.

A red emergency EXIT sign glows down in the corner.

ABOUT THE AUTHOR

REYoung was born in Pittsburgh, Pennsylvania and currently dwells in chthonic darkness in a limestone cave deep beneath the city of Austin, Texas. He is the author of the novels *Unbabbling* (Dalkey Archive Press, 1997), *Margarito and the Snowman* (Dalkey Archive Press, 2016), *Inflation* (TageTage Press, 2019), *The Ironsmith* (TageTage Press, 2020) and *Zol* (TageTage Press, 2020).

UNBABBLING

A NOVEL

In the tour de force called America, one of the tired, the poor, the huddled masses struggles upward to the penthouse of God, discovering too late he's taken the elevator marked down. Resurrected from the rubble of dreams as a messiah and accidental revolutionary, his cry for freedom echoes like a broken record as they lower him into the ground. Like a hopelessly lost coal miner, he digs on, deflating the gloom with slapstick, pensive as a clown, gathering strength for the next round.

MARGARITO AND THE SNOWMAN

REYoung

Margarito and the Snowman

A NOVEL

A nation buried in snow and ice in an obligatory 365 days a year Christmas celebration, a tribe of Mayan warriors in comedy troupe disguise, an existentially challenged hero known as the Snowman on a quest that takes him south of the border down ol' Mexico way, and a B-grade movie director named Boone Weller with his own agenda. Is it a book? A movie? Told in a shoot from the hip Texas style, *Margarito and the Snowman* is loose, rangy, battered with an attitude and bound to offend everybody.

INFLATION

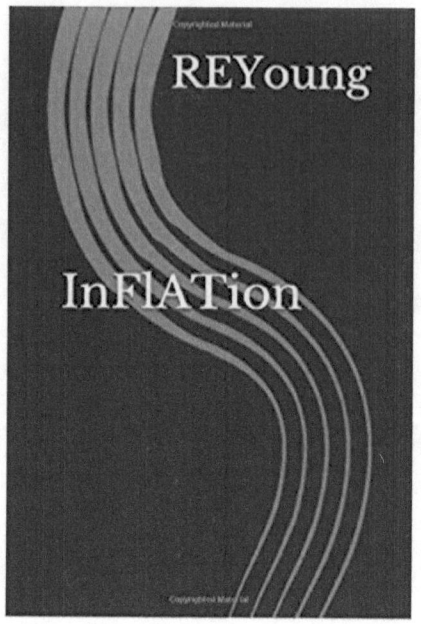

A NOVEL

Martin "Marty" Grasso (think Mardi Gras) wakes to find the world turned into a Dantesque "carnival of bloat." Excess consumption is patriotic, high fat and cholesterol diets are good, exercise is frowned upon, the price of fuel ticks upward by the second, and giant virtual billboards, or VRBLs, bombard citizens with advertisements for consumer products. As a mysterious vortex sucks up rapidly dwindling energy reserves and civilization faces famine, chaos and collapse, the impending catastrophe is blamed on a subversive element known as the sappers. Marty's quest for the truth intersects virtual worlds, utopian societies and ever-morphing nightmares—in a wild vaudeville cyber-punk noir romp that crosses into the twilight zone of "sic"-fi where nothing is ever what it seems.

THE IRONSMITH

A NOVEL

Born out of myth and fairytale, in particular the tradition of the wise old wizard mentoring a bumbling apprentice, and told in language echoing Homer, Beowulf, biblical scripture and John Coltrane, among others, *The Ironsmith* evolves into a surreal Bildungsroman of a self-perceived "monster," a painfully introverted young man whose obsession with the ancient sport of weightlifting causes him to withdraw into an increasingly delusional world that anachronistically intersects classical Greece, the Middle Ages, the Industrial Age, WWI and II, the tumultuous sixties, and the age of the Internet.

A NOVEL

In book two of the Margarito and the Snowman trilogy, the eponymous Snowman wakes up on a desert film set in B movie director Boone Weller's sprawling new epic, Zol. Told in a mix of melodrama, slapstick, documentary and cinema verité, and packed with drug cartels, coyotes, revolutionaries, fire-breathing dragons, human sacrifice and magic, this blockbuster unfolds in a Dalían landscape along a chimerical pan-American highway deep in the heart of Mexico as the Snowman continues his quest for a mythical place called Zol and an enigmatic friend named Margarito.